RAM LH

Dear Reader,

Deep down, doesn't ev~~~~~~~~~
about "rich boys"? W~~~~~~~~~~~

Right?

I think so.

I know I do, and I also love a reunion story, where lovers who
were torn apart in the past have to face each other again.
I believe that old sparks can be quickly ignited again, and
*Secrets and Lies* is a book that proves my theory.

Years ago I wrote the Mavericks series, which was composed
of *He's a Bad Boy, He's Just a Cowboy* and *He's the Rich Boy*,
all written for Silhouette Special Edition and all connected by
The Legend of Whitefire Lake.

In *Secrets and Lies*, two of those stories, *He's a Bad Boy* and
*He's Just a Cowboy*, come back to life again. You'll get to meet
"bad boy" Jackson Moore and Rachelle Tremont, the woman
he's never forgotten, no matter how hard he tried. Then there's
"cowboy" Turner Brooks, and Heather Tremont Leonetti, who
had his love child. Their story is included. Let me tell you, the
sparks fly when these people get together again!

I'm thrilled that HQN Books has repackaged some of my
earlier novels, and I'm sure you'll love the Mavericks of *Secrets
and Lies!* Look for the third book of the Mavericks series in
*Confessions*, coming soon from HQN. In that story you'll meet
Hayden Garreth IV (the rich boy) and the woman he could
never forget, Nadine Warne.

If you'd like to find out more about *Secrets and Lies* as well as
my other books, just visit me at www.lisajackson.com or my
Facebook fan page!

Keep reading!

Lisa Jackson

# LISA JACKSON

## SECRETS AND LIES

HQN™

ISBN-13: 978-0-373-77682-5

SECRETS AND LIES

Copyright © 2012 by Harlequin Books S.A.

The publisher acknowledges the copyright holder of the individual works as follows:

HE'S A BAD BOY
Copyright © 1992 by Susan Crose

HE'S JUST A COWBOY
Copyright © 1993 by Susan Crose

Recycling programs for this product may not exist in your area.

# CONTENTS

# HE'S A BAD BOY

# PROLOGUE

*San Francisco, California*
*The Present*

# *PROLOGUE*

THE WIND WAS BRISK, cold for early summer, as it blew off the bay and crawled beneath the hem of Rachelle Tremont's leather jacket. Rain began to fall from the leaden sky, and she hurried up the staircase leading to her apartment.

"Come on, come on," she muttered under her breath when she couldn't find her keys in her pockets. She rifled through her purse while rain dripped from an overflowing gutter and her black cat, Java, meowed loudly at her feet. "I'm trying," she grumbled through chattering teeth as she found the key in a side pocket of her purse. The door stuck, as it always did in the rain, and she had to shoulder it open.

Finally she was inside, dripping on the faded gray carpet, her hands like ice. She should feel good, she told herself; she'd finally made a decision to get on with her life—confront the past so that she could face her future.

She plugged in the coffeemaker and, after leaving a dish of milk for Java, replayed the single message on her answering machine.

The voice on the machine belonged to her sister. "Rachelle? Rachelle, are you there?" Heather asked. "If you are, pick up and don't give me some nonsense about deadlines or any of that guff.... Rachelle? Mom just called. She says you're going back to Gold Creek...that you're planning to rent the cottage! Are you crazy? Don't

you remember what happened there? Your life was practically ruined! For crying out loud, Rachelle, why would
you go back?" A pause. "This doesn't have anything to
do with Jackson Moore, does it? Rachelle? Rachelle?"
Another pause while Rachelle's heartbeat thudded so
loudly, she could hear it. "You call me," Heather insisted, sounding worried. "Before you take off on some
trip that's going to be emotional suicide, you call me...!
Listen, Rachelle, you're supposed to be the levelheaded
one. And you told me once if you ever thought about
doing anything as insane as returning to that town that I
was supposed to take a gun and shoot you. Remember?
Well, consider yourself shot! Don't go and do something
stupid! And just forget Jackson! You hear? Forget him.
He's bad news. Always was. Always will be.... I wish
you were home so we could straighten this out," Heather
added anxiously. "Okay, you call me. Okay?"

Finally a click and a beep and Rachelle let out her
breath. Her hands were trembling as she poured herself
a cup of coffee. Just the mention of Jackson could shake
her up. It had been twelve years. Twelve years! How
could she still be so affected by a man who had turned
his back on her when she'd been his only friend in a town
that had branded him and wanted him hung from the tall-
est tree?

The answer was simple—and complicated. Despite
her down-to-earth nature, Rachelle had once had a romantic side, a part of her personality that had believed
in fairy tales and castles and knights on white chargers.
And bad boys? Hadn't she believed in the myth of the
bad boy with the heart of gold? Well, Jackson Moore
had killed that fantasy, which, all things considered, was
probably for the best.

She shrugged out of her jacket and draped it over the

cane-back kitchen chair. Water dripped from the sleeves to the floor, but she didn't care. She considered calling Heather, but decided against it. Why have an argument with her younger sister? She could picture Heather, blond hair neatly cut, silk pants and matching top, perfect smile. One of San Francisco's elite, or she had been, during her marriage to Dennis Leonetti, a rich man whose father owned the Bank of The Greater Bay. Now Heather, divorced and a single mother, was trying to make her own living by converting the art she'd dabbled in for years into a career. She'd bought a loft, studio and gallery not far from Ghirardelli Square.

Heather had enough problems. She didn't need to worry about her older sister—the confirmed career woman, the reporter who was always championing the cause of the underdog and who thought nothing of storming into the office of any public official for a quote.

The reporter who still quaked at the mention of a man she hadn't seen for over a decade.

Rachelle glanced at the cluttered kitchen table and the manila envelope that contained a copy of the article she'd already left with her editor at the *San Francisco Herald.* Her first article explained that for the next ten weeks her syndicated column would be written from Gold Creek, California, the town where she'd grown up. Her introductory column in the series *Return to Gold Creek* would appear in newspapers across the country tomorrow. And her editor, Marcy Dupont, expected more—a lot more. Marcy wanted an interview, by telephone of course, with Jackson Moore. That request would probably prove impossible.

Frowning thoughtfully to herself, Rachelle kicked off her sodden boots. Her socks were waterlogged, and she yanked them off before tossing the wet hosiery into the bathroom sink. Padding barefoot into her single bed-room, she finger-combed her tangled hair and spent the next ten minutes braiding the wet strands into a single auburn plait that swung past her shoulders as she walked.

She'd decided to go back to Gold Creek and, come hell or high water, she was going. No amount of talking from Heather was going to change things. She'd already worked out the details with her job; Marcy was all for a column of self-examination about herself and the town in which she'd grown up. Rachelle bit her lower lip and felt a tiny jab of guilt that she'd have to draw Jackson into this. Too bad. Especially now, when she was over him—completely over him.

Now she had David—kind, understanding David. Hadn't he insisted she return to "find herself" or some such sixties mumbo jumbo? What he'd really meant was that he wanted her to be able to lock away the past once and for all and return to him. He wanted her to move in with him, marry him, and accept his teenage daughters as her stepchildren. And he wanted her to be fulfilled. Because he didn't want to start another family—not at the age of forty-five. David was sixteen years older than Rachelle, which wasn't all that much, but he'd done his fatherly bit and he wanted a new wife with no hang-ups about starting a family. A new, younger wife who would look good at company parties and cook his dinners for him, yet still have an interesting, vital career of her own. Rachelle filled the bill. Except she had a few problems of her own to work out first.

So she was returning to Gold Creek. For David. For her job. For herself.

*For Jackson?*

Not in a million years.

All she had to do now was pack. But she stared at her

closet, her throat dry. Her stomach tightened into a hard knot when she spied the yearbook of Tyler High, and next to it a scrapbook filled with yellowed, time-worn pages from her youth.

Knowing she was making a mistake that could cost her all of her hard-fought independence, she crossed to the closet, yanked out the scrapbook and slid to the floor where she sat cross-legged on the braided rug. One knee poked out of the hole in her jeans as she slowly opened the dusty volume and stared at the aged articles from the *Gold Creek Clarion*. The pictures were grainy, brittle with time, but Jackson Moore seemed as real now as he had then. He stared at the camera as if it were an enemy.

His eyes were dark and brooding, his sensual mouth curved into a defiant frown, his wet hair plastered to his head. He was looking over the shoulder of his black leather jacket and his hands were cuffed behind him. His jeans were dirty and crusted with blood. A policeman, riot stick in hand, was leading him through the glass-and-steel doors of the county jail.

Rachelle's heart slammed against her ribs and her eyes stung with unshed tears. The print in the newspaper had faded, the picture of Jackson was wrinkled and unforgiving, but in Rachelle's memory the night that had changed her life forever might just as well have been yesterday....

# BOOK ONE

*Gold Creek, California*
*Twelve Years Earlier*

# CHAPTER ONE

THE NIGHT WAS WARM, a harvest moon glowed behind a thickening layer of clouds and there was excitement in the air—a sense of adventure that caused Rachelle's seventeen-year-old heart to race. The football field shimmered green under the lights, the crowd loud and anxious and yet there was more: an undercurrent of electricity that seemed to charge the atmosphere.

Maybe it was because tonight was homecoming and the parade of students had serpentined through town. Maybe it was because the Tyler High Hawks were taking on the rivals from Coleville. Or maybe it was because Rachelle, after spending her life doing exactly what was expected of her, was about to step out of her quiet, studious, "good-girl" image. She'd already unwittingly lied to her mother and felt more than a tiny twinge of regret.

But she wasn't turning back. It was time to experience life a little, walk on the wild side—well, at least touch a toe on the wild side; she wasn't ready for out-and-out rebellion yet.

With an earsplitting shriek, feedback whined from the speakers.

Rachelle winced, but aimed her camera at the plywood platform that had been set up for the pregame ceremony. As a reporter for the school paper, she sometimes took pictures and tonight, because Carlie, the staff photographer, was scouting out drinks at the refreshment stand, Rachelle was stuck with the camera. She didn't mind. Looking through the lens sometimes gave her a clearer view of the person she was interviewing and actually helped her write her article.

She zeroed in on Principal Leonard, who, with a big show to the packed stands, turned to one of the students operating the public-address system.

"...And I want it on now! Oh. Testing, testing. Uh-oh, there we go." He managed a foolish-looking grin as he tapped the microphone loudly and his voice boomed into the stadium. "Well, now that we worked out all the bugs in the PA system, let's get on with the festivities." He droned on about Tyler High for a minute, then added, "I'd like to take this opportunity to thank Thomas Fitzpatrick for his generous donation to the school."

Across from the stands on the far side of the field the new electronic scoreboard flashed with a thousand lights. Fitzpatrick Logging was scripted across the top of the scoreboard and the company insignia was stamped boldly across the bottom. No one who ever witnessed a football game at Tyler Stadium would forget the Fitzpatrick name. Not that anyone in Gold Creek could, Rachelle thought with a wry smile.

Click. Click. Click. She snapped off several shots of the new lighted display and a few more of the small crowd in the middle of the field. Short and round, Principal Leonard was going on and on about the generosity of the Fitzpatrick family. Rachelle grimaced. The Fitzpatricks were one of the wealthiest families in Gold Creek, and Thomas Fitzpatrick never passed up an opportunity to show off his philanthropy.

The two men shook hands. Fitzpatrick was tall and handsome. With broad shoulders and black hair shot with silver, he looked like a politician running for office. It was speculated widely that with all his money, he would someday enter state politics—all the better for Fitzpatrick Logging, the primary employer for the town. And therefore, all the better for Gold Creek, California.

A roar of applause rippled through the stadium as Fitzpatrick flashed his often-photographed grin and hugged his wife, June, who stood, along with her three children, next to her husband.

Yep, Rachelle thought, rewinding the film, the Fitzpatricks looked exactly like what they were—the royal family of this California timber town. June was a tall, blond woman with delicate features, haughty brows and sculpted cheekbones. Her firstborn, Roy, was blond, as well, but solidly built, like his father. Just the year before, Roy had been the star quarterback for the Tyler High Hawks. Now his younger brother, Brian, was leading the team. Brian stood with the family. He dwarfed Roy because of the thick padding beneath his uniform and he carried his helmet under one hand. The youngest Fitzpatrick, a girl named Toni, stood a little apart from the family. She was only fourteen, but already promised beauty, and was rumored to be more trouble than both the boys put together.

"Rachelle. Hey, get a load of this!" Carlie sang out as she balanced two soft drinks and wended her way through the ever-thickening throng of people standing on the sidelines. Some of the soda had sloshed over the rim and she was licking her fingers. "Here's your Coke."

"About time you showed up," Rachelle teased. "You're supposed to be responsible for the pictures—"

"I know, I know," Carlie replied, her blue-green eyes dancing merrily. "Now, come on, there's something you've *got* to see."

"Just a minute." Rachelle finished taking her shot,

then traded her camera for the cup. The Coke was cold and slid easily down her throat.

"Look to the north of the field. Here, use these." Carlie stuffed her camera into her oversized bag and withdrew a small pair of binoculars. "No, no, not there. North! Now, see over there?" She pointed toward the far side of the stands.

Rachelle peered through the glasses. She swung her gaze past the green turf shimmering beneath the floodlights and the track surrounding the playing field. Beyond the track was a chain-link fence separating the athletic facility from the parking lot.

"You see him?"

"Who?"

Exasperated, Carlie gently grabbed Rachelle's chin and swiveled her head slightly. Rachelle's gaze landed on a motorcyclist straddling a huge black bike.

"Oh," she said, her throat suddenly dry.

"'Oh' doesn't do him justice."

Carlie was right. The boy—well, nearly a man—on the bike was tall, maybe six feet, with hair as black as midnight and harsh features that were drawn into an angry scowl of determination. His skin was tanned, but not dark enough to hide the cut beneath his eye or the bruise on his cheek. Backdropped by the lights of a strip mall, and set apart from the festivities by the fence, he seemed sinister somehow, as if his being ostracized were as much his idea as the rest of the crowd's. He stared through the mesh of the security fence, to the center of the field where the Fitzpatricks were posed like the quintessential family unit. The biker looked as if he'd like to personally tear into the whole lot of them.

Rachelle's heart drummed a little faster.

"It's Jackson Moore," Carlie told her, as if Rachelle

didn't know the name of Gold Creek's most notorious hellion.

"What's he doing here? I thought he left town." Rachelle focused the binoculars again, until Jackson's rough features were centered in stark relief. For a second she thought he was handsome with his knife-sharp features and thin lips, but it wasn't so much his looks as his attitude that made him seem mysterious—even sexy. Wondering if she were out of her mind, she let the binoculars swing from her neck, grabbed the camera and snapped in the zoom lens before clicking off several shots of the bad boy of Gold Creek.

"Print one for me," Carlie said as she lifted the binoculars to her own eyes.

Rachelle ignored her. "So you don't know why he's back?"

"Haven't you heard? He's in trouble big-time with the Fitzpatricks," Carlie said. "That's why he's giving them all the evil eye. My dad's a foreman for the logging company and he's usually up in the woods, but he had to come into the office for something—to fill out forms for an accident that happened the other day.

"Anyway, it was kinda late and Jackson was there, raising some sort of stink about his mom working for 'dirty Fitzpatrick money' I think was the quote. It's not like she's there all the time. She just puts in a few hours a week doing filing or something. Everybody thinks the old man hired her out of pity—they went to school together, I guess, and he's into causes, you know. Part of his political thing. Anyway, supposedly Jackson objected to his mother being another one of Fitzpatrick's charities."

Rachelle took another swallow of Coke, her throat parched from staring at Jackson.

Carlie rattled on. "It probably has something to do with the fact that Thomas Fitzpatrick gave Jackson a job a couple of years ago, then fired him. No one, not even my dad, knew why, but my dad figures Jackson was stealing tools or something and that Fitzpatrick didn't want to press charges." From the corner of her eye, Rachelle noticed the guilty look that passed over Carlie's face. "I wasn't supposed to say anything—"

"Your secret is safe with me," Rachelle replied, but wondered how many other people Carlie had told. Carlie loved gossip, and short of wiring her mouth shut, there was no way to keep her from spreading rumors. The news of Jackson Moore's confrontation about his mother was probably all over school.

Rachelle bit her lower lip and stared openly across the field to the spot where Jackson, balanced on the idling motorcycle, still stood. Suddenly his head swung toward her, his eyes searching the crowd. His gaze landed on her with a force that sent a jolt of electricity through her. Her throat tightened and her hands were clammy. She looked quickly away, then finished her Coke in one swallow.

It was stupid, of course. He couldn't pick her out of a throng; he had no idea that she was thinking about him or had even glanced his way, but when she slid another glance toward the fence, he was still staring at her and her blood seemed to pound at her temples.

Touching her throat with her fingertips, she felt tiny drops of perspiration collecting against her skin. She couldn't help a little feeling of fascination for the boy with the blackest reputation in Gold Creek. He was almost twenty-two, and though he was rumored to have straightened out some of his lawless traits, there had been a time when he'd raised nothing but hell. He lived with his mother on the outskirts of Gold Creek in a rusting single-wide mobile home. He didn't have a father—well, none that anyone in town could actually name—and he'd been in trouble with the law for as long as Rachelle could remember. As a minor, he'd stolen gas and hubcaps and shot mailboxes and had been kicked out of Tyler High for fighting on the school grounds. Somehow he'd managed to scrape together enough credits to get his diploma, though no one in Gold Creek thought he'd amount to anything.

He'd joined the navy for a hitch and had disappeared from town for a while. But now he was back—dressed in black leather and riding a thrumming Harley-Davidson, his tattered image of the troubled kid from the bad part of town still very much intact.

"Oh, Lord, he's looking right at you!" Carlie whispered loudly. "You know, he's got a face to die for."

"He's dangerous," Rachelle replied, crushing her cup.

Carlie's eyes widened and her blue-green eyes glinted impishly. On a sigh she said, "Of course he is. That's what makes him so attractive."

"LAURA SAID SHE'D MEET us in the parking lot—after she changed out of her cheerleading uniform," Carlie told Rachelle as they climbed out of the emptying bleachers an hour later. They'd stayed at the stadium to take some postgame pictures of the star players and get some quotes for the next week's edition of the school paper. Carlie had snapped a couple of pictures of Brian Fitzpatrick and Joe Knapp, the team's all-league wide receiver, who, after catching a wobbly pass from Fitzpatrick, had run fifty-three yards to make the winning touchdown. Carlie had taken the boys' pictures while Rachelle had gotten a few quotes from Coach Foster. Now they were to meet Laura, Carlie's friend and one of the most popular girls in school.

"There's her car!" Carlie said, pointing to a yellow Toyota. "She must be around here somewhere—oh, look, over there—"

Rachelle searched the lot and saw Laura standing next to a shiny red Corvette. Two boys were seated in the car, and another was leaning against the fender of a pickup parked next to the sports car.

"Oh my God, that's Roy Fitzpatrick!" Carlie whispered. "Do you think he's the new boyfriend she's been hinting about?" Before Rachelle could answer, Carlie was dashing through the few vehicles left in the parking lot and Rachelle was beginning to think that her new rebellious streak wasn't all it was cracked up to be. *Roy Fitzpatrick?* He'd earned a reputation for smooth words, quick hands and fast goodbyes. Rumors of his sexual appetite had filtered through the hallways of Tyler High and there had been gossip of a pregnant girlfriend in Coleville. Lately he'd been dating Melanie Patton, his best friend's sister.

Rachelle had met Roy only a couple of times—when she'd had to interview him for the school paper. She was probably the only girl in the entire school who didn't have a crush on him.

Ignoring the apprehension that followed her like a cloud, she wended her way through the parked cars, careful of the vehicles backing up and trying to find a way out of the crowded lot.

The night was muggy, the clouds overhead dark and threatening rain. Over the odors of exhaust and hot engines, a thinner smell, of stale beer and cigarettes, wafted on the breeze that rustled the dry leaves dancing across the asphalt.

The Corvette's glossy red finish shone under the glow of the security lights. Roy, the crown prince of Fitzpatrick Logging, was seated behind the wheel, his toe tapping restlessly on the throttle, the powerful car's engine thrumming anxiously.

Scott McDonald, one of his friends, sat in the passenger seat and Erik Patton leaned against the fender of his metallic blue pickup.

"Roy wants to take us for a ride," Laura said as Rachelle approached. She tossed her a triumphant glance, as if she'd caught a prize all the girls in town were wanting.

"Where?" Rachelle asked, feeling suddenly awkward. Though Roy and his friends were only two years older than she, they seemed so much more mature.

"Remember I told you I knew someone with a cabin on the lake?" Laura reminded her.

The Fitzpatricks did have a home at Whitefire Lake, but, in Rachelle's estimation, it was hardly a cabin. The house had to be four or five times the size of the small cottage in which she'd grown up. But then Laura had grown up with higher standards. Both her parents worked and she'd never had to go without anything she really wanted.

And now, from the looks of things, Laura wanted Roy Fitzpatrick. As if reading Rachelle's hesitation, she said, "Come on, Rachelle, why not?" Her eyes were bright and eager as she sneaked a peek at Roy.

Roy tossed them all—Rachelle, Laura and Carlie—his well-practiced all-American smile. His wheat-blond hair was clipped short, his athletic physique visible beneath the thin layer of yellow cotton in his polo shirt. "Yeah, why not, Rachelle?" Roy said, his gaze moving slowly up Rachelle's body with a bold familiarity that caused her stomach to turn over.

She swallowed hard. Until the past couple of weeks since she'd begun hanging out with Laura, not many boys had noticed her, and certainly not older college boys who practically owned the whole town.

"Yeah, why not?" Carlie chimed in. "We already planned to ditch the dance."

Laura had told Rachelle that if the dance was boring they'd go out cruising around town, maybe drive over to Coleville as none of the girls were dating anyone special from Gold Creek, then return to her house for a sleepover. But she'd never once mentioned going to the lake with Roy and his friends.

Rachelle hesitated. Everyone was staring at her. "Still the prude?" Roy taunted, and Rachelle's cheeks flamed. How would Roy know anything about her?

"I told my mom we'd be at the dance—"

"So?" Roy cut in a little irritably. "What your mom doesn't know won't hurt her."

Laura shot her a scathing glance. "We already worked out our story, Rachelle."

Rachelle bit her lip. This was her chance. She'd always been considered a "brain," a girl who'd rather study or work on the school paper or paint scenery for the drama club than show any interest in boys. But lately, with Laura's help in the makeup and hair department, boys had been calling and asking her out. She liked the feeling. But she didn't trust Roy.

"Well, what's it gonna be?" Roy asked, his smoldering blue eyes touching hers. "A mama's girl—or ya gonna have some fun? We can't wait around here all night."

"That's right," Erik agreed, glancing over his shoulder. His vintage truck didn't compare to Roy's sleek machine, but the Pattons didn't have the kind of money that had been passed down from one generation of Fitzpatricks to the next. As long as there had been people in Gold Creek, there had been money in Fitzpatrick hands.

"Come on," Carlie urged.

"Yeah, let's go with the guys," Laura agreed, smiling at the three college boys. She fanned herself with her fingers. "It's so hot tonight. The lake would be great."

Roy flashed his rich-boy grin—a slow-spreading smile that had been known to melt the most formidable ice maiden's resistance.

Laura leaned against the fender of the Corvette, her hands braced against the gleaming hood of the car, her heavy breasts outlined against her sweater. "I know *I* would *love* a ride."

"That's more like it. I was beginnin' to think that you girls were afraid," Roy drawled, his blue eyes flickering devilment at Rachelle. He pushed the throttle with his toe and the Corvette's engine rumbled eagerly.

"Yeah, come on, we'll show you a good time," Scott agreed. Whereas Roy was blond and blue-eyed, the all-American boy, Scott was shorter, more muscular and had thick brown hair and freckles.

Erik, unlike Scott and Roy, didn't seem as interested in Laura or her friends. "Let's get outta here," he grumbled. "There's no action. Everybody's takin' off."

He was right. The line of cars that had been streaming from the stadium lot had dwindled to a trickle. Even some of the boys from the team, freshly showered, were climbing into vehicles and heading back to the school for the postgame dance, the dance Rachelle had promised her mother she'd attend before spending the night with Laura. But Laura, it seemed, was only interested in Roy Fitzpatrick.

"There's action here," Roy replied, sliding a cocksure

glance Rachelle's way. "All the little ladies have to do is say 'yes.' We'll guarantee them the ride of their lives."

"Now what kind of ride are you talking about?" Laura asked in a sexy voice, and Rachelle nearly choked.

Scott chuckled deep in his throat, and Erik looked embarrassed.

Rachelle was flabbergasted by Laura's behavior. The girl was asking for trouble, more trouble than Rachelle thought she could handle.

"I don't think this is a good idea," Rachelle said, feeling Roy's hot gaze on her. She didn't want to be a wet blanket, but she could smell trouble. *A walk on the wild side.*

"Loosen up," Carlie said in a soft whisper. "When do you ever get a chance to go joyriding with Roy Fitzpatrick?"

"Three of us, three of you—we could have a party," Roy said.

"A private party?" Laura replied, flirting outrageously. Rachelle wanted to drop through the pavement, but she didn't move. There was no place to go. By now the parking lot was nearly empty. Except for a lone motorcycle rider astride his thrumming machine.

Rachelle's heart nearly stopped as she recognized Jackson Moore. He parked his bike about twenty yards away and didn't move. Just sat there...waiting, the Harley's engine idling loudly, the growl of a metallic beast.

Roy blanched at the sight of him. "Get lost, Moore," he yelled, but Jackson didn't flinch.

Rachelle couldn't take her eyes off him.

"We didn't finish our discussion the other day," Jackson said, and his lips curled into a sardonic smile as he rubbed the bruise beneath his eye.

"We've got nothing to talk about," Roy replied testily.

"Get out," he muttered to Scott McDonald, reaching over his friend and flinging the passenger door open. An old Doors song blared into the night.

Jackson didn't let up. Over the rumble of engines and Jim Morrison's deep-throated lyrics he yelled, "You and that old man of yours keep insulting my family."

Roy pretended not to hear. As Scott climbed out of his car, Roy crooked a long finger at Laura. "Let's go," he said. He took up the conversation where it had been dropped. "You said you're lookin' for a private party, well you found one. Hop in." His gaze moved quickly up and down Laura's curves as she climbed into the convertible. Roy's mouth twitched. "Now that's what I like—a girl who knows her own mind."

"We're not through, Fitzpatrick," Jackson reminded him.

"That does it. I'm sick of you, Moore. Just butt the hell out of my life!"

"As soon as you stay away from my family."

"Your family? God, that's rich. You're a stinkin' bastard, Moore. Or didn't you know? Everyone in Gold Creek but you knows that your mother's the town slut and that she probably can't even name the man who's supposed to be your father!"

Jackson's expression turned to fury. "You lying—"

Roy tromped on the accelerator. The Corvette lurched forward with a spray of gravel. Tires squealed and Roy wrenched hard on the steering wheel, heading the car straight at Jackson and his bike.

Rachelle screamed.

Laura, in the seat beside Roy, turned to stone.

Jackson gunned the engine of his Harley, but not before the fender of the Corvette caught the back wheel of the bike. The motorcycle shimmied, tires sliding on the loose gravel. Jackson flew off. With a loud thud he landed on the ground and his bike skidded, riderless, across the lot.

Roy laughed, shifted into a higher gear and tore out of the lot. Rachelle started running to Jackson's inert form. *He can't be hurt, he can't be,* she thought as panic gripped her heart. He lay flat and still on the gravel while the sound of a disappearing engine and the lyrics of "Light My Fire" faded on the wind.

Erik tried to grab her. "Leave him alone," he said, though his voice lacked conviction and his face was sheet-white. "He's okay. Only scared a little. That's all."

"I hope to God you're right." Heart in her throat, Rachelle jerked her arm away and ran to Jackson's inert form.

With a groan, he rolled over. His jacket was ripped down one arm and his pants, too, were torn. "Bastard!" Jackson groaned. "Damn bloody bastard." He slowly pulled himself to his feet and though he limped slightly, he headed straight for his bike.

Relief flooded through Rachelle's veins and she managed a thin smile. "Then you're okay?"

"Compared to what?" he muttered, righting his bike and frowning as he noticed broken spokes. Lips flattening angrily against his teeth, he winced painfully as he swung one leg over the motorcycle and switched on the ignition.

"But at least you're all right," Rachelle said, nearly sagging with relief.

"No thanks to your friend."

"He's not my—"

"Sure." Jackson sucked in his breath, as if pain had drawn the air from his lungs, then shoved hard on the kick start with his boot heel. With a roar and a plume of blue exhaust, the Harley revved.

"You...you might want to see a doctor—"

"A doctor?" he mocked. "Yeah, sure. I'll go check into Memorial. Have them patch me up."

"It was only...a...suggestion."

"Well, I *don't* remember asking for your advice."

Stung, she stepped back a pace. "I was just concerned," Rachelle said lamely, flustered at his anger. "Look, I'm on your side."

Dark, impenetrable eyes swung in her direction. His lips curled sardonically, as if he and she shared a private joke. "Let's get something straight. *No one* in Gold Creek is on my side. And that includes you."

"But—"

"You know Fitzpatrick, right?"

"Not really. He's *not* my friend and—"

"In case I don't catch up to him tonight, you can give him a message for me. Tell Roy-boy that if he knows what's good for him, he'll leave my family alone. And that goes for his old man. Tell the old coot to quit sniffin' around Sandra Moore. Got it?"

"But I don't know—"

"Just do it," Jackson ordered, his square chin thrust in harsh rebellion as he flicked his wrist and took off in a spray of anger and gravel. She watched him streak out of the lot and onto the street and listened as the bike wound through several gears. Her heart was racing as fast as the motorcycle's engine, but she attributed the acceleration to the near collision of sports car and cycle and the fact that she'd been talking to the bad boy of Gold Creek. His reputation was as black as the night and anyone in town would tell you that Sandra Moore's son was just plain bad news.

"Rachelle, come on!" Carlie called. She seemed to have shaken off her own fears that Jackson was injured and was deep in conversation with Scott and Erik.

With realistic fatalism, Rachelle glanced around the deserted parking lot. Aside from Laura's car, the acre of asphalt was empty. Rachelle sighed and shoved her hair out of her face. She knew she was stuck with Roy's two best friends. Not a pleasant thought. The wild side suddenly seemed like something she should avoid—unless she was with Jackson. Oh, but that was crazy. Jackson was no better than Roy and he carried a chip on his shoulder the size of Mount Whitney. Uncouth, rebellious and just plain nasty—that's what he was.

Still, she listened to the sound of the cycle, the engine whining in the distance. There was something about that boy that was just plain fascinating. Probably because he was so bad.

Despite the mugginess of the night, she stuffed her hands deep into the pockets of her jean jacket and retraced her steps.

"Was he okay?" Carlie asked, looking worriedly past Rachelle's shoulder to the spot where Jackson had been thrown.

"I don't know. I think so."

"He'll get even with Roy somehow," Erik predicted, and Rachelle thought about Jackson's cryptic warning. Erik looked nervous. He searched his pockets for his keys.

"Let's get out of here." Scott was already opening the door of the pickup and glancing anxiously around the empty lot, as if he expected Jackson Moore to come back and wreak his vengeance on Roy's friends. "We'd better find Roy."

"Roy? You want to find Roy after what he did? He

nearly killed Jackson! On purpose." Rachelle wrapped her arms around her torso and felt herself shaking from the inside out.

"He didn't, did he?"

"No, thank God!"

"You don't understand," Scott said a little impatiently. "Moore's been asking for trouble—begging for it—for weeks. There's always been bad blood between Jackson and Roy. It goes way back. But it's over tonight."

Rachelle wasn't sure. "Maybe not. Jackson could press charges."

"His story against Roy's."

"But we all saw it. Roy tried to run him down!" Rachelle pointed out.

"If he would've tried to run him down, he would've," Scott said. "Moore would be in the hospital now. Instead he and his bike are a little scratched up. No big deal."

"But it was a big deal!"

Erik, sullen, frowned darkly. "Come on," he ordered the girls. "Get in." He must've seen Rachelle's stubborn refusal building in her eyes because he added, "Unless you'd rather ride on the back of Moore's cycle, but you don't much look like a biker babe to me. Besides, he already took off."

Carlie didn't look convinced, but the night was drawing close around them. "We have to get hold of Laura."

"We could call—" Rachelle ventured.

"No phones at the summer house," Scott said.

"I don't think this is a great idea."

Scott lifted his hands, palms up to Rachelle. "Look, I'll admit it. Roy's a hothead. And when it comes to Moore, well, he just sees red. But that goes two ways. And Roy shouldn't have scared the hell out of Jackson, but then Jackson shouldn't have come nosing around, telling Roy what to do." He offered Rachelle a smile that seemed sincere. "Look, it was a bad scene, but it's over and everyone's okay. Now let's go and try to find Laura. If you want to come back later, I'm sure that Roy or Erik—" he glanced up at his friend for confirmation, and Erik gave a reluctant nod "—will bring you home."

Carlie shrugged. Obviously her worry for Jackson was long gone. "I say we go."

Rachelle's only other option was to walk to the school and call her mother and explain why she was stranded, since Laura had the keys to her car with her and Rachelle's overnight bag was locked securely inside the trunk. The thought of bothering Ellen Tremont and telling her about being abandoned by Laura in favor of a party at the lake wasn't appealing. Rachelle would probably end up grounded for life.

"Looks like we don't have much of a choice, do we?" Carlie asked, echoing Rachelle's thoughts. "And once we connect with Laura, we'll have these guys drive us back to the dance and no one will be the wiser." Carlie was already climbing into the cab of Erik's pickup. Her black hair gleamed, and she even managed a grin. "Let's not let this spoil our fun."

She had a point, Rachelle supposed, but it still didn't feel right. She slid into the truck from the driver's side and Erik followed her. Carlie perched on Scott's knees, bumping her head, trying to avoid more intimate contact.

Erik started the pickup and Carlie was thrown against Scott's chest. He was quick. His arms surrounded her and her backside was pressed firmly to his lap. Carlie giggled as Erik rolled out of the lot and turned east.

"Why is there bad blood between Roy and Jackson?" Rachelle asked, and Erik shot her an unreadable glance. She wasn't about to be put off. "Well?"

"Yeah, why does Roy hate Jackson?" Carlie asked, but Scott was tracing the slope of her jaw with one finger.

"Jackson's a nobody."

"But Roy almost ran him over!" Rachelle protested, her back stiffening. She'd always taken the side of the underdog and though Jackson had started the altercation with Roy, she felt that somehow he'd been wronged. "You don't run over a 'nobody' without a reason."

Erik pressed in the lighter and fumbled in his pocket. He withdrew a crumpled pack of Marlboro cigarettes and lit up. "Let's just forget it. Okay?"

Scott reached behind the seat to find a couple of bottles of beer. He opened them both by hooking the caps under the lip of the dash and yanking hard. Foam slid down the bottles and onto the floor. He tried to hand the first bottle to Rachelle.

"I don't think so," she said dryly.

"Your mistake." Erik grabbed the bottle and began drinking as he took the smaller streets to avoid the center of town.

"Maybe you shouldn't drink while you're driving," Carlie said, but Erik just laughed.

"Boy, are you out of it."

Rachelle's stomach twisted into a hard ball. This was all wrong. She'd made a big mistake in getting into this truck and now, as they headed out of town, she didn't know how to get out without completely abandoning Laura.

*She abandoned you, didn't she? Took off with Roy and left you with these two creeps.*

She stared into the rearview mirror, half expecting to see a single white light from Jackson Moore's motorcycle drawing up behind the truck. If the rumors surrounding Jackson's temper were true, Roy and his friends would have to answer to him sooner or later, which was probably why sweat had collected on Erik's upper lip. He took a long drag on his smoke, the tip of his cigarette glowing brightly.

"Forget about Moore," Erik advised, as if reading her mind. "He's nothin' but trouble."

WITH THE TASTE OF HIS OWN blood in his mouth, Jackson seethed. He slowed the Harley down and turned into the trailer park where his mother still lived. He'd moved back for a couple of months, but already this town was getting to him—Gold Creek was like a noose that tightened, inch by inch, around his neck. And he knew who held the end of the rope—who was doing the tightening. Roy Fitzpatrick.

He thought of Roy and his blood boiled again. *Ignore him,* one part of his mind said, but the other, more savage and primal male part of him said, *teach him a lesson he'll never forget!*

The pain in his shoulder had lessened to a dull ache and he knew his knee would bother him come morning. He'd been thrown hard from the bike, and his body would hurt like crazy tomorrow. He wanted Roy to feel a little of his pain. Roy was a stupid, spoiled brat and had been the bane of Jackson's existence for as long as he could remember. Roy hated him. Always had. Pure and simple, and though it sounded crazy, Jackson suspected that Roy was jealous of him. But why?

Roy had grown up in the lap of luxury, having anything he wanted, doing whatever he pleased. Jackson, on the other hand, had been dirt-poor, had never known his father and had spent most of his life helping support his mother. So why the jealousy?

It didn't matter. Jackson usually avoided Roy.

But tonight he'd had it. His mother had let the cat out of the bag. Her sister's girl, his cousin Amanda, in Coleville, had turned up pregnant last year while Jackson was still in the Philippines under the employ of the U.S. Navy. Rumor had it, the kid belonged to Roy. Amanda had dropped out of school, had the baby and given it up for adoption. Now she was regretting her decision and was involved in a messy court battle that was costly and gut wrenching for everyone involved.

Wincing, Jackson rubbed his shoulder.

Roy, of course, had denied his paternity and somehow, probably by Thomas greasing the right palms, Roy had come out of the sordid situation with hardly a scratch. But Amanda and the baby, and the couple who had adopted the boy, were paying and would be for the rest of their lives.

Roy deserved a beating, and Jackson intended to thrash him within an inch of his silver-spooned life. He cut the engine of the bike at his mother's door and stared at the black windows of the trailer. His shoulder was bruised from his embrace with the gravel, his leg hurt like a son of a gun, and the Harley's fender was bent and twisted. Other than that, the only thing wounded was his pride. And it was wounded big-time. Who the hell did Roy think he was?

Jackson knew the answer: Prince of Gold Creek. Keeper of the keys to the city. All-mighty jerk.

It was time Roy Fitzpatrick learned a lesson. And Jackson intended on being Roy's teacher. Roy and his father, Thomas, worked on a premise of fear and awe. And most of the comatose citizens of Gold Creek were either scared stiff of the old man or thought they should bow when he entered a room. It made Jackson sick.

Thomas Fitzpatrick believed that he could buy anything he wanted, including judges, doctors and sheriffs. Yeah, the old man was a piece of work and, in Roy's case, the apple hadn't fallen far from the tree. That went for the rest of the Fitzpatrick offspring, as well. The second son, Brian, was a snot-nosed wimp, and the daughter, Toni, though quite a bit younger, was already on the red-carpeted path to being a spoiled princess.

Sandra Moore's single-wide trailer showed no signs of life—no light in the window, no sound of radio or television. She was out again and she didn't confide in him where she went—just "out." Jackson supposed she was with a man and he only hoped that whoever the guy was, he'd treat her right. She'd never quite made the trip to the altar, though she'd come close a couple of times. But the love of her life had been his father, a sailor she'd met and planned to marry, but who had died before the wedding ceremony. Matt Belmont. She still carried his faded and well-worn picture in her wallet.

Jackson glanced up at the sky. The moon was nearly hidden by slow-moving clouds. The air was oppressive and hot. His cheek throbbed, his shoulder ached, and somewhere up by the lake Roy Fitzpatrick was having the time of his life with yet another girl. He supposed he shouldn't care, but the thought made his blood boil.

Tonight Roy was with the blonde—the Chandler girl, a flashy, big-breasted cheerleader who was just Roy's type, but soon Roy would get restless and bored and he'd move on. But to whom? Some college coed at Sonoma State where he went to school, or another small-town girl who thought the world began and ended with Gold Creek and the Fitzpatrick money? Maybe Roy would take a shine to one of the others who had been in his group. Perhaps the girl with the long red-brown hair, the one who had seemed genuinely concerned when Roy had tried to clip him.

Leaning forward, he rested his forehead on the handlebars.

He knew where Roy was. He'd heard about the party at the summer home of the Fitzpatricks. His chin slid to one side as he considered his options. Sweat trickled down his neck. He thought again of the girl who had run over to him to see if he'd been hurt. She was beautiful, as were all of the girls to whom Roy was attracted. Her hair was straight and thick, a glossy auburn sheath that fell nearly to her waist. Her face was small, with high cheekbones and eyes that were a shade between green and gray. Funny, how he'd noticed those eyes. They'd studied him with such intelligence, such clarity, that he couldn't imagine she was one of Roy's women. Still, he'd given her a rough time; tossed off her concerns. She was, after all, with Roy. Just another Gold Creek girl who wanted to get close to the Fitzpatrick money. They were all the same.

He spit blood onto the gravel drive and ran his tongue over his teeth. None chipped. He'd been lucky. Roy's fender had just clipped him, though Jackson doubted that Roy would really risk denting his expensive car. Or maybe he would. Daddy would always buy Roy a new one.

Closing his eyes, he rotated his head and heard his neck crack a little. A headache pounded near his temples. He should just leave Roy and Old Man Fitzpatrick alone. But he couldn't.

He kick-started the bike and wheeled around. No reason to stay in the dark trailer when he could settle things once and for all with the Fitzpatricks.

## CHAPTER TWO

THE FITZPATRICK "CABIN" was a mansion. Hidden behind a brick fence and wrought-iron gates, the rustic building was nestled in a thicket of pines on the shore of the lake. A sweeping front porch, awash with lights, was flanked by cedar-and-stone walls rising three stories.

Rachelle climbed out of Erik's pickup. The night smelled of pine, fir and water. Clouds gathered in the sky, blocking out the moon. The wind, too, picked up and rifled across the water, promising rain.

Music was throbbing through the open windows. Laughter and loud conversation were punctuated by the beat of a classic Eric Clapton tune. Though the night was muggy, Rachelle drew her jacket around her more tightly as she hurried up the stone path to the front door. She just wanted to find Laura and go home.

Even Carlie was getting nervous. She shot Rachelle a worried glance. "Maybe this wasn't such a good idea."

"It's a great idea," Scott said, throwing his arm over Carlie's shoulders. "Besides, Roy would be disappointed if you two didn't show up."

"He'd never miss us," Rachelle predicted.

"Oh, I wouldn't say that," Erik drawled. He and Scott exchanged a look and a smile that made Rachelle's blood run cold.

"What do you mean?"

"You'll see." Erik herded them onto the porch.

The door was ajar, and they walked into a two-storied foyer resplendent with Oriental rugs tossed over polished hardwood floors. Objets d'art and antiques were positioned carefully in the entry hall. A spinning wheel stood near the coat closet, a loom bearing a half-woven rug had been pushed into the far wall of the living room and a suit of armor stood near the staircase, a can of Coors clutched in its iron-gloved hand.

Laughter and music wafted from the back of the house.

"This way," Scott said, as he and Erik turned a corner and headed toward the rear of the house. Reluctantly Rachelle and Carlie followed. Rachelle regretted ever getting into the truck. What if someone called the police? What if no one was in any shape to take Carlie and her back to town? What if Laura was having such a good time, she didn't want to leave? Well, Rachelle could always call her mother. She winced at the thought and decided that if worse came to worst, she could hike the seven miles back to town.

The party was in full swing in the game room. Glassy-eyed heads of deer, moose and elk were mounted on the walls. In one corner, a player piano stood untouched, in another a Wurlitzer jukebox, straight out of the fifties, was playing records. A pool table, covered in blue felt, was centered on the gleaming floor and Foosball and darts were arranged in other parts of the room. A wall of windows, two stories high, offered a panoramic view of the lake, while against the interior, a set of stairs led to a loft. Smoke filled the air and glasses clinked.

Looking for Laura, Rachelle recognized some of the faces of the boys standing around a keg and telling jokes. Others were playing pool. Through sliding doors, to one side of the game room, steam rose from a glassed-in pool where a couple, dressed only in their underwear, was splashing and laughing.

"Have you ever in your life seen a house like this?" Carlie asked in an awed whisper.

"Never." Under other circumstances, Rachelle would have thought the rustic old house beautiful. Compared to the small cottage she lived in with her mother and sister, this "summer home" was palatial. Of course, the Fitzpatricks were the wealthiest family in town. They wouldn't have settled for anything less than the largest house on Whitefire Lake. But tonight the place gave her the creeps.

She kept telling herself to relax and lighten up, that she'd made the decision to come here, and she had to make the best of it. She sat on the piano bench, her fingers curling over the chipped edge, and tried to smile. But her lips felt frozen, even when she saw kids she recognized: older boys—Evan and Jason Kendrick—rich kids who knew the Fitzpatricks, and were playing pool while Patty Osgood and Nadine Powell were hovering nearby, ready to laugh at the boys' jokes and smile easily. Patty was drinking from a paper cup. She appeared a little unsteady on her feet and Nadine, the redhead, was leaning over the table, her face flushed as she flirted with Jason Kendrick. Both girls were wearing tight jeans and too much makeup. Patty, the reverend's daughter, was rumored to be fast and easy, though Nadine usually kept out of trouble. But tonight, both girls were definitely interested in the rich boys.

Gold Creek seemed to be a town divided—the haves and the have-nots, all of whom had collected at Roy's party. Rachelle wanted to go home more than anything right now. She had no business being here—

no interest in any of the people who'd come here to pay homage to the Fitzpatrick wealth.

"Surprised to see you here," Nadine commented, raising a brow at Rachelle.

"Yeah, don't you have a midterm to study for or somethin'?" Patty asked, then giggled and turned her attention back to her cup.

Rachelle felt the heat rise in her cheeks. Ignore her, she thought. Patty was drunk. As Rachelle watched, Patty draped one arm over Jason Kendrick's back while he tried a particularly difficult shot. The cue ball skipped and clicked against the eight ball, sending it whirling into a corner pocket.

"Too bad," Jason's older brother, Evan, said, but chuckled at his brother's misfortune.

Rachelle saw Carlie inching her way through the throng of kids, talking and laughing with several before plopping down on the bench beside Rachelle. "Where's Laura?" She was holding a cup, sipping beer and trying to look as if she'd done it all her life.

"Probably with Roy," Rachelle guessed.

"But where?"

"I wish I knew." Rachelle pretended not to be worried as she glanced around the room again, but she felt trapped. And Erik's cryptic words about Roy wanting the girls there made her uncomfortable.

Erik retreated to a corner with a group of boys. They were laughing and telling jokes, but Erik's dark eyes never glimmered with the faintest trace of humor. Scott hung out at the keg, but his eyes kept returning to Carlie. "He likes you," Rachelle said, and Carlie bit her lip.

"I know." She took a sip from her cup.

"Aren't you flattered?"

Before Carlie could reply, some of the football players showed up. Brian Fitzpatrick, of course, Joe Knapp and a few others swaggered in. They bellied up to the keg, started drinking and became louder and louder, replaying the game over, down by down, drowning out the music and other conversation.

Wouldn't Coach Foster be proud? Rachelle thought with a trace of sarcasm. She had no right to judge the football players, though, did she? She'd shown up here, too. Of her own free will. No one had pointed a gun at her head and forced her into Erik's truck.

Brian smiled when he noticed Rachelle and Carlie. "Joinin' the big boys, eh?" he asked, holding up his mug of beer. Some of the foam sloshed over his meaty fingers.

Rachelle managed a smile. "I think we're about ready to leave," Rachelle replied. "As soon as we find Laura. We just need a ride."

"Laura Chandler?" Brian said, grinning widely. "She's probably with Roy." He sniggered to his friends and then glanced to the loft. "She and Roy have been seein' a lot of each other lately, and I mean *a lot.*"

This caused a roar from the crowd and Rachelle couldn't stand it another minute. "Let's find her," she said to Carlie. She started toward the pool but stopped when she spied Laura slipping through the door. Her clothes were wrinkled, her hair a mess and mascara streaked her cheeks.

Rachelle and Carlie surrounded her. "Where have you been?" Carlie asked. "What happened?"

Laura ignored Carlie's questions. "So you made it," she said bitterly to Rachelle. "I was stupid enough to think you wouldn't show your face here."

"This was your idea," Rachelle reminded her.

"No it wasn't. It was Roy's." Laura's voice was filled with a cold fury. "That's why I started hanging out with you. Because he was interested in *you!* I thought I could change his mind, but I was wrong." She sniffed loudly and her eyes glittered. "He wants you, Rachelle. He just used me to get close to you."

"But I've hardly ever talked to him—"

"Well, it doesn't matter. He's seen you. At the games. At school. At your job with the *Clarion.*"

"It's only freelance—"

Laura laughed harshly. "Doesn't matter. Roy remembers you. You did a couple of articles about him when he was a senior. And, can you believe it, he's even impressed that you write for the school paper—that you're ambitious!" Tears had collected in the corners of her eyes and she wiped at them. "God, I need a cigarette."

Carlie dug into her purse, found an old pack of Salem cigarettes and shook one out for Laura. Grateful, her hands shaking, Laura lit up and blew smoke to the ceiling. "God, I'm such a fool," she whispered, her voice cracking as tears streamed again.

Some of the pool players glanced over their shoulders and a few of the girls stared openly at the cheerleader from Tyler High as she blinked rapidly and fought a losing battle with tears.

"Look, let's just get out of here," Rachelle suggested.

Carlie looked at Rachelle as if she were crazy. "How?"

"I don't know, but we'll find a way."

"You—you don't want to stay here?" Laura was flabbergasted. She took a long drag of her cigarette. "Roy will want to—"

"I don't care what Roy wants! *I* want to leave." Rachelle really didn't believe that Roy had any interest in her, but she wasn't going to argue with Laura now, not in the state Laura was in. And Rachelle didn't give two cents for Roy Fitzpatrick. "We can find someone to take us back—maybe Joe Knapp," she said.

Laura's chin wobbled and tears drained down her face, streaking her cheeks with mascara. "I love him," she said simply, and Rachelle felt a deep sadness for her friend—because she believed that Laura really did think she was in love. "I just…" Laura blinked hard but couldn't stop crying. "I'm so embarrassed." She wiped at the water-works in her eyes.

Carlie grabbed hold of her hand. "Come on. You can clean up in the bathroom."

"I left my purse outside. My makeup and wallet and everything…" She dissolved into tears again, and Rachelle felt more than one set of eyes staring at them. Erik Patton, from his position near the keg, lit a ciga-rette. Through the smoke, his eyes found Rachelle's and he shook his head, as if he found Laura's emotional con-dition pathetic.

"I'll get your purse," Rachelle offered. "And I'll find us a ride back."

Laura stubbed out her cigarette. Her hands were still trembling. "Thanks. I think I left it in the gazebo by the lake."

Rachelle didn't waste any time. "I'll meet you two by the front door in fifteen minutes."

While Carlie hustled Laura to a bathroom, Rachelle worked her way through the thickening crowd to the door. Outside, the air was heavy and close and the first fat drops of rain began to plop to the ground.

"Great," she murmured, hurrying along a lighted path that wound through the pines. The temperature seemed to drop ten degrees and the breath of wind blow-ing across the lake was now cool with the rain. Her feet slapped against the bricks, and her hair streamed out behind her as she ran up the two steps to the gazebo.

Roy Fitzpatrick was waiting for her.

"I was thinkin' I'd have to go in after you," he drawled, his voice smooth as silk.

She stopped dead in her tracks. "I just came for Laura's purse."

"Here it is." He picked up the purse by the strap and let it swing from his fingers. "Come and get it."

Fear slid down Rachelle's spine. "Why don't you just toss it over here?"

"What's'sa'matter? You scared of me?"

*Scared to death,* she thought, but shook her head. "Of course not." She stepped forward and grabbed for the strap, but Roy was quick. He caught hold of her wrist and pulled her down hard against him. "Hey, let me go!" she cried in surprise.

"Didn't Laura tell you I wanted to see you?" Roy asked. His breath reeked of beer and cigarettes, and his arms circled her back, holding her close.

"Laura's really upset," she replied, trying to wriggle free. This was crazy. What was Roy thinking? "Look, we're all leaving."

"You ain't going nowhere, honey," he whispered against her ear, and with a jolt Rachelle realized he wasn't kidding around.

"Roy, please—"

"Please what?"

"Just let me go."

"No way. I've been lookin' at you for a long time. Too long." Roy was strong, his muscles toned from years of athletics. As she pushed against him, he laughed and to her horror he placed a kiss against her hair. "Mmm, baby, you smell so good."

"Stop it," she warned, but his arms tightened and she was pressed hard against him.

Rachelle struggled, but her fight seemed to arouse him all the more. She tried to scream, but he covered her mouth with lips that were hot and eager. His tongue pressed anxiously against her teeth, trying to gain entrance. The heat of his body radiated into hers. "Come on, baby," he whispered, and she jerked her head away. His kisses brought a hot taste of fear to the back of her throat, but he wouldn't stop and the hands that held her were as strong as steel.

"Stop it," she ordered when he finally drew his head away. His expression in the darkness was intense. His eyes bored into hers in a savage way that made her insides curl. He transferred both her wrists to one of his hands and he kissed her again. This time his free hand slipped beneath her jacket to palm a breast.

She screamed then and tried to kick him, but he moved and covered her mouth with his hand. "No one's gonna come to your rescue here, girl. Don't you know that? All the guys—they're lookin' for their own fun."

She bit his hand and he yelped. "You bastard!" she shrieked as he flinched. She tried to scream again, but he flattened his lips to hers and kissed her hard.

"You know you want it," he whispered roughly, his breath tinged with stale beer. His fingers felt clammy and cold.

She kicked again, throwing all her weight into the effort as she aimed for his crotch. He shifted and her foot connected with his shin. He howled in pain but didn't let go.

"You little bitch!" He shoved her hard against the bench, and she screamed.

"Roy, don't—"

"*You,* don't. Ya hear?" he screamed in her face. "I'm the one giving orders and you're going to give me whatever I want and you're going to like it—"

Suddenly he was ripped off her and tossed across the gazebo like a rag doll. Her blouse tore with a horrid ripping sound.

Roy yelled, "Hey—what the—" as he crashed into the bench on the far side of the slatted structure.

"Leave her alone," Jackson thundered, appearing out of nowhere. Rachelle hadn't heard his bike or boots. She gulped back tears, limp beneath a tidal wave of relief at the sight of him. He glared over his shoulder at her. "Run!"

Rachelle tried to get to her feet, but she could barely move.

"I shoulda killed you when I had the chance," Roy yelled, struggling upward and lunging at Jackson. But the beer had made him sluggish, and as he scrabbled for Jackson's neck, Jackson shoved him back down.

"Leave her alone," Jackson ordered, then shot Rachelle a furious glance. "Damn it, I told you to run." He grabbed hold of her arm and yanked her to her feet. "Get outta here!"

A dozen of Roy's friends converged on the gazebo. There were shouts and hoots; the smell of a fight was heavy in the air.

Roy climbed to his feet, reached into his pocket and pulled out a jackknife. Jackson glared at him. Roy clicked the knife open. The blade gleamed wickedly in the night.

"No—Roy—" Rachelle cried, horrified.

But Roy smelled blood. He swung at Jackson, and Jackson spun, but not quickly enough. Roy drew back and the blade slashed downward. With a sickening rip, the knife connected with Jackson's leg.

Jackson sucked in his breath as Roy struck again, this time plunging the knife into Jackson's shoulder.

"Stop it, Roy!" Scott McDonald yelled.

"Butt out! This is my fight!" Roy snarled.

Jackson backed up and Roy slashed wildly.

Rachelle screamed.

"I'll kill you, man," Roy vowed, swinging at Jackson savagely, the blade slashing through the air as Jackson wheeled and dodged. Roy raised the knife again, and Jackson grabbed his wrist with one hand and landed a hard punch to Roy's midsection. The knife clattered onto the gazebo floor.

Jackson smashed his fist across Roy's cheek. Roy tumbled backward in a heap. Shaking his head, he spit and coughed. "You're a dead man, Moore! I'll kill you, I swear it."

"You'll never get the chance."

Jackson must've spied Rachelle from the corner of his eye. "Are you still here?" he demanded. "Get out of here before—"

"She stays!" Roy commanded, and Jackson lost no time.

"For crying out loud!" Grabbing Rachelle's arm firmly and half carrying her with him, Jackson vaulted the latticework of the gazebo. Together they landed in the bushes and scrambled to their feet. Jackson nearly stumbled as his leg gave out, and Rachelle pulled him upright. He was breathing hard and sweating. "Unless you want more trouble than you bargained for, you'd better get out of here now!" he advised.

"Listen, you illegitimate SOB," Roy bellowed, "she stays here!"

"No way!"

With Jackson still tugging on her arm, Rachelle started running with him, holding her tattered blouse and jacket together as they dashed through the shrubbery, Jackson spurring her on, though his gait was uneven and he was breathing heavily.

"Stop Moore—stop him!" Roy yelled but his voice was muffled now. Jackson led Rachelle through a garden and between trees to the driveway where his bike was parked. Three boys were standing guard and when they saw Jackson emerge from the woods, Erik Patton smiled wickedly.

"Well, look what you found—Roy's little piece," he taunted, but Jackson ignored them.

"Get on," Jackson told Rachelle, and without thinking she climbed astride the huge machine.

Erik lit a cigarette with exaggerated calm. "You're not gonna get far," he predicted, then cupped one hand around his mouth. "Hey, Roy, they're over here! Moore and the girl."

Jackson tried to start the bike. Nothing happened. Rachelle shivered visibly. Roy was coming. She could hear him. Her heart slammed in fear. "Come on," she whispered, and Jackson tried again. The engine wouldn't even turn over.

He glared at Erik for a heart-stopping second, then swept his gaze back at Rachelle. She didn't doubt if she weren't there that he would have climbed off the bike and torn Erik limb from limb.

"This way," he said, hopping off the motorcycle and dragging her along. They ducked into the woods again, and Rachelle wanted to cry. She was terrified of Roy, and knew instinctively that she was safer with Jackson, yet the night was too awful to believe. Roy had intended to rape her and Jackson, her savior, wasn't exactly a knight in shining armor. She only hoped her instincts about him were right, because she guessed by the way he touched her, by the glint in his eye, that beneath his bad-boy exterior, there was a trace of good. She clung to that notion like a drowning man holding fast to a life preserver.

Twigs and thorns tore at her skin and hair, but she took Jackson's advice and began running, as fast as her legs would carry her, toward the rocky beach surrounding the lake. She tripped twice on berry vines, but Jackson helped her struggle up and keep plunging forward. She didn't know if they were being chased, didn't want to take the time to look around and find out.

Her throat was hot and thick and tears streamed from her eyes. Rain poured down her neck. She couldn't forget the skin-crawling feel of Roy's body against hers, the terror that he wouldn't stop until he'd stripped her of her clothes, robbed her of her dignity and...oh, Lord, she couldn't think of that! She wouldn't.

The trees gave way and she was on the beach, running north, against the wind and rain that swept over the hills. Jackson's breathing was labored, and he ran with a limp. Now it was she who was pulling him, half dragging him up the beach. *Help me,* she prayed as the rain pelted them both and her legs began to ache. She held back sobs of fear and just kept running, clinging to Jackson's hand as if he were, indeed, the knight who was destined to save her from the evils of Roy Fitzpatrick.

# CHAPTER THREE

JACKSON WAS WEAK FROM the fight. By the time they turned from the beach and reentered the woods, he was limping badly and breathing hard. Even in the darkness, Rachelle could see the sweat standing on his face.

"We've got to get to the main road and hitchhike back to town," Rachelle said as he pulled up and braced his back against the rough trunk of a pine tree. He drew in a ragged breath, then placed his hands on his knees and lowered his head. "Come on," she urged.

"You want to take a chance on being picked up by Roy or one of his friends?" Jackson asked. He tilted his head to stare up at her in the darkness. His eyes were dark and unreadable—as black as the night that surrounded them. He swiped the back of his hand over his forehead. "Isn't that what got you into this mess in the first place?"

"You can't go much farther."

His lips twisted ironically. "Don't count me out yet. Come on, I've got an idea." He took her hand and led her at a slower pace through the forest. Trees snapped underfoot, and rain dripped in a steady staccato on a carpet of needles.

The night was so dark, she could barely pick a path; she continually stepped in mud and puddles. Her hair was drenched and she shivered as the wind whistled through the trees. Clutching her ripped clothes with her free hand, she didn't stop to think where they were going;

she wanted only to keep moving and put as much distance between Roy Fitzpatrick and herself as she could.

She wondered about Jackson's timing, how he'd found her with Roy in the gazebo. "Why were you at the party?" she asked.

"Fitzpatrick and I had some unfinished business."

"Is it finished now?"

He snorted. "I don't think it ever will be."

"Why does he hate you so much?"

Jackson threw her a dark glance. "Maybe he doesn't like me interrupting him when he thought he was going to score."

Rachelle felt as if she'd been slapped. "What're you talking about?"

"I didn't see what started it. But somehow you ended up alone with Roy. The way I figure it, you flirted with him, he responded and when things got a little too hot to handle, you panicked."

Rachelle's mouth tightened in indignation. "I went out there to get my friend's purse."

"And somehow ended up making out with him."

She stopped, breathing hard, her anger as bright as her tears. "You have no right to judge me. *No right.* I didn't tease or lead Roy on, if that's what you're hinting at. And anyway it doesn't matter. He attacked me. I said 'no' and he wouldn't listen. Look, you don't have to babysit me any longer. I can find my own way back to town."

He glanced at her, muttered something under his breath and sighed. "I guess I made a mistake."

"I guess you did." They stood staring at each other, the rain drizzling around them, their gazes locked. The woods smelled steamy and wet, and far in the distance the sound of music hummed through the trees.

Jackson grimaced. "I got to the party, decided that I

needed to cool off before I made an ass of myself with Roy, so I walked down toward the lake. I heard noises in the gazebo. When I got there, Roy was kissing you. I couldn't tell you were fighting back until you screamed."

He glanced away, his hands on his hips. "Look, I'm sorry. I just figured anyone who was with Roy and his crowd was asking for trouble."

She couldn't argue with that. Hadn't she, too, decided the very same thing? "I'm not a part of Roy's crowd."

"Just who are you?"

"A friend of Laura's, Rachelle Tremont."

Eyeing her for a moment, he said, "We don't have any time to lose. Come on, Rachelle." He took her hand again and they began picking their way through the undergrowth.

"Where're we going?" she whispered. She'd lost her sense of direction, but she felt as if they were circling back, heading toward Roy's party.

"I know a shortcut," he said. His grip tightened around hers and she felt as if the blood were all pooled in her hand. Jackson was wheezing a little, wincing each time he stepped on his right leg.

"You can't go on—"

"Shh!" he warned so loudly that some unseen creature scurried through the undergrowth.

Rachelle's heart was pounding in her ears, but she knew she was right. Closer than before, she heard the sound of voices and the gentle vibration of music. Jackson was leading them right back to Roy!

"You've got to be out of your mind!" she whispered.

"Maybe," he admitted with a sarcastic edge to his words. "But I don't think so."

They skirted the Fitzpatrick estate, staying in the trees that surrounded the thick stone walls. When they came to the private lane, Jackson hesitated, his muscles taut, his gaze moving swiftly through the forest. "Okay. Now," he whispered, half dragging her out of the cover of the woods to dash across the road and into the trees on the far side. They were heading east now, and the lake was visible through the trees. Dark and shimmering, the water rippled with the wind.

Rachelle's throat was dry and her body ached all over. Rain ran down her neck and seeped through her jacket. It seemed that they'd been wandering through the dripping trees for hours.

Jackson stopped for a second and rubbed his leg. Even in the darkness, she noticed the corners of his mouth turn white. "You need a doctor."

"I just need to rest awhile," he argued, taking her hand again and hobbling toward the lake. She followed him blindly, her fate in the hands of the bad boy from Gold Creek.

"Here we go," Jackson said as they used the beach to get past the fence that separated the estate and a huge house came into view.

"What's this?"

"The Monroe place."

She'd heard of it; a grand house that had stood empty during the winters when the Monroe family returned to San Francisco. "I don't think we should stop here," she said aloud, worrying, but Jackson had already run to the manor and was standing in a breezeway between the house and garage.

"No one will think we'd have the guts to stay so close to the party," he reasoned aloud. "They saw us take off in the opposite direction."

"But—"

"Stay here," he ordered, then checked all the doors and windows on the first floor.

"You're going to break in?"

"If they left it locked."

"But that's illegal."

Jackson sent her a glance that called her naive. "We won't get caught."

"That doesn't make it right."

"No, it doesn't. So you go ahead and stand here in the rain and figure out what else we're gonna do. In the meantime, I'll be looking for a way into this place."

He disappeared around the corner, and Rachelle shivered. She thought of Roy, how he'd tried to force her, and her stomach turned over. She'd been stupid and foolish and now, here she was, in the middle of nowhere, with a boy whose reputation was tarnished, breaking into the summer home of a wealthy family!

She'd wanted adventure, she'd longed to test her wings, and those very wings were about as sturdy as Icarus's had been against the heat of the sun. She'd plummeted in a downfall so great, she knew she'd crash and never find herself again.

Wrapping her arms around herself, she considered her options. Maybe Jackson was right. If they could just rest and warm up, then they could decide what to do. Inside the house, there could be a phone; she might be able to call her mother. Her stomach tightened at facing Ellen Tremont, or her friends again. What had happened to Carlie and Laura? What were they doing right now? Were they worried sick about her?

She heard a noise on the roof and her heart nearly stopped. Moving out of the cover of the breezeway, she looked up. Jackson had shimmied up the drainpipe and was working his way across the rain-slickened shakes to a window. She held her breath and crossed her fingers that he didn't slip, fall and break his stubborn neck. He rattled one lock, swore and moved to the next window. It, too, seemed shut tight.

To Rachelle's horror, he worked up the slope to the third story, where dormers protruded from the roof. At the second window, he stopped, withdrew something from his pocket, worked on the lock until with a sound of splintering wood, it gave way. A second later, he climbed through.

Great. Not only had they trespassed, but now they were breaking and entering. She waited impatiently, certain that someone from Roy's party would wander by and discover her. A full five minutes passed and she started to worry again. Had Jackson hurt himself, fallen down the stairs in the dark?

A lock clicked softly. The back door swung inward and Jackson stood with his back propping the door open, obviously pleased with himself.

She didn't wait for an invitation, but slipped inside, where some of the heat of the day had collected. They stood in the kitchen, dripping water onto the oak floor, listening to an old clock tick and the timbers creak. The furniture was covered in white sheets, and if she let herself, she could imagine that this particular house was haunted.

"Now what?" she asked him, suddenly aware that she was completely alone with him.

"We need a flashlight. The electricity's been turned off and I wouldn't want to use any lights anyway. Someone might see us and call the cops."

"No one will see us," she said, thinking how remote they were.

"Wrong. There's a marina across the lake and the bait-

and-tackle shop. Someone over there could glance this way, see a light that shouldn't be on and get nervous." He opened a cupboard and ran his fingers over the contents of the shelves, grunted, then started with the next cupboard. Before too long, he'd covered half the kitchen.

"This isn't going to work—"

"Hold on. What's this?" he asked, and she could hear the grin in his voice. "A candle. Primitive. But just the ticket."

He struck a match. It sizzled in the night, and in the small flame she could see his face, streaked with mud, a hint of beard darkening his chin, and the reflection of the match's flame as pinpoints of light in his dark eyes.

Carefully he lit the candle, then searched in the closet for more. Soon he had lit three candles and the kitchen seemed almost cheery in the flickering golden light.

"Aren't you afraid someone might see the candle-light?" she asked, but he shook his head.

"There's a den near the front of the house. It doesn't face the lake or the Fitzpatrick place. The blinds are already drawn. I think we'll be safe. If not—" He looked at her again and this time his gaze lingered a second longer than it should have. He shifted. "If not, we'll just have to face the music."

"We could call—"

"I tried. The phone's shut off."

"Wonderful," she murmured sarcastically, trembling inside. Things were going from bad to worse. "So what do we do?"

Jackson leaned one hip against the kitchen island. His hair was wet, golden drops ran down his face and neck. "I guess we wait, try to dry out and then figure out a way to get back to town. I imagine that if you don't show up somewhere at sometime, your folks will send out a search party."

Rachelle lifted a shoulder. "My mom works nights and I'm supposed to be staying overnight with Laura. My sister is with a friend. So no one's looking for me yet."

"What about your dad?"

That old knot in her stomach squeezed tighter. "He, um, he won't know. He and Mom are separated and he's living in an apartment in Coleville." She didn't add that he was probably with his girlfriend, a woman only a few years older than Rachelle. Glenda. Her father had found Glenda in the middle of his life and had decided that Ellen could raise the girls. He had living to do. "No one will call him," she said, trying to avoid thinking about her dad.

"But Laura's mother might call yours."

"I suppose."

Again Jackson looked at her and one side of his mouth lifted a fraction. "It's not so bad having someone who cares for you, you know. Believe me, it's better than the alternative."

Rachelle felt suddenly foolish. His mother probably had never cared when he came home and he'd never had a dad to worry over him or scold him or play catch with him or take him fishing.

He left the kitchen and, walking stiffly, holding on to the wall for support, headed for the den. Rachelle followed, carrying two candles and noticing how he favored his right leg. His jeans were soaked and streaked with mud, and the worn fabric clung to his thighs and buttocks as he limped down a short hallway. She forced her eyes away from his legs and found herself staring at the back of his battered old jacket, wide at the shoulders, tapered to the waist.

Over the scent of melting wax were the stronger smells of rain and musk and leather.

He placed his candle on the mantel of a river-rock fireplace and turned to face her.

She was shivering, her feet ice-cold in her wet boots. A crease formed between his brows, and he rubbed his chin. "You're freezing."

"A little."

"A lot. So am I." He checked the blinds again, closed the door to the room and then leaned over the fireplace. "I guess we'd better find a way to warm up." He reached into the chimney and pulled, opening a creaking damper and causing soot to billow onto the grate.

There were already logs piled on old andirons and newspaper and kindling neatly stacked in a box near the hearth. He bent on one knee and set to work.

Rachelle tried not to stare at him. "Isn't starting a fire asking for trouble?"

"Begging for it."

"Seriously."

"Maybe." He grabbed his candle and pressed the flame to the dry kindling and paper. In a few seconds the fire was popping and hissing, shooting out sparks and slowly warming the room. "Come over here," Jackson suggested, but Rachelle didn't dare move. She felt trapped in the seductive glow of the blaze, held prisoner by a man she found fascinating yet frightening.

To her horror, he stripped off his jacket, then his shirt. He hung his clothes over the screen and was left standing, half-naked, the golden light playing upon his dark skin and black thatch of hair at his neck. The wound to his shoulder had already stopped bleeding. He winced a little as he moved his arm.

"I—I can't do that," she pointed out, and he grinned—

not the sardonic smile that twisted his lips cruelly, but a genuine smile of amusement.

"We'll figure something out. At least take off your boots."

That, she could do. So she balanced herself on the edge of a couch and tugged on her boots. Her skirt was torn in spots where thorns had caught in the folds and her blouse was in tatters. Her jacket was in better shape, but wet all the way through. She kicked her boots onto the hearth, then self-consciously hung her jacket over the screen.

She felt every bit the virgin she was. She'd seen boys without their shirts before—many times while swimming at the lake or watching them scrimmage in basketball—but they had been boys, with smooth skin and only the smallest suggestion of body hair. Jackson, on the other hand, was a man. His muscles were developed and moved with corded strength, and his beard was dark against his jaw. The way his jeans hugged his hips, hanging low enough to expose his navel, caused her diaphragm to constrict. The back of her throat went dry, and she had to force her eyes away from the raveling waistband of his jeans.

His voice jerked her from her wicked thoughts. "I'll see if there's something around here that you can wear, so that that—" he pointed to her ripped blouse "—can dry out."

"It's fine."

"Is it?" He lifted a brow in disbelief. "We're in enough trouble as it is. I don't want to be responsible if you get pneumonia."

"I won't."

"And I don't want to get caught with you in something that was obviously torn from your body."

"Oh." She licked her lips nervously, aware that his gaze followed the movement. "Well, uh, I don't want to get caught—period."

"Amen." He limped out of the room and Rachelle let out her breath. Good Lord, what was she doing here? If she had any sense at all, she'd grab her boots and jacket and flee.

To where?

Anywhere! Any other place had to be safer than here, alone with Jackson. Her thoughts had turned so wanton that she was shocked. She, who had never much enjoyed being kissed. All that fumbling and groping and panting. She'd thought something was wrong with her because she'd never been "turned on" as some of the girls had confided. She'd wondered about the girls who said they'd trembled because they wanted to sleep with their boyfriends so badly.

Well, Rachelle had never been in love and her parents were a fine example of how love didn't work out. As for sex, Ellen Tremont had been embarrassed by the subject and had given her daughters minimal information on the subject. But Rachelle had learned a lot. From her friends. From the books she read. From movies. And she knew that something was wrong with her. Because she didn't want it.

Or at least she didn't think she did. Until now. For the first time in her life, she knew what her friends meant by thudding heartbeats and sweaty palms and a crackle of excitement—an electrical charge—between two people.

But Jackson Moore? Why not someone safe like Joe Knapp or Bobby Kramer? Someone who wouldn't intimidate her.

She was still standing in front of the fire, heating the backs of her legs and holding her blouse together when he returned with a couple of blankets. "No clothes," he said, and she accepted the blanket and tucked it over her shoulders.

"I'll be fine."

He smiled then and shook his head. "If either of us get out of this and are 'fine,' it'll be a miracle." She was suddenly so aware of him...of his maleness that she couldn't look at him and felt tongue-tied, though she was beginning to warm a little.

From the corner of her eye, she watched him. Half boy, half man and thoroughly fascinating.

He flopped onto the couch, then sucked in a sharp breath as he attempted to struggle to a sitting position. But his knee, stiffening, wouldn't bend. His face turned white with the effort, and he fell onto the cushions, wincing when his shoulder connected with the back of the couch.

"Your leg. It's hurting you and your shoulder..."

"Don't worry about it."

"You should see a doctor."

"I said I'm okay."

Rachelle wasn't convinced. Every time he moved, he blanched. "You're a lousy liar." She glanced down at his jeans and felt sick. A dark stain colored the fabric stretching across his knee.

"So sue me."

"Let me look at your leg."

He offered her a lazy, pained smile. "Why, Miss Tremont," he mocked, "are you suggesting that I drop trou?"

"No, I—"

"That's a new one on me," he cut in, "but if you insist—" He made a big show of sliding the top button of his waistband through its hole and she knew that he was expecting her to yell "stop," but she wouldn't give him the satisfaction.

Her heart was beating faster than the wings of a bird in flight but she watched, her fingers clenched tight in the folds of the blanket.

His gaze still pinned on her face, he yanked at the worn fabric and a series of buttons released with a ripple of pops. Rachelle's breath seemed to stop.

Despite his pain, his lips twitched in amusement.

Rachelle was certain he wouldn't go any further, yet she stared at him as he squirmed, lifting up his buttocks and sliding his pants down his leg with a grimace and groan of pain. For the first time in her life she saw a man in white briefs and she forced her eyes away from the bulge that was apparent between his legs.

"You could help me, you know. This *was* your idea."

"You want me to help you take off your pants? No way." The thought of grabbing that wet fabric, the tips of her fingers grazing his legs and hips brought a blush to her cheeks. He was injured, she told herself, she should help him, but she stood near the fireplace as if cast in stone. It wasn't a simple situation of patient and nurse; there were emotions charging the air, sensual impulses that she'd never felt before but recognized as sexual. Her insides quivered—in fear or anticipation—before she saw the gash that started above his knee and swept over the joint to dig deep into the flesh of his calf. Blood was crusted around the cut and her stomach turned over.

"That's horrible."

"One word for it," he said. His pants would go no further as he was still wearing black leather boots. Without a word, she grabbed one boot by its run-down heel and tugged, inching the wet leather off his swollen leg. The sturdy cowhide had spared his lower calf from further injury, but still the cut looked painful.

"Nice guy, Roy Fitzpatrick," Jackson mocked.

"A prince." She yanked off the other boot, and it slid off to the floor with a clunk. To keep busy, she set both boots by the fire, then turned to find him, nearly naked, staring up at her.

"What now?"

"You should go to a hospital, then press charges against Roy at the police station," she said flatly, still keeping her distance.

"Oh, sure. Like the cops would believe me."

"You had witnesses."

"Who will all say I started the fight, provoked Roy into it."

"I won't," she whispered, biting her lower lip. "I was there, Jackson. I know what happened."

"Our words against the son of Thomas Fitzpatrick. Do you know who the chief of police in Gold Creek is?" he asked, and Rachelle's heart did a nosedive. "So you do. Vern Kyllo. Thomas Fitzpatrick helped elect him. Vern's Thomas's wife's cousin or something like that. Anyway, there's no way Chief Kyllo is going to let anything happen to Roy."

"But Roy attacked you and me!"

Jackson shot her a look that called her a fool. "You're going to stand up to the Fitzpatricks?"

"Yes!"

He smiled and shook his head. "Then you'll lose."

"Someone's got to stand up to them."

"I just wouldn't want to see you hurt." His gaze touched hers, and for a crazy second her heart took flight. Her face was suddenly hot. "I've got a bone to pick with Roy. You don't—"

"I do after tonight!"

"I know, but if you start yelling 'attempted rape,' you'll be in for a lot of trouble."

"You mean no one will believe me."

His gaze touched hers. "It'll be tough."

"But you believe me, don't you?" Suddenly it was important that Jackson know the truth.

"Yeah, but I'm the only person in this damn town who sees Roy for what he is." He reached forward and touched her hand. "I'm sorry for that crack earlier—I know you didn't tease Fitzpatrick into attacking you." His fingers were warm and gentle. "I was just angry. It bothers me that you were with him."

"It does?" She bit her lip, her heart pounding as his fingers linked with hers.

"You're better than Roy, Rachelle. Better than the whole lot of Fitzpatricks. Don't let any of them get to you."

"I—I won't," she said as he dropped her hand.

Her heart was thudding so loudly she was sure he could hear it. "I—I'll go look for something to clean up your leg," she said, suddenly needing air.

Jackson flopped back on the couch, and for the first time she noticed that the water on his face wasn't all rain-drops. There was sweat beading against his upper lip and forehead and his teeth were clenched tight. Against pain. He'd only been keeping up a good front for her.

Using candlelight as her guide, she explored the down-stairs, found a bathroom off the kitchen and discovered not only scissors, iodine and cotton balls, but gauze and tape, as well. She didn't know the first thing about bind-ing wounds and warding off infection and whether or not a person would need stitches, but decided to be prepared for anything.

However, nothing could have readied her for the sight of Jackson lying on his back, eyes closed, firelight playing upon his bare chest, arms and legs. Black, straight lashes touched his hard-edged cheekbones and his wet hair was drying in a thick tangled thatch that fell over his forehead. The corners of the room were in shadow, and the room smelled of burning cedar and baking leather. Warm. Cozy. The sound of rain pelting the windows and wind rattling old shutters only added to the feeling of home. For the first time that night she felt safe.

Which was ridiculous, considering the circumstances.

She was alone, cut off from the world with the sexiest boy she'd ever met and all her emotions were on edge—tangled and confused. Her pulse was out of control when he opened one eye and slid his gaze her way.

"I'm not much of a nurse," she said.

"Probably better than I am."

"There's no water," she said, "but I suppose that the iodine will do."

Nervous couldn't begin to describe how she felt as she balanced on the edge of the couch, turned slightly and, with visibly shaking fingers, swabbed the cut with the dark liquid that turned yellow against Jackson's skin. He sucked in a swift breath and caught her wrist between steely fingers.

"Damn it, woman! What're you trying to do, burn a hole clean through me?"

"Of course it burns. That's how you know it's working," she replied, though she was only repeating her grandmother's words from long ago.

"Then it's working like crazy." He let go of her wrist. "Least you could've done is give me a bullet to bite or something."

She almost laughed. Except she had to touch him

again. Carefully she washed the cut again. Jackson flinched and ground his teeth together, his muscles tightening reflexively, but he didn't try to stop her.

The gash began to ooze more blood. Rachelle's stomach roiled. "I don't think this is working."

"Sure it is," he assured her through gritted teeth. "Just finish cleaning it and wrap the damned thing up."

"You need a doctor."

"Not when I've got you, Florence Nightingale."

She caught his eye and knew that he was trying to lighten the mood. "Give me a break," she muttered, but started wrapping gauze around a muscular leg covered with tanned skin and surprisingly soft black hair. She tried not to notice that her heart was thundering, that her insides had seemed to melt or that the little bit of heat climbing up her neck had seemed to start in a deep part of her that heretofore had been unexplored. She concentrated on her work, closing the skin and stopping the flow of blood, and refused to let her eyes wander upward past the slash that started on his thigh to his shorts and what lay beneath the thin fabric.

Being here alone with him was madness. She bandaged his shoulder, but the wound wasn't as deep as that on his leg. "We have to find a way out of here," she said. "You really do need a doctor."

"I'll be okay."

"Will you?" She tried to smile, but couldn't. "I don't know if, after tonight, either one of us will ever be okay again," she said, repeating the sentiments he'd expressed earlier. When he didn't reply, she moved off the couch and threw another chunk of wood onto the fire.

She started to explore a bit then, feeling his gaze upon her as she poked into a bookcase that covered one wall. Below the rows and rows of volumes were cupboard doors, and within the cupboard was an old quilt, hand-stitched and lovingly worn in places. "Just what you need," she said, withdrawing the blanket and shaking out its neat folds. "Voilà. Comfort and modesty all in one fell swoop." With a flourish, she snapped the comforter in the air and let it drift down over the couch to cover Jackson's long body.

"Does it bother you?"

"What?"

"The fact that I'm undressed."

"What do you think?" She couldn't even look at him then; the conversation was far too intimate.

"Haven't you ever seen your brothers—"

"Don't have any. Just one sister."

"Well, the brother of a friend?"

"No."

He studied her long and hard, as if trying to unravel a mystery that surrounded her. It was foolish of course. She wasn't mysterious, nor particularly interesting for that matter, and yet he stared at her as if she were the most fascinating creature on earth.

"Tell me about Rachelle Tremont," he suggested.

"Not much to tell."

"Well...tell me about yourself, anyway. What else have we got to do?"

The question stopped her cold. It implied that they had time, and lots of it, alone together. It implied that anything else they might consider would only get them in trouble. It implied that they were somehow bound together, obligated to share of themselves, and yet she couldn't imagine sharing only part of herself with this boy. This man. This male.

As she stood up, she glanced down at him, at his shoulders rising above the hem of patchwork pieces. "I should leave, Jackson. Try to get to town and find you a doctor."

"I don't want a doctor."

"You need one."

"No way."

She sat down on the edge of the couch, looking at him, wondering what it would be like to kiss him, and her gaze locked with his for a heart-stopping instant. The look was electric, and she glanced quickly away, aware of heat climbing up her neck.

"You okay?" he asked, his voice husky.

"No, but considering…" She shrugged. "I'm all right." She was so aware of Jackson that she tingled. "Thanks… thanks for saving me."

"No big deal—"

"It was!" She bit her lip then, surprised at her vehemence, and when she slid a glance his way, he was studying her face.

"I—I'm not sure—we should stay here."

"Neither am I," he admitted, his hand finding hers. His fingers were warm as they laced through hers. Still watching her, he tugged gently, silently insisting that she get closer to him. She knew she shouldn't. That she should resist. He was too dangerous. Too sexy. And yet her legs moved willingly to the edge of the couch and she didn't stop him from pulling her closer, so that she was sitting, half lying with him.

As she lowered herself, his hands moved, surrounding her waist, drawing her closer. He stared up at her with the firelight catching in his golden-brown eyes and the throb of his pulse visible in his throat.

One hand held the back of her neck, dragging her head forward until his lips were only inches from hers, his breath mingling with her own. She felt poised on the brink of an emotional river that promised to change her life forever. Not really understanding what was expected of her, and yet wanting to find out, she felt herself let go and dive into the current as his lips brushed gently over hers.

Her heart stopped and the noises of the night—the steady patter of rain, the tick of the clock, the hiss of the fire—faded into some dreamy corner of her mind. The kiss was slow and sensual, and though only their lips touched, the feeling seemed to reach every point in her body.

She felt his breath mingle with hers as his hands twined in her hair. Low and husky, his voice whispered a soft groan and she responded in kind. He drew her closer still until her breasts were flat against his bare chest and his tongue insistently prodded her teeth apart.

Willingly she accepted him. Never had she wanted to be kissed so thoroughly, never had she felt such passion. Eager to learn, quivering as his fingers brushed the bare skin at her throat, she kissed him with the same hunger she felt shudder through him.

"This is dangerous," he said, but didn't release her.

"I know." She licked her tingling lips nervously, and he groaned again.

"I think we should stop."

"I do, too," she replied, but didn't mean the words. Thoughts of pregnancy skittered through her mind, but were quickly forgotten when his fingers lowered, through the long strands of her hair to her back and he gently eased her forward until he could bury his face between her breasts. Her ripped blouse gave him easy entrance, and his breath was warm and wet against her skin.

She felt on fire and instinctively she arched closer, quivering when his tongue touched her flesh, wanting more of this delicious torture. An ache, deep and hot, burned between her legs as his lips slid downward, opening the flaps that had been her blouse and touching the lace of her bra.

His tongue delved beneath the sculpted edge and her nipple puckered in expectation. "You're beautiful, so, so beautiful," he said, shoving her blouse open and lowering the one silky strap.

Rachelle kissed the top of his head, wanting so much more.

She trembled as the strap was pulled over her arm and her breast, unbound, spilled into his waiting mouth. A shiver ripped through her as he began to suck and she moved against him, ecstasy and desire running like lava through her veins.

He cupped her buttocks and she felt a short second of panic before desire, like a living, breathing animal, turned panic into need. While he suckled and nipped at her breast, his hands moved downward, beneath her skirt to inch upward again, his flesh against hers.

"Stop me," he said, his eyes glazed as he stared up at her. "Stop me if this isn't what you want."

She was embarrassed, but couldn't control her wayward tongue. "I—I—uh, don't want to stop."

"You don't know what you're saying."

She reached down and held his face between her hands. "I've never felt like this before. *Never*. I don't know if I can stop."

He grabbed her hands, his fingers biting into her wrists. "For God's sake, Rachelle, you were nearly raped tonight. I have no right to ask you to—"

"What happened with Roy has nothing to do with this," she replied, surprised that he would compare the ugly scene with Roy to this tender, warm moment.

He stared up at her and clenched his teeth together as she shifted her weight. His eyes were tortured. "Too much has already happened tonight. I can't do this to you."

"Just kiss me," she said, knowing she was inviting trouble, but unable to stop. *A walk on the wild side?* Wasn't that what she wanted? But this—?

"Rachelle—no—"

She lowered her face to his and slowly drew his lower lip into her mouth. He clenched his jaw. She moved, and her bare breast rubbed against the hair of his chest.

With a groan, he buried his face in her abdomen and she bucked against him.

Jackson's control burst and he was kissing her again. His lips, wet and anxious, covered her bare skin with eager kisses. His tongue, a wild thing, licked and played, and she was moaning in his arms, consumed with an ache so painful, she only wanted him to fill it.

Her thoughts were blurred, the flame within her so hot that she knew nothing aside from the feel of his skin against hers. He was hard where she was soft, he was hot and sweating as was she and her clothes seemed to fall away effortlessly as he kissed her and whispered words that hinted of love.

Rachelle closed her eyes and let her hands explore every inch of his maleness. From his rock-hard shoulders to the scale of his ribs, she felt him. He kissed her eyes and throat and sucked from her breasts as if she were offering sweet nectar and when he, suddenly oblivious to pain, rolled over her so that she lay beneath him, she felt no fear. He parted her legs and hovered above her.

Only when he looked down and saw her completely naked did he hesitate. "This is wrong," he whispered.

"It feels right," she said, swallowing against a sudden

premonition that what was happening could never be undone. That he didn't love her, nor she love him. That she was a stupid teenager experimenting with something that could burn her forever.

Swearing at himself, he thrust into her and she cried out from the pain that seared between her legs. She flexed but he didn't stop. He moved within her, gently at first until once again the doubts were chased away and all that she felt was the swell of him in her, the calluses of his hands stroking her breasts, the fire that ravaged them both. His strokes deepened and came faster and Rachelle moved with him, wanting more of him, knowing in her heart that nothing that felt so beautiful could be wrong. She clung to him, her fingers digging into his shoulders, her hips arching up to meet his until, like an earthquake, a tremor rocked through her and she cried out.

He stiffened and threw back his head in a primal cry. As he fell against her, he tangled his hands in her hair and whispered her name over and over. She seemed to glide, like a feather on the wind, sinking slowly back to earth. She was breathing hard, but the soothing waters of afterglow wrapped around her as tightly as the frayed quilt and Jackson nestled beside her, holding her close, resting her head in the crook of his neck, telling her that she was like no other woman on earth. To her horror, a sob thickened her throat and tears formed in the corner of her eyes.

She didn't regret their lovemaking, oh, no, but she did cry—for something lost and something gained.

## CHAPTER FOUR

AFTER HOURS OF MAKING LOVE in the candlelight, Rachelle fell asleep in Jackson's arms, certain that their love—for that's what she told herself the emotions she was feeling had to be—would last forever. Midway through the night, she felt Jackson slip away from her, but only for a while. Soon he was back beside her, his skin cool, his hair smelling of pine trees, his lips pressing softly against her nape. She wrapped her arms around him and they slept, legs and arms entwined, one of his hands cupping her breast.

She didn't think of the morning or the problems they would face.

But those problems were worse than she imagined. She was still sleeping soundly when a loud banging against the door dragged her into consciousness.

"Moore?" A male voice boomed through the house.

Rachelle's eyes flew open. She was disoriented for a second and the room unfamiliar.

Jackson levered up on one elbow, his bare muscles tense.

She was confused. "Wha—"

Silently he placed a warning finger against her lips, cautioning her not to cry out. His eyes were dark as he slid off the couch and snatched his jeans from the floor.

The voice thundered again. "We know you're in there. Sheriff's department. Open up."

Rachelle felt instantly cold all over. *The sheriff's department?* Here? Searching for them? Panic and guilt tore through her. Had her mother called the police and hysterically claimed that her child had run away or been kidnapped? But how had the police tracked them down here?

Noiselessly Jackson tossed her skirt and blouse to her and motioned for her to get dressed.

She couldn't move. The thought of the police just outside the door made her feel sick with fright. What would happen to them? She began to panic, but Jackson's hand, strong and warm, settled over her shoulder.

"It'll be all right," he whispered, though she didn't believe him. But it was nice to have him try to comfort her, and she flew into action, throwing on her clothes before anyone saw her nakedness.

Jackson, too, was trying to get dressed. Wincing against the pain ripping down his leg, he struggled into his jeans. His calf and knee had swollen and with the added thickness of his bandage, he had trouble sliding his wounded leg into the tight-fitting Levi's.

The pounding on the door resumed, and Jackson, limping visibly, slipped to the back of the house, where he carefully peered through the kitchen windows. Rachelle followed him and watched his handsome face fall.

"No way out," he whispered, cursing under his breath.

"Maybe we should hide."

"From the sheriff's department? They've got dogs, Rachelle."

The thought of the police terrified her. Sirens, guns, lights, dogs… "But—"

His face was filled with compassion. "We've got no choice."

She glanced past him to the window. "You mean they've got us surrounded—just like in all those crummy old Westerns?" she asked, following his uneven strides back to the den.

"That's about the size of it." His gaze swung around the room where morning light was piercing through the shades and the smell of warm ashes, tallow and sex still lingered. The quilt had slid to the floor but throw pillows were still piled on the end of the couch that had supported their heads. Rachelle's throat tightened at the sight of this, their love nest.

"Moore! Come out with your hands over your head!" the deputy ordered, his voice hard.

"I hear you!" Jackson replied. "Give me a second."

"Now!"

Jackson swiped his jacket from the screen and tossed Rachelle hers. "Big trouble," he said, staring into her eyes so deeply that her heart turned over. "I'm sorry."

"Not me." She gulped, but tilted her chin upward. Panic seized her, and her stomach clenched into a hard ball.

"You will be," he predicted as he twined his fingers through hers. He sucked on his lower lip for a minute as he stared at her, then, in a gesture she'd remember the rest of her life, he drew her close, fingers still interlaced, and touched his lips to hers in a chaste kiss that melted most of her fears. "I'll never forget last night."

"Me neither." Tears threatened her eyes as hand in hand they walked to the front door. She felt dead inside, certain that her life—as she'd known it for the past seventeen years—was over, but at least she and Jackson were together, she reminded herself, tossing her tangled hair away from her face and holding her shredded blouse together. What a sight they must make.

"Comin' out," Jackson yelled as he opened the door with a decisive turn of his wrist. He and Rachelle stepped onto the front porch. It was early, just after dawn, and there was still a thick mist rising off the lake.

Three cars from the sheriff's department were parked in the drive. Six officers, weapons drawn, were staring grim-faced at them, sighting their guns as if Rachelle and Jackson were dangerous fugitives who had escaped the law.

Rachelle thought she might faint.

"Let her go," one deputy ordered, and Jackson released her hand as if it had suddenly seared him.

"No—" she whispered, but was cut off.

"You're Rachelle Tremont?" another officer demanded.

She nodded dully. What was this all about? They were trespassing, true, but the somber faces and loaded weapons of the officers reeked of much more heinous crimes than even a possible kidnapping charge. "Jackson?" she whispered.

"Move away from him," a voice barked.

"But—"

"Move away from him. *Now!*"

Her spine stiffened in silent rebellion though she was scared to her very soul. With her throat dry as a desert wind, she moved on wooden legs, feeling the distance between Jackson and herself becoming more than physical; as if by walking away from him, she was creating an emotional chasm that might never be bridged again. His expression turned harsh and defensive, and he only glanced at her once, without a glimmer of the kindness or even the cynical humor she'd seen the night before.

Slowly Jackson raised his hands, palms forward into the air, and the officers rushed him. Two grabbed his arms, while another threw him up against the side of the house and quickly frisked him. Rachelle looked on in horror.

"Hey, man, I'm not carrying—"

"Shut up!"

Jackson snapped his mouth closed while another deputy read him his rights.

Rachelle was nearly dragged by yet another to one of the deputies, down the steps and to the cruiser.

"What's going on?" she demanded, shaking and pulling back, her head craned to look over her shoulder so that she could keep Jackson in view. Her blouse gaped, and she caught it with cold fingers.

"Just get inside, Miss Tremont."

"But why are you doing this?"

Jackson was being stuffed into another car from the sheriff's department, and once the deputies had slammed the cruiser's heavy door shut, they slid into the front seat and flicked on the engine. With red and blue lights flashing, the car roared down the puddle-strewn drive.

"We're taking you to the department to ask you a few questions," a short deputy with a bushy red mustache explained. His name tag read Daniel Springer.

"Why?"

"We want to know what you were up to last night."

She swallowed hard and her cheeks began to burn. "I was here."

"All night?"

"Y-yes—after we, um, left the party—the party at the Fitzpatrick place on the lake."

"We know about the party."

"Jackson and Roy got into a fight. Roy almost killed him…."

"So you were here alone all night with Jackson Moore," Deputy Springer clarified.

"That's right."

"You'd swear to it?"

"Slow down, Dan," the other deputy, Paul Zalinski, insisted. He lit a cigarette, took a long drag and snapped his lighter closed. Smoke streamed from his nostrils. "We don't want to screw this up. She's a minor, for God's sake. We've got to talk to her guardian and probably a lawyer. Then we can get her statement."

"By then, she and Moore can get her story straight—"

"There's nothing to get straight," Rachelle interjected.

The men exchanged glances and told her to get into the waiting car. She had no choice. Nervous sweat broke out between her shoulder blades as she slid into the worn backseat of the cruiser. Deputy Zalinski ground his cigarette out beneath the heel of his boot before climbing into the Ford. Deputy Springer started the car. Soon, they were following the other police cars on their way back to Gold Creek, leaving the Monroe mansion, a rumpled couch and a night of lovemaking far behind them.

Rachelle tried to fight against the terror that she felt creeping into her heart. Arms hugging her middle, she huddled in the backseat of the police cruiser and silently prayed that this was all a bad dream and she'd wake up with Jackson stretched out beside her. She rubbed her arms and stared through the trees to the misty lake. What was the old Indian legend? Drink from the lake but don't overindulge and the waters will bring you good luck? Well, she was certain both she and Jackson could use a shot of magic water right now. They were in trouble. Deep trouble.

However, she wouldn't realize until hours later just how bottomless that trouble was.

Before the day was out, Jackson Moore, the bad boy of Gold Creek, would be formally charged with the murder of Roy Fitzpatrick.

"THAT'S CRAZY! JACKSON wouldn't kill anyone!" Rachelle cried, disbelieving. She leapt out of the hard wooden chair in the interrogation room at the sheriff's office.

Her mother, two deputies, a lawyer she'd never seen before, and even her father were with her, listening as she tried to explain the circumstances of the night before.

"You've got everything wrong!" She was nearly hysterical.

"Calm down, little lady," Deputy Springer advised. "We're just talkin' this thing out. Now, someone hit that boy over the head and drowned him in the lake last night, someone strong enough to hit him and hold him down, someone who was angry with him, someone who had a reason to pick a fight with him."

"But not Jackson," she replied staunchly, though her insides were shredding with fear and doubt and a million other emotions.

"You see 'em fightin' earlier?"

"Yes, but—"

"And didn't Moore stop Roy from...well, from attacking you?"

Rachelle took in a long breath. "That doesn't prove anything."

"A couple of witnesses say that Jackson was lookin' for a fight with Roy, that he'd already had words with Roy's daddy at the logging camp a few days ago, and that Roy had almost run Jackson down before the party."

Rachelle didn't say anything. Her throat was tight and hot, and she was more scared than she'd ever been in her life.

"Isn't that what happened?" Deputy Zalinski prodded.

Slowly, so as not to be misunderstood, she said, "I'm telling you I was with him the entire night." Her voice was raw from talking, and hot tears began to gather in the corners of her eyes. She felt shame that all of Gold Creek would learn of her night with Jackson, but more than shame she felt fear, sheer terror for Jackson. The charges were ridiculous, but the stony, solemn faces of the men who worked for the sheriff's department convinced her that they meant business. She had to save Jackson. She was the only one who could. "That last time we saw Roy, he was alive. Drunk, and a little beat-up, but *alive!*"

"And you were awake all night long?" Deputy Zalinski asked. He fiddled with his lighter, but she knew his concentration hadn't strayed at all. He waited, flipping the lighter end over end in his fingers.

Rachelle hesitated. She couldn't look her father in the eye. "I slept part of the time." She was mortified and tired and still in the dirty, ripped clothes she'd been in the night before. All she'd been given was a box of tissues and a glass of water. And her father's disgrace, so visible in the downcast turn of his eyes, made cringe inside.

Zalinski finally lit a cigarette. "Are you a heavy sleeper?"

"I don't know."

"She sleeps like a log—" her mother began, then snapped her mouth shut when the lawyer shot her a warning glance. Ellen Tremont went back to worrying the handle of her purse between her bony fingers.

"Isn't it possible that Jackson could have left you for a couple of hours and you would never have been the wiser?" Deputy Zalinski suggested. He took a long drag of his cigarette, and the smoke curled lazily toward the light suspended above the table. "The Monroe place is less than a quarter of a mile away from the Fitzpatricks'."

"He didn't leave me!"

"But you were asleep."

"He was hurt and…" She swallowed back her humiliation and tried not to remember the hours in early dawn when she'd felt him leave the couch to return later—she couldn't have guessed how long—smelling of pine needles and the rain-washed forest.

"And what, Miss Tremont?" Zalinski pressed on.

"He, uh, he didn't have his clothes on."

Her mother gasped, and Rachelle fell back into the folding chair. Somehow she managed to meet Deputy Zalinski's eyes. "He could barely get into his pants because of the swelling and bandage around his leg."

"He was wearing jeans this morning."

"Yes, but he had to struggle to get them on. And I watched him do that—after you had arrived and ordered us out of the house."

The deputy smiled patiently. "Then it was possible that while you were sleeping, he could've *'struggled'* into his clothes, left and returned before you even missed him."

"No!" she snapped quickly, and watched as Deputy Springer, propped against the corner of the room, jotted a note to himself.

Zalinski stubbed out his cigarette. "Miss Tremont—"

"Can I go now?" she cut in.

The answer was no. The interrogation lasted another two hours, at the end of which, on the lawyer's advice, her parents—in the first decision they'd agreed upon for two years—proclaimed that Rachelle wasn't to see Jackson again. They were both shocked and appalled that their daughter, the reliable, responsible one of their two girls, had gotten involved with "that wretched Moore boy." Though the police had assured her folks that Rachelle was not a suspect, not even considered for being an accessory, she was as good as convicted in their eyes. She'd slept with a boy she hardly knew, a boy with a reputation as tarnished as her grandmother's silver tea set, a boy who was now charged with kidnapping, trespassing, assault, breaking and entering and *murder*.

While Jackson sat alone in the county jail, unable to make bail, Rachelle was grounded. Indefinitely. Even her sister, Heather, who usually enjoyed adventure and took more chances than Rachelle, was subdued and stared at Rachelle with soulful, disbelieving blue eyes.

"I can't believe it," Heather whispered, gazing at Rachelle with a look of horror mingled with awe. "You *did it?* With Jackson Moore?"

"I don't want to talk about it." Rachelle, sitting on the edge of her bed, towel-dried her hair.

"But what was it like? Was it beautiful, or scary or disgusting?"

Rachelle ripped the towel from her head. "I said I'm not discussing it, Heather, and I mean it. Let it go!" she snapped, and Heather, for once, turned back to the pages of some teen magazine. To Rachelle, her sister, four years younger and a troublemaker in her own right, seemed incredibly naive and juvenile. In one night, Rachelle felt as if she'd grown up. She had no patience for Heather getting vicarious thrills out of Jackson's bad luck.

And bad luck it was. Jackson, before he was indicted, was branded as a killer by the citizens of Gold Creek, and Thomas Fitzpatrick swore that whoever murdered his boy would live to regret it. Thomas never came out and publicly named Jackson as Roy's assailant, but it was obvious, from the biting comments made to the press by

Roy's mother, June, that the Fitzpatrick family would leave no stone unturned in seeing that Jackson was found guilty of Roy's death. The Fitzpatrick money, lawyers and as many private detectives as it would take, would aid the district attorney in the quest to prove Jackson the culprit.

Rachelle was frantic. She would do anything to see Jackson again and she suffered her mother's reproachful stare. "Just pray you're not pregnant," Ellen Tremont said through pinched lips about a week after Jackson was hauled in. She was washing dishes with a vengeance. Soapsuds and water sloshed to the cracked linoleum floor as she scrubbed, her stiff back to her daughter. "It's bad enough your reputation's ruined, but think about the fact that you could be carrying his child!" She cast a look over her shoulder and her mouth curved into a frown of distaste. "And then there's venereal disease. A boy like that—who knows how many girls he's been with?"

"He's not like that!"

Her mother slapped down her dishrag and held on to the counter for support. She was shaking so badly, she could barely stand. "You don't know what he's like! And besides all that—" Ellen turned to face her daughter, and her teary reproachful stare was worse than her rage. Her chin wobbled slightly and the lines around her mouth were more pronounced. She looked as if she'd aged ten years. "How will you ever get a scholarship now? We can't count on your father anymore and...a scholarship's about the only way you'll be able to afford college. Lord, Rachelle, God gave you a brain, why didn't you use it?"

Rachelle couldn't stand to see her mother's pain any longer. Nor could she listen as Jackson's character was destroyed even further. She left the kitchen and slammed the door of her room behind her. But she felt sick as she flopped on her twin bed and stared across the room to her sister's empty bunk. She flipped on the radio and tried to get lost in the music of Billy Joel, but through the thin walls of the cottage, she could still hear her mother softly crying.

*God, please help us all. And be with Jackson. Oh, Jackson, I wish I could see you....*

Rachelle squeezed her eyes shut. She refused to break down and sob, but tears slid down her cheeks and she had to bite her lower lip to keep the moans of despair within her lungs. She wouldn't let her mother or anyone else in town see how much she hurt inside. She would abide the stares, the whispers, the pointed fingers and the knowing snickers, because she knew that she and Jackson had shared something wonderful, something special.

Let the gossip-mongering citizens of Gold Creek make it dirty. Let the damned *Clarion,* the newspaper where she had worked two afternoons a week and from which she had been fired, tear her reputation to shreds. In her heart of hearts, she knew that she and Jackson would never let go of the unique bond that held them together.

Was it love? Probably not. She couldn't kid herself any longer. But someday, if things worked out, and the circumstances were right, if given the chance, she and Jackson could fall in love. In time. And together she and Jackson would show everyone that what they'd shared was beautiful. He'd prove his innocence, the town would forgive him and everything would work out.

It had to.

# BOOK TWO

## Gold Creek, California
## The Present

## CHAPTER FIVE

RACHELLE SHIFTED DOWN and her compact Ford responded, slowing as she took the winding curves of the road near the lake. From the wicker carrier propped on the back seat, her cat growled a protest.

"We're just about there," Rachelle said, as if Java could understand. But how could he?

More than once Rachelle herself had questioned the wisdom of this, her journey back home. She told herself it was necessary, that in order for her to be happy as David's wife, she would have to resolve some problems that were firmly rooted in Gold Creek.

But now as she approached the lake where all the pain had started, her skin began to rise in goose bumps and she wished she were still asleep in her walk-up overlooking San Francisco Bay.

She shivered a little. The summer morning was dark, the last stars beginning to fade. Her headlights threw a double beam onto the rutted road and she flipped on the radio. Bette Midler's voice, strong and clear, filled the small car's interior and the words of "The Rose" seemed to echo through Rachelle's heart.

She flipped to another channel quickly, before the words hit home. She'd heard the song often in the days after Jackson's arrest—the days when she, along with he, had been branded by the town. The lyrics had seemed written for them and the lonely melody had only reminded her that aside from her family, only Carlie had stood by her.

Carlie.

Where was she now? They hadn't spoken in three or four years. The last time Rachelle had heard from her, she'd received a Christmas card, two weeks into January and postmarked Alaska. Most of the other kids had stayed in Gold Creek. A few had moved on, but the new generation of Fitzpatricks, Monroes and Powells had stayed. Even Laura Chandler, the girl who had never once spoken to Rachelle since the night of Roy's death, had married into the Fitzpatrick money by becoming Brian Fitzpatrick's bride.

The soft-rock music drifting out of the speakers was better. No memories of Jackson in a Wilson Phillips song.

She parked her car near the bait-and-tackle shop on the south side of the lake and knew in her heart that she'd come back to Gold Creek because of Jackson, to purge him from her life, so that she could start over and begin a new life with David.

The thought of David caused a pucker to form between her eyebrows. She told herself that she loved him, that passion wasn't a necessary part of life and that romance was a silly notion she'd given up long ago.

David sent her flowers on all the right days—straight from the florist's shop each birthday and Valentine's Day. He took her to candlelight dinners when he deemed it appropriate and he always complimented her on a new outfit.

A stockbroker who owned his own house in the city and drove a flashy imported car and knew how to program a computer. Perfect husband material, right? What did it matter if he didn't want a baby or that his lips curved into a slight frown whenever he caught her in a pair of worn jeans?

She shoved her hands into her pockets. Though the lake was still thick with mist, several boats were already heading into the calm waters, and fishermen were hurrying in and out of the old bait shop. Built in the twenties, it was a rambling frame structure that still had the original gas pumps mounted in front of the store. A bell tinkled over the threshold as customers came and went and the wooden steps were weathered and beaten. Rusted metal signs for Nehi soda and Camel cigarettes had never been taken down, though the lettering was faded, the paint peeling.

"Like stepping back in time," she told herself as she followed a trail past the store and into the woods. From this side of the lake, once the haze had disappeared, she would be able to look to the north shore, where the estates of the wealthy still existed. The Monroe home and Fitzpatrick "cottage" would soon be visible.

Rachelle wasn't superstitious. She didn't believe in ghosts. Nor Indian lore. Nor psychics, for that matter. She'd never had her palm read in her life and she wasn't about to have her chart done to find out about herself.

And yet here she was, standing on the shores of Whitefire Lake, the source of all sorts of legends and scandals and ghosts that were as much a part of the town of Gold Creek, California, as the Rexall Drug Store that stood on the corner of Main and Pine.

Hopefully she'd find answers about herself as well as this town in the next few weeks. And when she returned to San Francisco, she'd be ready to settle down and become Mrs. David L. Gaskill. Her palms felt suddenly sweaty at the thought.

And what about Jackson?

Jackson. Always Jackson. She doubted that there would ever be a time when she would hear his name and her heart wouldn't jump start. Silly girl.

Rachelle tossed a stone into the lake. The first fingers of light crept across the lake's still surface and mist began to rise from the water. Like pale ghosts, the bodies of steam collected, obscuring the view of the forests of the far shore.

*Just like the legend,* Rachelle thought with a wry smile. Impulsively she knelt on the mossy bank, cupped her hands and scooped from the cool water. Feeling a little foolish, she let the liquid slide down her throat, then let the rest of the water run through her fingers. She smiled at her actions and wiped the drops from her chin. Drying her hands on her jeans, she noticed, in the dark depths of the lake, a flash of silver, the turning of a trout, the scales on its belly glimmering and unprotected, as the fish darted from her shadow.

She felt a sudden chill, like winter's breath against the back of her neck, and the hairs at her nape stood. She knew she was being silly, that the old Indian legend was pure folly, but when she looked up, her gaze following an overgrown path that rimmed the water, she saw, in her mind's eye, a figure in the haze, the shape of a man standing not twenty feet from her.

Too easily, she could bring Jackson Moore to mind. She imagined him as she'd last seen him: dressed in a scraped leather jacket, battered jeans and cowboy boots with the heels worn down; his thumb had been hooked as he started toward the main highway. The look he'd sent her over his shoulder still pulled at her heartstrings.

"Bastard," she muttered, refusing to spend too much time thinking of him. The mirage, for that's all it was, disappeared.

The sun crested the hills and sunlight streaked across the sky, lighting the dark waters of the lake, turning the surface to golden fire. The mist closed in, pressing against her face, wet and cool.

She drew in a long breath and wrapped her arms over her chest. Maybe coming home hadn't been such a hot idea. What was the point of stirring things up again?

*Because you have to. Because of David.*

She smiled sadly when she thought of David. Kind David. Sweet David. Understanding David. A man as opposite from Jackson as a man could be. A man who wanted nothing more than for her to become his wife.

With one final glance at the still waters of Whitefire Lake, she dusted off her hands and walked up the gravel-and-dirt path to her car. The mist rose slowly and without the fog as a shroud, the forest seemed warm and familiar again. A chipmunk darted into the brambles and in the canopy of branches overhead, a blue jay screeched and scolded her.

"Don't worry," she told the jay. "I'm going, I'm going." She unlocked the door of her old Ford Escort and slid onto a cracked vinyl seat. Someday soon she'd have to replace the car, she knew, but she had resisted so far. This car, bought and paid for with her first paycheck from the *San Francisco Herald,* was a part of her she'd rather not throw away just yet.

With an unsettling grind, the engine turned over, coughed and sputtered before idling unevenly on the sandy road. Java meowed loudly. Rachelle sighed and turned on the radio. A song from years past reverberated through the speakers and she thought again of Jackson.

Rolling down a window, she breathed deep of the wooded air, then threw the little car into gear and started down the winding road that would lead her back to Gold Creek.

Jackson Moore. She wondered what he was doing right now. The last she'd heard, he was in the heart of New York City, practicing law, but still a rebel.

"I TELL YOU, THERE'S GONNA be trouble. Big-time," Brian Fitzpatrick insisted. He tossed a newspaper onto his father's desk and, muttering an oath under his breath, flopped into one of the expensive side chairs.

Thomas was used to Brian's moods. The boy had always been a hothead who didn't have the mental fortitude to run the logging company, but there'd been no choice in the matter. Not after Roy's death. At the thought of that tragic night, Thomas set his jaw. God help us all, he'd thought then. And now, as he stared at the Tremont girl's headline, he thought it again.

"Back to Gold Creek," the article was titled. Thomas's gut clenched. He skimmed the article and his lips thinned angrily. So she was returning. What a fool. She was better off living in the city, burying the past deep as he and the rest of his family had.

"Thomas? Did I hear Brian's voice?" his wife, June, called. He heard her footsteps clicking against the marble foyer of the house they'd called home for nearly twenty years. She poked her head into the den and her pale face lit with a smile at the sight of her son. "Weren't you even going to say 'hi'?" she admonished with that special sparkle in her eyes she reserved for her children.

"'Course I was, Mom," Brian replied. He was putty in her hands. Just as Roy had been. "Dad and I were just discussing business."

She rolled her eyes. "Always. So Laura isn't with you?"

At the mention of his wife's name, Brian forced a cool smile. "Nope. I came directly from the office."

"She should stop by more often, bring that grandson of mine over here. I haven't seen Zachary for nearly a month," June reprimanded gently—with a smile and a will of iron.

"I'll bring him over."

"And Laura, too," June insisted, and started for the door. But as she turned, she spied the newspaper, folded open to Rachelle Tremont's article. Her pale face grew whiter still. "What's this?" she whispered.

"Nothing to get upset about," Brian intervened quickly.

Wearily Thomas handed his wife the paper. She'd find out soon enough as it was. "Rachelle Tremont's coming back to town."

"No!"

"We can't stop her, June."

Two points of color stained her cheeks as she read the article. "I won't have it, Thomas. Not after what happened." Her throat worked and she clasped a thin hand to her chest.

"She has family here. You can't stop her from visiting."

"That little tramp is the reason that Jackson Moore wasn't convicted!" she said, her eyes bright. She collapsed on the couch and closed her eyes. "Why?" she whispered. "Why now?" The agony in her voice nearly broke Thomas's heart all over again.

"I don't know."

"If she comes, *he* won't be far behind," she predicted fatalistically.

"Who? Moore?" Brian asked. "No way. He was lucky

to get out of this town with his skin. The coward won't dare show his face around here."

"He'll be back," she whispered intently, unnervingly.

Thomas rounded the desk and sat on the edge of the couch, taking her frail hands in his. "He's a hotshot lawyer in Manhattan. He probably doesn't even know that she's coming back."

"He'll know. And mark my words, he'll be here."

"He could've come back any number of times. It's been twelve years."

Her eyes flew open and she looked over his shoulder and through the window, as if staring at the hills in the distance, but Thomas knew she wasn't seeing anything other than her own vision of the future and that the vision frightened her to her very bones. He felt her fingers tremble in his hands, saw her swallow as if in fear.

"He's a coward. A murdering, low-life coward," she said, her voice cracking. "But he'll be back. Because of her." With a strength he wouldn't have believed she possessed, she crumpled the newspaper in her fist and blinked against the tears that she'd held at bay for over a decade.

"He's in New York," Thomas assured her, and they both knew that Thomas had kept track of Jackson Moore ever since he'd left Gold Creek. There were reasons to keep track of him, reasons Thomas and his wife never discussed. "He won't come back."

But Thomas was lying. With a certainty as cold as the bottom of Whitefire Lake, Thomas knew that Jackson Moore would return.

THE HEAT OF THE DAY STILL simmered in the city and the air was sultry and humid, a cloying blanket that caused sweat to rise beneath collar and cuffs. Even the breath of wind slipping across the East River didn't bring much relief through the open window of Jackson Moore's Manhattan apartment.

He rubbed the kinks from the back of his neck, then poured Scotch over two cubes of ice in his glass and sat on the window ledge. The air-conditioning was on the fritz again, and his apartment sweltered while dusk settled over the concrete-and-steel alleys of the city.

As he had for the past six summers since he'd started working, he wondered why he didn't pack his bags and move on. New York held no fascination for him—well, nothing much did. He'd spent too many years chasing after a demon who probably had never existed, before giving up on his past and settling here in this city of broken dreams.

"Keep it up, Moore, and you'll break my heart," he told himself as he swirled his drink, letting the cubes melt as condensation covered the exterior of the glass. He didn't have it so bad. Not really. His apartment was big enough for one, maybe two, should the need arise, and he did have a view of the park.

By all accounts he was a rich man. Not a millionaire, but close enough. Pretty damn good for a kid from the wrong side of the tracks, he thought reflectively, a kid once considered the bad boy of a sleepy little Northern California town. Not that it mattered much. He tossed back his drink and felt the fiery warmth of the liquor mingle with the frigid ice as the liquid splashed against the back of his throat. A nice little zing. A zing he was beginning to enjoy too much.

He flipped through the mail. Bills, invoices and yet another big win in a clearing-house drawing where he would become an instant millionaire—all he had to do was take a chance. He snorted. He'd been taking chances all his life. The afternoon edition of the *New York Daily* was folded neatly under the stack of crisp envelopes and, as he had every Saturday since her syndicated column had appeared, he opened the paper to Section D, and there, under the small byline of Rachelle Tremont, was her article—if you could call it that. Her weekly exposés were little more than expressions of her own opinions about life in general—or her latest pet peeve of the week, usually on the side of someone she thought had been wronged. Not exactly hard-core journalism. Not exactly his cup of tea. Why he tortured himself by reading her column and reminding himself of her week after week, he didn't bother to analyze; if he did he'd probably end up on the couch of an expensive shrink. But each Friday evening, when the Saturday edition was left near his door, he poured himself a drink and allowed himself the pleasure and pain of tripping down memory lane. "Idiot," he muttered, and his voice bounced off the walls of his empty apartment.

He leaned a hip against the table and read the headline. Back to Gold Creek. Distractedly he read the editor's note that followed, indicating that the column would be written from good ol' Gold Creek, California, for the next ten weeks while Rachelle returned home to examine the small town where she'd grown up and compare that small-minded little village now to what it had been when she'd lived there.

Jackson sucked in a disbelieving breath. His gut jerked hard against his diaphragm. Was that woman out of her mind? She was always too inquisitive for her own good—too trusting to have much common sense, but he'd given her credit for more brains than this!

A small trickle of sweat collected at the base of his skull as he thought of Rachelle as he'd found her that night in the gazebo, drenched from the rain, her long hair wet and soaked against bare skin where her blouse had been torn. A metallic taste crawled up the back of his throat as he remembered how frightened she'd been, how desperate she'd felt in his arms and how he, himself, had unwittingly used her.

So now she was going back? To all that pain? He'd never thought her a fool—well, maybe once before. But this—this journey back in time was a fool's mission—a mission he'd inadvertently caused all those years ago.

He squeezed his eyes shut for a minute and refused to dwell on all the pain that he'd created, how he'd single-handedly nearly destroyed her.

So what was this—some sort of catharsis? For her? Or for him?

The demons of his past had never been laid to rest; he'd known that, and he'd accepted it. But whenever they'd risen their grisly heads, he'd managed to tamp them back into a dark, cobwebby corner of his mind and lock them securely away. And time, thankfully, had been his ally.

But no longer. If Rachelle tried to turn back the clock and expose that hellhole of a town for what it really was, if she attempted to tear open the seams of the shroud that had hidden the town's darkest secrets, the questions surrounding Roy Fitzpatrick's death would surface again. Jackson's name would surely come up and the real murderer—whoever the hell he was—might reappear.

What a mess!

He tossed his paper on the table and swore as he began pacing in front of the open window. His muscles tense, his mind working with the precision that had gained him a reputation at the courthouse, for he'd been known to become obsessed with his cases, living them day and night, he considered his options.

Until now, he'd managed to keep his past to himself. However, things had changed. It looked as if, through Rachelle's column in the *Daily* and a dozen other newspapers across the country, that the whole world would find out how he'd grown up on the wrong side of the tracks and left his hometown all but accused of murder.

"Great," he muttered sarcastically, glancing at the half-full bottle of Scotch on the bar. He plowed both sets of fingers through his sweaty hair and his thoughts took another turn. Not that it really mattered. His life was open. He'd been raised by a poor mother, gotten into trouble in high school and had shipped out with the navy. Eventually he'd gone back to Gold Creek, made a little money and had been accused of murder.

That's when he'd left. And along with the government's help and the money he earned working nights as a security guard, he'd made it through college and law school. He'd been hell-bent to prove to that damned town that he wasn't just their whipping boy, that he had what it took to become successful. And every time a news camera captured him on film, he hoped all the souls in Gold Creek who had condemned him, could see that the bad boy had made good. Damned good.

He'd never wanted to go back. Until now. Because of Rachelle. Damn her for sticking her pretty neck out.

If he returned to Gold Creek, he'd have some explaining to do. Rachelle, no doubt, hated him.

Not that he blamed her. She had every reason to be bitter. From her point of view he'd used her, then left her to fight the battles—his battles—alone. He snorted in self-derision.

Yanking on his tie and loosening the top button of his shirt, he thought about the town where he'd been sired.

Gold Creek. A small town filled with small minds. No wonder he ended up here, where a person could be as anonymous as he wanted, one man in seven million.

He scanned the article one last time and noted that she'd written it while she was still in San Francisco. The column explained why she felt it necessary to return to that godforsaken hamlet.

She seemed to think that she had to tell the whole nation about her past, which, given the circumstances, was cruelly knotted to his in a noose of lies and sex and death. He smiled grimly at the ironic twist of fate, because by purging herself, she would be dragging him back and, perhaps, putting herself in danger.

Only he wouldn't let her get away with it. Whether she knew it or not, Rachelle and her series were like a siren call to a place he wanted to forget.

He burned inside, thinking that she was manipulating him, forcing him to take a roller-coaster ride back in time.

Tossing back his drink, he knew what he had to do. It was something he should have done long ago. Now it was time to return to Gold Creek, to straighten out a past that had twisted his life for so many years, a past that had threatened his life, his career and his relationship with women; a past that had given him cause to become one of the toughest defense lawyers in the nation, his reputation tarnished or shining brightly depending upon which side of the courtroom a person favored.

He poured another drink, which he figured he owed himself, then checked the top drawer of his nightstand. His .38 was right where he'd left it, untouched, for six years. He picked up the gun, his fingers resting against the smooth handle. The steel was cold even in the heat of the bedroom.

Seeing his reflection in the mirror over the bureau, he cringed. His face had taken on the expression of a man obsessed by a single purpose.

*Bad boy. Son of the town whore. From the wrong side of the tracks. Bastard. Murdering son-of-a-bitch.*

The taunts and ridicules of the citizens of Gold Creek ricocheted through his mind, and his hands were suddenly slick with sweat.

He dropped the gun and slammed the drawer shut. Twelve years was a long time. Whoever had set him up for Roy Fitzpatrick's murder was probably confident that his secret was safe. And even if the culprit were dangerous, bringing a handgun along wouldn't help. He couldn't walk back into town packing a gun. The .38 would stay, but Jackson would return to Gold Creek.

And when he did step onto California soil again, come hell or high water, he was going to find out what had happened on the night that had changed the course of his life forever.

Rachelle Tremont and her series be damned. She had no business putting herself into any kind of danger.

He picked up the telephone on the nightstand and dialed the number of his travel agent, the first move toward returning to California.

And to Rachelle: the last person he'd seen as he'd shouldered his few belongings and hitchhiked out of Gold Creek twelve years ago, and the first person he intended to lay eyes upon when he returned.

## CHAPTER SIX

RACHELLE'S FIRST DAY IN Gold Creek wasn't all that productive. She'd spent hours unpacking and settling into the cottage where she'd grown up, the cottage her mother and Heather still owned. At present no one was renting the little bungalow, so Rachelle and Java moved in, cleaned the place and fought back memories that seemed to hang like cobwebs in the corners.

It was night before she donned her jacket and drove into town. Her first stop was the high school. She parked in front of the building and ignored the race of her heart.

Red brick and mortar, washed with exterior lights, Tyler High rose two stories against a star-spangled backdrop. The sharp outline of a crescent moon seemed to float on a few gray wisps of clouds that had collected in the sky.

Memories, old and painful, crept into her mind and she wondered again about the wisdom of returning to a town where she'd been born, raised and humiliated.

*Steady,* she told herself, and plunged her hands deep into the pockets of her jacket. Muted music and laughter, seeping through the open doors of the Buckeye Restaurant and Lounge, rode upon an early summer breeze, diminishing the chorus of crickets and the soft hoot of an owl hidden high in the branches of the ancient old sequoias that guarded the entrance of the school.

She remembered the taunts of the other kids—the

clique of girls who would giggle as she passed and the boys who would lift their brows in invitation. Her senior year had crawled by and when it was over, she'd worked the summer at a newspaper in Coleville and started college the following September. She'd refused to think about Jackson, for, after eight months of thinking he would return for her, she'd finally accepted the cold, hard fact that he didn't care for her.

Harold Little, her mother's second husband and a man she could hardly stomach, had lent her money to get through school. After four years at Berkeley, long hours working on a small, local paper and few dates, she'd graduated. With her journalism degree and her work references, she'd found a job at one small paper, and another, finally landing a job at the *Herald*. Her column had been well received and finally she felt as if she'd made it.

But not as big as had Jackson. Even now, standing in front of the school, she remembered the first time she'd seen him on television. His face was barely a flash on the screen as the camera panned for his famous client, a famous soap-opera actress whose real life paralleled the story line on her daytime drama.

Rachelle had dropped the coffee cup she'd been carrying from her kitchen to the den. The television set, usually on, was muted, but she couldn't forget Jackson's strong features, his flashing dark eyes, his rakish, confident smile, the expensive cut of his suit.

She'd heard that he'd become a lawyer and it hadn't taken him long to move to New York and earn a reputation. But seeing his face on the television screen had stunned her, and in a mixture of awe and disgust, she'd watched the screen and mopped the coffee from the floor. From that point on, she'd kept up with his career and wondered at his chosen path.

He'd never contacted her in twelve years. He probably didn't even remember her name, she thought now, alone in the dark. And yet she'd promised her editor she'd try to interview him by calling him in New York. What a joke!

GOLD CREEK HADN'T changed much.

Jackson drove his rental car through the night-darkened streets. Yes, the homes sprawled closer to the eastern hills than they had twelve years before and a new strip mall had been added to the north end of town. A recently built tritheater boasted the names of several second-run movies and, as expected, a lot of the real estate and businesses were tagged by the name Fitzpatrick.

"Some things never change," he said, thinking aloud as he passed yet another home offered for sale by Fitzpatrick Realty.

Fitzpatricks had *always* run the town. The first Fitzpatrick had discovered gold here and his descendants, too, had made a profit from the natural resources the hills offered and from the strong backs of other able bodies in town. From the early 1900s, when Fitzpatrick Logging had opened up wide stands of fir and pine in the foothills surrounding Gold Creek until now, Fitzpatrick Logging had been a primary employer of Gold Creek. Millions of board feet of lumber had translated into hundreds of thousands of dollars for the first timber baron in the county's history, and George Fitzpatrick had become a millionaire. His wealth had been passed on from generation to generation, spreading like some unstoppable disease until the majority of townspeople worked for Thomas Fitzpatrick, grandson of George and father of

Roy, the boy Jackson had been accused of murdering twelve years before.

Fitzpatrick Logging. Fitzpatrick Realty. Fitzpatrick Hardware. Fitzpatrick Development. Fitzpatrick Building Supplies. Everything in the town seemed to be a shrine to the influence and wealth of the Fitzpatrick family.

Jackson's hands tightened over the wheel of the Buick as he cruised past a local pizza parlor, thankfully named Lanza's. As far as Jackson knew, Thomas Fitzpatrick and his ancestors didn't have any Italian blood running through their veins.

He guided the Buick to a stop at the park situated in the middle of town. This little scrap of ground, less than an acre, was a far cry from Central Park in the heart of Manhattan, but Gold Creek was no New York City, he thought with a trace of sarcasm. Despite its problems, New York held more appeal.

Jackson climbed out of the car and stretched his legs, eyeing the surroundings. The hair lifted on his arms as he spied a gazebo that stood in the center of the green where several concrete paths met. The gazebo was larger than the lattice structure he remembered at the Fitzpatrick summer estate, but still, his skin crawled.

The walkways, illuminated by strategically placed lampposts, ran in six directions, winding through the trees and playground equipment of one square block of Gold Creek. The grass was already turning brown, and the area under the swings and teeter-totters was dusty. Flowers bloomed profusely, their petals glowing in the white incandescence of the street lamps. A few dry leaves, the precursors of autumn, rustled as they blew across the cracked concrete.

But the air was different from the atmosphere in New York City. In Manhattan, he felt the electricity, the frenetic pulse of the city during the day as well as the night. But here, practically on the opposite shore of the continent, the pace was slow and low-key. No one appeared in the dusky park, and the wattage of energy seemed to simmer on low.

Shoving his sleeves over his elbows, he made his way to the gazebo and read a carved wooden sign that noted that the park was dedicated to Roy Fitzpatrick, and listed his date of birth and death, a bare nineteen years apart. Ironic that the shrine for Roy had been a gazebo, similar in design to the gazebo on the Fitzpatrick property at the lake—the very spot where Roy had tried to force himself on Rachelle. Jackson's jaw grew hard. He supposed he should feel some pity for Roy, but he didn't. Though he'd never wished Roy dead, the kid had rushed headlong into tragedy. Roy had taken what he wanted, had felt no remorse and had believed that excess was his due.

No wonder someone had objected. It was just a shame that Roy had died. He ran his fingers over the inscription and wondered for the millionth time who had killed Roy. Probably someone they both knew, some coward who had let Jackson hang, twisting in the wind, for the murder. How far would the killer have let him go? If the case had gone to trial, if, by some fluke, Jackson had been convicted, would Roy's murderer have come forward? He doubted it. Whoever had killed Roy had been more concerned about covering his tracks than letting justice prevail.

But Jackson hadn't been indicted and he'd run. Like a jackrabbit escaping a coyote, he'd decided to run as far as he could and start a new life. Without any ties to Gold Creek. Without Rachelle. And he'd created that life for himself through hard work, determination and luck—something that was in short supply here in Gold Creek.

And now Rachelle was going to dig through the dirt all over again. Though her column hadn't said that was her intent, Jackson knew that the old scandal wouldn't stay buried, not with the ever-widening specter of dominion that was the Fitzpatrick family. It was time to settle this, once and for all. Before anyone—especially Rachelle—got hurt.

*And Rachelle? How does she fit into the plan?* He glanced up to the diaphanous clouds skirting a slit of a moon. He'd tell her to lay off, threaten her with some kind of fictitious libel suit, then leave her alone.

He only hoped she had enough sense to take his advice. He didn't really give a damn if she wanted to let the nation see the small town where she'd grown up, but he didn't want her fouling up his own reasons for being here.

Yes, she'd been the catalyst that brought him to the sunny state of California, but he wanted her to concentrate on the daily lives and anecdotes of the people in her town, and he wanted her to stay the hell away from the night that Roy Fitzpatrick died.

Roy's death was Jackson's business. Unfinished business that he intended to finally take care of. He didn't need Rachelle unwittingly stepping into danger.

Now all he had to do was find her. There were a couple of motels in town that he would check out and he knew the little house where she'd grown up. He'd start there.

RACHELLE TOOK A SIP FROM her tea and nearly burned her lips on the hot mug. "Blast it all," she muttered at the microwave she had yet to master. The house had changed in the past twelve years, as had her life. New coats of paint gleamed on the walls, the kitchen cabinets had been refinished and soft new carpet spread like a downy blanket over the battered linoleum floors. She could thank her sister, Heather, as well as Heather's money, for the restoration of this place. Heather had, for their mother's sake, invested in this house after their mother had decided she wanted to rent an apartment in the heart of town, closer to the man who was now her husband, Harold Little. Rachelle frowned at the thought of Harold. She'd never liked the scrappy, flat-faced man.

But Heather, God bless her stubborn streak, had tried to help their mother. She'd thought Ellen needed to meet other people, get on with her life and quit stewing over the fact that her husband had left her over a decade before. Rachelle had agreed, and Heather, confiding that she planned to let the tide of California inflation buoy the value of the cottage into the stratosphere, had bought the house. The plan had been great until the recession had hit and the tidewaters of big money had ebbed dismally.

Cradling her tea, Rachelle padded barefoot back to the small bedroom. Aside from a few clothes, her cat, Java, and her laptop computer, she hadn't brought much with her. Setting her mug onto the nightstand, she kicked a small pile of dirty laundry toward the closet.

She flopped onto the bed, the laptop propped against her knees and Java curled at her feet on the rumpled bedspread. This little room with its blond twin beds and matching dresser had been the girls'. The bulletin board was long gone, taken down in her senior year when her blackened reputation had made each day at Tyler High a torture and any reminders of high school had been burned, tossed out or locked in the attic.

Her dark thoughts shifted to the friends who had turned their backs on her, who had since become stalwart citizens of the town: teachers, bankers, waitresses and even a doctor who had avoided her. Now they were parents themselves, married, divorced, their lives as changed from their carefree days in high school as hers had been. She set her fingers on the keypad and started on her column, entitling it "Faded Flowers," and imagined interviewing the people who had shunned her.

Shivering, she picked up her mug, nearly sloshing its contents over the bed when the doorbell pealed. Java leapt off the bed and crawled beneath the dust ruffle.

"Chicken," Rachelle chided the cat. She set her drink down and walked quickly through the hall. "Coming!" she called toward the door, then noticed from the antique clock on the mantel that it was after ten. Aside from her mother, or possibly Heather if the whim struck her, no one would visit.

Flipping on the porch light, she peered through the narrow window next to the door—and froze, her spine tingling coldly. She'd been thinking of him tonight, yes, and not kindly. But she couldn't believe he was here, a handsome ghost of her past returned to haunt her! Her tongue clove to the roof of her mouth, and her heart nearly stopped as her eyes glued to the hard-edged features of Jackson Moore.

Time seemed to stand still. Rachelle's skin was ice as Jackson's inflexible brown gaze moved to the window to land full force upon her.

Her throat turned to cotton at the hard line of his lips, the tension in his jaw. He didn't smile or frown, and she knew instinctively that he wasn't pleased to see her.

Twelve years of fantasies shattered in that single second. For even though she'd told herself she hated him, that the mere sight of him on the news reports turned her stomach, a stupid little feminine part of her had wished that he still cared. From the intensity of his features and the unspoken anger in his glare, she'd been wrong about him. Shame washed up her neck as she realized, not for the first time, that the town, this damned town, had been right! She'd been a worse fool than even she had thought.

Obviously she'd meant nothing more to him than a one-night stand and an easy alibi for Roy Fitzpatrick's murder. It took all the strength she had to throw the dead bolt and open the door.

A night breeze crept past him, stealing into the room.

"I thought you were in New York," she said defensively, her reticent tongue working again. She decided she'd better set things straight before he had a chance to say anything. "Isn't that where you live now, righting all the wrongs against your innocent clients?"

His eyes glittered, and the whisper of a smile caught the edges of his mouth for just a second. "I didn't come here to talk about my practice."

"Just in the neighborhood?" she taunted, wanting to wound him and give him just a taste of the pain she'd suffered when he'd abandoned her. All those years. All those damned years!

His thin lips shifted. "Actually, I came to see you."

"A little late, aren't you?"

Did he wince slightly, or did the shadow of a moth flutter by the porch light, seeming to change his expression for just a second? "I guess I deserved that."

"What you deserve I couldn't begin to describe," she replied. "But phrases like 'drawn and quartered,' 'boiled in oil' or 'tarred and feathered' come quickly to mind."

"You don't think I suffered enough?" he asked, crossing tanned arms in front of a chest that had expanded with the years. He was built more solidly than he had been: broader shoulders, still-lean hips, but more defined muscles. Probably the result of working out with a private trainer or weight-lifting or some such upper-crust urban answer to aging. There wasn't an ounce of fat on him and he looked tougher in real life than he did on camera.

"You didn't stick around long enough to suffer," she said.

"What would that have proved?"

*That you cared, that you didn't use me, that I wasn't so much the fool....* "Nothing. You're right. You should have left. In fact, I don't know why you'd want to come back here at all," she admitted, some of her animosity draining as she stared at his sensual lower lip. Steadfastly, she moved her gaze back to the hard glitter in his eyes.

"I returned for the same reason you did," he said slowly.

"And why's that?"

"To settle things."

"Is that what I'm doing?" He was gazing at her so intently that her heart, which was already beating rapidly, accelerated tempo. Emotions, as tangled and tormented as they had been twelve years before, simmered in the cool night. The sound of traffic from the freeway was muted, and the wind chimes on her porch tinkled softly on a jasmine-scented breeze.

"I take the *New York Daily*," Jackson said, his hands in the back pockets of his black jeans. "It carries your column."

She waited, expecting more of an explanation, and avoided looking into his eyes. Those eyes, golden-brown and penetrating, had been her undoing all those years ago. She'd trusted him, believed in him, and it had cost her. Well, she wouldn't let his gaze get to her again. Besides, he couldn't. There was a new jaded edge to him that she found not the least bit appealing.

"I read that you're doing a series about Gold Creek."

"That's right." Her gaze flew back to his and she straightened her shoulders, determined to deal with him as a professional. An interview with Jackson Moore would be a coup, an article her editor, Marcy, expected, but Rachelle couldn't imagine talking with him, taking notes, probing into his life as it had been in Gold Creek all those years ago.

"I think we should discuss it."

"Discuss *it?*" she repeated, her backbone stiffening as if with steel. "Why would you want—?" She cut herself off, and, folding her arms over her chest, propped one shoulder against the door. "What're you doing back in Gold Creek?"

His eyes bored deep into hers and she realized suddenly what it must feel like to be a witness squirming on the stand while Jackson, slowly, steadily and without the least bit of compassion, cut her testimony to shreds. "I think you're about to get yourself into trouble, Rachelle," he said. "And I want to make sure that you don't get hurt."

She laughed. "I don't need *you* to protect me. And there's nothing to be afraid of, anyway."

"You don't know what you're getting into."

"I do. And if you're talking about the Fitzpatrick murder, I was there, too. Remember?" Deciding she was probably exercising a blatant error in judgment, she kicked the door open wider. "Why don't you come in and say whatever it is that's on your mind?"

"Off the record?" he asked.

"Afraid of what I might write?"

"I've been misquoted before." She thought of the past six years and his meteoric rise to fame, or infamy. He hadn't been afraid of taking on the most scandalous of cases, many involving the rich and famous, and he'd managed to see that his clients came out smelling like proverbial roses.

One woman, an up-and-coming actress who had a reputation with men, had been accused of shooting her lover after he'd been with another woman. Jackson had come up with enough blue smoke and mirrors to confuse and cloud the issue, and the actress, Colleen Mills, had walked out of the courtroom a free woman. Though the press had tried her in the newspapers and the evidence had been overwhelmingly against Colleen, she was now in Hollywood working on her next film. Rumor had it that she was giving an Oscar-worthy performance, as she had, no doubt, on the witness stand under Jackson's direction.

He walked into the house and she closed the door after him. He didn't look like a hotshot New York attorney in his faded black Levi's, boots and T-shirt. A leather jacket—black, as well—was thrown over one shoulder and she wondered sarcastically if he'd joined a motorcycle gang and roared up on his Harley.

She almost smiled at the thought and realized that he looked much the way she remembered him, though his features had become leaner, more angular with the years. His hair was still on the long side, shiny black and straight, and his eyes, golden-brown and judgmental, didn't miss a trick. Even the brush of thick lashes didn't soften his virile male features. His gaze swept the room in one quick appraisal and probably found it lacking.

"It's late. Why don't you get to the point?" She perched on the rolled arm of the old overstuffed couch.

"As I said, I read your column."

She couldn't help but let a cold smile touch her lips. "Don't try to convince me that you left your lucrative practice, flew across the country and came back to the village of the damned just because of something I wrote."

"That's about the size of it." He dropped onto the ottoman, so close that his jean-clad knees nearly touched her dangling bare foot. She refused to shift away, but part of her attention was attuned to the proximity of her ankle to the hands he clasped between his parted knees. She wondered if, beneath the denim, there was a faded scar, an ever-present reminder of that night—that one beautiful, painful night.

Her gaze moved back to his and she caught him watching her. She blushed slightly.

"I think it would be better if you didn't touch on the Fitzpatrick murder."

Rachelle lifted her brows. "Afraid your reputation might be smeared if it's all dredged up again?"

"My reputation is based on smears." He almost looked sincere, but, as a lawyer, he was used to playing many parts, being on stage in the courtroom, convincing people to say and do what he wanted. She wasn't buying into any of his act. "But there is a chance you'll scare whoever did kill Roy, into reacting—maybe violently."

"And you came all the way cross-country to tell me this?" she said, unable to keep the sarcasm out of her voice. Who did he think he was kidding?

"No," he admitted, stretching his legs before standing and walking to the fireplace. A mirror was hung over the mantel, and in the reflection, his gaze sought hers. "I'm going to be straight with you, Rachelle. When I said I was going to settle things, I meant everything." Turning, he faced her and his features were set in granite. "I'm going to look into the Fitzpatrick murder and clear my name. I don't want you poking around and getting in the way."

She should have expected this much, she supposed. Shaking her head, she said, "So you're afraid that I'm going to rain on your parade. That I might find out what really happened that night and steal your thunder."

"That's not it—"

"Sure it is, Moore. Look, I've read all about you. I know you don't give a damn about your reputation or what happened to any of the people you left behind when you hooked your thumb on the highway and made your way out of this town. But if you think you're going to come back here, cover up the truth and ruin my story, you'd better guess again." She climbed off the sofa and advanced on him, her chin lifted proudly, the anger in her eyes meeting his. "I'm not the same little frightened girl you left sniveling after you, Jackson."

"All grown up and a regular bad-ass reporter?" he drawled, baiting her.

"You got it."

He sighed, his mask slipping a little. "What happened to you, Rachelle?" he asked, some of his insolence stripping away as he stared at her.

She didn't want to see another side to him; didn't want to know that, beneath his jaded New York attitude, beat a heart that had once touched hers. Nor did she want him to guess that he had any effect on her whatsoever. She was over him. She was! Then why did her pulse jump at the sight of him?

Shaking inside, she walked to the door and opened it, silently inviting him to leave. Her voice, when she finally found it, was barely a whisper. "You did, Jackson. You're what happened to me. And for that, you're lucky I'm just holding the door open for you and not calling the police and demanding a restraining order."

His eyes glinted. "Does this mean the wedding's off?" he teased cruelly, and Rachelle's heart tore a little.

"This means that I never want to see you again, Jackson."

He crossed the room, but stood in the doorway, staring down at her. "I'm afraid that's impossible."

"I don't think so. Just walk out the door, find the nearest plane and fly back to the East Coast. Everyone here was doing fine before you showed up. We'll all manage to survive without you."

"Will you?" he asked, skepticism lifting a dark brow.

"Go, Jackson. Or I will call the police."

"And here I thought you'd be anxious for an interview with me."

The man's gall was unbelievable. But his reasoning was right on target. "Believe it or not, I'm not a Jackson Moore groupie," she replied, knowing that she was lying more than a little. She'd already half promised Marcy an interview with Gold Creek's most notorious son.

"You were once," he said, and his voice sounded softer, smooth as silk.

Her throat caught, and she remembered vividly how she'd lost her virginity with this very man. She'd tried to blame him for that loss over the years, but she couldn't. Even now she realized that she'd given herself to him willingly. But what was worse, was the knowledge that she might, given the right circumstances, do it all over again.

"That was a long time ago, Jackson, when I was young and naive and believed in fairy tales. I trusted you, stood up for you and told everyone how innocent you were. But I'm all grown up now and I'll never believe you again." She forced a cold smile she hoped would pierce that insolent armor he wore so boldly. "Even fools eventually grow up."

His eyes burned black. "I'm innocent."

She let out a slow breath, her fingers clenching around the hard wood of the door. "Innocent?" She shook her head. "I believe you didn't kill Roy Fitzpatrick twelve years ago, I believe you think you're here to clear your name, but, Jackson, we both know you're far from innocent."

# CHAPTER SEVEN

JACKSON WAS STILL STANDING on the threshold when the phone rang.

"I've got to get that," she said, but he didn't budge. Fine. Let him wait. She left him at the door and picked up the phone on the fourth ring.

"Rachelle?" David's voice was warm and familiar. She heard him sigh with relief and a part of her melted inside. David was safe. She could count on him. He would never treat her as Jackson had.

"Hi." She sneaked a peek at Jackson—still so darkly sensual. Well, his good looks and bloody sexuality did nothing for her. *Nothing!*

"You didn't call," David said, gently reprimanding her. His voice was filled with concern. "It's getting late and I was worried."

"Sorry," she said automatically. "I just got in this morning and the phone wasn't installed until four." She tried to concentrate on the conversation, but slid a glance at Jackson, who didn't seem the least bit bothered that he was eavesdropping. He didn't even *try* to look interested in anything other than her.

"Well, so you're okay?" David persisted.

"Fine. Just fine."

"But you miss me," he guessed, and she heard the tiny wheedle in his voice that was there every time he didn't feel secure.

"Sure," she replied. "Of course I miss you."

"Good. Good. Look, I'm going to work the rest of this weekend, but I'll get some free time at the end of next week and maybe I can come up and see you for a few days. Just you and me in the wilderness? Hmm?" he said suggestively, and Rachelle had to bite her tongue to keep from snapping at him. He had no idea that half their conversation was being dissected.

"I, uh, don't think that would be such a great idea." She felt heat climb up her neck. She turned her back to Jackson, tried to pretend that he wasn't only a few feet from her, and attempted to ignore the knocking of her heart.

"Why not?" David asked in his suggestive voice. "We could have a good time."

"I know we could, but this is serious stuff. I'm working."

He sighed again, long and loud. Not quite so friendly. "It's just a few columns, Rachelle. I thought we agreed that you'd go back, write whatever it is you have to, and then come back here. Pronto."

"If it works out that way."

"Well, try, won't you? I miss you already."

"Me, too," she replied before saying goodbye and hanging up. She wanted to sag against the wall; there was something about her recent conversations with David that seemed to suck all the life right out of her. He wasn't a controlling man, not really, not like Jackson, but he did try to manipulate her subtly, and that bothered her. He deftly attempted to mold her way of thinking to his. She would have preferred an out-and-out confrontation. She would have preferred an honest fight with someone like Jackson.

She brought herself up short. She didn't mean that, of course; she couldn't mean it.

"Trouble in paradise?" Jackson said with just a trace of sarcasm.

"No trouble. And definitely no paradise."

He glanced at the phone. "Your husband?"

"Afraid not," she replied breezily.

"Boyfriend?"

"Look, I don't think it's any of your business."

Java slunk out of the bedroom. The black cat took one look at Jackson, arched her back and sidestepped back down the hall.

"Friendly," Jackson remarked.

"You already told me to steer clear of the Fitzpatrick murder and I told you that I was going to do my job as I saw fit, so what is it you want from me, Jackson?" Rachelle finally asked. "I thought I made it clear that you weren't welcome."

His eyes held hers for an instant too long, and the back of her throat tightened in memory. "What I want..." he said with a twisted smile. He rubbed the back of his neck, his hair, still slightly on the long side, brushing his fingers. "That's not easy."

"Not what you want," she clarified. "What you want from me. There's a big difference."

He crossed to the kitchen and hoisted one leg over a barstool. Seated at the bar, he could watch her as she wiped the kitchen counter for the third time. He leaned forward, elbows on the tile, hands clasped in front of him. "What're you trying to accomplish by all this?"

Maybe it was time for honesty. "I needed to come back here, clear up my feelings about the past, reexamine this town because it's time I got on with my future."

"With the guy on the phone?"

She met his gaze boldly. "Yes."

"He gonna give you everything you want?" Jackson asked, and when she hesitated, he added, "You know, I'm surprised. I thought by now you'd probably be married and have a couple of kids."

She flinched inside at the mention of children. For as long as she could remember, she'd wanted a baby, a child to raise. For a short time, twelve years ago, she'd fantasized about being pregnant and having Jackson's child. All things considered, she was lucky she hadn't conceived.

"You may as well know," she said, tucking the towel into the handle of the oven door. "Monday morning I'm interviewing Thomas Fitzpatrick."

Jackson's expression changed. His smile fell and his eyes turned dark. "Why not start at the top?" he asked sarcastically.

"Whether you like it or not, he's the single most important man in this town. For the past twenty-five years, he's shaped the future of Gold Creek."

"Lucky him." He climbed off the stool. "I'm surprised he agreed to talk to you."

"So was I. But he probably decided that he couldn't dodge me forever and even if he tried, it wouldn't look good. Remember the man is supposed to have political aspirations."

Jackson's eyebrows quirked. "You like to live dangerously."

She stared at him long and hard. "I did once," she admitted. "But that was a long time ago."

She walked to the front door again and held it open. "I don't think we have much more to say to each other, Jackson," she whispered, though the questions that had bothered her for twelve years still swam in her mind.

*Why had he never called? Once he was released from jail, why didn't he stop by? Why had he left her to battle the town all by herself? And why, oh why, had he never so much as mentioned the night that she'd given herself to him, body and soul?*

This time he left. He paused only for a second at the door, and for an insane instant Rachelle thought he was going to kiss her. His gaze caressed hers then moved to her mouth.

Her lungs stopped taking in air as his gaze shifted back to hers. "I hope you find what you're looking for," he said as if he really meant it. Her heart ached dully for an instant, and when he traced her jaw with one lean finger, she didn't have the strength to pull away.

"I think you should go," she said, and he touched her lips with his thumb. Inside she was melting, her pulse rocketing, but she didn't move a muscle.

"Do you?" he said, and in his expression he silently called her a liar.

"Absolutely." She grabbed hold of his wrist and shoved his hand away from her face. Beneath her fingertips she felt his own pulse, quick but steady, and the smell of him, all male and clean, filled her nostrils. "Just because we're back in the same town, doesn't mean we have to see each other."

A sardonic smile curved his lips. "No?" he asked, disbelieving. "You think we can stay away from each other?"

"It hasn't been a problem for the last twelve years."

"But now we're back in Gold Creek, aren't we? I doubt that we can avoid each other."

"We can try." She dropped his hand and refused to acknowledge his insolent grin.

"Gold Creek's a small town. But you're right, we

can try." Without so much as a goodbye, he crossed the porch, grabbed hold of the rail and vaulted into the yard. Within seconds, he'd disappeared into the shadows.

Jackson Moore.

Back in the town that had cast him out.

Back with a vengeance.

And she needed a damned interview with him!

Rachelle closed the door and threw the dead bolt into place as the sound of a car's engine roared to life.

JACKSON MENTALLY KICKED himself all the way back to his motel. What in God's name had he been thinking? He hadn't intended on making a pass at Rachelle. In fact, he'd faced her just to prove to himself that his memory of her was skewed; that she wasn't as attractive today as she had been on that long-ago emotion-riddled night.

He'd dealt with his guilt over leaving her by telling himself that they'd made love, she'd lost her virginity because of the circumstances, because they were thrust together·and scared, because they were young and stupid. He'd convinced himself that he'd overdramatized their lovemaking in his mind and that she wouldn't affect him now as she had then.

Wrong.

He'd been stunned at the sight of her. While in high school, she'd been pretty, now she was beautiful, not in a classic sense, but beautiful nonetheless.

But beauty usually didn't get to him. He was surrounded by beautiful women, women who were interested in him because of his notoriety or his money. He usually didn't give a damn.

Rachelle was different. She looked more womanly now than she had twelve years before; her face had lost all the round edges of adolescence. Her cheekbones were more pronounced and her body language gave the impression that she was a woman who knew what she wanted and went after it. Until she'd taken the phone call. The atmosphere in the room had changed then; she'd seemed more submissive somehow, a little less secure.

Whoever the guy was on the other end of the line, Jackson didn't like him. And so, he himself had come on to Rachelle.

He pulled into the parking lot of his motel and gritted his teeth. *Leave her alone,* he kept telling himself as he pocketed his keys and climbed the stairs to his room on the second floor. *She doesn't want you and she's better off with the jerk who called her.*

Inside the room, he tossed off his jacket and headed to the bar. He needed a drink. Seeing Rachelle again was a shock. His reaction to her was even more of a shock. And what he was going to do about the next couple of weeks scared the hell out of him.

AVOIDING JACKSON DIDN'T prove to be easy, Rachelle learned to her chagrin. Gold Creek was just too small to get lost in. She'd seen him walking into the Buckeye and caught him having breakfast at the Railway Café. She'd even watched him work an automatic teller machine at one of the two banks in town.

Now Rachelle half expected to see him at Fitzpatrick Logging where she was rebuffed by a sweet-smiling receptionist. "I'm sorry, but there must've been some mistake. Mr. Fitzpatrick is out of town for several days," she was told.

"But I've got an appointment with Mr. Fitzpatrick," she replied firmly. "My editor set it up a week ago."

The receptionist, Marge Elkins, lifted her plump shoulders and rolled her palms into the air. "I'm sorry.

There must've been some mix-up, but if you'd like to speak to Mr. Fitzpatrick's son, Brian, I could fit you in within the next couple of days."

Why not? Rachelle thought. She may as well start with someone she knew, someone at the top of Gold Creek's economic ladder. "I'd like that."

"Mmm." Marge flipped through an appointment book. "He's free Wednesday morning," she said. "How about eleven?"

"That would be fine," Rachelle agreed, her curiosity aroused. "So Brian works here with his father?"

"Oh, yes, Mr. Fitzpatrick, Mr. *Brian* Fitzpatrick is president of the company," the friendly woman told Rachelle as she scratched a note in the appointment book. "His father only works a few days a week—more of a consultant than anything else. He's busy with the rest of his businesses. Oh, here—our annual report." She reached into a drawer and pulled out a glossy folder. Inside, along with pictures of the board members, which consisted mainly of the Fitzpatrick family, were graphs and charts on productivity at the logging company as well as a list of other enterprises that comprised the Fitzpatrick empire.

Rachelle thumbed through the report as she walked away from the receptionist's desk. Brian? In charge of the logging company? Rachelle was surprised. In school, Brian had always been more interested in sports than academics. She'd heard from her mother that Brian had married Laura but, of course, Rachelle hadn't been invited to the wedding. During the remainder of their senior year at Tyler High, Laura had made a point of keeping her distance from Rachelle.

All because of Jackson, Rachelle thought with a trace of bitterness. Though, if given the same set of circumstances, Rachelle would have stood up for him again. He was innocent, damn it, and no matter what else happened, she'd never believe him capable of murder.

Frowning at the turn of her memories, she shoved open the door and stepped outside. The air was clear, a hint of sunshine permeating thin clouds. Behind the low-slung building housing the offices of Fitzpatrick Logging was a huge yard surrounded by a chain-link fence and guarded by a pair of black Doberman pinschers who paced in a kennel that ran along the fence. Warnings were posted on the chain link. A few signs cautioned employees to wear hard hats and work safely. Other signs threatened would-be trespassers.

Trucks, loaded with logs, rumbled in and out of the yard. Cranes lifted the loads from the trucks, to be stacked in huge piles, while other trucks hauled their cargo away from the yard, presumably to a sawmill down the road.

Rachelle's boots crunched on the gravel of the parking lot and so immersed was she in the report she'd received from Marge Elkins, she didn't notice Jackson leaning against the dusty fender of her Escort.

"Short meeting," he commented, and she nearly jumped out of her skin.

"Wha—oh!" Her hand flew to her throat and she almost dropped the shiny-paged report. Though she'd thought he might show up, still he startled her. "What're you doing here?"

"Waiting for you."

"Why?"

"Because I thought we got off on a bad foot the other night and I decided maybe I'd come on a little strong."

"A little?" she mocked, unlocking her car door and refusing to look at his long, jean-encased legs that were propped in the gravel for balance as he rested his hips against her car.

"A lot, then. I was just worried, that's all."

"Worried? About me?" She almost laughed at the irony of it. "Too late, Jackson." Years ago, when she'd needed him, he'd left her high and dry to stand up for herself, to stand up for him, to endure the taunts, the smirks, the jokes at her expense. She'd earned a new nickname. Risqué. And the boys who'd call her by the name would let their eager gazes rove all over her. And where had Jackson been then? Hitchhiking to God-only-knew-where. "I don't need you to worry about me."

To his credit, he winced a little. "I can't help it."

"I can take care of myself." She opened the car door and tossed her bag onto the passenger seat.

He caught her by the hand before she was about to slide behind the wheel. "Wait."

"I'm through waiting for you. I did enough of that twelve years ago." She tried to yank her arm away, but he wouldn't let go. His fingers were warm and as seductive as his voice.

"I didn't mean to hurt you," he said, and she believed him. The honesty in his angular features couldn't be faked. "I did what I thought was best. Maybe I was wrong. Maybe I should have stuck around here. Maybe I should have stood by you. Married you."

"What?" she gasped, but a little part of her wanted to cry at the tenderness in his words. *Don't be an idiot, Rachelle!*

"That's what this is all about, isn't it?"

"I never wanted to marry you," she replied, stung at how close he came to the truth. But her teenage fantasies had nothing to do with her feelings for him now.

He dropped her hand, though his enigmatic brown-gold gaze wouldn't let go of hers. "Then I guess I made a mistake. I thought all the rage that you're holding inside had something to do with me."

"I *lied* for you, Jackson. I perjured myself for you." She thought of the painful days he'd spent in jail, the police who had badgered her, the way she'd waited for him when he'd been released and the charges dropped. She'd been so foolish.

Now he didn't move. The silence in the air was thick.

Rachelle glared up at him. "You weren't with me all night, were you? You left sometime after midnight."

He didn't deny it. But the look in his eyes was hard as glass and his mouth compressed into a furious white line. "You think I killed Roy?"

"No. If I did, I would never have lied. I just wanted you to know that I pulled out all the stops for you. Because, believe it or not, I trusted you. With everything I had."

"So now I owe you one, is that it?"

She wanted to slap him, to tell him that he was the most frustrating man she'd ever met, but she slid into the warm interior of her car and rummaged in her purse for her keys. Her emotions were shredding. With each second she spent with him, all her hard-fought independence seemed to unravel bit by bit. Slowly she dragged in a long breath. Honesty. She had to be truthful with him. Even if it killed her. But she didn't have to bare her soul, did she? Not entirely. "I stood up for you, Jackson. When no one in this town could say your name without verbally crucifying you, I told everyone that you were innocent, that I knew you couldn't have killed Roy because I was with you. All night long."

His lips pinched slightly. "And you've blamed me ever since."

"Yes!" she cried. "For abandoning me. I lost my reputation, my job, my friends and all my self-respect. Even the teachers knew that I'd slept with you—that I'd spent all night with a boy I barely knew, a boy whose reputation was the worst in town, a boy who used me and then left me without once looking over his shoulder, without once calling. You were a coward, Jackson," she said, tears stinging the back of her eyes. "And that's why I can never forgive you."

"I never used you! I cared, damn it."

"Can't prove it by me." She wrenched the car door closed and stared up at him through the open window. She couldn't help blinking back tears as she palmed her keys. "Leave me alone, Jackson. And while you're at it, go to hell."

With a flip of her wrist, she started her car. Gravel spun beneath the Escort's wheels as she floored the throttle and took off.

Jackson jumped backward and was left staring after her, silently damning himself and knowing that most of what she'd said was true. Though she didn't know his reasons. Cowardice hadn't driven him from Gold Creek. No, he could have stood up to all the gossip-mongering citizens of the town; he could have suffered their stares and their remarks and their unspoken innuendos.

But he'd left because of her. Any more involvement she may have had with him would only have destroyed her further. True, she'd suffered. But the pain would have been much worse if he would have stayed here, stood by her and married her.

The thought struck a painful chord in his chest. Not that he hadn't considered marrying her before. Lying on the dirty bunk in his jail cell, he'd had plenty of time to come up with alternative plans to prove to everyone that they were wrong about him. He'd considered marrying Rachelle, just to clear her reputation and prove himself capable of one decent act.

But what would have come of a hasty marriage between two kids who had nothing in common but one night of sex? With no education and the suspicion of murder hanging over him, he would have been able to offer her next to nothing. Their romance—if that's what it was—would have faded quickly when he couldn't find a decent job in Gold Creek and she would have had to move away from her friends and family and give up her dreams of a college education and a career in journalism.

No, marrying Rachelle would have been a mistake. A big mistake. One they both would have regretted for the rest of their lives. They would've ended up hating each other.

*And is she so fond of you now?*

He didn't care. It was best if she hated him, he told himself, but he couldn't convince himself to stay away from her. The fire in her eyes that had attracted him twelve years ago had only mellowed to a quietly burning flame that captivated him all the more. She was long-legged and sleek, with mahogany-hued hair that still swung to her waist. He remembered getting lost in the fragrant, damp strands of her hair that night. He could still recall the firelight casting deep shadows of red into the auburn waves.

He'd drowned in the scent and feel of her, losing all sense of right and wrong while letting her agile body be the balm that he'd so desperately needed. He hadn't thought about the future, only about the present and about the incredibly hot desire she'd aroused in him.

He'd made love to her. Over and over. Putting aside the pain from his wounds, and the thoughts that somehow they'd be found out, he'd driven into her sweet warmth again and again, fusing with her flesh until all he could feel, taste and smell was Rachelle.

Naked in the light from the dying fire, her supple body stretched out beside him, her breasts crushed against his chest, she'd been more beautiful than any woman he'd ever met. He'd told himself that he'd loved her, that no matter what had happened, that night was special and right, that nothing so perfect could go wrong.

What a fool he'd been. What a pitiful, young fool.

*And now you're an older fool,* he thought, staring after the cloud of dust that trailed after her car. *Because like it or not, Moore, Rachelle Tremont with her sharp wit and even sharper tongue is still in your blood.*

RACHELLE LEFT FITZPATRICK LOGGING with her heart in her throat. Why was he here? She didn't want to see him or deal with him. Just being around him reduced her to childish emotions that she'd hoped she'd grown out of. Love, hate, anger and frustration. One minute she was ready to slap him, the next she was moved to tears. What was wrong with her? Jackson Moore was just a man, for crying out loud, a man who'd hurt her once but wasn't going to get another chance.

Yes, she had to see him again—to ask for an interview. But then, by God, she'd keep the conversation professional, even if it killed her!

The two-lane road passed beneath the Escort's wheels in a blur. Only when the asphalt dipped a bit as she drove under the old railroad trestle, did she bring herself back to the present. She smiled at the skeletal rigging of the bridge that had survived two major earthquakes and a fire that had swept through town in the fifties. The rickety-looking trestle seemed as indestructible as the Fitzpatricks.

She spent the next couple of hours poking around town, noticing the new businesses as well as the old. The same dress shop was still on Seventh Street, owned by a woman who must now be in her seventies, while other stores had changed hands over the years.

She grabbed lunch in a café that had once been part of the old movie theater and walked through the park, only to stop and stare at the memorial—a gazebo of all things—to Roy Fitzpatrick.

No matter what she did or where she went, the memory of the night Roy died followed her. It seemed as if the town of Gold Creek had changed permanently that October evening. The course of history had been altered. And she and Jackson were a major part of that change.

Who had killed Roy? She'd asked herself a hundred times and never found an answer. Maybe there wasn't one. Maybe the past was so buried beneath prejudice against Jackson and gossip about her, that the other facts surrounding Roy's death were conveniently forgotten. No other suspect had ever been hauled into jail, though the sheriff's department and the Gold Creek police had questioned nearly everyone who had been at the homecoming game that night, as well as a few citizens who hadn't. Every kid who'd shown up at Roy's party had been interrogated, but when the dust had cleared, Jackson had been the only suspect.

Roy's murder had been left unsolved, though everyone in Gold Creek assumed that Jackson was the culprit.

She climbed back into her car and stared at the green. It had all been so long ago, and yet, in some respects, it was as if time had stopped in Gold Creek.

And now Brian was running the logging company—a job Roy had been groomed for. Things would be different in Gold Creek if Roy had survived, and things would certainly be different between Jackson and her. But she wasn't going to think about Jackson. Not today.

She had work to do.

She drove back through town and under the railway trestle again. But she didn't drive as far north as the logging camp and stopped at Monroe Sawmill Company, where some of the workers were just getting off. Still, others were arriving for the swing shift.

She approached a man she didn't recognize and hoped he didn't know her name as she introduced herself. He didn't even lift a brow as she explained her reasons for returning to Gold Creek and began asking him questions about his family, the town and what he wanted from life.

"I just want to work and support my family," he said after staring at her long enough to decide he could trust her.

"And you've found that opportunity here?"

"I did until all the dad-blamed environmentalists decided it was more important to save some bird's habitat than it was to keep men's jobs. I got a wife and two kids, a mortgage and car payment. I don't give a rat's rear end for some dang bird."

She quickly took notes as the man rambled on, and she decided the complexion of Gold Creek had changed little in the past decade, though there was more talk about environmental concerns that affected the timber town. When jobs depended upon cutting down trees and slicing them into lumber, no one really cared about the fate of endangered species of wildlife.

"Sure, we care," a man admitted, as he wiped his work glove over his face and brushed off the sawdust that clung to his hair and his mustache. "But if it comes to the damned owls or my family, you'd better bet I'll pick my family every time. It's time those big-city environmentalists got a look at real life. Who's in the corner of the little guy, hmm? Who's protecting *my* environment—my job? I'm just a workin' man. That's all. And you can print that in your paper."

He'd finished his coffee then and headed back to work. Rachelle watched as he climbed aboard a forklift, shifted some levers and began moving stacks of lumber.

She didn't see Erik Patton until she'd started back to the car. He was standing by three other men, hard hats in place, gloves stuffed in back pockets. He was bigger than she remembered, and the start of a beer belly had begun to hang over his thick belt. At the sight of Rachelle, he stopped talking for a second, then muttered something to his friends and walked over. Hitching up his pants, he almost swaggered and Rachelle braced herself.

"Heard you were back in town," he said, stopping only a few feet from her. He fished in his pocket for a crumpled pack of cigarettes. "Stirrin' up trouble again, right?"

"I don't think so."

"No?" He squinted through a cloud of smoke as he lit up. "Moore's back, too. Quite a coincidence."

"Isn't it?" she replied, then decided Erik would be an interesting subject to interview. He'd been here from the day he was born and his college career had either been cut off or he'd decided he loved sawmilling. "Do you mind if I ask you a few questions? I'm doing a series of articles for the *Herald* and—"

He waved off her explanation and removed his hat. His hair, shot with the first few strands of gray, was creased where the band of the hard hat had fitted against his head. "I heard about it. Why would you want to talk to me?"

"Because you've been here the whole time I was gone. You've seen the changes in town—"

He snorted. "What changes? This place is just as dead today as it was twelve years ago." He took a long drag on his cigarette and cast a look at the sawmill, where men bustled in and out of sheds and heavy equipment kept the logs moving.

"Why didn't you leave?"

He shot her a dark look—the same brooding glance that she remembered on the night he'd driven her to the Fitzpatrick summer home in his pickup. "Some people have roots here."

"But you were going to college..." she pressed on, and his lips turned into a tiny frown of disappointment.

"Sonoma State and I had a parting of the ways," he said. His cigarette dangled from the corner of his mouth, and smoke curled in the clear air. "I don't know what good this is going to do, Rachelle," he said with more candor than she'd thought him capable of. "Moore should have stayed away and left things as they were. And you—" he motioned toward her pocket recorder "—you were better off in the city. No one here is ever going to forget that night, you know. And you and Jackson back in town just bring it all up again. You're not going to be very popular."

"It's not the first time."

He took a final tug on his cigarette, and as smoke streamed from his nostrils, he tossed the butt onto the ground and settled his hat back onto his head. "You were a smart girl once. Do yourself a favor and go back to

LISA JACKSON                    141

wherever it is you came from. And tell Moore to do the same. Believe me, there's nothing here but trouble for both of you."

## CHAPTER EIGHT

AS SHE UNLOCKED THE DOOR to her cottage, the phone began to ring. She dropped her purse and sack of groceries on the counter and picked up the receiver before the answering machine took the call.

"I was about to give up on you!" her mother scolded gently.

Rachelle rolled her eyes to the ceiling and twisted the phone cord in her hands. She'd only been on the phone ten seconds and already she was on a Mom-inspired guilt trip. "I've been busy." The excuse sounded lame.

"Too busy to have dinner with me?"

"Never," Rachelle replied as she stretched the phone cord taut and shoved a quart of milk into the refrigerator. "In fact, I was planning on asking you out."

"Nonsense. It's already in the oven." They talked for a few minutes and neither woman brought up Jackson's name, but Rachelle braced herself for the evening ahead. No doubt it would be an inquisition. Ellen Tremont Little made no bones about the fact that she thought Jackson Moore was the cause of all Rachelle's problems.

Within half an hour Rachelle had changed and driven the two miles to her mother's small house. She carried a bottle of wine with her as she pushed the doorbell.

The door opened and Ellen waved her inside. Her mother looked smaller, more frail than she had on her last visit to San Francisco and her eyes were red, as if she'd been crying. Her permed hair was unkempt and frizzy, and she was nervous as she hugged her daughter. "Thank God you're here," she whispered, clinging to Rachelle and smelling of cigarettes and perfume. She dabbed at her eyes with her fingertips.

"Mom, what's wrong?" Rachelle asked, but deep in her heart she knew. Her mother's second marriage had been rocky for several years.

"Harold moved out," Ellen replied as Rachelle glanced uneasily around the small rooms, glad not to find her stepfather, pipe stuck in the corner of his mouth, reading glasses perched on the end of his tiny nose. He was a small, round man with a nasty temper and cutting tongue. From the day he'd married Ellen, he hadn't been satisfied with anything she or her daughters had done.

"Are you okay?" Rachelle asked, holding her mother's shoulders at arm's length.

"I think so." Her mother offered a wan smile. "When your father left me for *that woman,* I thought I'd die. I couldn't imagine not being married." She wrung her hands together as she motioned Rachelle into a tired kitchen chair that Rachelle remembered from her youth. "It wasn't just the money, you know. It was the company. The fact that I'd be alone. When your father left me, he took our social life with him." She sighed heavily. "And it was hard to accept the obvious fact that he'd rejected me—rejected me for a younger woman." She shook her head and her lips tightened at the corners. "You can't imagine the shame of it…everyone in town whispering about me…. Well, maybe you do understand a little." Her sad eyes filled with tears as her gaze met Rachelle's.

*I understand more than you'll ever believe,* Rachelle thought, but held her tongue.

"Anyway, I was at a loss." Ellen threw up her hands.

"All my friends were married. My social life—what little there had been of it—was gone. I felt betrayed, alone, miserable and then...well, you know. I met Harold. I knew he wasn't perfect, but he was a way out of the money problems and the loneliness.... Oh, God, Rachelle," she whispered, working hard against tears, "I'm going to be alone again." She held her face in her hands, and Rachelle hugged her tightly.

"Being alone's better than being with Harold," Rachelle said, but felt more than a little stab of guilt. Harold, though a mean, self-important man, had, when she was struggling in school, loaned Rachelle enough money to make ends meet until she graduated from the University of California at Berkeley. She'd paid him back with interest, but still, she couldn't forget that he'd helped her when she'd needed it.

"I know I'm better off without him, but it's so hard. So damned lonely." Ellen sniffed and rubbed her forearms as if suddenly cold.

"You're sure it's over?"

Ellen waved away the question and her face knotted. "He, uh..." She looked about to confide in her daughter, but changed her mind. "We've agreed. All we have to do is work out the details with the lawyers. I just—I just don't know what I'll do," she said in a voice choked with bitterness.

Rachelle's heart went out to her mother. "You could come to the city. Live with me."

Ellen's face crumpled for a second and then she started to smile. "Live with you?" she repeated. Suddenly she was laughing or crying or both. Tears streamed down her lined face. "Then we'd both be miserable."

"It would only be until you got on your feet."

"I couldn't even drive in San Francisco. No, honey,

I'm a small-town girl. Born and raised here. I guess someday I'll die here. Probably earlier than I should if I don't give up these," she admitted, reaching into a drawer for a carton of cigarettes. Her fingers shook as she opened the cellophane wrapper of a new pack. Lighting up, she let out a smoky sigh. "I don't know how many times I've tried to quit." She studied the tip of her cigarette and lifted one side of her mouth. "I think I've got to go out and find a job. Isn't that a hoot? At forty-eight. I never worked a day in my life. What can I possibly do?"

"You'll find something," Rachelle predicted.

"I hope so." Ellen drew long on her cigarette, then set it in an ashtray near the sink. Without another word, she started moving food from the oven to the table, and Rachelle helped put the napkins and flatware on the place mats. She stubbed out her cigarette just before they sat down, then, in a ritual that had been with the family for as long as Rachelle could remember, she folded her hands and sent up a silent prayer.

"No matter what happens, we've got to thank the Lord," Ellen said, an explanation Rachelle and Heather had heard a hundred times over after their father had walked out.

The meal—pork chops, gravy and squash—was delicious. Rachelle was so full, she could barely move, but her mother wouldn't hear of her declining dessert, "her specialty" of strawberry-rhubarb pie topped with whipped cream.

Rachelle ate three bites and had to quit. "I can't, Mom. Really. It's wonderful. The best. But I swear I'm going to pop."

Ellen laughed and seemed almost happy as she licked the whipped cream from her fork.

"I like cooking for someone," Ellen said sadly as she

wrapped the remainder of the pie in plastic wrap. "I enjoyed cooking for your father and even Harold. Now who am I going to cook for?"

"Yourself."

Her mother threw her a disbelieving glance. "Cooking for one is worse than cooking for a dozen. You should know that."

Rachelle ignored the little dig about her marital state. Her mother had been pushing her toward the altar for years and didn't understand why she hadn't yet taken the plunge, even though she herself was soon to be twice divorced.

Ellen reached for her pack of cigarettes and a lighter. "Heather says you're thinking of getting married."

Rachelle, if she'd been able to find her sister at that moment, would gladly have strangled her.

"David, I assume," Ellen added.

"He thinks it's time," Rachelle hedged.

"And you?"

"I don't know if I'm ready."

"You're going on thirty. David's a nice man, has a good job and seems to love you."

She couldn't argue with such straightforward logic. But her mother wasn't finished. While her cigarette burned unattended in an ashtray, Ellen began clearing the dishes. "You know, I read your column every week," she said simply, and a touch of envy entered her voice. "You're the first woman in this family to have completed college and that's always been a source of pride to me. I thought that—" she leaned against the sink to gather her thoughts "—I thought that you, of any of us, would be a survivor. You'd find the right man. Even after that mess with Jackson Moore."

"Mom—"

Ellen held up a hand to hush her daughter. "But I've heard that Jackson is back in town."

"Yes."

"You've seen him?"

Rachelle's shoulders stiffened. "A couple of times."

"Oh, honey!" The words were a sigh, and again tears threatened her mother's tired eyes. "We don't have a very good track record, the women in this family. I've married twice and never found happiness, and Heather...well, she's living proof that money isn't everything. That husband of hers was worth a fortune and still it didn't work out." The lines of strain were visible on her face. "But I always thought with you it would be different. You would find Mr. Right."

"And you think David might be Mr. Right," Rachelle stated.

"I only know that Jackson Moore isn't. And I think it's more than a coincidence, Rachelle, that he's back in town at the same time you are."

"So?" Rachelle picked up an apple from a basket of fruit on the counter and began tossing it in the air and catching it, avoiding eye contact with her mother.

"So, I want to remind you of all the pain that man caused you and this family. I've made mistakes, I know, but I hope that you don't follow in my footsteps."

"By getting involved with Jackson again," Rachelle guessed, a headache forming behind her eyes. She placed the apple back in the basket.

"He's no good, Rachelle," Ellen said, turning off the water and drying her hands on a nearby dish towel before smoking the rest of her cigarette. "We all know Jackson's bad news, Rachelle. Even you. You can't forget how you felt when he walked out of town and left you holding the bag. You were the one who had to walk down the streets of Gold Creek and hold your head up while people talked." She touched Rachelle's hair and smiled sadly. "Just don't do anything as foolish as getting involved with him again, baby. I don't know if you could stand getting hurt a second time."

HER MOTHER'S ADVICE HAUNTED her all night and into the next day; Rachelle couldn't shake the feeling that she was marking time. So far, this Wednesday morning had been a waste. She'd spent some time in the library, doing research, and then had driven to the logging company for her interview with Brian Fitzpatrick.

He wasn't overly friendly. Seated behind a solid wood desk, he managed a thin smile and motioned her into a chair. He ordered coffee for them both, but he squirmed a little in his chair and she wondered if he, too, was remembering the night when they'd last spoken, the night Roy had attacked her, the night Roy had died.

He was a stocky man, his football physique beginning to sag a little around the middle. His hair was straight and brown and just beginning to recede.

His office wasn't the plush room she'd expected. His desk was oak, the chairs functional, the decor wood paneling had seen better days. A family portrait of Brian, Laura and their boy adorned the wall behind his desk and the few chairs scattered around the room were simple and sturdy. The portrait bothered Rachelle. Because of Laura. She was smiling, her hands on her son's shoulders, Brian's arm slung around her waist. Wearing a wine-colored dress and pearls, her blond hair piled in loose curls over her head, she looked elegantly beautiful, but though she smiled, she didn't seem happy, as if the painter had forgotten to give her the sparkle, the bubbly, flirtatious personality that Rachelle remembered.

She studied the carpet, which was thin in some areas, and the brass lamps which were showing a little bit of tarnish. The office wasn't decorated in the flamboyant Fitzpatrick style. But then Brian had never been as flashy as his older brother, or even his father. She'd heard the rumors around town that Fitzpatrick Logging was having some financial difficulties, but she'd dismissed the news as gossip. The Fitzpatricks had attracted attention and speculation—be it good or bad—since they'd first settled in Gold Creek.

"I didn't think you'd ever come back," Brian said after they'd gone through the motions of a less-than-enthusiastic handshake and Rachelle had turned on her recorder. Though he attempted to be civil to her, the temperature in the room was cold and he didn't bother smiling.

"I decided it was time to visit."

"Why?"

"I'm supposed to be asking the questions," she replied with a smile.

But he ignored her attempt to change the course of the conversation. His eyes narrowed and he tugged thoughtfully at his tie. "I just thought you were smarter than that, Rachelle. There's nothing for you here, and any column you write about Gold Creek isn't going to be all that interesting."

"We'll see," she replied, taking out her notepad.

"You know my family doesn't much care for you," he said slowly. "I said I'd do this interview just because I thought a little publicity wouldn't hurt the company, but no one's forgotten that you stood up for that lyin' bastard who killed my brother." He said the words with such deadly calm that she thought he must've rehearsed them a hundred times.

"Jackson didn't kill anyone," she maintained, her spine stiffening.

"Sure he did. There just wasn't enough evidence to put him away. Everyone in Gold Creek knows it and you know it, too. And, from what I hear, he's back. Probably to make trouble again."

"Why would he do that?"

Brian threw his hands up in the air. "Who knows? Can anyone figure out why he does anything he does? Look at the cases he tries, for God's sake. He's always defending some loser who shot a lover or stole from his boss or forged a million dollars' worth of checks. I have no idea why Moore does the things he does. As far as that goes, I can't even figure out why you're here. Just what is it you want from me, Rachelle?" He picked up a paperweight—a crystal golf ball—and polished its clear surface over and over again with the corner of his sleeve.

"I'd just like some answers about the company. Gold Creek, is, after all, what a lot of people would consider a company town. Or it was when I left here eleven years ago. The Fitzpatricks are an integral part of the town's history as well as the primary employer. What Fitzpatrick Logging does, affects most of the citizens in town."

Mollified somewhat, he leaned back in his chair.

"Just tell me, Brian, what's changed around here in eleven years? You've lived through it—you've never lived away from Gold Creek, not even when you went to college. Even then you commuted. And you've been in charge, right? You were promoted to president of Fitzpatrick Logging the minute you finished school." He seemed flattered by the statement and relaxed a bit.

"What's changed around here," he repeated thoughtfully. "Not a whole helluva lot. I'm the boss now, but everything else is about the same."

"But the Fitzpatrick organization has stretched into other businesses."

"Not me. My dad has a little."

"A little? Just about everything in town has the Fitzpatrick name on it."

"That's Dad for you," Brian said. He told her of the changes at the logging company, which were a result of the environmental issues—clear-cutting timber, water rights and habitats for endangered species. He explained the value of "old growth" timber and reforestation, and talked at length about import problems and quotas. But throughout his well-rehearsed answers, he maintained a distance from Rachelle, keeping his responses short and to the point. He was obviously uncomfortable, not with the subject matter so much as the woman doing the interviewing.

"I'll still want to talk to your dad," she said when she'd run out of questions, and Brian had checked his watch for the fifth time.

"I don't know if he'll go along with it."

"Not even for free publicity? Rumor has it he plans to run for the state senate."

"Rumors can be wrong." Brian stood, and he paused at his desk, tapping the pads of his fingers along the smooth surface as Rachelle collected her briefcase and recorder.

"You may as well understand something, Rachelle. The night Roy died, my dad changed. Our whole family changed. Mom was…'inconsolable' would be putting it mildly, and everyone else paid." He gazed thoughtfully through the window, to the lumberyard where trucks and men were milling about. "Toni and I—don't get me wrong, my folks loved us, still do—but Toni and I have never quite measured up. Roy was special—the golden boy. Everyone knew it. Hell, I'm not telling you anything you don't already know. And Mom and Dad have never gotten over the fact that he was cut down in his youth." Brian leveled hard eyes at her. "As far as my mother is concerned, you gave Jackson Moore his alibi. She figures you lied just to save Jackson's useless hide. That goes for my dad, too. So don't be surprised if, when you start asking questions of the old man, you get a door slammed in your face."

The intercom on his desk buzzed and Marge Elkins's nasal voice filled the room. "Mr. Fitzpatrick? Your wife's here." Her voice grew softer for a minute as if she'd turned her face from the receiver. "No, wait, he's with someone. You shouldn't go in there just yet. Mrs. Fitzpatrick— Oh, dear, I'm afraid—"

Before Marge could finish, the door to the office burst open, and Laura, dressed in a royal blue suede skirt and jacket, walked quickly into the room. Her blond hair was cut shorter than it had been in high school, her nails were polished a deep rose and her makeup was perfect. She was as gorgeous as she had been in school, maybe even more so. Her gaze swept the room, paused for a second on her husband, and landed with full glacial force on Rachelle. "I heard you were back in town," she said, forcing a cold smile. "And I've got to tell you, I'm surprised."

"You and everyone else in Gold Creek," Rachelle replied with a smile. She stood and offered Laura her hand. "How are you, Laura?"

Laura looked at Rachelle's outstretched palm, then ignored it. Rachelle, embarrassed, let her hand drop to her side.

"How am I? You really want to know? Well, I'm upset, Rachelle, really upset. I thought we'd put the past behind us, gotten on with our lives." She shivered and rubbed her arms. "My family has been through a lot...." She glanced up at her husband with worried eyes. "...And now you're back. You and Moore." She shook her head. "It's hard to understand."

"I came back to write a series of—"

"I know, I know," Laura replied, waving off Rachelle's explanation. "But what about Jackson Moore? What in God's name is *he* doing here?"

"Good question," Brian said. He'd rounded the desk and stood next to his wife. "What *does* Moore want?"

"You'll have to ask him," Rachelle said, deciding she couldn't be his spokesperson. If the Fitzpatricks wanted to know what was on Jackson's mind, they could ask him themselves.

"No way. He's got to stay away from the family," Brian said firmly. "My mother's very frail. Her health's declined ever since Roy died, and I'm sure Dad would refuse to see Moore. There's just no point to it."

Laura clutched Brian's sleeve, but she stared at Rachelle. "Don't you remember all the pain, all the agony that the Fitzpatricks have been through? Why would you want to put any of us—or yourself for that matter—through it all over again?" She fumbled in her purse, found her lighter and cigarettes and lit up.

"I'm not here to hurt anyone," Rachelle said, surprised at Laura's outburst.

Laura's lips softened slightly. She touched Rachelle on the arm. "Then take some advice, and let things lie. As for Jackson Moore, if I were you, I'd avoid him. He's trouble, Rachelle. The man *killed* Roy."

"He didn't," Rachelle replied quickly.

"Oh, Rachelle, it's over. You don't have to protect him anymore—"

"I didn't. He's innocent, Laura," she replied quickly.

"I can't speak for Jackson, but as for me, I'll see anyone I want to while I'm here in Gold Creek."

"That could be a mistake," Brian said.

"No doubt, but that's the way it is." With a quick "thank you for your time," she walked stiffly out of the offices of Fitzpatrick Logging and tried to stem her temper. She hadn't liked being told what to do when she was in high school and now, at twenty-nine, she was even more independent. Where did Laura get off, telling her whom she could see and whom she couldn't?

Frustrated, she tossed her purse onto the passenger seat and slid into her car. *Calm down,* she told herself. The Fitzpatricks had reasons to be suspicious of Jackson, though she didn't buy their reasoning. Why, if Jackson really had killed Roy, would he come back here to clear his name? No, it didn't make sense. The Fitzpatricks were just too tunnel-visioned to think that one through.

She stuck her key into the ignition and the Escort's little engine turned over. The interview with Brian had gone badly. But she still had to face Thomas Fitzpatrick. Trying to question Roy's father would probably end up being torture—for both of them.

"More fun," she said sarcastically, her anger stemming a little as she glanced to the yard where log trucks were being unloaded. She thought she saw a familiar face—a face from the past. Without thinking, she turned off the car, pocketed her keys and climbed back out of her car. Half running across the parking lot, she stopped at the high chain-link fence separating the yard from the business offices. Eventually, one of the truck drivers noticed her. He waved to the foreman, Weldon Surrett, who spotted her and, a sour expression on his face, strode her way.

Beneath his hard hat, Surrett's eyes were stern, and

when he recognized her, his lips pulled into a scowl. "I heard you were back in town," he said.

"Hello, Mr. Surrett." Still foreman of the company, Weldon Surrett was a big bear of a man. He was Carlie Surrett's father, and Rachelle hadn't seen him in eleven years. He'd aged a great deal in that time.

Near retirement, he was a little stoop-shouldered and he walked with a slight limp, as if arthritis had settled into his hips. His hair was still jet-black and thick, but craggy lines marred his otherwise-handsome face, and a day's growth of bristly dark beard shadowed his jaw. He yanked off his rough leather gloves, fished in the back pocket of his jeans and pulled out a can of snuff.

"I s'pose you're lookin' for Carlie."

"Is she around?"

"Nah." He stuck a pinch of tobacco against his gum. "She don't come home much."

"Where's she staying?"

"Been ever'where. New York, Paris, Rio de Janeiro—you name it. Big career, y'know. Modelin'. Made more in a day than I take home in a month. Now, I guess, she's givin' that up and becomin' a photographer up in Alaska, I think. Her mother knows. I can't keep up with that girl."

"You must be proud of her."

He shook his head and spat a thin stream of tobacco onto the ground. "Proud? Humph. Nope. She's got no business gallivantin' around the world dressed in underwear, all painted up like a cheap hussy. She shoulda stayed here, settled down and had me a couple of grandkids—that's what she shoulda done." He eyed Rachelle and a sadness seemed to radiate from him. "But she couldn't wait to shake the dust of this town off her feet. After all that stink with the Fitzpatrick kid, and the trouble with the Powell boy, there wasn't nothin' good enough in Gold Creek for her. Nosiree. She became Missy Big Britches, that's what she done." He didn't say it, but the stare he sent her accused Rachelle of making the same mistake. "That's the trouble with kids today. They don't stick around and take care of their kin. Well, it's not the way we raised our girls, and sooner or later, Carlie'll come to her senses and come home."

It sounded like an old man's final hope—a hope he didn't dare believe himself.

"Do you have an address where I can reach her?"

He stared at her sullenly. "Yer not fixin' to drag her into all this again, are ya? I heard yer writin' about the town—what's become of it—and I know that the Moore kid's back, bringin' a whole passel of trouble with him. I don't want Carlie mixed up with any of that business. It's no good, I tell ya. All it'll cause is a lotta hurt feelin's and Thomas and June Fitzpatrick have had more'n their share already."

"I'd just like to talk to Carlie—catch up with her," Rachelle replied.

He rubbed his chin and ruffled his hair before placing his hard hat back on his head. "Call the house. Thelma's got it somewhere." He spat another long stream of brown juice, then donned his gloves and headed back to the yard.

Rachelle was left standing alone, feeling a fool and wondering if this series of articles she'd felt so compelled to write were worth the trouble. Everyone in Gold Creek seemed to resent her—including Jackson himself.

"The price you pay," she told herself as she settled behind the wheel of her little car and with one final glance over her shoulder at Fitzpatrick Logging, drove back through the open gates and headed to Gold Creek.

JACKSON AVOIDED RACHELLE for three days. He told himself he didn't want her, that getting involved with her would only complicate his life, that she obviously hated him and that he should, if he had a decent cell in his body, leave her alone.

But he couldn't. Not now, probably not for the next few weeks. He walked to the window of his motel room and stared outside. Twilight was descending over the town, purple shadows lengthening along the sidewalks and streets. The first few stars glimmered seductively and the moon began to rise.

Jackson curled his fists around the windowsill and rested his head against the cool glass, hoping the cold would seep through his skin and into his blood. He had no right to her. He'd given up all claims he might have had long ago. And yet…and yet the hardness in his jeans made him groan. He was over thirty, for God's sake, and his blood was on fire. Why was he as anxious and hot as a nineteen-year-old?

He gritted his teeth, trying to force back the desire that thundered through his brain. Just the thought of her caused an unwilling reaction in his loins.

As long as he knew she was in the same town, he realized with fatalistic acceptance, he would be unable and unwilling to let go of her.

He'd tried. God, how he'd tried. After she'd thrown him out of her house, he'd wanted to turn his car around, pound on her door and when she opened it, grab her and kiss the shock and anger from her face. But he'd managed to talk himself out of going to visit her again and by sheer matter of will he refused to follow her all over Gold Creek. The times he'd run across her had jarred him to his very bones, especially when she'd half accused him of Roy's murder!

And for years he'd thought she was the one person in town who had believed in him. "Damn it all to hell," he whispered, because he knew now that she doubted him, as well. He should forget her. Leave her alone. Even find another woman to keep his mind off her. But that was impossible.

For the life of him, he couldn't get her out of his mind. No way. No how.

Though he didn't believe in the rubbish of physical chemistry, there was something about her that kept him awake nights and brought sweat onto his skin.

*Lust.* Nothing more. He wanted her. There was a uniqueness in her spirit, a defiance that he felt compelled to tame. Like a randy stallion with a herd of mares, only one of which was unwilling, he wanted that single female he couldn't have.

"Damn you," he muttered, clenching his eyes shut and losing his resolve. The fact that she was so near was dangerous and like a magnet near iron, he couldn't stop himself from giving into her incredible pull.

Before he realized what he was doing, he snagged his jacket off the back of the couch and grabbed his keys from the small table. He'd just go talk to her again, that was all. Find out what she'd learned. But he'd keep his hands off her. That much was certain.

Maybe she could help him. Though he'd at first disdained her aid, he now convinced himself he needed her insight. So far, he'd come up with dead ends on the Fitzpatrick murder. He'd spent a day in the library, going over old newspaper articles about Roy's death. He'd even called in a few markers, asking for information from a man who worked in the governor's office and had once been Jackson's client. The man had promised to get hold of whatever information he could from the local D.A.'s office.

And he'd hired a private investigator in San Francisco, a man named Timms who was supposed to be, according to Jackson's partner, the most thorough detective in California. So far, the man had come up with nothing.

Jackson was out the door and down the steps before he could think twice. He drove to Rachelle's house and found it dark. When he knocked on the door, no footsteps hurried to greet him and the only sound he heard was the tinkle of wind chimes and the growl of her damned cat that was perched on the windowsill.

*Well, what did you expect? That she would be waiting for you?* Angry with himself, he refused to acknowledge any sense of disappointment, but the thought did cross his mind that maybe the guy on the phone had shown up and he'd taken Rachelle out for a night of dining, dancing and romance. *You had your chance, Moore, and you blew it. Years ago. The woman's entitled to her own life, her own boyfriend, her own lover. You've got no claims to her. None!*

He drummed his fingers on the steering wheel and decided to wait.

THE DAY HAD BEEN A DISASTER. Once again, Rachelle had been stood up by Thomas Fitzpatrick and this time the receptionist hadn't been friendly. She hadn't gotten much information from the library and later, at the sheriff's office, when she'd wanted to interview some of the cops who'd been on the force for twelve years, she'd been asked politely to leave.

She was tired, hungry, and had no idea what the subject matter of her next column would be. She'd have to mail something by five o'clock tomorrow, or she'd miss her deadline for the first time in all her years as a reporter.

She turned the corner to her mother's cottage and she nearly slammed on the brakes. She recognized Jackson's rental car parked near her drive. Her hands grew clammy over the wheel. "You can handle this," she told herself as she remembered their last harsh conversation. "You can."

She pulled into the drive. Jackson was out of his car before she'd locked hers. Though she was still angry with his high-handed attitude, a small part of her heart warmed at the sight of him. "I'm warning you," she said, finally twisting the key, "I've had a bad day."

"Me, too," he admitted. "Seems as if the citizens of Gold Creek don't appreciate my presence."

"Well, at least we have one thing in common," she replied as they walked across the lawn to the front porch. The door stuck, and Rachelle, turning the lock, finally resorted to kicking the door open. "No one's gone out of his or her way to make me feel welcome, either."

He hesitated on the threshold, and Rachelle debated whether or not she should let him inside. There was something dangerous about having Jackson around, and the closer he got to her, the more menacing he seemed.

"Aren't you going to invite me in?"

"Seems like I just threw you out a couple of days ago."

"I'll be good," he said, swallowing a smile and Rachelle couldn't help the little laugh that escaped from her lips.

"You? Good? And destroy your image? I don't think so."

"Give me a chance," he said softly, and Rachelle's heart twisted.

"I gave you chances, Jackson. Lots of them. You threw them back in my face."

He moved swiftly, gripping her arm. "I did what I had to, damn it." All kindness had been erased from his features. His lips pulled back to display his teeth and he seemed bitter and hard. "I did what I thought was best for both of us."

"You could have explained it to me."

"I will. If you'll listen."

"I mean, you could have explained it to me then. I was only seventeen, Jackson. *Seventeen!* I trusted you." He paled a little, but his grasp wasn't less punishing. "I gave you everything, everything—my trust, my heart, my body and my reputation. And what did you do?"

His eyes narrowed, but he didn't back away. "You didn't trust me completely, now did you? You thought, because I left the house for a while, that I might have killed Roy."

"I never thought you killed anyone," she replied. "But I wondered why you didn't tell me about it. Or why you never mentioned to the police that you'd taken a post-midnight stroll."

"Probably for the same reasons you didn't," he snarled back.

She lifted her chin a fraction. "You walked out on me, Jackson. Walked out and never looked back. It didn't matter to you that I had nearly an entire year left of high school, that I had to suffer for your guilt—or your innocence."

His skin was stretched taut over his face and his eyes glittered at the injustice of her words.

"It's hard for me to even talk to you," she admitted.

"You hate me that much?"

She hesitated a second, paused on the brink of the

abyss she was certain would swallow her if she admitted
to having any feelings for him. All the scars of the past
were slowly being opened, hurting again, aching. Her
head began to throb, and she swallowed with difficulty.

"Oh, God, Rachelle. Don't hate me," he pleaded, his
voice a low rasp. Desperation shadowed his eyes.

She thought her heart might break all over again. She
had to remind herself that Jackson was the one who had
broken it in the first place. Finally, after all those years,
the pieces were healing. With a little love and tenderness,
all the pain would soon disappear into vague memories
that she would lock away forever.

"Talk to me," he commanded in a voice as dry as a
winter wind.

"I—I can't."

His fingers gripped her flesh. "What is it?"

Her throat ached with unshed tears, but she forced
the words over her tongue, and once they started, she
couldn't call them back. "You asked me not to hate you,"
she said, shaking her head. "Well, I have no choice. I hate
you for what you put me through, I hate you for ruining
my parents' trust in me and I hate you for making me
love you, because I did, you know. I thought I *loved* you."
She laughed and felt the sting of improbable tears at her
confession. "I felt like Joan of Arc, or some other mar-
tyred saint, because I knew, deep in my heart, that you'd
come back, that you'd explain that you cared for me, that
you'd prove you were innocent and everything would be
all right." She blinked hard at her own foolishness. "I
was stupid enough to believe that you'd come back for
me, Jackson, and I clung, like the silly fool I was, to that
hope for years." She yanked her arm away from his rough
hand and shook her head. "So excuse me if I don't invite
you in, okay? I'm just not up for any more heartache."

"I didn't mean to hurt you," he said simply.

"But you did. Every day that you didn't call. Every time I walked to the mailbox hoping for a letter and finding nothing. Every night when I waited, patiently, praying that you'd come back. You hurt me. Maybe that's not fair, maybe you could tell me that I was a fool and that I only hurt myself, and you may be right. But it's easier, after all this time, to just blame you."

His tortured gaze searched hers. "I never figured you for taking the easy way out."

That hurt. Like the sting of a wasp. "Like you did?"

"I had no options," he replied, but she noticed the doubts surfacing in his eyes, the regret and pain.

"Everyone I've seen in this town has given me only one piece of advice," she said, "and for once, I think I'll take it."

"Let me guess—"

"They say that I should stay away from you, that you've always been trouble and always will be trouble."

"They're right."

"Then you won't mind if I say good-night." She didn't wait for a response, just reached for the door and started to swing it shut, but he pressed his palm against the peeled-paint surface and flung the door open with such pure physical force that the knob banged loudly against the wall. Java scurried down from the windowsill and, hissing, dashed into the night.

"I do mind," Jackson told her. "I mind a lot."

"Jackson, just get out of here—oh! What're you doing?"

He grabbed her so quickly, she couldn't escape. His arms were around her and constricting her body. She tried to push away, but he was so much stronger. Then his head lowered and he pressed his lips to hers.

As if he realized what he was doing, he snapped his head back sharply and eyed her. "I didn't mean to—" He broke off, as if seeing her own uncertainty, and kissed her again.

She didn't want the feel of his mouth on hers and told herself that she would fight him tooth and nail. But his lips were warm and supple; they demanded her to yield, which she steadfastly refused to do.

Her blood grew hot, and she convinced herself that she was having a purely animal response. Yes, Jackson was a masterful lover—she knew that from years ago. And he'd undoubtedly had a lot of practice. But she wouldn't succumb to his charms; she wouldn't! He moved against her, forcing her backward until her shoulder blades and hips met the resistance of the wall. And still he didn't stop the plunder of her senses as he kissed her with a hunger so wild she thought she might faint.

Her body responded, and she silently cursed herself. She would ignore the tingles crawling up her spine if it were the last thing she did in this lifetime. And she wouldn't feel the persuasive stroke of his hands against her back, or the inviting feel of his tongue rimming her lips. She wouldn't! She'd hit and kick and struggle to make him stop.

But his lips were magical. They chased away all her hard-fought intentions. The smell of creaking leather and musky aftershave brought back bittersweet memories that caused tears to clog her throat. The wall of his chest was familiar and felt as right this night as it had all those years ago...

His tongue pressed against her teeth, and she, unwillingly, opened her mouth to him. She tingled as their breaths mingled and his tongue danced with hers.

*This is crazy. This is wrong. This is exactly the kind of madness you should avoid!*

She thought of Roy and how he'd tried to force himself upon her all those years ago, but this was different; a part of her longed for Jackson's touch, a small portion of her wanted to believe that they had shared a passion that was as enduring as it was hot.

And yet her struggles slowly diminished, and her lips, swollen from the ravenous passion of his kiss, wanted more. Her knees sagged and she only stood because she was pinned against the wall, Jackson's hard body pressed into her chest and abdomen, her back squeezed against the plaster.

Desire flared like a match and ran quick as wildfire through her veins. His fingers wove through her hair, touching her neck, her throat, her breasts through her sweater. And she didn't stop him. Couldn't. Weak with lust, she clung to him until he stepped away from her.

"Don't ever tell me you don't want me," he said, breathing hard, "because I'll never believe you."

She slapped him. With a smack, her palm smashed into his face. "And don't you ever try anything like that again," she shot back, hoping to wound him as deeply as he'd hurt her. She was still reeling from the sting of his words. "I'm more than a few female body parts that you can will into submission. If you ever come at me like a caveman again, I'll have you up on charges so fast, your head will spin!"

His fist curled, but he stepped away from her, his mouth drawn into a hard, uncompromising line.

Rage consumed her and she was shaking. "Don't ever touch me again, Jackson. You saved me once, from Roy. And then you seduced me. But it won't work again."

He lifted a dark brow that silently and insolently

called her a liar. "Who seduced whom, Rachelle? Am I mistaken, or weren't you the one who wouldn't stop, who wanted a taste of adventure, who *wanted* to experience sex?"

She reached up to slap him again, but he caught her wrist and drew her close. His face was mere inches from hers and his breath, hot and angry, washed over her. "Don't even think about it," he warned, and she shivered from a mixture of fear and anticipation.

"I *never, never* wanted sex from you! I just got caught up in the moment. I assume, from the way you took off after the police investigation, that you felt the same. My problem was that I romanticized what we did into something more than what it was. But that's over, Jackson. I'm grown up and believe in reality, not some silly romantic fantasy about you and me."

"So why're you back in Gold Creek, Rachelle?" he asked as he slowly released her.

"What?"

"If you're not here because of me, I'd like to know why you felt compelled to return."

"I told you—I'm doing a series of columns on—"

"Bull!"

"Excuse me?" she asked, astonished at the man's gall.

"You're here for the same reason I am. You're just not admitting it to yourself. You want to get on with your life and you can't, not while there's so much of the past still unsettled."

He'd hit so close to the mark, she was stunned and she knew her surprise registered on her face. Yet she couldn't allow him the satisfaction of that particular admission. "You have nothing to do with the reasons I came back."

He barked out a short, mirthless laugh. "Tell that to someone who'll believe it, Rachelle," he said as he sauntered back through the door and left.

# CHAPTER NINE

NOTHING WAS SETTLED. In fact, things were worse now than when he first set foot back on Gold Creek soil.

Lying on the motel room bed, Jackson tossed his key ring into the air and caught it. He'd figured on a lot of things when he'd returned. He hadn't been surprised at the cool reception he'd received in town and he'd expected a hassle when he went to the Gold Creek police department and asked for information, but he hadn't guessed that one feisty little woman would get to him. And she had. In a big way.

Ignore her. Stay away from her. Keep your distance. He'd warned himself off her a hundred times in the past twenty-four hours and yet he couldn't get her out of his mind. Swinging his feet from the bed in frustration, he stretched. His entire body was tense, coiled, as if ready to strike. And seeing Rachelle hadn't helped relax him at all. He'd been in town nearly a week and in that time he'd learned next to nothing. His friend at the attorney general's was still "working on things" and Timms, the private investigator he'd hired, told him, "This kind of work takes time. Hell, it's been twelve years, what's the rush?"

The rush was Rachelle. She'd been the siren's call that had brought him back here and now she was intent on shoving him out the door. As if she, too, weren't here to settle old scores.

Well, things were going to change. He hadn't traveled across the country just to stroll through the shrines built to the Fitzpatrick family. He had business to do, and he'd better do it and get out of town while his feelings for Rachelle were still somewhat under control.

What a laugh! Who was he kidding? Whenever he was with her, control was the last thing on his mind. When he thought of the last time he'd seen her, how he'd physically shoved her up against the wall and kissed her—forced her into submission—his stomach churned. When it got down to basic animal lust, maybe he and Roy Fitzpatrick hadn't been so different after all! The thought disgusted him and he told himself that from here on in, he wouldn't push himself on Rachelle. He'd take it slow. Despite the freight train of adrenaline that rushed through his body every time he set eyes on her.

The phone rang and he answered it with a gruff, "Moore."

"So you're still alive and kicking, eh?" his partner, Boothe Reece, asked over a poor connection that linked him to New York. "I thought maybe you'd taken a permanent powder."

"I've been busy," Jackson said, walking to the window and stretching the cord of the phone so that he could survey the day. Warm rays of California sunshine were flooding the street outside. A kid on a bike rode by, a dog chasing after him in a slow lope. Gold Creek. Homey. Warm. Cozy.

Unless you were Jackson Moore.

"Things are heating up here," Boothe said, bringing Jackson back to the conversation. "We've got a case I think you'll be interested in. Since you said you didn't want to be bothered while you were in California, I tried to brush her off, but the client insists she wants to deal with you."

He should feel the first rush of adrenaline now—that spark of interest whenever a new case was brought his way, but he didn't. "She'll have to wait."

"She doesn't have much time. The D.A.'s pressing hard."

Jackson scowled and, still watching the kid and dog ride through the park, rested one shoulder against the wall. "What's the deal?"

"The client is Alexandra Stillwell—ring any bells?"

"Vaguely." He tried to remember. Then it clicked. Stillwell Oil—a small, independent company that had survived without yet becoming part of the bigger, national oil conglomerates.

"Well, she's money—big money. Heiress to an oil fortune."

"I'm with you. Her father died recently, right?"

"Killed two weeks ago. Freak accident on his sailboat. Alexandra was there. Some people think it was just that—an accident—that the old man's number was up. He'd been drinking, popping some pills and slipped on the stairs, knocking his head. Others are conjecturing that it was suicide, some of the old man's debts were being called and he didn't have enough cash to cover them, and he didn't want to sell his company. So some people figured he was going to kill himself one way or the other."

"But not everyone thinks this way."

"Nope. There are a few others, including our illustrious district attorney, who thinks Alexandra did the old man in. She claims she's innocent, of course, that even as sole heir she would *never* do anything to hurt her father."

"You believe her?" Jackson asked, trying to keep the

skepticism from his voice. For every client he represented, he turned a dozen away.

"I can't tell. But it doesn't matter. She won't deal with anyone but you."

Jackson plowed a hand through his hair. A week ago he would have jumped at a case like this. Now the scandal and notoriety didn't intrigue him. "I'm gonna be tied up here awhile."

"She can't wait."

"Then she'll have to get someone else."

There was a long sigh on the other end of the line, and Jackson could imagine Boothe drumming impatient fingers on the desk. Boothe, a veteran of the Vietnam conflict, was fifteen years older than Jackson and, in Jackson's opinion, twice as tough. He didn't like taking no for an answer and was as stubborn as a mule when he wanted to be.

"Look, I don't get it, man," Boothe cajoled. "You've spent the last four years making a name for yourself and now a case like you've never dreamed of is dropped in your lap and you're not interested."

"I didn't say I wasn't interested. Just that she had to wait."

"Why? What could possibly be more intriguing in that little fork in the road than the Stillwell case?"

What indeed? Jackson thought as he told his partner to have someone do the preliminary work and promised to fly back to Manhattan for a day or two later in the week. Maybe he needed a little time and space away from Gold Creek to put his reasons for coming here into fine focus. Ever since seeing Rachelle again, he seemed to have lost his sense of purpose. Instead, his purpose had shifted to her.

He needed to get out of Dodge, so to speak. He'd personally visit the investigator he'd hired in San Francisco. The man hadn't returned any of his calls for four days, and Jackson wondered if he'd skipped out with his two-thousand-dollar retainer.

As for what he found so fascinating in Gold Creek, the answer to his partner's question was simple: Rachelle Tremont and an old murder case that had never been solved.

He decided he couldn't sit around and wait for the phone to ring any longer. He was going out of his mind. He had to keep moving, start making things happen.

First things first, he decided, snagging his leather jacket by the collar. Thomas Fitzpatrick was back in town, and Jackson figured it was time they met. He had only one stop to make on the way and that was at a motorcycle dealership on the outskirts of town. The rental car bored him, and he felt the yen of a bike. He'd lost something in Manhattan—something of himself. A part of him that had been wild and free and wanted to race with the wind. The edge.

In New York he didn't drive often; he only did when he left the city. And the Mercedes that sat in his garage for days on end was a symbol—a symbol he'd grown to hate.

With a grim smile he walked outside and climbed into the rental. He drove to the agency, handed over the keys and paid his bill. Then, stuffing his hands deep into the pockets of his jacket, he started walking. The motorcycle showroom was a mile away, but the day was warm and he needed the fresh air to clear his head.

THE MOTORCYCLE DEALERSHIP was small, with black bars across the windows and eight bikes displayed side by side. He picked out his machine without a second glance

at the other cycles. He bought the big, black Harley—a
newer model of the bike he'd left in Gold Creek years
before.

For the next half hour, he toured the town and surrounding hills, putting the bike through its paces, getting
used to the machine and feeling the long-lost exhilara-
tion of the wind against his face.

Satisfied that he'd mastered the beast, he took off. In
a roar of exhaust, he ripped through the gears and drove
straight to the Fitzpatrick home, a brick-and-stucco Tudor
set upon a hill on the outskirts of the town.

Fortunately, the wrought-iron gates were open and
Jackson drove up the lighted brick drive for the first time
in his life. The Fitzpatricks had lived here for years, but
never before had he been on the grounds. The lawn was
lush and trimmed and a rose garden was just beginning
to bloom. A tiered fountain sprayed water to a series of
man-made ponds that were the home for schools of or-
ange-and-black fish that swam beneath the surface, their
scales glinting in the sunlight as they moved between
spreading lily pads.

The grounds were trimmed meticulously, shade trees
planted in strategic locations, flowers blooming profusely in wide terra-cotta planters on the front porch.

All in all, the estate looked like what it was: a castle
fit for the king of Gold Creek. Jackson didn't hesitate.
He parked on the circular drive and walked swiftly to
the front door. He expected a liveried butler or a maid
dressed in traditional black-and-white to answer the bell,
but as the door swung open, he found himself standing
face-to-face with Thomas Fitzpatrick.

The old man hadn't changed much. A little older, of
course. The salt-and-pepper hair was now pure silver, but

Thomas Fitzpatrick was still trim and athletic, his features strong, his stare as cold as Jackson remembered.

"You've got a lot of nerve," Thomas whispered tightly. Stepping outside, he closed the door softly but firmly behind him. He saw the bike, and his lips pinched at the corners. "Still the rebel, are you?"

"This town just seems to bring out the best in me," Jackson quipped sarcastically.

Frosty blue eyes assessed him with refined repugnance, but Jackson didn't flinch. In his line of work in Manhattan, he'd met more than a dozen men and women who could've bought and sold Thomas Fitzpatrick.

"You have no right to be here," Thomas said sternly.

"I think I do."

"After what you did—"

"Look, Fitzpatrick, I didn't kill Roy," Jackson said, standing toe-to-toe with the man who had been his nemesis for years. Beneath his tan, Thomas paled slightly, and deep in his eyes there was more than rage and indignation brewing. Other emotions stirred, emotions Jackson couldn't begin to name. But the old man was made up of more layers than Jackson would have ever thought.

"Look, Jackson, just because there wasn't enough evidence—"

Jackson snapped. All the years of being the whipping boy for the Fitzpatrick clan got the better of him. He grabbed hold of Fitzpatrick's shirtfront and crumpled the smooth silk in his fingers. "I didn't do it, okay? There wasn't enough evidence because I didn't do it. If you would have spent a fraction of the energy you've spent on hating me on looking for the truth, you probably could've nailed the real killer and saved us all a lot of trouble."

Thomas's lips curled and he shoved Jackson away.

"You impertinent pup. You weren't satisfied with getting off scot-free. You had to come back, didn't you? I'd thought—no, I'd hoped—that you were smarter than that."

"The way I see it, I've still got a black mark or two to erase."

"But why?" For the first time, Thomas's anger seemed to lessen a bit, turning into frustration and even exasperation. "There's no reason."

"Not if you don't care who killed your son." Jackson watched the old man, noticed the change in his emotions. He'd dealt with enough liars in his profession to smell when someone wasn't telling the truth and dear old Thomas was hiding something—something that affected them both. "What is it, Fitzpatrick? Something's bothering you."

"*You're* bothering me."

"But there's something else, isn't there? Something about Roy's death that doesn't sit well with you."

"Nothing about it 'sits well.'"

Jackson wouldn't give up. Like a dog after a bone, he just kept digging. "You want to blame me, have me hauled away to jail and hope that the sheriff will throw away the key. You wanted to get rid of me."

"You killed my son," Fitzpatrick replied stoically, but he didn't meet Jackson's gaze—almost as if he didn't believe the charges he'd leveled at Jackson. The old man was a puzzle, and Jackson intended to take him apart, piece by crooked piece.

"If I'd killed Roy, why would I come back? Why would I want to dig everything up again? If there were a chance that I could be convicted, don't you think I'd be taking one helluva risk coming back to Gold Creek and inviting the police to open up the case again? I may be a lot of things, Fitzpatrick, but I'm not stupid and I'm not a murderer. Now, the way I see it, if you really want to find the person who killed Roy, you could work with me on this, or, if you're satisfied with things the way they are, you can butt the hell out. But if you fight me, then I'll start to wonder why. What is it you've got to hide?"

Thomas's spine was stiff as an iron spike. His voice was low, but rang with an authority honed by years of being in charge, an authority few dared challenge. His stony blue gaze collided with Jackson's. "I just don't want my family hurt anymore," he said slowly. "My wife's not in the best of health and my other children...they've all suffered because of this. It's better to let it die, Jackson. Leave it alone."

Jackson studied Fitzpatrick's face—perfect and patrician, the rough edges smoothed by money and power. "I can't leave it alone," Jackson finally said, remembering how June Fitzpatrick had sworn to see justice done and that "justice" was to destroy him. "It's my life we're talking about. My reputation. And as for your family, I would think that they would be glad to settle this matter once and for all." He inched his face closer to the older man's. "Just what is it that scares you so much?"

A vein throbbed in Thomas's forehead, but the old man didn't respond.

"I'll find out, you know."

"Go to hell."

"'Fraid I can't," Jackson replied. "I'm already there. Have been for twelve years." He sauntered back to his bike and swung one leg over the black leather saddle. As he cocked his wrist, he kick-started that monster of a machine. The bike's engine raced with a powerful roar and Jackson rode off, the gears winding as he screeched out of the drive.

HE'D PROBABLY KILL HIMSELF, Thomas thought with a jab
of guilt.

Thomas stared after him, a bad taste in his mouth.
The boy was a wild card, that was for sure. And Thomas
was the first to recognize and applaud an independent
and rebellious nature, as long as that independence and
rebellion could be turned to his own good use. Many of
the men he'd hired had come to him as insubordinates
who had experienced their share of difficulties with the
law. Thomas had spent a lot of time and a good deal of
money molding those very men into loyal, innovative
workers.

Jackson Moore could have been one of those men.
Except for his innate hatred of the Fitzpatricks and the
fact that now, Jackson was a rich man in his own right.
A pity. He probably couldn't be bought, and therefore
couldn't be manipulated. With grudging admiration for
a man who had started with less than nothing and made
himself a visible, if slightly notorious, lawyer with a fat
bank account, Thomas walked along a shaded path and
through a garden fragrant with early summer flowers.

Jackson Moore. He had to be handled. Some way.
Somehow. But not by the usual methods. There were just
too many painful memories that were connected with
Sandra Moore, her son and Roy. What a mess. Thomas
should have cleaned up the whole affair years ago—suffered the consequences and started fresh. But he hadn't.
Because he'd been weak. A coward.

The back of the house was already in shadows as the
sun settled behind the mountains to the west. Thomas
felt older than his fifty-seven years and the burden of his
youth seemed heavy. He'd made mistakes in his life—
too many mistakes to count, most of them when he was
younger, and they lingered. Some of his past errors in

judgment haunted him every day of his life—like shadows that were invisibly attached to him and couldn't be shaken off.

The soft leather soles of his shoes scraped against the bricks of the sun porch.

His wife was there. Reclining in a chaise longue, her eyes closed, her fingers absently stroking the back of a Persian cat who had settled on her lap, she said softly, "What is *he* doing back here?"

Thomas felt the thickness in the air. Over the scent of lilacs and the drone of insects, he sensed the change in atmosphere that his wife, through her bitterness, brought with her. Though in repose, June was ready to fight and he knew, from a marriage of over thirty years, that there was nothing he could do to avoid the confrontation. He walked to the portable bar and poured himself a straight shot of Scotch. "He's poking around. Claims he wants to clear his name."

June sighed loudly. "He can't. He's guilty."

"I suppose."

Her eyes flew open. "You *know* he did it, Tom." She moved quickly on the chaise, and the cat, startled from his nap, leapt onto a table and, sending glossy magazines flying, scrambled off the porch to slink through the shrubbery.

"It was never proven that Jackson did it."

"Because he's slick. Like oil on water." She shuddered, and her pale skin grew whiter still. "He single-handedly took Roy's life. Maybe it wasn't premeditated, I'll give him that. But he killed him, sure as I'm sitting here. That miserable bastard killed my boy! Our son, Tom! Our firstborn." Tossing a sweater over her shoulders, she stood, walked to the bar and poured herself a healthy glass of gin. She fiddled with the bottles and added a sniff of vermouth before plopping an olive into her glass. The air in the porch was as cold as an Alaska wind, and the old pain of betrayal and death hung between them, just as it always had.

Thomas took a long swallow of his drink, feeling the liquor splash against the back of his throat and warm his stomach. This was a no-win argument. "I miss Roy as much as you do," he said, conviction deep in his throat.

"But not enough to see that the man who killed him paid for his mistake."

"I hired the best attorneys, the most highly recommended private detectives and Lord knows the D.A. went after Jackson with everything he had. It just wasn't enough."

June turned accusing, icy eyes up at him before taking a long sip of her martini. She licked a drop from her lips and measured her words. "You didn't try hard enough, Tom. That was the problem. Because, deep down, you didn't want Jackson to hang for our son's murder!"

RACHELLE WALKED INTO THE post office on Main Street. A few people were waiting to buy stamps and to mail packages or just chat with the postal workers who had manned the counter for years. The floor was worn near the counter and the small warehouse smelled of paper, dust and ink. Pressing the stamps firmly on her manila envelope, she mailed her second article—a column about changing attitudes in Gold Creek. She focused the article on the issue of company towns that had lost their natural resources, and the desperation of families who had grown dependent upon the timber industry for their livelihoods. She felt the article would have merit in other parts of the country where jobs were dependent upon the auto industry or the oil industry or even the farming industry, wherever small towns across America counted on one main source of revenue to keep their citizens in jobs.

Next week she'd tackle the environmental issue and compare how people in town felt about the environment now to how they'd felt about it twelve years ago. The next article would deal with people who had lived in Gold Creek for generations, how they expected to stay and live in this small town, marrying within the community and having no dreams of moving on.

She thought of some of her classmates, and Laura Chandler came to mind. Laura had only wanted to marry the richest boy in Gold Creek, if not Roy Fitzpatrick, then his younger brother, Brian. Rachelle snorted and slung the strap of her purse over her shoulder. She doubted she'd ever get to talk to any of the Fitzpatrick clan again. Every time she'd called the offices of Fitzpatrick, Incorporated and tried to set up an appointment with Thomas Fitzpatrick, she'd been told icily that Mr. Fitzpatrick was "out of town on business." The receptionist had promised to call her when Mr. Fitzpatrick returned.

Rachelle didn't believe the faceless woman on the other end of the line; being a reporter, she'd been put off enough times to recognize a stall job when she was on the receiving end. She'd give Fitzpatrick a couple more days, then she'd start really digging.

In the meantime she'd help her mother sort out her life without Harold. There were bills to pay, credit to establish, a job to find...but at least Rachelle could help her, and Ellen, for once, wasn't fighting her elder daughter.

Rachelle planned to start another article, this time about people who had moved from Gold Creek to make their mark on the world. People like herself. People like Carlie. People like Jackson Moore.

She wondered about Carlie. Where was she? After

speaking with Mr. Surrett, Rachelle had called Carlie's folks a couple of times, but the line had always been busy or unanswered. No machine had picked up, so she hadn't been able to leave a message.

As for Jackson, she'd managed to avoid him for a few days, but she hadn't stopped thinking about him. She wondered if they would ever be able to talk civilly or if there would always be anger between them, passion that eroded common sense?

She walked outside and started toward her car.

"Rachelle?" The voice, a woman's, was unfamiliar. Turning, she found a pretty redhead standing beside a beat-up old hatchback filled with mops, cleaning supplies and two blond boys who were wrestling in the backseat. "You're Rachelle Tremont, aren't you?" The woman's nose was dusted with freckles and her eyes were a deep, vibrant green. "I thought I saw you near the lake the other morning."

"Yes…yes, I was there," Rachelle replied, recognizing Nadine Powell.

"I live on the south side," Nadine explained, then turned to the car and the back window, which was barely open a crack, "Knock it off, you two."

"We're gonna be late, Mom," one of the boys said.

Nadine checked her watch and rolled her eyes. "The story of my life," she said. "Look, I heard you were back in town and writing some articles about Gold Creek, which beats me. I can't believe anyone would be interested in what's been happening here. But if you'd like to talk to someone who's lived here all her life, give me a call. I'll buy you a cup of coffee."

Rachelle grinned. "I will—"

"Mom! Come *on!* Mrs. Zalinski is gonna kill me if I'm late again!"

Rachelle's heart nearly stopped. Zalinski. Zalinski. The deputy who had arrested Jackson!

"Hold your horses, I'm coming!" Nadine shook her head. "Gotta run." She slid into the Chevy and eased out of the lot, and Rachelle wondered if Nadine, a girl she'd barely known in high school, a girl rumored to have run with the fast-and-loose crowd, would turn out to be her only friend in Gold Creek.

HOURS LATER, RACHELLE SHOVED back her library chair in frustration. She glanced out the large windows, noticed that the afternoon sunlight had faded and wished she could find something, *anything,* about the Fitzpatrick murder that she didn't already know. But the articles she read were filled with the same worn-out phrases that she'd read a thousand times years ago. Why was she even dredging it up again? Probably because Jackson had told her that Roy's death was off-limits. And because the night of Roy's death had marred her forever. Until she dealt with her own old, hidden feelings regarding that night, she'd never be able to look to her future—a future with David.

She frowned and bit the corner of her lip. Since arriving in Gold Creek, she'd thought less and less often of David. The old theory that absence made the heart grow fonder didn't seem to hold true. At least not in this case, though years ago, while pining for Jackson, she had convinced herself that she loved him more and more with each passing day that she couldn't see him.

She hadn't been allowed to visit him in jail. Her parents—independently, of course—had forbidden any sort of visitation and she'd been underage, ineligible to see an inmate unless accompanied by an adult. In desperation, she'd even pleaded with an older girl to loan her some ID to prove that she was old enough to visit a jailed inmate, but the security guard had laughed in her face as she'd extended her friend's driver's license. "Go home, Miss Tremont," he'd told her, shaking his head and clucking his tongue at her embarrassment. "You're only making things worse for yourself. And worse for him."

She'd hoped that the county cops wouldn't remember her, but of course they had. She was, after all, a key witness. And a fool to have gone to the jail. The word had gotten out and fallen on her mother's keen ears. All Rachelle had accomplished was to make the trouble at home worse and to ensure that her trampled reputation was battered even further.

A reporter had gotten wind of the story and the very paper she'd worked for, the *Gold Creek Clarion*, had written a follow-up story about her aborted attempt to see her jailed lover. She'd been the laughingstock of the school, though, thankfully, the school newspaper where she'd still logged in some hours didn't cover the story.

"Hey, Rachelle, how about a date—at the state pen?" one boy had hooted at school the following Monday.

"See your murderin' friend, huh?" another boy had called. "How was old lover boy?" The kid had made disgusting kissing sounds that followed Rachelle down the hallways as the group of boys had laughed at her expense. Tears had stung her eyes and she'd hidden an entire period in the darkroom of the school paper.

Even now her guts twisted at the thought. Was it worth it? All the old pain—was it worth facing it again?

She dropped her head in her hands and wished the headache that was forming at the base of her skull would go away. Her emotions were a yo-yo, coiled and ready to explode one second, strung out and pulled tight the next.

*Just hang in there,* she told herself. *It's going to get better. It has to!*

Except that Jackson was back in town—a wrinkle she hadn't expected.

She turned back to the screen and began again to search through old newspapers on microfiche. Her eyes were tired and strained, and she nearly jumped out of her skin when Jackson appeared behind her machine and leaned lazily over the glowing monitor.

"What're you doing here?" she whispered, and several people seated at old tables turned their attention her way.

"Looking for you."

"I thought we weren't going to see each other."

"That was your idea, not mine."

"Shh!" A grouchy, bespectacled man with bushy gray eyebrows glowered at them, then snapped open his newspaper and began reading again.

Jackson grabbed Rachelle's hand and tugged.

"Hey, wait a minute. What're you doing?" She remembered their last encounter, which she'd sworn was to be their final one. And here he was, smiling and charming and wanting something from her, no doubt.

"Let's get out of here."

She considered the way he'd kissed her—and her stupid heart fluttered. "I don't think—"

"I just came from Thomas Fitzpatrick's house."

"He's back in town? But he canceled an appointment with me—" She was rising from her chair, scooping up her purse and jacket before she even realized what she was doing. From the corner of her eye she saw the bushy-eyed man purse his thin lips and watch her escape with Jackson.

Outside, the afternoon sun had disappeared, the wind

cool with the coming night. Shadows lengthened across the asphalt parking lot. Rachelle pulled her hand away from his and stopped. "*You* spoke to Thomas Fitzpatrick?" she asked suspiciously.

"That's right."

"When?"

"This afternoon at his house."

"Oh, sure. And he just opened his door to you, invited you in for a drink, welcomed you as an old family friend."

A grin tugged at the corners of Jackson's mouth. "Not quite. I didn't get in the front door, or even the back for that matter."

"Are you crazy? Why would you go there? The man hates you! Don't you remember what he did to you?" she cried, using the same arguments with Jackson that her sister, Heather, had used with her.

A middle-aged couple, approaching along the cement walk, stared at them, then exchanged knowing glances. The man leaned over to the woman who covered her mouth with one hand and whispered into his ear.

The back of Rachelle's neck burned and Jackson took her hand once more, pulling her toward a huge motorcycle. Images of another night flashed through her mind. "Wait a minute. What're you doing?"

"We're getting out of here."

"On that?" She pointed a disbelieving finger at the bike.

"Mmm."

"You and me on the bike together? Oh, no. I don't think—"

He swung a leg over the gleaming machine. "Just get on, Rachelle."

"No way. I'm not going to let you bully me into..."

She let her words drift away when she spied Scott McDonald walking briskly down the street. He'd filled out over the years, but she still recognized him.

"Another one of Roy's friends," Jackson observed, his eyes following Scott as the man shoved open the door of the pharmacy and walked inside. "Didn't any of them leave?"

"Not many," Rachelle said, and when he looked sharply at her, she shrugged. "I've done a lot of research for my articles. It seems the people closest to the Fitzpatricks stuck around Gold Creek."

"Small town, small minds."

"Not entirely," she replied, surprised that she would stand up for anything to do with this town. She'd suffered here at the hands of many of her peers as well as an older generation of townspeople. There had been no haven. She'd been tormented in school, at the newspaper office where she'd been fired for no apparent reason other than she was on Jackson's side, even in church, where several of the women had tossed looks over their shoulders that silently damned her as a sinner. She wouldn't have been surprised if Mrs. Nelson had come up and asked her to wear a scarlet *A* on her blouse.

Her mother had tolerated her own share of pain. Not only had her husband run off with a younger woman, but her older daughter had proved she was no better than her philandering father had been. Ellen Tremont had dropped out of her bridge club, avoided church gatherings and generally cut off her social life.

Yes, Rachelle's one night with Jackson had scarred most of the people she loved.

"Well?" Jackson was waiting. His jaw was clenched hard and a muscle worked double-time in his jaw. He was straddling the bike and had turned on the engine. It thrummed loudly in the quiet street—an invitation.

She glanced up at his face, saw a glimmer of tenderness in his eyes and her resistance melted. *You're being a fool—a crazy, masochistic fool!*

Despite all her arguments to the contrary, Rachelle climbed onto the back of the huge machine, still not touching him.

Jackson stuffed her purse and notes into a side pouch and cast her a glance over his shoulder as he guided the bike into the slow stream of traffic. "Where to, lady?"

She lifted a shoulder and slowly placed her arms around his torso. "This was your idea."

His mouth lifted into a wicked smile. "You're going to let me take you wherever I want?"

Her pulse rocketed at the innuendo and she had to force a cool smile onto her lips. "You're in the driver's seat, Jackson."

# CHAPTER TEN

RACHELLE KNEW SHE SHOULDN'T have gotten onto the motorcycle with Jackson, just as she'd known she shouldn't have climbed into Erik Patton's pickup twelve years earlier. She couldn't believe she'd made the same mistake twice, but she had. Her gut was coiled tight as a clock spring as Jackson took off on the north road, roared under the old railway trestle and headed toward the lake.

"The lake? We're going to the lake?" she shouted above the roar of the bike. She couldn't hide her disbelief.

"Why not?"

"You really are a masochist, aren't you?"

"The lake is where it all started," he replied with a thread of steel in his voice as he shifted down and they hugged a corner.

"You know what people will say—that the criminal always goes back to the scene of the crime."

He cast her a hard look over his shoulder. "Let them talk."

"But—" She snapped her mouth shut. He'd made up his mind; he was driving the damned bike and nothing she could say would change his mind. She felt a jab of irony at the situation. How many times after Jackson had left town had she daydreamed that he would return for her, that he would take her back to the lake, and there, against a backdrop of pine and rising mists, they would make love, sealing their destiny to be together?

Well, she'd grown up a lot since spinning those tender dreams where Jackson was always the hero and she the persecuted, but eventually vindicated, heroine. Now, going to the lake sounded like a nightmare.

They passed through the night-dark hills and the wind rushed hard against her face, tangling her hair. Rachelle trained her eyes over Jackson's shoulder. She tried not to notice the scent of leather and aftershave, or the way his stomach tightened whenever her hands shifted. Pressed this tightly against him, her breasts crushed against his back, it was nearly impossible to keep her thoughts from straying to the very obvious fact that he was a male, a very virile and potent male, and she was no more immune to him tonight than she had been twelve years ago.

"Going back to the lake might put things in perspective," he said. He didn't glance back over his shoulder, just stared straight ahead, into the night, his concentration on the beam the headlight threw in front of the cycle.

They passed Monroe Sawmill where most of the trees cut by Fitzpatrick Logging were turned into lumber or pressed into plywood. The night was turned to day as the swing shift worked toward quitting time. Lights glared from sheds where employees in hard hats, jeans, flannel shirts and heavy gloves stood at the green chain while the raw lumber was moved by conveyor belts and sorted.

In another shed, a barker peeled the rough outer layer from buckskin logs and huge saws, spraying sawdust, sliced the naked logs into thick cants, which would soon be cut into smaller lumber and sold, adding to the profits of the sawmill while lining the pockets of the Monroes and the Fitzpatricks.

Rachelle had driven by the sawmill a hundred times in her lifetime, but now, riding in the dark with Jackson, she was reminded of the night that had bound them together forever. She stared at the formidable line of his jaw, just barely visible over his shoulder, and felt the tension in each of his muscles. His thoughts, no doubt, had taken the same turn as hers.

The road twisted upward through the forest. Rachelle's stomach tightened into a hard knot as they passed by the Fitzpatrick estate. Was he taking her here? But why? She couldn't imagine that trespassing on Fitzpatrick land would be of any help and she didn't want to see the gazebo where Roy had attacked her, and Jackson, thank God, had come to her rescue.

He drove on, along the winding road and he didn't stop until he came to the grounds of the Monroe house. The wrought-iron gates were closed, the thick rock walls surrounding the estate seeming unscalable.

"Now what?" she asked as they parked and Jackson sat with the beam of his headlight washing the stone and mortar. Her chest felt tight and she knew, from the charged air between them, that, tonight, she was going to do something she shouldn't. Jackson would try to convince her to go along with him, just as he'd convinced her to come with him up here.

"Now we break in—"

"Oh, no! We did that once before, remember? You ended up in jail—"

He turned and faced her, one of his hands grabbing hers. His touch was warm and his fingers found the soft underside of her wrist, finding her pulse as it began pounding erratically. "I do remember, Rachelle," he said quietly. "That's why we're here." The night air seemed to crackle between them.

"This is wrong, Jackson. We both know it. And it's dangerous. Think what happened the last time—all the trouble. I'm not going to take a chance on being charged with trespassing or breaking or entering or anything!"

"Where's your sense of adventure?"

"Where's your brain? This is crazy. *C-r-a-z-y!*"

"And I thought you reporters would do just about anything for a story," he chided.

"There's no story here." It was a lie. In fact, she'd promised her editor an interview with Jackson in order to have her series of articles approved. She bit her lip.

"Oh, I think we can scrounge up a little bit of copy—a few interesting column inches." He looked at her darkly and his eyes seemed to smolder. Her throat turned to dust as she thought he'd kiss her again, but he let go of her hand suddenly and swung off the bike. Tossing her the keys, he said, "You can come. Or you can leave."

"I don't even know how to drive this thing…Jackson, wait!"

He disappeared. Half running, he made his way through the trees and Rachelle wished she were anywhere but here. Damn his miserable hide! They weren't a couple of kids any longer. This was big trouble. Major trouble. Both of their careers could be affected, even ruined.

If she had a functioning brain, she would stuff the keys into the ignition, turn the bike around and, God only knew how, leave him to hitchhike back to town. It wasn't as if he hadn't done that sort of thing before, she thought with more than a trace of bitterness. Her heart squeezed painfully. So why was she here, along with him, back at the very spot where she'd given him her virginity all those years before?

*Because you're a fool, girl. A romantic fool!*

A small smile crept over her lips, for, despite the pain, the heartache, the bitterness she felt for him, a tiny part of her still treasured those few tender hours they'd shared as lovers. Even now, years later, there was still a fondness—a cozy feeling in her heart—when she remembered his lovemaking. Their passion had been explosive, but there had been a tenderness to him, as well, a gentle side, that few had been allowed to see. She'd often wondered if anyone but she had gotten a glimpse of that inner part of him.

The idea was ridiculous, she supposed. He could have made love to dozens of women and each of his lovers might well think that she held the exclusive hold on his heart, that she alone was witness to his pain, that she had helped balm his wounds, that she, and she only, had caught a glimmer of the kinder man beneath his hard and calloused exterior.

To her horror, she looked at the wall surrounding the estate again, and there he was, on the other side of the gate, fiddling with some gadget—the controls no doubt. Within minutes, the huge gates began to swing, creaking open. Jackson ran to the bike, hopped on and—plucking the keys from her fingers—winked. He started the bike and drove onto the grounds.

"You are out of your mind," she whispered, but she clung to him, her arms snug across his abdomen.

He shot her a dangerous look over his shoulder. "Maybe."

"There's no 'maybe' about it."

The lane was dark, the asphalt chipped and cracked. Jackson drove slowly and Rachelle's insides squeezed together. This was a mistake, a horrid mistake, she thought as he parked near the house.

The house was as she remembered it—three stories with a sharply pitched roof complete with dormers. She wondered if the furniture was the same, if the old couch was positioned near the fireplace.

"Looks like no one's been here for years," she said, eyeing the overgrown grounds.

"I don't think the Monroes come up here any longer." He got out of the car and stared up at the house. "I never could figure out how the sheriff's department found us," he said. "I decided they must've done a house-to-house search once they found my bike and learned that Roy and I had been in a fight." He walked to the front door and tried to open it, but the latch was securely fastened.

He took her hand and they walked toward the lake. The moon cast shadows in the trees and the overgrown shrubbery snagged their jeans as they passed. The air was warm, but still, and the sounds of the night were soft—the gentle lapping of the lake, the rumble of a distant train rattling on ancient tracks, the splash of a trout as it jumped for an unseen insect in Whitefire Lake.

"I made a lot of mistakes, Rachelle," he said as they reached the shore. Across the lake, the lights of the marina winked on the water, and cabin windows glowed a warm gold.

"What is this? An apology?"

He paused, glancing down at her. "An explanation. That's all. Take it any way you want. I didn't mean to hurt you. I just did what I thought was best at the time."

He stood at the shoreline, his jaw hard, his proud expression etched upon uncompromising features. He hadn't mellowed in the decade since she'd seen him last; if anything, he'd become more jaded and cynical than she remembered. His tender side was buried deeper than ever.

"I waited," she said softly as a tiny breeze teased her hair. She thought she saw pain in his eyes, but the shadows were probably induced by the night. "I kept telling myself that you'd come back for me."

His eyes narrowed. "I didn't make any promises—"

She touched his lips, surprised at the warmth of his skin. "I know. I knew it then, but I was young enough, naive enough to believe that we'd shared something special, something sacred."

"And now?" he asked. "What do you believe now?"

She met his gaze, her eyes unwavering. "That spending the night with you was the single biggest mistake of my life," she said, her admission tearing her in two. "I was a fool—a schoolgirl who lived in a dream world. You taught me a lot about reality, Jackson. For that, I suppose, I should thank you." She couldn't keep the bitterness from her words. "I trusted you, slept with you, lied for you."

"You didn't lie."

"And you weren't with me for all of the night."

His teeth flashed white as he bit out an oath. "You didn't trust me."

"I didn't know you."

"I did go back to the Fitzpatrick place," he admitted, his voice low. "I wanted to get my bike—either drive it or push it—but by the time I got there, the party had broken up and my cycle was gone. You know, I never saw it after that night."

Her pulse was hammering in her head; she remembered that the bike had been stolen, but she hadn't really thought Jackson had returned to the party. Why? Just for his bike? Or to settle a score with Roy? Her tongue froze and her throat worked; surely he hadn't...

"Hell, Rachelle. You don't believe me. You think I killed Roy!" He muttered another string of oaths.

"I do believe you. I…I just wonder why you never told me before."

"So that the story was simple."

"But it wasn't the truth."

"It was," he said. "I never saw Roy again."

Her heart turned to stone. He'd lied—and caused her to perjure herself. To save his hide. Her stomach rolled over, and for a second she thought she might be sick. Her voice, when she spoke, quavered. "I thought more of you than this," she whispered, her disappointment a gaping wound.

"It was a mistake. I should have told you everything."

He reached for her, but she backed away, her ankle twisting on a rock near the shore, but she didn't notice. "God, what a fool I was. I'd half convinced myself that you were some knight in shining armor, saving me from Roy. I'd even imagined that I was in love with you—"

"I never said anything about love!" he cut in, his eyes glittering ominously.

"I know. But I was naive enough to believe that sex and love went together. I know better now."

"Do you?" He eyed her speculatively and her breath stopped at the base of her throat.

"Oh, Jackson, no—" She pushed him away, but there was no stopping him.

Gathering her in his arms, he kissed her, long and hard, his lips molding expertly over her mouth, his body pressed intimately against her softer contours. Her blood began to pound at her temples and she told herself that kissing him was madness, would surely lead to the same torment she'd suffered in the past, but she couldn't stop.

"You lied," she choked out when he finally lifted his head. "I trusted you and you lied!" Tears drizzled down her cheeks, and he slowly brushed them aside.

"If I could change anything, Rachelle, I would. But I can't. God knows I've regretted a lot of things in my life, but I should never have kept my silence. I didn't know you knew I left and I…I should have explained everything to you. I thought I was protecting you."

"Oh, Jackson…" Her cold heart melted and she wanted to believe him, to trust him again, but the pain of the past was real and agonizing and she wondered if she *ever* could trust him again.

"Believe in me," he whispered, and kissed her again, this time so chastely that her heart nearly shattered into a thousand brittle pieces. Yielding, she wrapped her arms around his neck and told herself to forget about the past, ignore the future and live for the moment. She was here, alone with Jackson, in his arms on the shores of Whitefire Lake.

The night surrounded them, and the smell of pine and musk and moist earth mingled as his weight dragged her toward the sandy beach. She felt herself being pulled to the ground and tried to utter a protest, but her words came out as a moan. Cold sand pressed against her back and Jackson was lying atop her, his face close to hers, his breath soft as a midnight breeze. "I don't know what it is between us," he admitted, his breathing labored, his gaze as tortured as her own. "But it's something I can't control." His lips twisted into a line of torment. "I want you, Rachelle. More than I've ever wanted a woman, any woman."

She understood. Gazing into his eyes, she felt the same emotional magnetism that she was powerless to fight. Her body craved his. Even now her hips were pressing upward, silently begging him to stroke and caress her, to strip her of her clothes and take her as if she were his first and only lover. And yet her mind told her this was wrong—so very wrong. Just because pure animal lust existed was no reason to give into it.

He kissed her again, and his hand gently cupped her breast. Heat seared through her blood. Desire pulsed in hot, demanding waves as his mouth moved, his lips grinding against hers in imitation of his hips, which were locked to hers.

The hard swelling in his loins pressed hard against her abdomen and she ached inside for the feel of him. His tongue explored her mouth, but it wasn't enough. She wanted more, more—all of him.

She began to move and he rocked with her, his hands moving beneath her sweater to scale her ribs and grasp both breasts in anxious hunger. "Let me make love to you," he whispered against her ear, and she only moaned in response.

He shifted suddenly, straddling her abdomen with his knees. Slowly he lifted her sweater over her head, baring her torso except for her scanty bra. In the cool night, her nipples turned to hard buttons and her skin was blue-white in the light from a slice of moon.

Licking one finger lazily, he watched her as he placed that wet finger against her breast. She groaned and writhed, the ache within her growing and pulsing. Sweat collected on her skin, a reflection of the drops she saw on his forehead. Her fingers worked at the waistband of his jeans and soon he'd discarded his shirt so that she could touch the thin wall of muscles that surrounded his navel. Her fingers inched upward and she explored the swirling hairs that hid the muscles of his chest.

"This is dangerous," he whispered, unhooking her bra and letting her breasts fall free.

"Everything with you is dangerous," she whispered, hardly able to breathe. He rubbed the inside of his legs against her bare ribs and she bucked against him. She couldn't think, wouldn't reason, and as he fell down upon her, covering her hungry lips with his own, she arched upward.

His hand slipped to the small of her back, pressing her up against him, making her all the more aware of the urgency of his need. He kissed her face, her throat, her shoulders, and swept lower to brush her nipples with his lips.

Rachelle was melting inside and she needed his sweet rhythm to end her agony. She clung to him and ran her tongue across his chest. Groaning, he unsnapped her jeans, tore them from her and disposed of his own. He hesitated for only a second, his naked body poised over hers in the moonlight, his eyes searching hers for answers to questions he couldn't voice.

"It's all right," she whispered, anxious hands running down his sides. She felt the scar on his shoulder, a reminder of Roy's wicked knife. "You don't have to love me," she said, though she felt that they were bound by the threads of fate that wove their lives together. "Just make love to me."

"Oh, Rachelle, this isn't right." But he couldn't stop, and he plunged into her with a fevered thrust that caused her breath to stop in her throat. She closed her eyes as he began to move in a rhythm that melded with the night. Fighting tears, caught in an emotional maelstrom that tossed her backward in time, Rachelle clung to him. There was a desperation to his lovemaking, as if he never expected to hold her in his arms again and she, too, was desperate, feeling his body move within her, slowly at first and more quickly as his resistance gave way.

"Rachelle, Rachelle," he whispered hoarsely. "I can't stop.... Oh, oh, please, baby..." She barely heard his words over the sounds of her own breathing and the pounding of her heart. Her body bucked and arched and she cried out. The world spun faster and Jackson stiffened, shuddered and let out a primal cry that echoed off the lake. With a final tremor, he fell against her and she wrapped her arms around him, burying her face in his throat.

*I love you,* she thought and tears collected at the devastating reality of it. *Damn it, I love you.* Her tears slid from the corners of her eyes and a cloud of afterglow caught her in its misty folds. If she could just stay here forever with this one special man.

She heard him sigh, not happily, but as if a great weight had settled upon his shoulders. Lying beside her, his hands smoothing the hair from her face, he whispered, "What am I going to do with you?"

Swallowing back a sob, she said, "You're not going to do anything with me, Counselor. It's what I'm going to do with you that's the problem."

He laughed at that and she smiled through her tears. Their lovemaking had to happen. They'd been on a collision course since returning to Gold Creek and the questions of their sexual involvement when they were barely more than children had begged to be answered. Unfortunately, she had responded to him as she had twelve years before. The physical chemistry was just as raw and electric as it had been. The bad boy of Gold Creek was as good a lover as she remembered. Maybe better.

*And you love him!*

Oh, Lord, what a mess. He was the one man in the world she couldn't afford to love, the one man who could shred her heart into a million tiny pieces. She had to get away from him, to clear her head, before she did something even more foolish than she just had by making love to him.

In the dark she reached for her clothes, but a male hand clamped over hers. His expression was dark. "Things haven't changed," he said, studying her in the weak light from the moon. "I still haven't made any promises."

"Neither have I," she shot back, determined to hide her feelings. "I've grown up a lot, Jackson," she lied, still groping for her jeans. If only she could find her clothes and get dressed, she wouldn't feel so damned vulnerable. Her fingers came in contact with her belt and she snagged it. "Look, I don't expect a proposal just because we made love. I don't even expect you to try and see me again."

His jaw worked. "This is easy for you?"

"No." She wasn't going to lie. She found her jeans. Good. Her underwear was certainly nearby.... "I've lowered my expectations over the years."

A trace of anger registered in his eyes. "So you can love 'em and leave 'em?"

"Yes," she said, ignoring the furious line of his mouth as she struggled into her jeans. If only he knew. Tonight had been the first time she'd made love since she'd slept with him, twelve years ago. She'd come close a couple of times and disappointed more than one man, but she'd never been able to give herself to another...not even to David, which, she'd decided, was why he was so anxious to marry her. Over the years, she'd told herself that she was flawed, or at the very least scarred from Jackson's tender lovemaking and then quick exit from her life. She'd learned not to trust men who spoke words of love in the throes of passion.

Although Jackson alone couldn't be blamed. Her

mother's track record with men hadn't been good, and Heather, too, had failed at marriage. Tremont women just weren't good at picking partners. Her feelings for Jackson were a case in point.

He studied her for a minute as she worked at the buttons of her sweater. His eyes followed the movement of her fingers and she blushed. He was still naked, still somewhat aroused, and his dark skin and sinewy muscles reminded her that his body could do to hers what no other man had ever dared try.

"You don't fool me, you know. All this tough act—the hard-nosed reporter bit—I don't buy it."

"No one's asking you to." She straightened her sweater and stood. What had she expected? Champagne and roses? Moonlight and promises of love? With Jackson Moore? She had to be kidding!

He, still silently seething, jerked on his jeans and quickly buttoned his shirt.

When she started for the motorcycle, he grabbed hold of her hand. "We're not through yet."

Her throat closed. How much more of this emotional roller-coaster ride could she take? "Oh, I think we are."

"We have one more place to visit."

She knew what he was considering and the idea turned her cold inside. Was he crazy? The man certainly had a death wish. "I don't think it's a good idea to go snooping on Fitzpatrick property."

"You've come this far."

"My mistake."

He cocked a thick black eyebrow. "I don't think so. Come on, reporter. Let's go face our past." He tugged gently on her hand and reluctantly she fell into step with him. The lake was dark and quiet and the night felt suddenly cool. Going back to the place where Roy had been killed chilled her to her very bones. They walked in silence along the shore and she wondered what Jackson was thinking. They'd just made love and he acted as if their lovemaking had never happened.

Just like before.

Maybe this was how he dealt with all his lovers.

Her heart wrenched as they crossed unseen property lines along the lake, keeping near the water's edge, passing huge, empty estates until they came at last to the Fitzpatrick property, the most prestigious on the entire north shore.

They walked along the creaking dock, their footsteps loud in the quiet night. Rachelle could hardly breathe. She felt that they were being watched, that at any second someone, the police or the Fitzpatricks, would leap from behind the trees and point the muzzle of a rifle at their chests.

*Please, God,* she silently prayed, *let us get out of this.*

The boathouse was locked, the dock gray and bleached in the moonlight. The path to the gazebo wasn't lit as it had been on the last fateful night that they had been here, and the scrape of flagstones beneath her feet caused a chill to race down her spine. Her heart knocked in her chest. She felt as if there were eyes in the huge sequoias and pines that guarded the house.

No laughter or music or smoke tonight. Rachelle rubbed her arms. "This place gives me the creeps."

"Where're all your reporter's instincts? Your natural curiosity?"

"I'm not curious about this place."

"Well, I am," Jackson said, surveying the shrine of the Fitzpatrick empire. "Someone who was at the party that night killed Roy and was happy to pin it on me." He frowned as he studied the lines of the manor.

"But who?"

Jackson shook his head. "I wish I knew. It could've been anyone, even someone who hadn't been invited to the party—like me." Together they walked toward the dark house, which seemed to melt into the black trees surrounding it. "Roy had stepped on lots of toes. He just barreled through life not giving a damn about anybody else."

She glanced at him from the corner of her eye. "Why did you hate him so much?"

Jackson thought for a moment, his hands stuffed into his jeans. "It was mutual. For some reason Roy detested the sight of me. I didn't know it, until I was about thirteen, I guess. Then, all of a sudden, I was the object of his ridicule. I was older, but he was bigger—had more friends. He made a point of always putting me down."

"So you hated him."

"Wouldn't you?" He smiled at a private irony. "And I was probably jealous. The kid had everything. A rich, good-looking father who gave him anything he wanted, a big house, a respectable mother, nice clothes—the whole nine yards."

"So why would he give you a bad time?" Rachelle eyed the house warily.

Jackson shrugged. "That's just the way he was. He always put someone down to make himself look better."

"Prince of a guy," Rachelle said.

Jackson rubbed the back of his neck. "A few years later, I worked for Fitzpatrick Logging. But my career was cut short."

"Why?"

"I don't know. I was working in the woods—setting chokers. You know what they are—the cables that're hooked around the cut timber. Once they're set and in place, the logs are winched up the hill to the road where the trucks are waiting to be loaded."

"I've heard of chokers," she said dryly. "You're forgetting that I grew up with them. So what happened when you worked for the logging company?"

"The old man fired me."

"Why?"

"Well, I was never quite sure," Jackson admitted, his gaze narrowing thoughtfully. "The long and the short of it was that I was working, setting chokers one day, and there was an accident. The bull line snapped and, because of the tension, flew at me. I dived out of the way, skidded down the hill and hit my head—woke up in an ambulance. I was examined in the emergency room, stitched up and held overnight for observation. I had a private room, and I was groggy, but once, in the middle of the night, I woke up and the door of the room was cracked a little. I could see out into the hallway."

He chewed on his lower lip. "I couldn't believe it. I heard my mom talking, so I know she was there, but the only person I could see was Thomas Fitzpatrick. I don't know what he was telling Mom—his voice was too low—and later, when I asked my mom about it, she told me that I'd been delirious, that I'd imagined the whole thing, that Fitzpatrick had never been in the hospital."

A chill crawled down Rachelle's spine. "That wasn't all of it," Jackson said quietly. "Someone else was with Fitzpatrick that night, I think, but I can't remember who. I didn't hear another voice, but I *sensed* that someone else was there. It's strange—just an impression. Anyway, I got out of the hospital and found out I didn't have a job any longer."

"Why?"

Jackson shrugged. "Who knows? I was just a kid—I

didn't question it and my mother didn't bother explaining, just told me that I'd have to look somewhere else for work. I always blamed Roy, but I'm not sure he had anything to do with it."

"Why would your mother lie and say you were delirious if you weren't?"

"I don't know. But she lied. I spoke with one of the orderlies. He'd seen Thomas Fitzpatrick there that night."

Rachelle hugged herself and walked a few steps closer to the imposing house, a symbol of the lifestyle of the Fitzpatricks.

"The night Roy died, you were furious with him," she said.

"We'd already had a fight a few days before," Jackson said. "He'd started spreading rumors about my mother and I couldn't handle it. I confronted Roy and he hit me, cut me under the eye." Jackson stared to the far shore where the lights of cabins glimmered seductively. Moonlight cast shadows over the smooth water, and high overhead a night bird swooped over the hills.

"There's always been bad blood between our families," Jackson admitted. "While I was in the navy, Roy started seeing my cousin, Amanda. She lived over in Coleville and thought she was in love with Roy. Anyway, she ended up pregnant and Roy wouldn't marry her— claimed the baby wasn't his. It was a time before they could do DNA testing and it wouldn't have mattered anyway. Amanda's father was swayed by the all-mighty buck and Thomas bought him out. Amanda put the baby up for adoption and some couple now has an eleven- or twelve-year-old kid. Amanda regrets giving the baby up, but she got a college education out of the deal—bought and paid for by Granddaddy Tom."

Rachelle felt sick. "So that's why you hated Roy."

"One reason. But there were lots of other people who hated him. Lots of people were jealous of his money, hated the way he threw his name around town...how his old man bought him favors. Even Erik Patton had a bone to pick with Roy. Roy had promised to marry Melanie, but he got sidetracked."

"By Laura," Rachelle said.

"And then you." Jackson turned and faced her. "It was you he wanted, you know."

"I don't think so."

"Oh, yeah. Laura was just a means to an end. She was pretty and willing and Roy was happy enough to show her a good time until he could get to you. But you posed a challenge and Roy liked nothing better than a challenge."

"But I never knew he was interested in me," she protested. "Until that night I didn't have a clue."

Jackson's eyes turned hard. "Roy wasn't known for longevity. He was just used to having anything or anyone he wanted. If he made a mistake, Daddy took care of it. He figured it was only a matter of time before you'd be interested in his wealth or his car or him. But he got too drunk to be subtle. You showed up in the gazebo and he reacted."

"How do you know all this?"

"I've had a long time to piece it all together."

"And are the pieces beginning to fit? What happens when you find out the truth?"

He grinned, his teeth flashing white in the darkness. "Then I've made my point to this town."

"And that's it?"

"One chapter in my life closed."

They walked down a short path and suddenly the gazebo was in front of them. Paint peeled from the weathered slats, a step sagged in the middle and the roof had lost a few shingles, but it stood, neglected in the same grove of pines that Rachelle remembered. Rachelle's heart thudded painfully and her insides turned as cold as a long, dark well. She remembered Roy struggling against her, pressing his anxious body over hers, his breath sour with beer as he'd tried to tear off her clothes.

"Oh, God," she whispered as the memory of Jackson and the fight slid through her mind.

The taste of bile rose in her throat. She could have been raped and beaten if not for Jackson. He'd risked his life for her, rescued her and been falsely accused of murder. It had happened long ago, but tonight, faced with the decaying ruins of the gazebo, Rachelle felt all the fear and pain of the past.

Shivering, she looked away and stared at the water of Whitefire Lake. She felt Jackson's arms surround her, felt the warmth of his body seep into hers as he drew her against him. His chest was pressed firmly to her backside and he buried his face into her hair. "I've never been in love," he said, his voice as low as the wind in the pines. "I wouldn't know what it felt like."

"Maybe you're not missing anything," she said, fighting a losing battle with tears.

"I don't have room in my life for a wife or a family."

"Did I ask you?" She whirled on him. "Is that what you're thinking? That I want you to propose to me? That I want to start making babies with you?" she demanded, frustrated tears hot as they ran down her cheeks. "You arrogant, self-important bastard!"

She tried to break away from his embrace, but he wouldn't release her. The harder she pushed, the stronger his arms tightened around her.

"Let go of me!" she ordered, the thin web of her patience unraveling.

"Not until you hear me out!"

"I've heard enough for one night!" She shoved hard and was rewarded with his mouth crashing down on hers in an angry kiss that plundered and took. But instead of reacting as her silly heart told her to, she kicked him in the shins.

Sucking in a swift breath, he finally let her go.

"I don't know the kind of women you're used to, Moore," she said in absolute fury, "but I'm not one of them. And I can't be 'tamed' or 'controlled' by a kiss. Either treat me as a woman, an equal, or leave me the hell alone!"

He smiled slowly. "Oh, God, if you only knew," he said, pinching the bridge of his nose in frustration. "I wasn't trying to control you. I was trying to control myself. And that's what I was trying to tell you. I can't seem to control myself around you. You turn me inside out. I've never, *never* wanted a woman the way I wanted you—the way I still want you. But I'm not the right guy for you. You should try and work things out with that guy in San Francisco. He can give you what you want."

"Which is?"

"A house. A family. A man to take care of you."

She advanced upon him, poking him in his chest, hiding the fact that she cared about him. "I don't want or need a man to take care of me, Jackson. And what I do want or need you couldn't begin to understand. So just leave it alone. Don't think you have to court me, for crying out loud."

"I wouldn't."

"Good!"

"But I can't stay away from you."

"You did a damned good job for twelve years!" she threw back at him, and in the moonlight he blanched. "Just keep doing what you've been doing for the past decade and don't concern yourself with me. I'm fine."

"We made love."

She swallowed hard, and all her tough facade shattered around her. "My mistake."

"Mine."

"It won't happen again. Don't worry about it. It was natural," she said, with false bravado, though her voice shook a bit. "We just wanted to see if the same chemistry was there."

"And now we're going to turn it off?" He touched her again, his fingers grazing her cheek, and with all the courage she could muster, she shrank away.

"Yes, Jackson," she said over the lump in her throat. "It's over. I think we should leave."

He glanced around the Fitzpatrick estate once more, as if he could still see everyone who had been at Roy's party that night. "Come on." He reached for her hand, but she drew away from him. On the way back to the motorcycle, they walked along the edge of the lake, not touching, keeping at least one step apart from each other.

## CHAPTER ELEVEN

DURING THE DRIVE BACK TO town, Jackson didn't say anything and Rachelle didn't bother with small talk. They were well past the small-talk phase, past reacquainting themselves. They were lovers again. And they weren't in love; no more than they had been in the past. They knew each other's bodies, but didn't understand each other's minds. What a shame. Once again she hadn't been able to resist the lust that he inspired. Blushing, she was grateful for the darkness.

They passed the sawmill and Fitzpatrick Logging and finally, after what had seemed hours, the outskirts of Gold Creek came into view. Streetlamps and stoplights, flickering neon signs and other headlights destroyed the darkness and the sense of intimacy, the feeling that they were all alone.

When she couldn't stand the tension a moment longer, she asked about his mother.

"She left Gold Creek about the same time I did." He paused at a stoplight, the red beam steady through the gathering fog.

Rachelle was surprised. She'd assumed that Sandra Moore, like her own mother, had been rooted so deeply in Gold Creek that she would never leave. "Where did she move to?"

He glanced over his shoulder, throwing her a hard glare. "This going to be in the paper?"

That hurt. Stung, she said, "Of course. Right after the paragraph where I explain that you and I trespassed and made love on the shores of Whitefire Lake."

Flashing her a mirthless smile, he revved the cycle's engine. "Just checking."

"What do you think I am?" she asked, appalled that he would think she would use their relationship to get information from him. And yet, wasn't that exactly what she'd done when she'd promised her editor an interview with Pine Bluff's most notorious alumnus?

"I'm trying to figure it out. Ever since we met again, you've been hard at work convincing me that you're a reporter—hell-bent to get a story. So I'm just making sure. No surprises."

"The light's green," she said as a horn blasted behind them. "And I didn't come back to get a story on you. If I wanted to write about you, Jackson, I would've called you in New York."

"So your paper isn't interested in me?"

Her jaw began to ache. "I didn't say that," she replied, remembering Marcy's exact words as she'd brought up her idea in her office. It had been raining, but Rachelle's editor always kept the windows open, and the cold air had filtered into the office, ruffling papers and bringing the scent of rain-washed streets into the small office.

"Sure, you can go up to Gold Creek," Marcy had told Rachelle. "Show how the town's changed and grown, but concentrate on the people, and if there's anything that will jazz up your columns, go for it. No boring trips down memory lane—be sure to add a lot of local color. We can use some homey pieces about the oldest lady in town and her ten or twelve cats and her embroidery piece that won at the state fair, but you need to dig deeper, check the town for any hint of scandal."

Rachelle, though she felt as if she'd suddenly grown stones in her stomach, had gambled. "Jackson Moore grew up in Gold Creek."

"*The* Jackson Moore?" Marcy had asked dubiously. A petite blond woman with short, spiky hair and over-sized glasses, her eyebrows had elevated over the thin copper rims. "As in lawyer to the rich-and-famous? The guy who has all the celebrity clients and somehow gets them off?"

Big mistake, she thought, but there was no getting out of it now. "One and the same." Rachelle had already begun regretting saying anything.

Marcy had grinned widely. "Well, what'd'ya know! I heard that he had trouble with the law before he turned into a lawyer and I knew he came from some little town around here, but I never guessed it was your old stomping grounds."

Rachelle had nodded.

"Did you know him?"

"A little," Rachelle had acknowledged. Sooner or later Marcy would find out. As would the world.

"Well, good. We know he's in New York, but you might be able to talk to some of his relatives and friends, people who knew him well. Then you can try a telephone interview. The guy is always in the papers. He won't care. Maybe he'd like to give a former acquaintance a shot in the arm."

Rachelle had doubted it, but the promise that she'd do a story on Jackson had cinched the deal and Marcy had sent her packing to Gold Creek....

"Looks like you've got company," Jackson observed, startling Rachelle as he wheeled the motorcycle into the drive.

Rachelle's heart plunged. David's silver Jaguar was

purring in the drive. At the approach of the motorcycle, David killed the engine, opened a sleek door and climbed outside. He was tall and trim, over six feet, with blond hair that was beginning to thin. "Rachelle?" he asked, obviously perplexed to see her straddling a Harley behind a man he'd never met before.

Jackson cut the bike's engine and Rachelle swung her feet onto the ground. "David! I didn't expect you," she greeted, knowing in her heart that she could never love him as he deserved, never love him as she already loved Jackson.

He slid a glance in Jackson's direction, but didn't comment.

Rachelle finger-combed her hair and motioned toward Jackson while making hasty introductions. The two men shook hands, though stiffly, and Rachelle could've screamed at the glint of amusement in Jackson's eyes. Whereas David appeared uncomfortable, Jackson, the bad boy turned New York City attorney, enjoyed the confrontation.

They walked inside and Rachelle nervously made coffee. She shot Jackson a few swift glances, hoping that he would pick up on the hint and leave, but he didn't. Instead he threw one jean-clad leg over a barstool and watched her as she poured water into the coffeemaker.

"Jackson Moore," David finally repeated as Rachelle handed him a steaming cup. His puzzled expression cleared a bit. "The attorney for Nora Craig?"

"I was," Jackson acknowledged.

Rachelle wished they would both disappear. They each represented the best and the worst in her life and each, in his own way, threatened her hard-earned independence. She didn't need this. Not now. Not after giving herself to Jackson again. What she needed was time alone—time to think and sort things out.

"Cream, honey?" David reminded her and, biting her tongue, she padded back to the kitchen and dutifully pulled a carton of skim milk from the fridge. She carried it back to David. "Nothing stronger?" he teased.

"That's it."

With a sigh, David checked the expiration date and, eyebrows puckering, poured a thin stream of milk into his coffee.

Jackson's lips tugged upward at the corners.

"You want cream, too?" Rachelle asked sarcastically.

"Black's fine," he said, and Rachelle watched as he swallowed back the urge to call her "honey" and mimic David, who slowly stirred his coffee and stared at Jackson.

"I didn't know you two knew each other," David said quietly, his eyes darting to Rachelle and asking her a thousand unspoken questions. She wanted to drop right through the floorboards, but she couldn't. Somehow she had to get through this ordeal.

"Didn't Rachelle tell you?" Jackson said. "We go back a long way. Just haven't kept in touch much over the years."

David looked at Rachelle, as if for an explanation, his eyes searching hers. She felt dirty and cheap. Only hours before she'd made love with Jackson and here was David, hoping that she would come back to San Francisco and marry him. Now, because of Jackson, she knew she'd never be able to walk down the aisle and become Mrs. David Gaskill. She wouldn't be content to raise his half-grown children on weekends, and she wouldn't ever embrace the same lifestyle, predicated on making money and doing things the "right" way. Nor would she be able to be his showpiece—his pretty, younger woman whom he displayed much as one would a prized Thoroughbred.

Since Jackson wouldn't take the hint, she decided she'd have to be blunt. "I'd like to speak to David alone," she said, and from the corner of her eyes she saw David's face light up. Cringing inside, she sighed. She hadn't meant to give him any encouragement, but he'd read more into her asking Jackson to leave than there was.

Jackson managed a cool smile as he swung off the stool. "Wouldn't want to be accused of not being able to take a hint," he said, and Rachelle walked him to the door.

He pulled her out onto the porch with him. "I thought you'd like to know that I'm leaving town for a couple of days," he said, reaching into the inner pocket of his jacket.

"Had enough fun here in Gold Creek?" she quipped, though disappointment coiled over her heart. The thought of being in Gold Creek without Jackson seemed suddenly pointless.

"I'll be back," he promised, and pressed his business card into her palm. "But if you need me—"

"You'll be a continent away."

His forehead wrinkled at that. "Call me."

"I don't think I'll need to. I can take care of myself."

He touched the corner of her mouth. "I care," he said softly, and the noises of the night seemed to fade into the distance. The traffic was suddenly muted and the wind chimes seemed to be instantly wrapped in cotton.

Her throat tightened and she bit her lip. "You don't have to say anything—" she protested, but he silenced her with another kiss. His trademark, it appeared.

"I care," he repeated.

Tears touched the back of her eyes at his tenderness.

He folded her into the warm embrace of his arms and sighed into her hair. "This is probably unfair of me— God knows I've always been accused of breaking the rules, but…" He squeezed her and his words were lost, as if he'd suddenly changed his mind.

"But what?"

"Oh, hell," he muttered, angry at himself. "Listen, I can't tell you how to run your life, Rachelle, but whatever you do, don't settle."

"Pardon me?" Again the little squeeze.

"Don't settle for less than you deserve." His gaze touched hers for an instant, and the back of her throat turned to sand. "I'm not the right man for you, and my guess is, that guy—" he hooked his thumb toward the open door "—isn't, either."

"You have no right to—"

"I know." He kissed her again, more passionately this time, and then let go of her quickly. Without looking over his shoulder, he stepped from the porch, swung onto his bike and roared away.

"A motorcycle?" David asked, as she walked back into the house, her lips still tingling from Jackson's kiss.

David was seated on the couch, sipping coffee, his eyebrows inched high over his thin-rimmed glasses. "Is the guy going through midlife crisis or what?"

"I don't know…. David…"

He looked up at her then, really stared at her, and his lips tightened a bit. "You don't have to say it," he muttered, setting his cup on the table and running an impatient hand through his hair. "You're involved with him."

It wasn't a question.

"You don't have to answer. It's written all over your face. Oh, God, Rachelle, what happened?" He was standing by this time, his fists opening and closing in frustration.

Rachelle leaned her back against the door. "I don't think *involved* is the right word."

"No?" He let his gaze rove slowly up her body and she realized how she must look. Her clothes were wrinkled and soiled, her hair a tangled mess, her makeup probably streaked from tears. "Well, just what is it then? Because from where I'm sitting, you and he are more than friends."

"I don't think Jackson and I were ever friends."

David rolled his eyes. "You know, Rachelle," he said, rubbing his fingers and thumbs impatiently, "I expected more from you than this, that you weren't like all those women who ran after the macho type, that you were too levelheaded to be interested in tough guys with bulging biceps."

"I haven't done anything to be ashamed of," she said, lifting her chin a fraction.

His gaze was positively damning. "I guess I'm the fool. I drove all the way up here thinking that you'd be missing me by now, that you would have had enough of this stupid town to want to come running back home. But, no—instead I find you riding a motorcycle with Mr. Bad News himself. God, what was wrong with me? Was I blind?"

Rachelle's heart twisted a little. She didn't want to hurt David. "It's hard to explain about Jackson," she finally said as she walked into the kitchen and poured the rest of the coffee down the sink. "He's someone I knew a long time ago."

"Ahh." He nodded sagely, as if the slow-coming confession he'd anticipated was about to be revealed.

"Ah?"

"I knew there was someone back here, Rachelle. Someone important. Someone who had done you serious emotional damage." Frowning, he picked up his coffee cup and carried it to the kitchen sink. "I was hoping that the man would be a heavyset middle-aged logger with a wife and a couple of kids. I guess I was wrong."

"You don't understand—"

"Probably not everything," he agreed, reaching for the jacket he'd hung on the coatrack near the door. "But I know that Jackson Moore, *the* Jackson Moore, was someone you cared about very much. Someone you obviously still care about."

She wanted to argue, to tell him he was wrong, but she couldn't. David had been good to her and the least she could do was to be straight with him. "I don't have a future with Jackson."

David shoved an arm into the sleeve of his jacket. "But you do have a past, Rachelle. And right now you have a present. As for the future…who knows? Maybe you and I are the future." He looked at her long and hard. "I'd like to think so."

"I—I can't make any commitments—"

"Yet."

She swallowed against a thick lump in her throat. She cared for David, if only as a friend. "About the future, I don't think I have one with you, either."

He studied the zipper tab of his jacket. "Are you telling me that you don't want to see me again?"

It sounded so final. Like a death knell. "I'm just saying that you and I want different things in life, David. I want kids—at least two."

"I've got the girls—"

"I mean I want my own children. They could be adopted—that wouldn't matter—but I want to start with them as babies and raise them as my own."

His mouth pursed into a hard knot. "If my children aren't good enough—"

"They're good enough, David. Don't start this argument again. You know I love your girls. But they're nearly grown. I feel cheated out of a lot of years. I wasn't there when they took their first steps, when they learned to ride a bicycle, when the neighbor boy taunted them and they ran home with tears in their eyes. I didn't get to teach them silly songs when they were three, or have them stand on chairs and help me bake cookies, or help pick out their dresses for their first dances. I wasn't there when one of their friends said something cruel, I didn't nurse them through their ear infections or buy them milk shakes when they had their braces tightened.

"It isn't enough, don't you see?" she asked. "I'd always be a stepmother to them, nothing closer and I want—no, I *need*—to have a child of my own, to raise my way."

"And Moore will give you that?" he said with a sneer, a bitterness she'd never seen before suddenly appearing. "Anyone can sire a child, Rachelle, but it takes more than a quickie in the woods to be a father."

A small cry escaped her lips. "You don't understand."

"No, but I'm beginning to," he replied. He was angry now, his face turning red as he grabbed hold of the doorknob. "You've kept me at arm's length for an eternity, Rachelle. I thought you were frigid, that you'd probably have to see a shrink to come to grips with your own sexuality, but it turns out I was wrong. Because you're still hung up on the guy that gave you all the problems to begin with."

"That's not how it was!"

"Oh, no? Well, you're probably right. But then, I

wouldn't know how it was, would I? You never let me in
on any of your little secrets, did you? You wouldn't let me
into your life, Rachelle, not really. Do you realize that I
don't know a damn thing about your past except that you
have a sister and that your parents were divorced when
you were in high school? Other than that, I have no idea
how you grew up." In frustration, he wrenched open the
door. "Oh, hell, I'm tired of all this! If you want me, you
know my number." He strode off the porch and climbed
into his car, leaving the door open wide and letting in
the cool night air.

Rachelle wanted to crumple onto a corner of the couch
and cry. In the span of fifteen minutes, she'd watched
the two single most important men in her life walk out.
Though she felt a whisper of freedom in David's departure, she was still reeling from the night and everything
that had happened.

She'd made love to Jackson, and the passion that had
rocked her body had shocked her to her bones. She'd
thought that her memories of her one-night stand had
been colored by time, that the passion she'd never felt
with another man had been exaggerated in her mind.
But she'd been wrong. Tonight his kiss and his touch
had aroused that same dark, slumbering desire that had
infiltrated her body and soul twelve years before.

Java, who had been hiding outside, strolled in and
rubbed against Rachelle. Absently she reached down and
petted the cat. "What am I going to do?" she wondered
as Java wandered off in the direction of her water bowl.

Goose bumps rose on Rachelle's flesh and she walked
over to the door and shut it, latching the bolt and telling
herself that everything was for the best. Now, at least, she
knew that she wasn't "frigid," that she could experience
desire as white-hot as a lava flow, that she could make

love to a man and wish the lovemaking would never stop. And David was gone. The parting hadn't been overly painful and now she had to answer to no one but herself. That little bit of freedom was worth a few hurtful words.

David had been right. She'd never let him get really close to her. She hadn't told him about Jackson or the night that had bound their lives together forever. Several times she'd tried to explain to David about Roy Fitzpatrick, about the fact that he had attacked her, but she'd kept quiet, hiding that secret in a locked chamber in her mind. She hadn't been fair to David, she supposed, but right from the start she'd known that his expectations had been different than hers.

Once, he'd asked her to change her outfit when they were going out with an important client of his. Another time, he'd introduced her as "my little princess." Rachelle had suffered those two indignities and sworn she'd never suffer another. She hadn't and their relationship had become strained. No wonder David had encouraged her to return to Gold Creek. He hadn't expected her to run into Jackson Moore.

Nor had she. And now Jackson was gone. She looked at the business card she still clutched in her hand. He was on his way back to New York. As soon as they'd made love, he'd found a way to leave—just like before. Well, this time, she didn't need him; she wouldn't sit around waiting for him to call or come back. Despite the ache in her heart, she told herself that his leaving was for the best and she didn't care if she ever saw him again. That was a lie, of course, but one she was going to stick to. Waiting around for Jackson had cost her dearly in the past and she wasn't going to make the same mistake twice. With a rush of independence, she tore his card into half, then quarters and eighths and dropped the fluttering white pieces into the nearest trash basket, trying not to think that those jagged snips of paper looked much like her heart.

THOMAS FITZPATRICK WOULDN'T see her. He wouldn't return her calls, nor agree to meet with her. Whatever had happened between Jackson and him had insured Rachelle of not getting an interview. She called Fitzpatrick, Incorporated and was given the runaround by Thomas's secretary. Even Marge Elkins at the logging company found excuses for not scheduling an appointment with him. Rachelle left messages at his home and never heard from him.

The man was avoiding her. There were just no two ways about it. But Rachelle wasn't about to give up. Thomas Fitzpatrick was the single largest employer in Gold Creek, and as such, he was an integral part of her series.

She decided to take matters into her own hands. She drove to the offices of Fitzpatrick, Incorporated and waited until she noticed his white Mercedes roll into his private parking spot. Within seconds, he was out of his car and inside the building, a yellow-brick, three-storied structure that had once housed the Gold Creek Hotel.

Rachelle climbed out of her Escort and walked into the lobby. Though recently renovated, the office complex retained its turn-of-the-century charm. Thick Persian rugs were tossed over gleaming oak floors and philodendron and ivy grew out of polished brass spittoons. A stained-glass skylight, positioned three stories above, allowed sunlight to pool in variegated hues on the walls and floor.

Thomas Fitzpatrick's office was on the third floor. Bracing herself for yet another rejection, Rachelle took the elevator. Within seconds she was pleading her case with a receptionist who couldn't have been more than twenty-two.

"I'm sorry, Mr. Fitzpatrick is tied up all afternoon," the girl said with an understanding smile.

"Then I'd like an appointment with him."

"Certainly," the receptionist said, though she was nervous and Rachelle had no doubt that the president of Fitzpatrick, Incorporated had left specific instructions that he wasn't to see one Rachelle Tremont. She started thumbing through the pages of a calendarlike appointment book, while avoiding looking directly at Rachelle. "There doesn't seem to be any time—"

Rachelle pointed to a blank page. "What about here?" she asked, tapping her finger on the empty squares representing the hours of Thomas Fitzpatrick's life.

"No—he's busy with a client, I think. They play tennis on Tuesdays."

"Wednesday, then." She flipped the page for the flabbergasted receptionist.

"No, Wednesday won't do."

"Why not?"

"Wednesday is golf with Dr. Pritchart—"

"Thursday."

"I'm afraid not—"

Rachelle slammed the book closed and leaned over the younger woman's desk. In her years working for the paper, she'd had to get tough with more than her share of reticent interviewees and had been forced to deal with some secretaries who would defend the door to their boss's office with their very lives. "Look—" she glanced at the brass name plate positioned on the corner of the desk "—Rita, we both know he's ducking me. The problem is, he can't duck me forever, and I'll find a way to talk to him. You could save us both a lot of time and effort."

Rita licked her lips and the phone rang. Relief painted her face with a smile. "If you'll excuse me—" She reached for the receiver and turned her attention to the caller. "Fitzpatrick, Incorporated."

Rachelle didn't wait. Opportunity wasn't about to strike twice. She walked swiftly past the reception desk and through inlaid double doors only to find herself up against another obstacle. She hadn't entered Fitzpatrick's private office at all; instead she was in the foyer of a suite of rooms and his secretary was positioned in front of another set of doors.

The woman, about Rachelle's age, was busy taking dictation. Her back was to the reception area and she was wearing a headset while her fingers flew over the keys. She glanced up as Rachelle entered and her expression turned from vague interest to disbelief. "I thought I told you he was busy," she said, stripping off her headgear and tossing thick black hair over her shoulders.

Rachelle's stomach sank. Thomas Fitzpatrick's private secretary was Melanie Patton, the girl Roy had promised to marry and then dumped when he took up with Laura.

Melanie was on her feet. "You can't be here. Mr. Fitzpatrick is a very busy—"

Rachelle wasn't about to be waylaid. She'd come this far and without another thought to Melanie, she rounded the desk and shoved open the door. "Mr. Fitzpatrick, I'd like to talk to you," she said as she spied the object of her quest. He was taller than she remembered, and trim. His shoulders were broad beneath an expensive navy blue suit, his white shirt crisp. He turned clear blue eyes in her direction and she nearly froze under the sheer power of his stare. "I'm sorry to barge in on you, but believe me, I've tried conventional methods and they just didn't work."

Thomas didn't seem the least surprised to see her. He was seated at a large teak desk, one hand poised over the telephone. He was a handsome, imposing man and though there was an edge of wariness in his expression, he didn't explode into a rage as she'd thought he might.

"Sit down, Miss Tremont," he said in the well-modulated tones of a would-be senator. "Since you're so hell-bent to interview me, I guess I'd better talk to—"

"I've called Security." Melanie marched into the room in a cloud of indignation. Rita was right on her heels— like a puppy.

"Oh, Mr. Fitzpatrick, I'm so sorry," Rita wailed, wringing her hands. Her skin had turned rosy with embarrassment, and she glanced at Melanie nervously, as if expecting the dressing-down of her life.

"You can throw me out," Rachelle said, her gaze meeting the arrogance of Fitzpatrick's, "but I'll be back. Either here or at your home. I'm doing a series of articles—"

He waved off her explanation. "I know what you're doing, Miss Tremont."

"Then you realize that I have to talk to you. Fitzpatrick, Incorporated is the single largest employer in Gold Creek. For years, at least during the timber boom, Gold Creek was practically a 'company town,' and you, your father and grandfather were the company, as were the Monroes with their sawmill. For as long as anyone can remember, the Fitzpatrick and Monroe families have been an important part of Gold Creek's industry."

Melanie opened her mouth, but shut it as Thomas motioned Rachelle into one of the chairs near his desk.

"Close the door as you leave," he told Melanie, "and tell the guard I won't be needing him."

Melanie hesitated a second. "You're sure—"

"Absolutely."

Rita was already scurrying out of the office, and Melanie, spine stiff with disapproval, walked quickly behind her. The doors whispered shut and the latch clicked softly in place.

Thomas leaned back in his chair and, resting his hands over the hard wall that was his belly, he stared at Rachelle. "All right, Ms. Tremont. You've got my full attention." He glanced to the door again. "I've got to tell you, you've got nerves of steel. I know grown men who wouldn't mess with my secretary."

"Or with you?"

He lifted a shoulder.

"Maybe they aren't as dedicated as I am." She reached into her purse for her pocket recorder and notepad. At the sight of the equipment, Thomas's features grew grim.

"Before we get started, we should get a few things straight."

"The rules?" she asked, unable to hide the sarcasm in her voice.

"The facts. I have a long memory and I remember very clearly that you were in Jackson Moore's camp when my son was killed. Your statement saved his neck."

"Jackson didn't kill Roy."

His eyes flickered a second, but he didn't appear angry. In fact, Thomas Fitzpatrick's reactions weren't what she'd expected at all. "Jackson and Roy were at each other's throats ever since Jackson blew back into town. It only makes sense—"

"He wasn't convicted, Mr. Fitzpatrick. You and all your fancy lawyers and the sheriff and the chief of police tried your best to convict an innocent man, but in this country a person is innocent until proven guilty."

"Is that right?" He studied his nails for a second, then turned his gaze back on her. "You accused my son of assault." The words were a blast of cold air.

"I, what—"

"Roy was dead, *dead,* damn it, and you had the gall to accuse him of attempted rape."

That old fear, cold as a knife, caused her bones to shiver a little. "I just told the truth, Mr. Fitzpatrick."

"No, Ms. Tremont, what you did was dirty my son's name. He was already gone, and you and Jackson Moore tried like hell to ruin his reputation, to put a black mark on my family. Do you have any idea what that did to my wife? To me? Or don't you care?"

"I only told the truth, and my story, of your son's attack, was corroborated by more people than Jackson. Several of the other kids came forward and recounted the fight and what they'd seen. That's why the police suspected Jackson."

"Bah—" He waved off her arguments and glanced pointedly at his watch. "What is it you want to know? I don't have much time."

The air was charged and she realized he didn't trust her any more than she trusted him. She wanted to shake some sense into him, to tell him that he was blind as far as his firstborn was concerned, but she knew she was lucky to be interviewing him at all. She flipped through her notes, to the questions she'd already prepared and began asking him about the town and his position in it, about the people he hired and how he dealt with his employees as well as the union. She asked about the benefits of working for Fitzpatrick, Incorporated now as opposed to ten years ago. She brought up Monroe Sawmill again, owned by Garreth Monroe III, Thomas's brother-in-law.

He answered succinctly, not giving any more information than the bare bones. He leaned back in his chair, tented his fingers and pondered each question, as if he were afraid of slipping up. He hadn't even run for office yet and already he was acting like a politician.

Eventually she brought up his family, his notorious and nefarious ancestors, as well as his remaining son and daughter. Thomas was remarkably candid about his family's history, but when Rachelle started asking questions about his personal life and his wife, his good humor fled and he was once again cautious.

"This isn't an essay about me," he said, resting the tips of his fingers against his lips. "I don't think your readers want or need to know about my family."

She wasn't ready to give up yet. "It's been rumored for years that you have political ambitions. How does your wife feel about your interest in a political career?"

He was wary. "My wife is very supportive, as always."

"But if you enter politics, your entire life will be examined and Roy's death will come up again."

His jaw thrust forward a fraction. "I'll cross that bridge when I come to it. Now, if you'll excuse me, I have an appointment." He stood up with a cold smile, but didn't offer her his hand.

She had no choice but to follow suit. "Thank you for your time," she said, but he didn't respond. His features, as rugged as his wife's were refined, were set in granite. He was truly a handsome man and his arrogance, his hard shell, reminded him of many men she'd known. In many ways, he wasn't unlike Jackson. They were about of the same build and stature, their pride their flaw, the edges of their personalities honed sharp.

He escorted her to the door. "Don't ever barge past my secretary again. She takes her job very seriously."

As she walked through the outer reception area, Thomas closed the door behind her. Melanie, settled in front of her word processor, looked up, glanced at the closed door and ripped off the headgear of her Dictaphone.

"Can't you leave Thomas alone?" she whispered as she fell into step with Rachelle. She shoved open the double doors and told Rita, "I'm taking a break. Handle everything."

Rita, upon spying Rachelle, turned a shade of crimson.

"I'll only be a couple of minutes," Melanie said. They walked into the elevator together, Melanie tossing long curls over her shoulder, her mouth pinched in anger. She was a pretty girl with expressive dark eyes and a sleek figure. Her clothes were a cut above what most of the women in Gold Creek wore, more elegant. As beautiful as she was, Melanie could have walked off the pages of a fashion magazine. Her dress was silk, a deep royal blue, her black heels a soft calfskin. A thick gold necklace surrounded her throat and matched a bracelet and earrings that dangled nearly to her shoulders. She fairly reeked of money, much more money than she made as a secretary—or at least more money than Rachelle's friends who were secretaries in San Francisco made.

Only when they were outside standing at the door of Rachelle's car, did Melanie say anything. "Listen, Rachelle, I don't know what you thought you'd accomplish by coming back here, but you're only causing trouble. Whether you know it or not, lots of people are nervous—they don't like the idea of their quiet little town being splashed all over the pages of national newspapers."

Rachelle couldn't help but smile. "You think I'm exploiting the citizens of Gold Creek?"

"Using them," she replied. "To sell papers."

"I just thought it would be an interesting series."

"Oh, yeah, right. Like people in Chicago, or New York, or Washington, D.C., are going to give a rip about how this little town operates." She shook her head and sighed. "Don't give me any of that crap. I know better. You're here because of Roy Fitzpatrick. That's why you pushed your way past me to get to his dad, that's why Jackson Moore decided to show up and that's what's turning this town inside out. It's over, Rachelle, so forget it. A boy died. Period. End of story."

"Is it?" Rachelle asked, studying the lines of Melanie's pretty face.

"Absolutely. And if you don't leave it alone, I'm afraid you might find yourself in big trouble."

"You're threatening me?" Rachelle laughed. "I can't believe it. What do *you,* what does this town, have to hide?"

"Take my advice, Rachelle. Leave it alone." She turned on her heel and half ran down along the path that led to the back door of the building.

Rachelle blew her bangs from her eyes and glanced up to the third floor. Her heart nearly stopped as she saw a flicker of movement at one of the windows. Thomas Fitzpatrick, his expression murderous, stared down at her.

So he'd witnessed her exchange with Melanie. So what? Though feeling as if he'd spied her doing something she shouldn't have been, she waved to him and slid into the warm interior of her car. It was silly of her to take Melanie's warning seriously, sillier still to be frightened of Thomas Fitzpatrick. From all accounts Fitzpatrick was a decent man, a philanthropist, for God's sake. And he'd been more than civil during the interview.

So why did he, with a single look, cause her to grow cold inside? If only Jackson were still here, she thought, then jammed her key into the ignition. Jackson was long gone and she could handle everything herself. She didn't need a man to lean on for God's sake! But she couldn't shake the cold dread that settled in her heart.

JACKSON LEANED OVER THE desk of the private investigator and glared at the weasel-eyed man. "You're telling me that there's nothing new you can dig up on the Fitzpatrick murder?"

The man, Virgil Timms, held up his palms, showing off yellow stains on his fingers from the cigarettes he smoked one after another. A Winston cigarette was burning unattended in the ashtray on the desk. "Nothing significant. But I'm still working on it."

"I'm paying you a lot of money to find out the truth," Jackson said, pacing to the window and staring through the streaked glass to the bustling streets below where pedestrians, bicyclists and motorists vied for room. Timms worked in Chinatown in San Francisco, and the pace of the city seemed frenetic compared with Gold Creek.

"Hey, I'm doin' my best."

Was he? Jackson wasn't convinced. He'd hired Timms on the advice of his partner. Boothe and Timms had served together in Vietnam, and Timms had gained a reputation, though the man seemed shady to Jackson. Not that it mattered. The shadier, the better in this case. "Did Fitzpatrick get to you?"

"What'd'ya mean?"

Jackson walked back to the desk. His muscles were tight and a knot was forming between his shoulders. "I mean, did he pay you to quit nosing around?"

Timms had the decency to look offended. "Hey, *you're* my client."

"Fitzpatrick has a lot of money. He's used to spreading it around to get what he wants."

"I didn't sell you out, man. Take a look." He shoved a file across the desk. The manila folder was marked Moore/Fitzpatrick.

Jackson rifled quickly through the pages, reading small biographies on each of the suspects in the Fitzpatrick case, including his own. No wonder the police hauled him in. Of all the potential murderers of Roy Fitzpatrick, Jackson had been the only one with a reputation for brushes with the law—even though they'd been minor.

"Is this mine?" he asked, his brows knitting as he began to digest some of the information.

"You paid for it. Hey—" Timms took a drag on his cigarette before crushing it in the ashtray already heaped with ashes and cigarette butts "—you still want me on the case?" He dumped the full ashtray into a wastebasket before lighting up again.

"I suppose," Jackson agreed.

"Good. But let me clue you in on one thing. It's not easy getting information out of that town. At the mention of the Fitzpatrick name, those people zip their lips like nobody's business. And the police—forget them. It's like the old man is some kind of god or somethin'."

"Or something," Jackson agreed dryly.

"He owns the whole damned town. Him and his relatives."

"Garreth Monroe," Jackson thought aloud. Brother-in-law to Thomas and a man who was just as greedy. He owned the place on the lake where Rachelle and he...

"Garreth Monroe III, mind you. Yep, unless you work for one of those two guys, you don't have much of a chance in that town."

"That, I already knew."

Timms's thin lips twisted into the semblance of a smile. "Well, there's a lot you might not know in that folder—things people didn't want me to find out. If I didn't know better I'd swear Gold Creek should be named Peyton Place." He laughed at his own joke and ended up in a coughing fit. "I gotta cut down," he said, holding up his cigarette. "Now, listen, you want me to dig as deep as I can?"

"Deeper."

"Even if you find out something you don't want to know?"

The question jarred Jackson. His jaw slid to the side and he had to remind himself that Timms was on his side. "I don't know what you're insinuating, but as far as I'm concerned, I want you to turn that damned town upside down and shake it until all the secrets spill out. Got it?"

"If you're sure."

"Damn right, I'm sure." Jackson grabbed the manila folder and tucked it under his arm. "I'll call you when I get back from New York."

## CHAPTER TWELVE

"MAYBE HE'S GONE FOR good," Brian said, yanking off his tie and tossing it onto the back of the couch.

"I wouldn't bet on it." Thomas walked down the two steps to his son's living room, a huge, spacious room decorated with stark white couches, white walls, white carpet and accented in red and black. The room reminded him of his daughter-in-law, who had overseen the decorating. Everything with Laura was black and white, no gray. "Jackson will come back to finish what he started."

Brian threw open the French doors and stepped onto the veranda. "Why doesn't he just crawl back under his rock in New York and leave us all the hell alone?" He leaned against the rail of the veranda and sighed heavily. Thomas noticed the beads of sweat that had collected on his son's brow.

"He wants vindication." Thomas stared over the grounds of Brian's estate, past the tended grass and shrubbery to the forest that grew along the banks of Gold Creek. Leaning his elbows on the rail, he wished he didn't have to ask the question that was foremost in his mind, a question that had nagged at him for years, but a question he'd managed to bury deep. Until Jackson Moore returned. "The night your brother died," he said gently, "you can swear to me that no one but Jackson had words with him?"

Brian looked up sharply. "What is this? Are you

asking me if *I* killed Roy?" A heartbeat passed and Brian trembled. "I don't believe this. I friggin' don't believe this! You, my own father, can stand there and accuse me of murdering my own brother? But why? To inherit this?" He motioned toward the house dismissively. "Do you honestly think I would have done it?"

"I haven't accused you of anything," his father said softly. "But it'll happen. The police are bound to be involved again—Jackson's already hired a private detective. He means business."

"Brian? Brian, are you home?" Laura's voice sang softly through the rooms and out the open door. Carrying his tie and a bag from a boutique in Coleville, she joined them on the porch. "This doesn't belong on the couch," she chided gently, lifting the tie and wiggling it. She caught her husband and father-in-law's somber expressions. "Is something wrong?"

"Moore's poking around."

The tie dropped from her fingers to coil at her feet on the bricks. "What now?" she asked, setting her shopping bag near the door.

"Jackson talked to Dad, and your friend, Rachelle, has spoken with both of us."

"I remember seeing Rachelle at your office," she said stonily.

Brian licked his lips nervously. "Dad's afraid they won't give up until they find out the truth."

"But the truth is that Jackson killed Roy..." she started, then let her sentence drift away.

"Jackson doesn't think so," Thomas said slowly. "And I don't want any surprises. I came over to talk to you so that you could refresh my memory of that night."

"It was so long ago—"

"I know. But let's go over it again. If either of you

know anyone who had anything to do with Roy's death, I want to know about it and I want to know about it now!"

"We would've told you then," Laura insisted, and her clear blue eyes met his. However, her hand shook and she had to slip it quickly into the pocket of her skirt. She blinked hard and glanced at Brian. "This is crazy."

Thomas wasn't about to be put off. "Let's just get a few things straight. I know about the problems you've been covering up at the logging company. Profits are way down and, say what you will, I can't believe it's all because of the environmentalists or the union."

"But—"

"I know you've been skimming," he said bluntly to his son, and the pain in his heart ached all the more. He'd lost one boy and had found out that his other was a thief. His daughter, Toni, was already a hellion....

Laura gasped. "No, that can't be true." Laura took a step toward her husband. "Brian—"

"Shut up, Laura."

"But this is a lie—"

Brian's face was flushed and the sweat on his forehead was drizzling down his chin. "I said, 'shut up!'"

Brian swallowed hard and Laura looked positively stricken.

Thomas didn't have time to worry about their emotions. "So now that we know where we all stand, let's get down to it, shall we?"

"Dad, listen, I just needed a little extra cash for the house."

Laura's mouth dropped open.

"I know what you needed it for," Thomas said tightly, his gaze cutting. Brian had a reputation. With the horses and with the women. No, he never should have trusted the boy to run the company. There were others who would have done better.

His son's hand was on his sleeve. Tears glistened in Brian's eyes. "I'm sorry."

"Forget it. Pull yourself together."

"Does Mom—"

"Does she know?" Thomas shook his head. "It's our little secret." He glared pointedly at Laura. "Let's make sure it stays that way, but, if you ever need money again, I suggest you come to me."

"I will. Oh, God, you know I will," Brian said, blinking rapidly in relief. Thomas felt sick that this spineless man was his only legitimate son. Then he felt a deep pang of guilt. If Brian had turned into a common, even stupid, thief, who could he blame but himself? Maybe if he hadn't lavished so much attention on his firstborn...

"Brian..." Laura touched him gently on the arm, but he shook off her fingers, just as he'd shaken off anything he had had to do with her since the wedding day. That, too, was probably Thomas's fault. He'd insisted that Brian marry Laura when he'd found out the girl was pregnant. He'd lost a bastard son by Roy, and he wasn't about to lose any more of his grandchildren.

He clapped his son on the shoulder. "Buck up," he said. "Now, you can help with this. Roy had lots of people who didn't like him. Jackson Moore was only the most visible. Who were the others?"

"Mom wouldn't approve of this," Brian ventured.

"Your mother is never to know. This conversation is private," Thomas said, and the glint in his eyes was enough to convince both Brian and Laura that he meant business. "I've spent most of my life protecting her and I won't let you ruin everything. So let's start with everyone who had a grudge against Roy and then tell me about

Rachelle Tremont." He turned his gaze on his daughter-in-law. "You knew her. You were friends, weren't you?"

Laura shrugged. "I only knew her a little while."

Thomas thought about his encounter with Rachelle. "She's as bullheaded as Jackson, and you can't tell me she isn't back here because of him." Irritated, he rested his hip against the rail and crossed his arms over his chest. "So tell me everything you know about her."

THE LAST PERSON RACHELLE expected to find camped out in her cottage was her sister. But Heather was waiting for her and the house had been picked up and cleaned. Heather was, and always had been, a compulsive neatnik.

With her five-year-old son, Adam, balanced on her lap, Heather swayed back and forth in the rocking chair near the fire. Adam's head lolled against his mother's shoulder and his eyes were closed.

Flames crackled over mossy logs and the scent of burning wood and clam chowder filled the rooms.

"Surprised?" Heather mouthed as Rachelle closed the door behind her. With one finger to her lips, she carried Adam into the spare bedroom.

"Shocked would be more like it," Rachelle admitted, as Heather closed the door at the end of the hall and padded quickly into the kitchen. Rachelle slung her jacket over the back of a chair and ignored her sister's pointed look of disapproval. They'd always been different, and Rachelle hadn't discovered her sister's need to keep a spotless house. Thank goodness!

Heather lifted the lid on the soup pot. The aroma of clams and spices escaped in a thick cloud of steam. Rachelle's stomach grumbled.

"Hungry?" Heather asked.

"Famished."

Heather grinned, showing off dimples. "Good."

"So how long have you been here?"

"Just an hour," Heather admitted with a chuckle.

"And in that time you washed the windows, scoured the sink, scrubbed the floors, changed the beds and had enough time left over to whip up a batch of chowder?"

Heather laughed. Her culinary talents left a lot to be desired. Rachelle often joked that her sister didn't cook in order to keep her kitchen spotless. Aside from cleaning, Heather's talents were limited to sculpting, painting and interior decorating. Her expertise, or lack of it, in the kitchen was an old family joke.

"Very funny," Heather responded, her blue eyes twinkling. "Actually, I bought the soup at a little bistro near Fisherman's Wharf."

"Ahh. You had me worried for a while there."

"And all this time, I thought I was the only one who worried." Heather tossed a lock of honey-blond hair over her shoulders. "Mom called yesterday and she sounded really upset, so I let my assistant handle the gallery and I packed Adam up and here we are. But we're not staying here. Mom wants us to camp out over at her place." Heather tasted the soup and winced. "Too hot."

Snagging an apple from the basket on the counter, Rachelle asked, "Is Mom still upset about the separation?"

"That's a big part of it," Heather hedged. She put the lid back on the soup kettle.

"But there's more," Rachelle guessed, knowing her mother's concerns about Jackson.

"Tons," Heather admitted with a nervous little shrug.

"Meaning Jackson Moore and yours truly."

"She mentioned you'd been seeing him."

Rachelle polished her apple on the edge of her blouse. "We've run into each other a couple of times."

"Oh." Heather sat at the table, propped her chin in one hand and said, "Spill it, Rachelle. Jackson Moore didn't travel over two thousand miles for no reason. Did he come back because you're here?"

"No."

Heather raised a skeptical brow, and Rachelle took a large bite of her apple. She'd never really dissected Jackson's reasons for returning; he'd said he had come back to close an open door on his past, clear his reputation— and she'd believed him.

"It's sure a coincidence that you and he are back here together."

"I don't want to hear it," Rachelle snapped, her patience worn thin. "He's back in New York right now."

"Permanently?"

She lifted a shoulder.

"How long has he been gone?"

"A couple of days, I think," she hedged, because it seemed like an eternity, though she hated to admit that fact to anyone, including herself. She frowned thoughtfully. "Everyone I've talked to in this town, and that includes Mom, seems to think that Jackson's primary purpose in life is to make trouble for me. I just don't think that's the case. Sure, the first article in my series was catalyst for returning to Gold Creek, but that doesn't mean anything—"

"Has he seen you?"

"Yes, but—"

"Once?" Heather asked with innocent guile.

"At least."

"Twice? Three times? Four?"

"I haven't kept count."

Heather leaned back in her chair in order to survey her sister. "And what does David have to say about all this?"

Rachelle steeled herself, but decided to tell Heather everything. It was going to come out sooner or later anyway. "David and I broke up."

The "I told you so" forming on Heather's lips didn't get past her tongue because at that instant the sound of a motorcycle engine split the night. "Oh, don't tell me," Heather whispered, walking to the window and peering through the blinds. "I don't believe it!"

Rachelle's heart soared. He'd come back. Just when she'd convinced herself that, like before, he wasn't going to return, he was back! "Believe it."

"But a motorcycle? Is he going through his second childhood or what?"

"I don't know."

"Mommy?" Adam, his eyes glazed, a tattered blanket wound in one chubby fist, walked groggily into the room.

"Oh, sweetheart. You woke up." In an instant all thoughts of Jackson disappeared as Heather picked up her son and clung to him with a desperation that seemed out of proportion to the circumstances. She nuzzled his neck and he ducked her kisses. "Are you hungry? I've got soup and bread and salad."

"I *hate* salad!" Adam said. He had one arm thrown around his mother's neck and he peeked at Rachelle over Heather's shoulders. His skin was paler than usual, Rachelle thought, and she was surprised that he was napping at this time of day. His light brown hair was sticking up at all angles and his gray eyes didn't hold their usual sparkle. Maybe it was the change in his routine.

Rachelle's thoughts were interrupted by the doorbell.

She didn't know if she had the stamina to deal with Jackson at this moment, but, obviously, she had no choice. She opened the door and he entered with the scent of fresh air and pine. His hair was windblown, his cheeks red, his gaze touching hers for an instant before landing full force on Heather. "I heard you talked to Fitzpatrick—"

"This is my sister, Heather," Rachelle cut in. "You remember?"

Jackson didn't crack a smile, but then his contact with Heather had been minimal and only after the sordid mess with Roy had been exposed. "We've met."

Heather's smile was brittle. "I heard you came back to Gold Creek."

"Looks like I'm not the only one."

"Heather's here visiting Mom," Rachelle explained as the tension in the air fairly snapped. What was it about Jackson that made everyone bristle?

"And who's this?" Jackson asked, spying the boy. His features softened as he touched Adam's chin.

To Heather's credit, she didn't shrink away. "This is my son. Adam, this is Mr. Moore."

"Heather was married to Dennis Leonetti. You remember him…." Rachelle explained.

Jackson's lip curled a bit. The Leonetti family, from Coleville, was associated with banking and money.

"We were divorced a couple of years ago," Heather said, and then, as if to change the subject, she handed Adam to Rachelle and turned her attention back to the stove. "If you haven't eaten…"

"Be delighted," Jackson drawled, though his expression was about as far from delight as a person could get.

Rachelle sliced bread and poured each adult a glass of wine. They all needed to relax a little. Even Adam, usually animated, seemed out of sorts. He wouldn't touch his soup and ended up curled on a corner of the couch, his blanket clutched tightly to his chest, an old quilt tossed over his slim shoulders.

The meal was tense, the conversation stilted and Rachelle poured herself a second glass of wine. Heather asked about Jackson's work and his reasons for being back in Gold Creek and he responded quickly, admitting that a particularly interesting case had lured him back to Manhattan for a few days, but that he'd returned on the first possible flight. The glance he sent Rachelle turned her cheeks a vibrant pink.

Heather didn't miss the exchange and, blowing her bangs from her eyes, shook her head. "So you came back," she said to Jackson.

"I've got some unfinished business here." Again his gaze touched Rachelle's as he poured them each a final glass of wine. Her heart was thundering under his stare, and yet she tried to act calm and nonchalant in front of Heather. He shoved his empty soup bowl aside.

"Your business here?" Heather persisted. "Legal matters?"

He smiled a crooked half grin. "You could say that." He studied his wine, rotating the glass between his fingers.

"Big client?"

He leaned forward, balancing his elbows on the table. "I'm working for myself."

Rachelle explained, "Jackson's decided to clear his name. He's going to try to find out who killed Roy Fitzpatrick."

Heather eyed him skeptically. "It's been eleven years."

"Twelve," Jackson corrected.

"A long time to cover up the truth."

"A long time to live with a lie," Jackson replied, his gaze cutting as it moved from Heather to Rachelle.

Somehow they finished the meal. Heather made excuses about getting Adam to his grandma's and putting him to bed, and Rachelle was relieved that the inquisition was over, at least for the time being. She hugged Adam thoroughly and promised that the next time she saw him, she'd have something special for him.

"Will ya really?" Adam asked, his eyes growing bright for the first time that evening.

"You betcha, sport."

He kissed the crook of her neck and whispered that he loved her and even though he was responding to her bribe, she squeezed him all the tighter. "I love you, too," she agreed, knowing that this special feeling she had with Adam was one of the reasons she couldn't marry anyone who didn't want children. There was just so much love she could give a child—her child.

"We'll see Aunt Rachelle again tomorrow," Heather said, peeling her son from Rachelle's arms.

"And she'll bring me a surprise."

Heather's gaze caught her sister's. "If she remembers."

"You'll 'member, won'cha?" Adam demanded.

"'Course I will." She rumpled Adam's hair and he giggled, some of his color returning as Heather carried him outside.

"I hope you know what you're doing," Heather whispered to Rachelle as she carried Adam down the steps.

"Trust me."

Heather cast a dubious look Jackson's way, then bit her lower lip. "I know you haven't asked for my advice," she whispered to Rachelle.

"But you're going to give it to me anyway."

"Right. Don't listen to Mom. Or Dad. Or anyone else

in this town. I know I called and said some pretty horrid things about Jackson, but you can't blame me. He *did* hurt you." She touched Adam's button of a nose. "But if you love him, and it's my guess that you do," she added quickly when Rachelle was about to protest, "then stick by him."

"This isn't the kind of advice I'd expect from you."

"I know. But I think it's important to be happy and follow your heart."

Rachelle thought she read something more in her sister's serious gaze, but Heather stepped off the porch and nearly slipped on the bottom step. "I guess we'd better fix that," she said, eyeing the rotting wood. "I'll talk to Mom about it." She hauled Adam to her car. Rachelle stood on the porch and waved; Jackson, who had lingered in the doorway, stood next to her. They watched as Heather's sleek car pulled out of the drive.

"I thought you'd end up like her, you know. Husband, kids, house with a white picket fence and a station wagon in the garage. The whole bit."

"It didn't work out that way." They walked into the house together and Rachelle was aware of the ambiance of the little cottage—the fire, the near-empty bottle of wine, the cozy rooms with shadowy corners. The curtains were drawn, the lights turned down. The setting was too intimate, inviting romance. Though what she and Jackson shared was as far from romance as a couple could get.

"Why not? Why didn't you settle down?"

Her heart ached a little and she felt him near her, smelled his masculine scent. "Didn't meet the right guy, I guess."

At the table, he turned a chair around and straddled it. "What about this David? Is he the right guy?"

Rachelle couldn't lie. She shook her head. "I don't think so. What about you?"

He laughed, his eyes glinting. "Maybe I just haven't met the right woman."

"I don't think there is a right woman for you."

"Oh, no?" His gaze moved lazily up her body, inch by inch. Her heart began to hammer, and to break the seductive spell he was weaving, she began stacking dishes in the sink. She should tell him to leave, to just go jump on his motorcycle and leave her alone. But she didn't. Because, damn it, she didn't want him to leave. There was something compelling about Jackson, something innately dangerous and yet strong and safe. She was pulled apart when she was with him, wanting to prove her independence one instant while ready to lean on him the next.

She turned on the water, nearly scalded herself and swore softly. Jackson unnerved her. She couldn't do anything right when he was near.

She didn't hear him approach but sucked in her breath when his arms surrounded her waist and he pressed the flat of his hands against her abdomen. A warm desire spread through her and she swallowed hard. She didn't want him to touch her, knew the dangerous territory to which it would lead, and yet she couldn't form the words to make him stop.

"We don't need to be at each other's throats," he said, pulling her closer still, breathing in the scent of her hair.

She felt her resistance ebb as his smell and touch enveloped her. Her buttocks rested against his thighs and she felt his hardness.

Deep emotions stirred within her, but thoughts of refusing him had already disappeared. His lips were on her throat as he turned her in his arms.

"I told myself I'd never kiss you again," he admitted, his voice a low rasp. "But even then I knew I was lying."

His mouth found hers with a hunger that stole the breath from her lungs. She closed her eyes and let the kiss consume her, knowing the fires he was stoking deep in her soul were sure to burn hotter still.

She opened her mouth to him, let him carry them both to the floor, and when he began to remove her clothes, she didn't stop. Instead her own fingers discovered the buttons of his shirt and the snap at the waistband of his jeans. She touched the naked wonder of him and explored each supple curve of his body. Her fingers traced his spine and pushed his pants over his buttocks as he disposed of her clothes.

Firelight cast flickering shadows over their bodies and sweat began to collect on their skin.

Jackson kissed her eyes, her lips, her throat, her breasts, and she tasted the salt on his skin as she kissed him back. Their arms and legs twined and she was so hot, she could barely breathe.

He stretched out beside her, one big hand resting on the curve of her waist. His eyes held hers and she felt as if she were losing herself to him. She tried to break the spell, but was unable. "Make love to me, Rachelle," he whispered, and kissed the fine shell of her ear.

She moaned her response, her arms winding around his neck as she dragged his head close to hers and met his eager mouth with her own. Staring up at him, she watched as his lean body moved ever so slightly so that he was astride her.

"I can't stop this," he said in near apology.

"Neither can I." Again she kissed him, her tongue delving deep into his mouth. With a shudder, he urged her legs apart with his knees.

"I can't get enough of you," he admitted as he plunged into her warmth. It was as close as an admission of love as she was going to get, and Rachelle clung to him, wrapping her arms and legs around him and meeting the passion of his thrusts and closing her eyes as the tide of desire swept her closer and closer to that whirling climax that ripped through her soul.

With a cry, Jackson fell upon her, flattening her breasts and breathing hard. He twined his fingers in her hair and held her face between his hands. Gazing down at her in wonder, he kissed her forehead. "I didn't plan this, you know."

"Neither did I."

"I didn't want it."

"I know."

"But I just can't seem to stop. I tell myself to keep my hands off you. I give myself a list of reasons to stay away from you that is completely logical. But I can't stay away."

She smiled softly and touched the corner of his mouth. "Neither can I, Counselor," she said with a giggle. "It's crazy…I know that as much—maybe more—than you do."

"What're we going to do?"

She looked up at him and raised a wicked eyebrow. "For the rest of the night?"

"For the rest of our lives?"

A thick lump formed in the back of her throat. She could barely breathe. "I think we should take it slow."

"Slower than twelve years?"

She had to laugh then. To her surprise, he rolled off her, picked her up and carried her stark naked into the back bedroom. "I think it's time we did this properly," he said, dropping her onto the old double bed.

"You? Proper?" She giggled again, and this time he flung himself down on the bed beside her. "Don't make me laugh."

"Actually, I was thinking of making you do a lot of things, lady. But laughing wasn't near the top of the list."

"What is?" she asked, a naughty spark lighting her eyes.

"I'll show you." And then, throwing the covers over them, he kissed her hard and didn't stop for a long, long time.

THE NEXT MORNING RACHELLE awoke to the smells of hot coffee and burned toast. She touched the bed where Jackson had lain, but the sheets were cold. Stretching, she smiled to herself. Waking up with Jackson felt right. She threw on her robe and found Jackson seated at the table, sipping coffee and staring at the contents of a file folder. He glanced up at her approach. "'Morning."

Spying his work spread out on the table, she said, "Look, before you bury yourself in that, I think you should know that I lied to you."

He stiffened, his eyes narrowing a fraction. "What about?"

"About the fact that I really do need an interview with you...my editor was insistent. You were so damned arrogant about it, I couldn't admit that you were right." She tossed her hair from her face. "Forgive me?"

He tapped a pen to his lips. "I guess," he said, then grinned.

"What's this?" she asked, covering her mouth to stifle a yawn as she gazed at the file folder that held his attention.

"Homework."

"From New York?" She wandered over to the coffee-maker and poured herself a cup of the fresh brew.

"Not exactly." He leaned back in his chair and smiled up at her. "I've had a change of heart. Remember when I asked you to stay out of my business?"

"How could I forget? Subtle isn't your middle name."

"All right, all right, so maybe I made a mistake."

"What? An apology?" She feigned surprise as she shoved her hair from her face.

His eyes narrowed in good-natured anger. "Are you going to hear me out or give me a bad time?"

"Hopefully a little of both." Cradling her cup, she plopped down in a chair next to his. "What's this?"

"The information I got from a private investigator."

"On?" she asked, her stomach dropping. Had he hired a detective to look into her life?

"On everyone who could've been involved in Roy's death." All the teasing light dimmed in his eyes. "You're here, as well as your friends."

Rachelle's stomach knotted as she began scanning the individual reports. Jackson was right. Her name fairly leapt off the page—along with her phone number, address, Social Security number and California driver's license number. A credit report and her credit history came next, then a quick résumé of her accomplishments, her education and her current working address and job description.

With the turn of each page, she became more furious; she felt that Jackson had asked a perfect stranger to put together her life, file and label it accurately, then stuff it into a neat envelope for Jackson to dissect as he pleased.

The typewritten biography started with her birth, her parents, her sister, even including how much money her father and mother made. She read about her parents' divorce, her father's affair with a younger woman and her own involvement with Jackson. The report mentioned her termination of employment at the *Clarion* and the fact that she gave up most of her extracurricular activities after the night Roy Fitzpatrick died. The investigation went further, following her through college and her career. David was mentioned, as was her boss, Marcy, and friends she'd made over the years. Attached to the back page were photocopies of newspaper reports, primarily from the *Gold Creek Clarion,* about her as a witness—the sole witness—who could get Jackson Moore off the hook for Roy Fitzpatrick's murder.

By the time she'd finished reading, her insides were shredding. "Thorough, isn't he?" she asked, her lips pressed hard against each other. She felt betrayed by Jackson. He had no right to order out a copy of her life and study it as if it were some new cure for a fatal disease.

"I hope he is. Otherwise I paid him a lot of money for nothing."

"Except to get your jollies from reading the dirt on everyone in town."

He looked up sharply. "You're offended?"

"Wouldn't you be?"

"I'm only trying to get to the bottom of this."

"By having me investigated? You didn't trust me—even after I stood up for you."

He sighed, set his cup down and leaned back in his chair. As if the strain of sitting for hours was beginning to get to him, he rubbed his eyes. "I didn't want to put any restraint on Timms. I figured I needed a fresh outlook on an old crime. So I told him to look into everyone involved, including myself."

"That's crazy."

He shuffled through a pile of reports and tossed one to her. Sure enough, it was labeled Jackson Moore and listed his address, phone number and place of employment.

"I don't understand...."

His smile was cynical. He motioned to the report. "Read it if you want. It paints a pretty grim picture. For years I thought the police just had it in for me, that they were somehow on Fitzpatrick's payroll, but if you read the facts objectively, you can see why I was the prime suspect. However," he added, before draining his cup, "I'm not giving up on the bribe theory. Fitzpatrick hates my guts."

She looked over the reports, reading familiar names: Thomas Fitzpatrick, Brian Fitzpatrick, June Fitzpatrick, Laura Chandler Fitzpatrick, Carlie Surrett, Erik Patton, Scott McDonald, Melanie Patton and on and on. It was an incredible compilation of history.

She finished her coffee and walked into the kitchen to grab the glass pot and return with it. As she poured coffee into Jackson's empty cup, she glanced at him. "Does all of this help?"

"I don't know. But I've discovered some interesting facts." He grabbed her wrist as she finished pouring. His fingers caught on the tie of her robe and he gently tugged, helping the knot to loosen. "By the way, you look great."

She rolled her eyes and clutched her robe closed. Without makeup, her hair a tangled mess, she thought "great" was a tad overdoing it. Nonetheless his hasty compliment brought a small smile to her lips. She finished pouring and took the coffeepot back to the kitchen to heat. "What interesting facts?" she asked as she returned to her chair.

"Erik Patton and Roy weren't that crazy for each other. His sister, Melanie, was supposedly engaged to Roy when he took up with Laura. Melanie even tried to trap him and claim she was pregnant, but she was lying apparently."

Rachelle thought back to that night and Erik's sullenness; he had seemed preoccupied, but he'd still definitely been in the Fitzpatrick corner. She remembered him laughing when Jackson, trying to flee, couldn't start his motorcycle. *Well, look what you found—Roy's little piece…. You're not gonna get far,* he'd predicted before calling to Roy.

"Erik thought I was Roy's girl," she said with a shudder.

"Erik probably knew that Roy was using Laura to get to you. It doesn't change the fact that there was bad blood between the two supposed best friends." He glanced up at her and shoved his hair from his eyes impatiently. "Puts a different slant on things, doesn't it?"

"I'd say so."

They then spent the next hour going through the files, scrutinizing the secrets of Gold Creek. Melanie Patton was hired by Fitzpatrick right out of high school as a receptionist and with each passing year, she was promoted until, at the age of twenty-nine, she had become Thomas's private secretary and administrative assistant.

Her brother Erik, too, had been employed by the Fitzpatricks, or their relatives, the Monroes, ever since he'd dropped out of college, two months after Roy's death.

Rachelle took a shower, dressed, then read the private investigator's reports until her head swam. What she read only confirmed what she already knew: Gold Creek was a small town and most of the local families had roots that went back for generations. People married, had children and watched those children grow up to marry someone in town only to start the cycle over again.

Jackson scraped back his chair in frustration.

"Restless?"

"A little."

"Come on, let's go for a ride."

He grinned. "On the motorcycle?"

"Why not?"

He didn't need any more encouragement. They rode through the hills, the wind pressing hard against their faces and tangling their hair. The sun was bright, casting shadows through the limbs of trees that hung over the country roads as they raced through the valleys and towns surrounding Gold Creek.

At a small general store a few miles from the lake, they purchased sandwiches and a bottle of wine, which they took to a strip of beach on the south side of the lake. Seated on a stump near the water's edge, they ate their lunch and watched the ducks swim on the lake. A few fishermen cast their lines into the still waters of Whitefire Lake and chipmunks, looking for a handout, scampered nervously along the shore.

"You believe in the old Indian legend?" he asked, sitting behind her as she half lay against him.

"I don't know." She remembered the first morning she'd come to the lake, how the mist was rising and how she, feeling adventurous as well as silly, had drunk from the lake. But then good fortune had come to her, hadn't it? Just days later Jackson had returned to Gold Creek. "I'm not really superstitious."

"Neither am I." He kissed the side of her head and nuzzled her neck. "I thought coming back here would be the end of my life here in Gold Creek—that I would resolve the parts of my life that were still unsettled."

"And have you?"

"Not until I find Roy's murderer and clear my name."
He climbed off the stump and kicked at a stone on the
shore. "But that might not be enough, either."

"No?" She hopped from the stump and joined him at
the edge of the lake.

He smiled sadly and his gaze drilled into hers. "Because I didn't count on you," he said, frowning. "I knew
you were here, of course. Hell, I planned to breeze into
town, land on your doorstep and convince myself once
and for all that you were nothing but a nice part of a bad
memory."

She remembered their first meeting when he'd shown
up on her doorstep and within minutes antagonized her
and kissed her with a hunger that had stolen the very
breath from her lungs. "But you came back."

"My motives weren't very pure," he admitted.

"Are they ever?" she teased, her heart drumming at
his confession.

"I wanted to make love to you—as often as possible—
as long as I could and I thought if I did, that I would quit
fantasizing about you, that I would quit falling into the
nostalgia trap of thinking something long ago was better
than today. But I was wrong." He stared deep into her
eyes and drew in on his lower lip. "I didn't know I was
capable of being so wrong."

She couldn't stop the elation that thundered through
her blood. He was standing only inches from her, not
touching her, claiming that he cared.

"I don't know if I can leave you," he said, a small,
self-deprecating smile tugging at one side of his mouth.
"I came here to conquer, to prove my innocence and all
I've proven is that I'm stupid enough to fall in love."

There it was—the confession hanging on the air. Tears

touched the back of her eyes and she couldn't smile because her chin was wobbling.

"I love you, Rachelle. I think I always have."

With a startled cry, she flung herself into his arms and let the tears of joy flow down her cheeks. Her fingers clenched in the soft folds of his leather jacket and she sobbed openly. "You don't know how long I've waited to hear you say those three words," she said. "I've loved you forever!"

His arms were around her and he swung her off her feet. Her sobs gave way to laughter as the world spun around them. The lake shimmered like glass and the air was fresh with the scent of pine and musk. He kissed her face, her neck, her hair, tasting her tears and holding her so fiercely that she could barely breathe. But she didn't care. All her worries seemed to float away and she knew that no matter what the future held, she would love Jackson forever.

When at last he let her go, she dashed away from him and he chased after her. Startled birds flew from their path and a squirrel scolded from the upper branches of a pine tree.

"You can't hide from me," Jackson warned, laughing as he bore down on her.

"You haven't caught me yet," she teased, scrambling over a rock to hide in the shadows. He saw her and she started running again, but he caught up with her easily and grabbed hold of her.

She laughed and tossed back her hair.

"So what're we going to do about this?" he asked, breathing as hard as she was.

Her gaze lingered in his and her heart melted. "Do we have to do anything?"

"I think it's proper to propose."

"And we know that above all else, Jackson, you're proper. Right?"

"Absolutely." He slapped her rear playfully. "Always the gentleman."

"Save me," she whispered, and he shook his head.

"No, you save me." He gathered her into his arms again, and in the shifting shadows of the fragrant pines, he kissed her forehead. "Marry me, Rachelle," he whispered, and her throat clogged all over again.

"You're serious?" She couldn't believe her ears.

"Marry me and have my children and grow old beside me."

Her world tilted and joy coursed through her blood. "In a heartbeat," she whispered, pressing her anxious lips to his as his knees gave way and they dropped onto a bed of pine needles.

# CHAPTER THIRTEEN

MRS. JACKSON MOORE. The name sounded right. She pinched herself to make sure she wasn't dreaming, even though she'd spent another night in Jackson's arms and had spent hours planning their future. They hoped after a few months' separation to be married and then she would join him in New York, where she could still write her columns.

Things were looking up, she told herself, as she walked into the Rexall Drug Store in search of a toy for Adam. The store was as she remembered it. Paddle fans circled the air lazily overhead and a bell tinkled when the front door was opened. More than a pharmacy, the store offered everything from cookbooks to baby clothes, from cosmetics to Band-Aids, from hair dye to costume jewelry. In the toy section, Rachelle eyed several games before deciding upon a model dinosaur. After purchasing her gift at the cash register, she walked to the back of the store where an old-fashioned soda fountain offered lunch.

Carlie's mother, Thelma, was "tending bar" as she used to call it by whipping up a gooey concoction of chocolate, marshmallow crème, milk and ice cream in the blender. She poured the frothy mixture into a tall waxed paper cup and slid it into the eager hands of a boy of about ten or eleven who was seated on the end stool. "There ya go, Zach," Thelma said with a wink.

Rachelle eyed the boy, a handsome child with pale blond hair and blue eyes. He reminded her of someone she'd known in grade school, but she couldn't remember whom until she spied the boy's mother walking quickly through the store. "Ready to go?" Laura asked her son.

"Sure."

Laura's gaze met Rachelle's in the mirror behind the counter. For a second, fear registered in Laura's eyes, then she offered a cool smile. "So you're still here," she said, flipping a lock of blond hair over her shoulder. "I thought by now you would have had more than enough material for your articles."

"It takes a while," Rachelle admitted. "I'm working on a couple of pieces, one about people who've moved out of Gold Creek and then come back and another about the people who've stayed for most of their lives."

"Would any of your readers really care?"

"I hope so."

Laura was tugging on her son's arm. "It's time, Zach. Daddy'll be home soon."

"I thought maybe I could talk to you," Rachelle said, and Laura visibly started.

"Me? I don't think—"

"Come on, Laura. We were friends once," Rachelle said, and a sadness stole across Laura's features. For a second she looked as if she might break down and cry.

"That was a long time ago, Rachelle. We don't even know each other anymore. Let's *go,* Zach." She tugged on the boy's arm and he yanked it quickly away.

"I'm comin', I'm comin'," he muttered, clutching his drink and trudging after her down an aisle that displayed wrapping paper and hundreds of greeting cards.

"Well, now, what can I do for you?" Thelma asked, her eyes lighting up. She was still an attractive woman, though she'd gained a little weight around her middle and her short dark hair was shot with gray. "You still like cherry cokes and banana splits?"

Rachelle's stomach turned over at the thought, but she was in such a good mood that she wasn't interested in counting calories, and if she had a stomachache later, so what.

"Give me a double," she replied with a smile.

"Oooh, you're a brave one." Thelma worked quickly, scooping ice cream and adding dollops of strawberry, chocolate and pineapple sauce to a boat that was over-flowing. She'd worked behind this counter for as long as Rachelle could remember, and Rachelle and Carlie had spent many a Saturday afternoon sitting on these worn stools, devouring French fries, hot-fudge sundaes and sodas until they were gorged.

"I heard you saw Weldon," Thelma said as she set the drink and ice cream in front of Rachelle.

"He told you that I asked for Carlie's address."

"Mmm." Thelma wiped her hands on a towel. "I'll write it down for ya. She's in Alaska, takin' pictures."

"So she really gave up modeling?"

"Quite a while ago." Thelma's lips tightened at the corners. "She ran into some trouble and she's back on the other side of the camera now. Like she was in high school."

"But she's all right?" Rachelle asked, sensing that there was more to the story.

"She's fine. Comin' home later in the summer. She sure would love to see you." Thelma scribbled Carlie's address on the back of a receipt and ripped it off, hand-ing the information to Rachelle.

"I'll write her. Maybe we can get together," Rachelle said. She wanted to ask more questions about Carlie, but didn't get a chance. The counter started to fill up, and Thelma and the other waitress, a girl of about nineteen, were busy. Rachelle finished half her banana split and wondered how she could have eaten a whole one when she was a teenager.

She'd finished her drink and left money on the counter when Thelma spied her and took off her apron, announcing to the other waitress that she was taking a short break. She grabbed her sweater and walked with Rachelle through the old oak-and-glass door of the pharmacy. Outside, on the sidewalk, she said, "I know you're getting a lot of flak from everyone around here, but I want you to know that I'm in your corner—and in Jackson Moore's, as well. He got a bum rap way back—he didn't have anything to do with killing that boy."

"I think you're the only person in town who feels that way."

"It's simple really. Jackson had nothing to gain by murdering Roy Fitzpatrick. If you ask me, and mind you no one around here wants my opinion, but I think it was someone else who held a grudge against him—someone with a bone to pick or a lot to gain." She glanced nervously at the plate-glass window of the drugstore. "I know my opinion isn't popular, but it's the way I feel, the way Carlie feels."

"Thanks. It's good to know we're not completely alone."

"Yes, but you just be careful. You and Jackson bein' here has stirred up a lot of folks who'd like to pretend that the whole mess never happened. And this town, God love it, can be vindictive. I've lived here all my life and I love Gold Creek, but sometimes…well, sometimes the town can turn on ya. It happened to Carlie, you know."

Rachelle's mother had once told her that Carlie had

left town suddenly, after one of the Powell boys, Kevin, had committed suicide. Some people claimed he took his life because of her; others said he was depressed because of money problems. But Carlie's name had been blackened, as had Jackson's.

"When Carlie calls, tell her I want to see her," Rachelle said, her fingers tightening over her package as she dashed across the street.

TIMMS WAS WAITING FOR HIM in the lobby of his hotel. The tiny man sat, eyeing the door. A cigarette was burning in the ashtray on the table next to his chair. He stood when Jackson swung through the lobby. "I thought we should talk in person."

Something was up. Something big. The little man was nervous and he looked as if he wanted desperately to hide.

"Come on." Jackson checked his messages and with Timms in tow, took the stairs. He couldn't imagine what had set the P.I. on edge, but maybe this whole ordeal was coming to a close. He hoped so. Because, for the first time in twelve years, he really didn't give a damn. Sure, he'd like to clear his name, but now he had another purpose in life, another reason to live.

Rachelle was going to be his wife. He couldn't believe it. Jackson Moore, the self-confessed bachelor, the bad boy of Gold Creek was going to settle down with one woman. He couldn't help smiling. No matter what Timms was going to tell him, it wouldn't compare with the emotional high he'd been on since yesterday. They walked down the short hall, with Timms nervously looking over his shoulder as Jackson inserted the key in the door.

Once inside, Timms locked the door behind them,

tossed his jacket over the back of a chair and wiped the sweat from his brow.

"What's up?" Jackson asked.

The small man met his gaze. "Sit down, Moore," he suggested, kicking out a chair. "I think I've found the key to the Fitzpatrick case."

RACHELLE'S MOTHER COLLAPSED into a kitchen chair. "You're not serious," she said, disbelieving.

"Yes, Mom, I am. I'm going to marry Jackson."

Heather smiled. "Well, I think it's a wonderful idea."

Ellen slashed her youngest daughter a horrified look. "You've certainly changed your tune."

"I met Jackson," Heather said, "and...well, I saw how Rachelle was around him. Mom, it's so obvious they love each other." She winked at her sister and Rachelle smothered a smile. "I think Rachelle should follow her heart, do what she *feels* is best."

"You always were an incurable romantic," Ellen whispered, reaching around the counter and pulling out the drawer where she kept her carton of cigarettes. "But you—" she looked at Rachelle beseechingly "—I always thought you had more sense."

"I love him," Rachelle said.

"Love," Ellen muttered in a puff of blue smoke. "What's love got to do with anything? I loved your father and he left me for a younger woman. And Harold... Well, love didn't much enter into it."

Heather touched their mother lightly on the shoulder. "You're just feeling a little down, right now, Mom. Things'll get better."

Ellen managed a smile, and Adam climbed onto the chair next to hers, happily walking his toy dinosaur around a bowl of cut flowers. "Well, at least we've got you, eh, baby?" Ellen said, brightening a bit as she ruffled Adam's hair.

He wrinkled his nose. "Am *not* a baby."

"Oh, right." Ellen laughed, and cocked her head in the boy's direction as she looked at Rachelle. "Well, maybe if you and Jackson can give me a couple more grandkids, I'll come around."

Heather bit her lower lip and looked as if she were about to cry. She turned to the window quickly. "Sure. Rachelle and Jackson can have a dozen children," she said with forced cheeriness.

Rachelle stared at her sister and was about to say something when the phone rang and Heather reached for the receiver.

She left a few minutes later. Climbing into her car and smiled inwardly, Rachelle let her thoughts wander.

WITHOUT REALLY THINKING, Rachelle turned north on the main road and headed toward Whitefire Lake, toward the Fitzpatrick summer estate. The last time she'd been there, with Jackson, she was walking an emotional tightrope, but today her mind was clear. Maybe she could sort out the truth by facing the past.

Knowing she couldn't be defeated, she smiled as she passed the sawmill. The day shift was just getting off and she spied Erik Patton as he headed for his pickup. Erik Patton and Scott McDonald, Melanie Patton and Laura Chandler Fitzpatrick, Thomas and June Fitzpatrick, Amanda Gray and Brian Fitzpatrick; names and faces swam before her eyes. Someone, probably one of those closest to Roy, knew what had happened to him. And Rachelle was determined to find out the truth.

TIMMS LIT A CIGARETTE AND slid a slim manila folder across the small table in Jackson's hotel room.

"Does this tell me who killed Roy?" he asked.

Timms drew hard on his cigarette. "I don't think so."

Jackson was irritated. "Then why're you here?"

"Just read the material, man."

Grumbling, Jackson opened the file folder and saw his mother's name on the first page. "What the hell is this?" he demanded, but the detective slid his gaze to the window.

"I didn't ask you to check into my mom."

"Read it."

The dead tone in the little man's voice convinced him that he had no choice, but as he read, Jackson felt as if red-hot coals had set fire to his gut; a burning sensation started in the pit of his stomach and seared his nerves. "No," he mouthed, reading still further, learning the secrets of his birth and his mother's betrayal. Before he was through, he crumpled the report in one huge fist and banged his hand on the table. "Where did you get this garbage?" he ground out, dropping the report and grabbing the investigator by his collar.

"It's the truth, I swear."

"Like hell. This is more of Fitzpatrick's filthy lies. That's all." Jackson's eyes burned with a cold fire. "Now, either you've been paid off, are lying or are the most pathetic excuse for a detective that I've ever seen!"

Timms's eyes bulged, but he didn't back down. "Thomas Fitzpatrick's your old man."

"Like hell!" Jackson gave the man a shake.

"Why would I lie?" Timms looked desperate.

"For money!"

"Why would Fitzpatrick pay me?"

"To get you off his case—"

"No way!" He reached to the table and fumbled for

the file folder, turning it open to the last page. "It's all here, Moore. See for yourself."

Jackson, still holding Timms by the shirtfront, slid a glance at the open folder. A notarized copy of his birth certificate was there and the name under the slot for Father was listed as: Thomas Fitzpatrick.

"It's a fake! I've seen my records! When I was in the navy..." he argued, though he felt his confidence begin to waver while his stomach roiled.

"This one is before the other was changed," Timms said, his voice tight.

Jackson slowly let the other man go. His gaze was fixed to the old copy and the letters spelling out Thomas Fitzpatrick as his father. A thousand emotions screamed through him—hate, betrayal, disbelief...denial. No way would his mother have slept with Fitzpatrick! No damned way! He rubbed his forehead and felt the beads of sweat that had collected on his brow. Matt Belmont was his father! Matt Belmont! He'd died before he could marry Sandra! The checks from the navy...

His gaze dropped to the file again and Timms flipped the page. Another copy. This time of a check made payable to Sandra Moore for five thousand dollars. The signature on the check was flamboyant and belonged to Thomas Fitzpatrick.

"Your mom got one of these every six months," Timms explained. "There are more copies—"

Jackson shoved the file off the desk. This couldn't be happening! There had to be some mistake! No way could that monster, that vile, hypocritical excuse of a man, be his father! It just couldn't be! "You made a mistake!"

"No way."

"I won't believe it!"

"Then don't. You don't have to believe me, but you

can ask your mother. You know, she and Fitzpatrick went way back!"

Flashes of memory, like bolts of lightning, seared through his brain. Sandra Moore had gone to school with Thomas Fitzpatrick, she had been able to get a job at the logging company whenever she needed one and he had been at her side when Jackson had been involved in the accident while setting chokers for Fitzpatrick Logging. Was it possible? His head throbbed. Still he wouldn't believe the damning evidence.

"Why do you think Roy hated you so much?" Timms asked, and the bottom of Jackson's world fell away as the truth hit him with the force of an avalanche. "He knew. He found out when he was in his early teens and from that point on, he took it out on you."

"Oh, God," Jackson whispered, hating the truth, hating the fact that he was spawned by a man he detested, hating the world.

"Look, Fitzpatrick probably would've paid me big bucks to keep my mouth shut, but you've been straight with me and I figured you deserved the truth." The private investigator reached for his jacket. "There are a lot of secrets in this town, Moore. I don't know if you want to find out anything else."

Jackson sat on the edge of the bed, his fists curled at his sides. "Who killed Roy?"

"I don't know," Timms admitted, "but if I were you, I'd start with the man with all the answers."

"Fitzpatrick."

"Bingo."

THE GATES TO THE FITZPATRICK summer house were locked and Rachelle wasn't about to try to break them down or climb the wall surrounding the estate. Instead, she drove around the lake to the north shore marina and rented a boat. Clouds had gathered, blocking out the sun, and the wind had picked up, but she slid into the small craft, sat at the stern, her hand on the throttle. The little boat chugged across the choppy water and the Fitzpatrick home came into view, imposing and grand, though in need of some repair.

Rachelle's heart began to knock as she pulled alongside the dock and threw the anchoring line over a post. She walked up the slippery pier and found the path leading to the gazebo. Her heart nearly stopped. This was where it all began, she realized, her throat suddenly like sandpaper. Here was where Roy used Laura, then attacked Rachelle.

She closed her eyes and imagined the laughter and music filtering from the house, smelled the fear that had held her captive.

She walked up the two short steps to the gazebo and gazed at the bench where Roy had attacked her. If it hadn't been for Jackson coming to her rescue, what would have happened?

It took all her fortitude to sit on that bench, all her courage not to run back to the boat and leave this miserable place with its monstrous memories behind. But she, too, had to confront the past, just as did Jackson, in order that they could start over and find a future untarnished.

The wood felt rough beneath her fingers and the pine trees seemed dark and foreboding. What happened that night? What happened? Why had someone killed Roy? Was it because of her?

She didn't think so.

Erik Patton held a grudge against his friend, and he'd been adamant about Rachelle leaving the past alone. But would he have killed Roy? Because of his sister?

And Melanie—could she harbor a grudge against the Fitzpatricks and then work for Thomas?

And what about Thomas and the whole Fitzpatrick clan? Surely they wouldn't kill their firstborn son—the boy who was groomed to inherit everything, their favorite....

The thought hit her like a lightning bolt. Roy had been the golden boy—the crown prince. Brian and his sister, Toni, had been their other "children," neither one better than the other, neither one coming close to Roy, neither one quite good enough in their father's eyes.

Rachelle swallowed hard. The answer was Brian. He inherited everything when Roy died—including Laura. He became his father's favorite. And it was rumored that he was running the logging company into the ground.

Rachelle with her reporter's instincts guessed that if Brian hadn't killed his brother, he had a good idea who had, at least better than anyone else.

So it was time to pay him a visit. She thought about being frightened, but wasn't. She'd known Brian for most of her life and believed, that confronted with the truth, he'd either lie or break down. He wouldn't resort to violence.


JACKSON'S FIST THUNDERED against the door of the Fitzpatrick house. "Fitzpatrick!" he yelled, pounding all the harder. His hand ached, probably bruised, but he didn't care. The pain in his hand didn't compare with the agony cutting his soul. "Fitzpatrick!"

The door opened suddenly and Thomas's wife stood on the other side of the threshold. "What do you want?" she asked, her skin nearly translucent.

"To see the old man."

"He's not here."

Jackson didn't have time for games. "I checked at the office. Melanie Patton said he was at home. Now some-one's lying. I'm guessing it's you."

June's lips compressed into a line of pure hatred. "Leave us alone! Haven't you caused this family enough grief?"

"Not by a long shot."

"My son's dead—"

"And I didn't do it," Jackson said beneath his breath, "but you know that, don't you?" He saw a flicker of fear in her cold blue eyes. "You just wanted to use me as a scapegoat, to make sure that I was out of your life."

"Oh, God," she whispered, her hand flying to her throat.

"That's right, *Mrs. Fitzpatrick*. I know about your hus-band and my mother and if it makes you feel any better, I don't like it any more than you do. But I think it's time he and I had a chat."

"He's not here," she said staunchly, and to her horror, Jackson brushed his way past her and walked through the house. "You have no right!" she screamed after him. "No right!" A maid, standing in the hallway, took one look at the situation and mumbled something in Spanish. "I'll call the police!" June said, reaching for the phone.

"Go right ahead."

"I'm not joking—"

"Neither am I." He spun and, towering over her, felt a wash of pity for the woman who had vowed to stick by Thomas Fitzpatrick in good times and in bad. "Call the police. Tell them I'm trespassing. And I'll tell them I'm Tommy's long-lost bastard."

Tears welled in her eyes and he felt a jab of empathy for the woman who had wanted more than anything in the world for him to be convicted of a murder he hadn't

committed. It would have made things so much tidier.
"Go to hell," she whispered, visibly shaking.

"Don't worry, lady, I'm there." He stormed through
the rooms, found no one but a couple of servants and,
convinced the old man had taken off, turned on June.
"Where is he?"

"I don't know!"

"Tell me."

"I don't know," she repeated, and a triumphant gleam
lighted her cold eyes.

"Then I'll find him myself." Jackson strode out of
the house and climbed on his bike just as the first few
drops of rain splattered from the sky. He barely noticed
the drizzle sliding down his collar or the rain-washed
streets. All he cared about was confronting his father—
his lying scum of a father—with the truth!

"RACHELLE!" LAURA STOOD ON the other side of the door
and for a second she resembled the girl who had once
been Rachelle's friend. How had they grown so far apart?
"I don't think you should be here."

"I want to speak with Brian."

Laura was instantly wary. "Why?"

"Because I think he knows who killed his brother."

Laura tried to speak, failed and finally, though her
eyes bore a desperate sadness, let the door open. "Brian
doesn't know anything," she said, but her heart wasn't
in it.

"Do you?"

"Only that Jackson's the culprit."

"We both know that's a lie."

Laura led the way into the house, through the marble-
floored foyer to the living room, a stark room that reminded Rachelle of an arctic winter. Only a few splashes

of color—bloodred and ebony—gave any depth to the interior. Laura opened a cabinet and found a glass. "Would you like a drink?"

"No, thanks."

Lifting the lid of an ice bucket, Laura found the tongs and carefully dropped a couple of cubes into two glasses. Ignoring Rachelle's request, she poured them each a healthy portion of Scotch. With an inward shudder, she handed one glass to Rachelle and sipped from the second. "Brian doesn't know anything about Roy's death."

"You're sure?" Rachelle guessed Laura was lying.

"Absolutely. He's convinced that Jackson is guilty. Everyone in the family thinks so."

"They're wrong."

"Oh, Rachelle, why don't you give up on this? Jackson got off, didn't he? So what does it matter?"

"It matters a lot."

The back door opened, and Laura jumped. Her drink sloshed onto her slacks and dripped onto the couch. "Damn."

"Laura?" Brian's voice fairly boomed through the house. "You home?"

"In the living room," Laura called back, her fingers fluttering nervously to her throat. "Rachelle Tremont's here—"

"Damn!" Brian burst into the room, his tie loosened, his expression hard. "I thought we were through with you."

Rachelle decided to get right to the point. "I think you killed your brother."

"I—I—what?" he stammered, stopping at the landing two steps above the sunken living room. His father joined him there and Rachelle's heart dropped.

"You think what, Miss Tremont?" Thomas demanded, his eyes slitted.

This was no time to back down. "I think Brian killed Roy—"

Laura's hand was on Rachelle's sleeve. "You're wrong."

"I think he killed him, took his place, inherited his position and his girlfriend and began running the company right into the ground."

"That's crazy!" Brian protested.

Thomas didn't say a word.

"Dad...Dad, you don't believe that I—" Brian swiped at the sweat on his forehead. "Good God, you think I would kill my own brother?" His voice came out in a squeak. He looked at Laura and worked his way to the bar where he poured himself a drink.

"Of course he doesn't," Laura said, but her confident smile faltered and her skin had turned white as milk. "This is all so ridiculous. Rachelle, I don't know what you think you're doing here, but you'd better leave before I call the police—"

A pounding on the front door echoed through the house. "Now what?" Laura asked, but seemed relieved to leave the room. A few seconds later, Jackson, his hair wild, his eyes gleaming with a furious flame, strode into the room.

"You miserable, lying son of a bitch," he growled at the sight of Thomas Fitzpatrick. Lunging at the man, he grabbed the lapels of Fitzpatrick's jacket and nearly ripped the cloth as his fingers clenched in the soft weave.

"What the hell's going on?" Brian asked.

"Stay out of this, *brother*," Jackson said with a sneer, and Thomas turned a shade of gray that looked positively unhealthy.

"I don't know what you're talking about—"

"Save it, Fitzpatrick. Save it for your yes men and your gofers and your legitimate children."

"Brother?" Brian repeated, and the back of his neck burned red.

"Oh, no," Rachelle whispered, and everyone in the room went quiet. The air was charged as Jackson glared at the man who had sired him. Standing there, eye-to-eye, Rachelle saw the resemblance and felt the hatred flowing between the two men. Her heart wept for Jackson. If this were true. If Thomas Fitzpatrick were his father...

"I don't understand," Laura whispered, but Brian swore loudly and drained his drink.

"You tried to pin Roy's murder on me so that you could get rid of me once and for all." Jackson released Thomas with a shove and looked disdainfully down at the man who hadn't claimed him. "You're the poorest excuse for a father I've ever seen."

"Now wait a minute—" Brian cut in.

"Shut up!" Jackson turned on him. "And you—you're no better. My guess is you know who killed Roy or you did it yourself. No one else gained from his death. Only you."

Brian visibly shook. He cast his wife a pleading look. "I didn't do it."

"Then who did?"

"No—" Laura cried as Brian pointed a finger in her direction. "Please, no—"

"*You?*" Thomas roared, pain ripping through him. "You killed my boy?"

"It was an accident," Laura said, tears streaming from her eyes. She backed up until her buttocks met the glass of the French door.

"An accident?" Thomas repeated, his voice cracking, his eyes moving from Laura to Brian. "And *you knew?*"

"No, Dad, I swear—"

"Liar!" Laura cried, tears streaming down his face. "Roy…he…oh, God, he and I made love…and then, and then, he…he told me to get Rachelle. That he needed a real woman…."

Rachelle was thunderstruck. She couldn't speak, she could hardly believe the confession that was coming from Laura's mouth.

"I…I ran back into the house and Carlie helped me clean up. Rachelle went to get my purse and that's when Roy attacked her—"

"You don't have to say anything more," Brian said. "We can get an attorney—"

She laughed bitterly through her tears. "Why? To save your hide?" The animosity between them throbbed through the room. "Later, after Roy's fight with Jackson, I left Carlie to find him, to try to patch things up. He was near the lake, and could barely stand up. He'd had too much to drink and the fight had taken a lot out of him. We argued. He called me horrible names," she said, her voice hardly more than a whisper, her gaze focused on the floor, "then we began to fight. We struggled and I pushed him down. He hit his head on something under the water. I tried to pull him up, but he sank and he wouldn't breathe and I got scared and…and…" She took a deep breath. "…And that's when I ran into Brian. He checked Roy out, knew he was dead and promised that he'd take care of me, that I wouldn't go to jail for killing him, that everything would be all right."

Thomas was stunned. His skin was still a pasty gray. Jackson didn't move. His anger seemed to have ebbed but his disgust at Laura's story showed on his features.

Laura appeared resigned, but Brian was still trying to set things right.

"It was an accident. Laura didn't mean to—"

"You should have come forward—told the police," Thomas said, his eyes filled with bitter disappointment.

"But Laura could've been charged with murder—"

"And instead, Jackson was," Thomas said, his voice a low whisper.

"Dad, you've got to understand, Laura and I—we did what we thought was best."

"What *you* thought was best," Laura clarified. "*I* wanted to go to the police. But you wouldn't let me and you held it over my head for twelve years. And why? Because you wanted to use me just like Roy did! It gave you a thrill that I'd been Roy's lover—"

"That's enough!" Brian raged.

But Laura wasn't through. "Problem was, I got pregnant and you couldn't just throw me away for someone else. You were stuck with me!" More tears streamed from her eyes, streaking her mascara as she sobbed, turned and walked out the door to stand on the veranda. Brian walked out and put his arm around her slim shoulders, but she shrugged his hand off and stepped away from him.

Thomas, a beaten man, fell onto the soft cushions of the couch. "I didn't know," he said, his eyes red, his prideful jaw still set as he stared up at his bastard child. "I didn't know who killed Roy."

"But you knew I was your son."

"Yes." He looked out the window, unseeing. "I loved your mother, you know."

"But you married someone else. Someone with money. Someone with social status. Someone respectable."

"I won't apologize for my mistakes," he said, "but I

took care of your mother in my own way, and my own family suffered."

"And I was almost hanged for a murder I didn't commit."

"I wouldn't have let it come to that," Thomas returned.

"Your lawyers, your money, your friends in the sheriff's department—"

"Couldn't build a case against you, could they? Nor did they rig the evidence and railroad you into a conviction, did they?" His clear eyes met his son's. "If you believe nothing else, believe that I would never have let you go to jail for a crime you didn't commit, but you have to remember, I, along with the rest of the town, didn't know the facts."

"And your wife wanted me wiped out of her perfect life."

"Yes."

"And what does she say about this?"

Thomas shook his head. "She accused me of not trying hard enough to send you to prison."

"Well, now she has her answers. Her truth. And she has to live with it."

"So do I," Thomas said. "If it's any consolation, I've already had a trust deed drawn up that assures you of your part of the estate. It's in my office—"

With cold assessing eyes, Jackson scanned the man who had sired him.

"I know it doesn't make up for everything," Thomas said, his chin inching upward. "But you are my son—"

"Never! And as for your damned trust deed, you can take it with you to hell!" Jackson's neck burned scarlet. "And just for the record, don't ever, *ever* call me 'son' again and I won't bother calling you 'dad.'"

Jackson stormed out of the house and Rachelle followed him. His motorcycle was parked next to her car and he kicked at the bike's tire. "Well, now we know the truth, don't we?" he muttered, glaring up at the dark sky and letting the rain wash his face.

"You're absolved of Roy's murder."

"And ended up being Thomas's son. I wonder which is worse."

"Come on," she said. "Take me for a ride, Jackson."

He hesitated.

"Please." She touched his shoulder, felt the wet leather. "I love you."

He smiled then, but the smile was filled with pain. "You mean you'd climb on a bike with a Fitzpatrick?"

"I don't care if your name is Benedict Arnold, Counselor. You're *not* a Fitzpatrick."

"Amen." He didn't laugh, but some of the lines of strain left his features. He climbed on the bike and she settled into the seat behind him.

With a powerful kick, he started the bike. He ripped through the gears, leaving the Fitzpatricks and all their selfish deeds behind.

Rachelle held him tight. The wind screamed past, catching in her hair, bringing tears to her eyes. She buried her face in his jacket, smelling the leather and racing wind and knowing she belonged beside him forever.

THAT NIGHT, JACKSON MADE love to her with a desperation that nearly tore her heart in two.

"I love you," he told her well into the night, holding her close and claiming her for his own. "Don't ever leave me."

"Never," she promised, snuggling close to him.

Before dawn, he woke her up with soft kisses and told

her to put on her clothes. In the cool morning, they drove to Whitefire Lake where they made love again.

As the sun climbed above the hills, streaking the sky with golden light, the mists of the lake rose like ghosts from the past. Rachelle smiled as she remembered the old Native American tale. Jackson dipped his hand into the water and held it to Rachelle's lips. "Forever," he whispered, kissing her cheek as the water drizzled through his fingers.

"Forever," she agreed with a smile as she pledged her life, and her love, to the bad boy of Gold Creek.

* * * * *

# HE'S JUST A COWBOY

# PROLOGUE

*Gold Creek, California*
*The Present*

## PROLOGUE

*SOME MEN YOU NEVER forget.*

Heather Leonetti parked her Mercedes beneath a deep green canopy of pine branches. Her head pounded and her heart beat an icy tempo. Through the windshield, she stared at the calm waters of Whitefire Lake and wondered how she would find the strength to undo the string of lies that had started six years before—lies she hadn't meant to utter, lies that weren't supposed to hurt anyone, lies that had her so bound, she didn't know if she could untangle them.

Her mother had said it all, years ago. "The trouble with lyin' is, once you start, you never can seem to stop. Your father, for example. Just one lie after another, one Jezebel of a woman after the next...."

Heather closed her eyes and rubbed her temples. Soon her mother would know the truth, as would everyone in Gold Creek. As would Turner.

She had to tell him first. He deserved to know. Too late, she realized. He should have known six years before. She should have found a way to reach him, to let him know that he had become a father. Instead, after a few feeble attempts to reach him, she'd taken the easy way out. And now, Adam, her son, her reason for living, was paying. It just wasn't fair.

Tears collected behind her eyes and clogged her throat, but she wouldn't give in to the pain. Not yet. Not while there was hope. She squeezed her eyes shut for a minute and sent up a prayer for strength. Somehow she had to undo all the wrongs; somehow she had to give her boy a chance to live a normal life. And Turner might be the answer. Although the horrid disease was now in remission and the doctors seemed to think that Adam had as good a chance as any for beating leukemia, Heather was scared to death...as she had been for nearly two years. It was time to face Turner.

Gritting her teeth, she forced her eyes open and knew she had to face Turner again.

*Some men you never forget.* Turner Brooks was that kind of man—all bristle and gruffness with brown hair streaked with gold, a rugged profile too cynical for his years and eyes that saw far too much. A cowboy. A rodeo rider. A penniless no-good, as her mother would say.

Heather hadn't seen him in six years. She couldn't imagine his reaction when she showed up on his doorstep, trying to undo those cloying lies, and begging for his help. She knew that he hadn't returned her calls, that her letter had gone unanswered. He obviously didn't want her to be a part of his life. But he couldn't reject his son.

Or could he?

Heather's heart cracked, because she didn't really know the man who was her son's father, had barely known him six years before.

"Help me," she whispered, refusing to break down. Pocketing her keys, she climbed out of the car and left the door ajar. A quiet bell reminded her that she should close and lock the Mercedes, but she didn't care. Pine needles muted her footsteps as she stuffed her hands into the pockets of her jacket and walked the short distance to the shore.

From the boughs overhead a hidden squirrel scolded

brashly and a flock of quail rose in a thunder of feathers into the thin fog. The lake was quiet; there were only a few fishing boats in the misty dawn. Heather was reminded of the old legend about the waters of Whitefire Lake as she crouched down among the sun-bleached stones of the bank and ran her fingers through the cool depths. Her left hand mocked her. Naked, stripped of her diamonds when she and Dennis were divorced nearly two years before, it waved ghostlike beneath the clear surface.

She sent up a silent prayer for her son, then skimmed a handful of the lake water and drizzled it against her lips. She'd been greedy in the past and she'd taken too much from life—too much for granted. Her expensive car, her house in San Francisco, her studio and all her clothes and jewels meant nothing to her now. All that mattered was Adam.

She didn't really believe in the legend of the lake, but she was willing to try anything, *anything,* to save her son's life.

Even if it meant confronting Turner.

She shivered, feeling a tiny icicle of dread against her spine. As she stared into the clear waters of Whitefire Lake, she remembered the summer six years ago so clearly, it was almost as if she were still eighteen and working at the Lazy K Ranch....

# BOOK ONE

*Lazy K Ranch, California*
*Six Years Earlier*

# CHAPTER ONE

THE AIR WAS THICK AND SULTRY, filled with horseflies and bees that buzzed around Heather's head as she shook the old rag rug. Dinner was long over and the guests of the Lazy K had broken into groups. Some had retired early, others were learning to play the guitar in the main hall and still others were involved in games of checkers or poker in the dining room. Laughter and music spilled from the windows, floating on a thin evening breeze.

Every bone in Heather's body ached from the twelve-hour days she worked in the kitchen. Her feet were swollen and she smelled as bad as some of the ranch hands. Deep down, she knew she wasn't cut out for ranch life, and yet here she was, kitchen maid at an obscure dude ranch in the foothills of the Siskiyou Mountains. Well, things could be worse. She could be back in Gold Creek.

Shuddering at the thought of the sleepy little town where she'd been born and raised, she stared at the distant hills. There were too many painful memories in Gold Creek for her to ever want to stay there. Even though some families like the Fitzpatricks and Monroes seemed to spawn generation after generation of citizens of Gold Creek, Heather wasn't planning on putting her roots down in a town so small...so full of gossip.

Her family, the Tremonts, had been the subject of the Gold Creek gossip mill for years. First there had been her father and his affair with a younger woman. Eventually her parents had divorced, her mother bitter and unhappy to this day, her father involved with his new young wife. And then there had been the incident involving Heather's sister, Rachelle, and the boy she'd been involved with— Jackson Moore.

Heather remembered all too vividly some of her mother's "friends" and how they'd whispered just loud enough so that Heather could catch a few of the key words. "...Never believe...all their hopes on that one, you know...no scholarship now...so hard on Ellen. Poor woman. First that no-good skirt-chasing husband and now this...and the younger one doesn't have a lick of sense...if there's a God in heaven *that* one will marry the Leonetti boy and give her mother some peace!"

Heather's cheeks had burned as she'd heard the wagging tongues in the checkout line at the Safeway store, in the dining area of the Buckeye Restaurant and Lounge, and even on the porch of the church after services. There was no way she was going to spend the rest of her life trapped in Gold Creek!

But ranch life? It wasn't a lot better. Though she planned on staying only for the summer. Only until she had enough money to enroll in art school. Only so that she didn't turn out to be one of those weak women who marry a man for his money, to get what she wanted. Only so she didn't feel compelled to marry Dennis Leonetti, son of one of the wealthiest bankers in Northern California.

Heather tossed the old rag rug over the top rail of the fence and stared across the vast acres of the Lazy K. Horses gathered in the shade of one lone pine tree, their tails switching at bothersome flies, their coats dull from rolling in the dusty corral. Sorrels, bays, chestnuts and one single white gelding huddled together, picking at a few dry blades of grass or stomping clouds of dust.

A hazy sun hovered over the ridge of mountains to the west, and she spied a lone rider upon the ridge—one of the ranch hands, no doubt. Squinting and shading her eyes with her hand, she tried to figure out which of the hands had chosen a solitary ride along Devil's Ridge. He was tall and wide-shouldered, though his broad chest angled to a slim waist. Against the blaze of a Western sunset, he sat comfortably in the saddle—as if he'd been born to ride a horse. She could see only his silhouette, and try as she would, she couldn't recognize him. Her mind clicked off the cowboys she'd met, but none of them seemed as natural in the saddle as this man.

A breath of wind tugged at her hair and caused goose bumps to rise on her skin as the stranger twisted in the saddle and seemed to look straight down at her. But that was impossible. He was much too far away. Nonetheless, her heart leapt to her throat and she couldn't help wondering who he was.

He kicked his mount and disappeared into the forest, leaving Heather with the impression that he hadn't even existed, that he was just a figment of her healthy and romantic imagination.

Her palms had begun to sweat. Nervously she wiped her hands down the front of her apron.

"Heather—you about ready to help clean this kitchen?" Mazie's crowlike voice cawed through the open window of the ranch house.

Heather jumped. Guiltily she yanked the rug off the fence and shook the blasted thing frantically, as if the fabric were infested with snakes. Dust swirled upward and caught in her throat. She coughed and sputtered and beat the life out of the rug.

"You hear me, girl?"

"In a minute...." Heather called over her shoulder. "I'll be right there."

"Well, mind that you git in here afore midnight, y'hear?" Mazie insisted, mumbling something about city girls more interested in cowboys than in hard work. She slammed the window shut so hard the panes rattled.

Swiping at her sweaty forehead, Heather hauled the dusty rug back to the ranch house. She hurried up the steps, through the long back porch and into the kitchen where other girls were scouring pots and pans, washing down the floor and scrubbing the counters with disinfectant. No dirt dared linger in Mazie Fenn's kitchen!

"'Bout time you got back here. Why don't you take care of the leftovers—take those pails onto the back porch for Seth's pigs," Mazie suggested. Seth Lassiter was one of the cowboys who worked at the Lazy K during the day, but lived on his own place where he raised pigs and his own small herd of cattle.

Jill, a redheaded waitress who was one of Heather's roommates, smothered a smile as she glanced at the two heaping buckets of slop. Carrying out the heavy pails was one of the worst jobs on the ranch, and it tickled her that Heather seemed to always inherit the job. Jill bit her lip to keep from giggling, then threw her shoulders into her own work of mopping the yellowed linoleum until it gleamed.

Heather gathered the heavy buckets of milk, corn bread, potatoes and anything else that was edible but for one reason or the other hadn't been consumed by the guests and staff of the ranch. Without spilling a drop, she hoisted both pails to the porch and told herself not to linger, though she couldn't help staring at the ridge where she'd seen the lone rider.

All her life her mother had accused her of dreaming romantic fantasies, of being "boy crazy," of living in an unreal world of heroes and heroines and everlasting love. Her older sister, Rachelle, had been the practical nose-to-the-grindstone type, and time and time again their mother had shaken her head at Heather's belief in true love.

"If you want to fall in love, then why don't you let yourself fall for Dennis Leonetti?" Ellen had asked her often enough. "He's cute and smart and rich. What more could you want?"

Heather sometimes wondered herself. But there was something about Dennis—something calculating and cold that made her mistrust him. Why he wanted to marry her, she didn't know; she only knew that deep in her heart she didn't love him and never would. Marrying him seemed like admitting defeat or becoming a fraud or, at the very least, taking the easy way out. Heather, despite her fantasies, didn't believe that there were any free rides on this earth. She had only to look at her mother's hard life to see the truth.

"Heather?"

Drat! Mazie again. Heather couldn't afford to look lazy; she needed this job. She dashed back to the kitchen.

"I thought we lost you again," Mazie said as she lit a cigarette at the little table near the windows. "Mercy, I've never seen anyone whose head is higher in the clouds than yours!"

"I'm sorry," Heather said as she wiped the top of the stove to look busy. Most of the polishing and cleaning was done, and three girls were huddled together near the swinging doors that separated the kitchen from the dining room.

"It's all right. Your shift's over." Mazie honored Heather

with a rare smile. "Besides, you're missin' all the fun."
Taking a puff on her cigarette, she motioned to the girls
crowded around the swinging door. "The boys are back."

"The what?"

"...I told you he was gorgeous," Jill whispered loudly.
Mazie chuckled.

"They all are," another girl, Maggie, said, her eye to
the crack between the two doors. She let out a contented
sigh. "Hunks. Every one of them."

"But they're trouble," Sheryl added. She was a tall,
thin girl, who, for the past six summers, had worked at
the Lazy K. "Especially that one—" She pointed, and
Jill shook her head.

"What's going on?" Heather couldn't hide her curiosity.

"The cowboys are back for a while. Between rodeos,"
Jill explained a trifle breathlessly.

Cowboys? Heather wasn't particularly interested in
the rough-and-tumble, range-riding type of man. She
thought of Dennis, the banker's son, and he suddenly
didn't seem so bad. But dusty, grimy, outdoorsmen
smelling of tobacco and leather and horses...? Well, most
of her fantasies were a little more on the sophisticated
side.

However, she remembered the ridge rider and her
heart did a peculiar little flop. But he was a man of
her dreams, not a flesh-and-blood cowpoke. She didn't
bother peeking through the crack in the door. Instead,
to atone for her earlier idleness, she hauled the sacks of
potatoes and onions back to the pantry where she dou-
ble-checked that the plastic lids on huge tubs of sugar
and flour were secure.

Cowboys! She smiled to herself. If she were to believe the image on the silver screen, cowboys spit tobacco

juice and tromped around in filthy scraped leather boots and tattered jeans. They loved the open range as well as horses and booze and country music and loose women in tight denim skirts.

And yet there was something appealing about the cowboy myth, about a rugged man who was afraid of nothing, about a man who would die for what was right, a man who disdained city life and health clubs and sports cars.

Even Rachelle—stalwart, sane, levelheaded Rachelle— had fallen for a rogue of sorts. Jackson Moore, the reputed bad boy of Gold Creek, the boy whom everyone believed had killed Roy Fitzpatrick. Rachelle had stood up for Jackson when the whole town had wanted to lynch him; Rachelle had given him an alibi when he had desperately needed one; and Rachelle had stayed in town, bearing the disgrace and scandal of having spent the night with him, while he'd taken off, leaving her alone to face the town.

*And that short love affair had scarred her and their parents forever.*

"I'm not going to sit around and watch you make the same mistake your sister did," Ellen had told Heather as she'd nervously taken a drag from her cigarette. "And she was the levelheaded one! You, with all your fantasies and silly notions about romance…ah, well. Unfortunately, you'll learn in time." She'd stubbed out her cigarette, and concern darkened her eyes. "Just don't learn the hard way. Like Rachelle did. That no-good Moore boy used her, he did. Spent one night with her, then left town when he was accused of murder. Left her here alone to defend him and mend her broken heart." Ellen had shaken her head, her loose brown curls bobbing around her face. "You listen to me, Heather. Romance only causes heart-ache. I loved your father—was faithful to him. Lord, I had supper on the table every night at six...and what happened? Hmm? He flipped out. Wanted a 'younger model.'" Ellen scowled darkly. "Don't fool yourself with thoughts of romance. Make life easy for yourself. Marry Dennis."

Heather frowned at the memory. Closing the pantry door behind her, she crossed the kitchen and headed up the back stairs to the room she shared with the other girls. She changed quickly, stripping off her apron and uniform and sliding into a pair of shorts and a T-shirt.

Within minutes, she'd caught and saddled her favorite little mare, Nutmeg, and was riding along a dusty trail through the pines. Telling herself she needed the ride to cool off, that her interest in exploring the trails had nothing to do with the rider she'd seen, she urged Nutmeg steadily upward, through the foothills. The sun had disappeared, and a handful of stars was beginning to wink in the evening sky. For the first time that day, Heather felt free and content. Her blond hair streamed behind her, and she even hummed along to the tempo of Nutmeg's steady hoofbeats. She met no one, didn't so much as hear another horse neigh.

So much for the solitary ridge rider.... Another fantasy.

Clucking gently to the mare, Heather followed the trail that led to the river. The air was fresher there, though the drone of insects was constant. She smiled as she spied the natural pool she'd discovered, a deep hole that collected and slowed the water where the river doglegged toward the mountains.

"I deserve this," she told Nutmeg, as she slid to the ground, and without a thought to her horse, stripped quickly out of her clothes, dropping them piece by piece at the river's edge. She ran along the rocky shelf that jutted over the dark water and with a laugh, plunged into the cold depths.

Frigid. So cold she could barely breathe, the icy water engulfed her, touching every pore on her body, sending a shock wave through her system. The river sprouted from an underground spring and the water was close to freezing. She didn't care. After battling the heat of the kitchen oven and the hot summer sun all day, the cold water was refreshing. She felt alive again.

Surfacing, she swam to the far shore, feeling the tension slip from her muscles as she knifed through the water. As the sky darkened, she dived down again, touching the rocky bottom with her fingers before jetting upward and breaking the surface. Sighing happily, she tossed her hair from her eyes and nearly stopped breathing.

She wasn't alone.

A tall, rugged man stood on the shelf of rock jutting over the water's edge. Dressed in dirty jeans, scratched boots and work shirt that was unbuttoned to display a rock-hard chest, he stared down at her with eyes the color of gunmetal. His lips were thin and compressed, his tanned face angular and bladed.

Without a doubt, this was the very man she'd seen earlier riding the ridge.

Her heart nearly stopped.

Romantic fantasies fled.

She didn't know this man, didn't know what he was capable of. He could be dangerous, and from the looks of him she didn't doubt it for a moment. Though his brown hair was streaked with gold, there was something about him, something about the arrogant way he stood in front of her bespoke trouble.

He was nearly six feet or so and looked to be in his

midtwenties, and Heather wanted to crawl behind the nearest rock and hide. But, of course, it was too late. In one hand he held the reins to his mount, a huge buckskin gelding, in the other, he dangled her clothes off one long, callused finger.

Heather swallowed hard and wondered just how menacing he really was. She didn't want to find out.

"Lose something?" he asked in a lazy drawl.

She rimmed her lips with her tongue. What could she say? She was obviously naked—the clothes had to belong to her. She decided to take the offensive before things really got out of hand. "Just put them down," she said, eyeing her shorts swinging from his finger. She treaded water in the deep part of the pool, hoping he couldn't see too much of her body through the darkening ripples of the river.

"I'm not talking about these." He tossed her shorts, T-shirt, bra and panties close to the water's edge—almost within her reach.

He was playing with her! Dear God, why hadn't she told anyone where she was going? Feeling a fool and very much afraid, Heather swallowed back a lump of fright in her throat and studied him more carefully. A cowboy, no mistaking that. His Stetson was pushed back on his head, displaying a ring of grime that matted brown hair to his forehead. His jean jacket was torn and dirty, his Levi's faded and tight, his shirt, a plaid cotton that was open to display a dusting of hair on a sun-bronzed chest. He looked hot and tired and disgusted. "Your horse," he prompted, and her gaze flew to the edge of the forest where she'd left Nutmeg grazing only minutes before. The mare was nowhere in sight.

"Oh, no—"

"She's halfway back to the stables by now," he said,

and his flinty eyes showed just a flicker of amusement. "Looks like you have to hike or hitch a ride with me."

For a fleeting instant she thought he was handsome, almost sexy, in a coarse sort of way, but she didn't dwell on his looks as she was busy trying to keep herself covered.

"Don't worry about me. I'll make it back," she said, knowing that riding with him would only spell trouble.

"Will ya, now?" he drawled in a voice as rough as sandpaper.

"Yes." She eyed her clothes and prayed for the cover of darkness.

"What's your name?"

Did it matter? "Heather." Anything to get rid of him so she could fetch her clothes and get dressed.

"Hmmm. You work in the kitchen?"

"That's right." So he was one of the men the girls were fawning over.

He didn't say anything to this bit of news, just stared down at her, and she wondered at the picture she must make—pale skin beneath the dark ripples, hair wet and plastered to her head, face awash with embarrassment, white legs moving quickly as she tried to stay afloat. "Look, if you don't mind, I really could use some privacy."

A slow smile spread across his chin. "What if I do mind?"

Drat the man! Her fists curled for one frustrated second and she started to sink, her chin sliding under the water's cool surface. Sputtering, she accused, "You're no gentleman."

"And I doubt that you're much of a lady," he said, working the heel of his boot with the toe of the other.

Heather nearly jumped out of her skin. He wasn't

really thinking of diving in and joining her, was he? To her horror, he kicked off both boots, yanked off a pair of dusty socks and started pulling his arms out of the sleeves of his jacket. "Wait a minute," she said, surprised at the breathless tone of her voice.

"Wait for what?"

"Whatever it is you think you're going to do—"

He stripped his jacket and shirt from a torso as tough and lean as rawhide. There wasn't an ounce of fat on him and only a smattering of gold-brown hair that arrowed down over a tanned, hard chest and a washboard of abdominal muscles. *Lean and mean.* Even in the darkness she saw a bruise, purple and green, discoloring the skin across one shoulder. "I don't think I'm gonna do anything. I *know* I'm goin' for a swim."

"But you can't—" she cried, as his shirt and jacket fell onto the pile of boots and socks.

"Why not? I've been swimmin' here since I was ten."

"But I'm here and..."

"You won't bother me." A devilish, off-center smile flashed in the coming darkness and he didn't pause once at the waistband of his jeans. They fell away with the *pop, pop, pop* of buttons.

Heather averted her eyes. She'd never seen a naked man before, and she was certain this man wasn't a good one to start with.

"You're not the first girl to swim here with me."

"That's comforting," she said, her voice filled with sarcasm. "And I'm not a girl—"

"That's right. My mistake. You're a *lady.*"

Heather felt a tide of color wash up her neck. She was out of her element. Way out of her element. And yet she was fascinated as, from the corner of her eye, she saw him yank off his jeans and in one lithe motion, dive into the river. She caught a glimpse of white—his underwear as he dove—and that was all it took. As quickly as he was in, she was out, scrambling into her clothes.

Dear God, how had she gotten herself into this mess? One minute she was fantasizing him and the next he was there, taunting her, teasing her with his smile, playing dangerous games with his gaze.

Her hands were cold, her body wet and her clothes clung to her skin. She didn't bother with her bra or panties; she was only interested in covering up as much as possible in the shortest amount of time. Heart thundering, icy fingers fumbling, she found the tab of the zipper of her shorts just as she heard him break the surface of the water. All she wanted to do was get out and get out fast!

She started for the path.

"Leavin' so soon, darlin'?" he yelled across the rush of the river. "I didn't scare ya off, now, did I?"

*Miserable beast!*

He still thought this was a game! She tried to ignore the challenge in his words. "I was done anyway."

"Sure," he taunted.

"I was." What did it matter? *Just take off, Heather. Leave well enough alone!*

"Well, you sure as hell weren't troublin' me."

"Good. Because you troub—you bothered me."

He chuckled, deep and low. "I'll take that as a compliment."

"Take it any way you please," she threw back, not understanding the emotions that seemed to have control of her tongue. The man scared her half to death, yet she was fascinated by him. He couldn't be more than twenty-five or -six, and yet he wore the jaded cynicism of a man twice his age.

"You'd better be careful of that tongue of yours," he said and, from the corner of her eye, she saw him swim closer, his head above water, his gaze never leaving her. "Could get you into a heap of trouble."

"Thanks for the warning."

"My pleasure." Again that deep, rumbling chuckle. At her expense. He reached the ledge and threw his elbows onto the rocks, content to stretch in the water. Heather was mesmerized by his sinewy forearms as they flexed.

There was something about him that got under her skin, something irritating, like a horsefly caught under a saddle that just kept biting the horse. Though she knew she was playing with fire, she couldn't just walk away, letting him think that he'd bested her—by seeing her naked and forcing her, for propriety's sake, to leave.

A plan of revenge started to form in her heart. Oh, but was she willing to pay the price? He obviously worked at the Lazy K. If she angered him, he might make the next two months of her life miserable. But it was worth the gamble. "I didn't catch your name."

"Didn't give it to you." His gaze found hers again, and for some reason she had trouble finding her breath. "Turner Brooks."

Not just one of the cowboys. Turner Brooks was nephew to the owner of the Lazy K. A drifter who followed the rodeo circuit. A man with a past that she'd only heard snatches of. Something about his father and a woman...maybe a girlfriend... Then there were the rumors of all the hearts he'd broken over the past few years—women along the rodeo circuit waiting for his return. "What're you doing back at the Lazy K?"

"Got to work between rodeos," he said.

"Aren't you good enough to make a living out of riding broncos?" She heard the sarcasm in her voice, but he didn't seem to mind. In fact, damn him, he grinned again—that irreverent I've-seen-it-all kind of grin that caught her by surprise and made her heart beat unsteadily.

"I'm good," he said, his dark gaze moving slowly up her body and causing a tingle to spread through her limbs. "Very good."

Her throat turned to dust. She swallowed with difficulty.

"I just came here to help out and earn a little extra spending money. Hurt my shoulder a while back and it's givin' me some trouble. Thought I'd take a rest." His gaze hadn't left her face, and she felt as naked as she had in the water. Though she was dressed, she knew that she had no secrets from him; her clothes were little shield. He'd seen her completely unclothed, had his fun at her expense; now it was time to turn the tables on him. She eyed his pile of clothes, wondering how he would feel if she took his worn jeans and work shirt. As if he guessed her intent, he clucked his tongue. "Don't even think about it unless you want more trouble than you can even begin to imagine." She bit her lower lip. Stealing his jeans seemed too childish and not punishment enough. Besides, he would catch her. But not if she took his horse. What more humiliation for a cowboy than to have a mere woman steal his pride and joy? No more had the thought entered her head than she turned and caught the gelding by the reins.

"I wouldn't do that if I were you," he warned. "Sampson doesn't like people he doesn't know."

"Then I guess I'd better introduce myself," she ridiculed. She wasn't going to let him bluff her. She climbed into the saddle and kicked the big buckskin, pulling hard on the reins. In a ripple of muscles, the horse whirled and leapt forward, covering the open ground at a breakneck pace. Heather clung to his mane and leaned forward as Sampson's long strides carried her into the woods. Trees rushed by in a blur. Heart pounding madly, she prayed the gelding's hooves were sure because the forest was gloomy, the trail uneven. She felt a quick little thrill of showing up the cowboy, and yet she knew that what she'd done was dangerous. Turner would never forgive her.

She glanced over her shoulder, half expecting to find Turner, wet and naked and furious, yelling and running barefoot through the trees. But Turner didn't start hollering or giving chase, and that worried her. He didn't seem the kind of man to roll over and accept defeat so easily.

She could imagine the consternation in his gray eyes, the anger holding his features taut.

A loud, low whistle pierced the forest. Heather's skin crawled. The gelding slammed to a stop, nearly pitching her over his head.

"Hey—wait a minute," Heather whispered, giving the buckskin a quick kick.

Another whistle curdled the air and sent a shiver of dread down Heather's spine.

With a snort, Sampson wheeled and Heather was nearly thrown to the ground. She wound her fingers more tightly in the gelding's coarse mane and pulled hard on the reins with her other hand, but the stubborn rodeo horse had a mind of his own.

"No, you don't," Heather commanded, as Sampson broke into a lope and headed back to the river. Back to Turner. Back to whatever terrible punishment he intended to mete out. She could do nothing but hold on. "You miserable lump of horseflesh," she muttered, still yanking on the reins, but the gelding had the bit in his teeth and he didn't even break stride.

Damn, damn, damn and double damn! Now what? Within seconds the forest seemed to part and the river rushed before her, a night-dark swirl that cut through the canyon. Turner, dressed only in his jeans and boots, was sitting on the rocks, his face a stony mask, fury blazing like lightning in his eyes. Drops of water still clung to his hair and drizzled down his chin.

"Nice try," he said to Heather's mortification.

"You *are* a bastard."

"Just as long as I'm not a gentleman," he drawled, shoving himself to his feet and dusting his hands.

"Never."

"Good. Glad that's settled." He walked over to the gelding, and before Heather could scramble off, he'd hopped onto Sampson's broad back, wedging his thin hips between Heather's rump and the back of the saddle.

"Hey—just a minute—"

"At least I'm not a horse thief."

"It was only a prank." Heather's mind was racing and her heart pumped wildly. "Look, I'm sorry. Now, I'll walk back to the ranch—"

"Too late. We're doin' this my way," he said, clucking to Sampson and taking the reins from Heather's reluctant fingers. His arms surrounded her, his scent filled her nostrils and his breath, hot and wild, seemed to caress the damp strands of her hair. Lord, what a predicament!

Her heart was drumming so loudly, she was sure he could hear its loud tattoo. The back of her shirt, still damp, was pressed into the rock-solid wall of his chest and his legs surrounded hers, muscle for muscle, thigh to thigh, calf to calf. Worst of all, her buttocks were crushed intimately against the apex of his legs, moving rhythmically as the horse headed home. One of his hands held the reins, the other was splayed firmly over her abdomen, his thumb nearly brushing the underside of her breasts.

"I'll walk," she said again, her voice a strange whisper.

"No way."

"Then *you* walk."

"Sampson can handle us both."

*But I can't handle you!* she thought, clenching her teeth in order to keep her wild tongue silent. She'd just try to pretend that he wasn't slammed up so close to her that she could feel the tickle of chest hair through her T-shirt. She'd attempt to ignore the scents of river water mingling with musk and pine as he swayed in the saddle so intimately against her. She'd disregard the fact that his breath blew gently against the nape of her neck, causing delicious tingles to spread along her skin, and she wouldn't even think about the fact that his body was molded so closely and intimately to hers that she could scarcely breathe.

They rode in silence. The sounds of the night—the flurry of air as bats took flight, the gentle *plop* of Sampson's hooves, the drone of insects and the steady rush of the river fading in the distance—were drowned out by the rapid beat of her heart and her own ragged breathing. This was crazy! Being alone with him was dangerous and tricking him had been asking for trouble. Why, oh why, had she been so impulsive and foolish?

"Look, really, I can walk...." She glanced at him from the corner of her eye and caught the hard line of his lips.

"And have me be accused of not being a gentleman?" he replied with more than a trace of derision. "I don't think so."

"But—"

Sampson broke free of the woods, and beyond a few

dry fields the ranch loomed before them. Harsh security lamps flooded the parking lot, drenching the barns and stables in an eerie blue-white illumination, and the ranch house, two stories of sprawling night-darkened cedar, was surrounded by dusky pastureland and gently rolling hills. The windows were patches of warm golden light. The French doors were swung wide and on the back deck several couples were learning the Texas Two-step to a familiar country tune by Ricky Scaggs. Some of the soft notes floated on the breeze and reached Heather's ears.

The couples laughed and danced, and Heather wished she were anywhere else in the world than imprisoned in the saddle with this cowboy. How could she ever have thought of Turner as a romantic figure, riding alone along the ridge this afternoon?

A few animals stirred as they passed the corrals, and Heather noticed some of the ranch hands. Their boots were propped against the lowest rail of the fence, the tips of their cigarettes pinpoints of red light that burned in the night. A thin odor of smoke mingled with the dust and dry heat.

Turner rode into the main yard, and several of the cowboys, lingering near the paddock, glanced their way and sniggered softly amongst themselves.

*Great.* Just what she needed—to be branded as Turner's woman. No doubt they made an interesting sight, both half-dressed and wet, wedged tightly into the saddle.

She didn't wait for an invitation. When Sampson slowed, she swung one leg over the gelding's neck and half stumbled to the ground. Without a word, she spun and started for the back of the house.

"Aren't you gonna thank me?" Turner called.

She stopped, her hands clamped into tight little fists.

"Thank you for what?" she asked, inching her chin upward as she turned to face him again. "For humiliating me? For forcing me to ride with you against my will? Or for being a voyeur while I swam?"

"Don't flatter yourself," he said lightly, but his eyes didn't warm and his jaw remained stiff.

"Go to hell!"

"Oh, lady, I've already been," he said with a mocking laugh that rattled her insides.

Heather turned again, and without so much as a backward glance, she hurried up the back steps to the kitchen and tried not to hear Turner's hearty laughter following after her like a bad smell.

She barely got two steps into the kitchen when Mazie, seated at the small table in the corner, glanced up from balancing the kitchen's books. "Trouble?" she asked.

"No—"

"Your horse came back alone. Zeke's none too happy about that and he was worried sick about you. He was just about to send out a search party. You'd better talk to him."

"I will," Heather promised. She wanted to drop through the floor. Mortified already, she didn't need to be reminded of her carelessness with Nutmeg. "Where is he?"

"In his office," Mazie replied, staring for a second at Heather's state of dress and tangled hair before turning back to her books and chewing on the end of her pen.

Heather ran up the back steps and slid into her room. Jill was on her bed, reading some teen-idol magazine. She glanced up when Heather shut the door behind her.

"What happened to you?" she asked, eyeing Heather with a curious gleam.

"I went swimming."

"In your clothes?"

"No," Heather said managing a smile. "I just didn't have a towel to dry off."

"Heard you lost your horse."

"That's the abbreviated story." In the mirror, her reflection stared back at her. Without makeup, her hair wet and limp, she looked about twelve years old. Turner Brooks probably thought she was just a kid. *Except he's seen all of you—breasts, the triangle of hair...*

"Great," she muttered, swiping a towel from the vanity and rubbing it hard against her long blond hair.

Jill tossed her magazine aside. "So what happened? And I don't want the *Reader's Digest* condensed version."

"It's boring," Heather replied, lying a little.

"I doubt it."

Heather stripped out of her dirty clothes and stepped into clean underwear, a denim skirt and pale blue shirt. She clipped a silver belt around her waist, combed her hair into a quick ponytail and contented herself with fresh lipstick.

"Does this have anything to do with Turner Brooks?" Jill asked. She drew her knees beneath her chin and smiled knowingly up at her roommate. "I saw Turner ride out that way."

"Did you?" Heather turned her attention back to the mirror in order to hide the tide of embarrassment she felt climbing up the back of her neck.

"Isn't he something?" Jill sighed contentedly.

In the reflection, Heather saw the girl close her eyes and smile dreamily.

"He's just the kind of man I'd like to marry."

"Turner Brooks?" Heather was aghast. The same slow-

talking, sarcastic man she'd met? What kind of a husband would he make?

"God, he's beautiful."

"But there are rumors…about his past."

"I know, I know, but I don't care." Jill grinned wickedly. "Besides, a man with a past is a little more interesting, don't you think?"

"What I think is that Turner Brooks is a conceited,
self-centered jerk who—"

"So you did run into him!" Jill's eyes flew open. "Oh,
I wish I'd been there with you."

"Me, too," Heather replied under her breath. Before
Jill could say anything else, she hurried out of the room
and clambered down the stairs. She had to face Zeke and
explain that she hadn't meant to lose Nutmeg, and hope
that he wasn't too angry with her.

Zeke's office was in the front of the house and with
each step Heather felt a mounting sense of dread. She
couldn't lose this job. She just couldn't! All her dreams
of art school and escaping Gold Creek would turn to dust
if she didn't save enough money to move away from her
mother's little cottage.

Steeling herself, Heather tapped lightly on the door.

"It's open."

Mentally crossing her fingers, she entered. The room
was small and cozy. Filled with rodeo trophies, Indian
blankets and worn furniture, the office smelled of tobacco, lingering smoke and leather. Antlers of every
shape and size were mounted on the plank walls, and
sprawled in one of the cracked leather chairs in front of
the desk was none other than Turner Brooks himself. He
turned lazy eyes up at her, and Heather nearly stumbled
on the edge of the braided rug.

"Come on in," Zeke ordered, his voice softer. He was a

man few people forgot. With snowy-white hair and thick muttonchop sideburns, he was a big man—over two hundred and twenty pounds and six foot one or two. Though he was huge in comparison to Turner, Heather barely noticed the older man. All her senses were keyed in to Turner—the slant of his knowing smile, the mockery in his gray eyes, the smell of him, a scent that seemed to cling to her nostrils. "You've already met my nephew."

Turner nodded in recognition and Heather swallowed hard. "Yes. Earlier." She forced her unwilling eyes back to her boss. "Look, Mr. Kilkenny, I need to talk to you."

Zeke leaned back in his chair and the old springs creaked. "So talk."

"I mean in private."

Zeke smiled. "We got no secrets here, Heather. At the Lazy K, we're all family." He waved her into the chair near Turner's. "Sit down and tell me what's on your mind."

Balancing on the edge of a chair, Heather tried not to think about the fact that Turner was only bare inches from her, that at any moment his hand could brush hers. "I…I'm sorry about losing Nutmeg. I was careless. It won't happen again."

"No harm done," Zeke said, rubbing his chin. "Nutmeg hightailed it back here for her supper. But it could've been worse."

"I'll be more careful," Heather promised, surprised she was getting off so easy. The horses were the life and blood of the ranch, and Zeke Kilkenny had a reputation of caring more for his animals than he had for his wife of twenty-odd years.

"Well, I know you haven't been around horses much— you livin' in town and all—and you're a good worker. Mazie says you're one of the best helpers she's had in

314 HE'S JUST A COWBOY

the kitchen and she's trained more'n her share, let me tell you."

Heather could hardly believe the praise. From Mazie? The woman who single-handedly was trying to work her to an early grave?

"I could warn you off the horses, but, the way I see it, that's unnatural. Horses and men—or women—they just go together." Zeke leaned forward, and his smile was friendly. "Turner here came up with the perfect solution to our little problem."

Heather's blood ran cold. A suggestion from Turner? She tried to say something but for once her tongue tangled on itself.

"Why don't you tell Heather your idea," Zeke invited.

Turner leaned closer to her. "I thought that you might need some lessons handlin' a horse."

"I don't—"

"And Turner here's offered to teach you," Zeke cut in, so pleased he beamed. "You couldn't get a better teacher. Lord, Turner could ride before he could walk!" He chuckled at his old worn-out joke, and Heather felt as if her life were over.

She imagined the grueling lessons where Turner would take his vengeance and his pleasure in making her ride so long, she'd be sore for weeks, by having her groom every horse in the stables, by having her clean out every stall and shed on the ranch. The summer would never end. When she found her voice again, she held on to the arms of her chair in a death grip and said, "Surely Turner has more important work here—"

Zeke waved off her reasoning. "Always time to get someone in the saddle. So that's it. Starting tomorrow, right after you work your shift, you're Turner's!" He slapped the desktop and the phone jangled.

The meeting was over. Heather stood on leaden feet as Zeke picked up the receiver. Riding lessons with Turner Brooks? She'd rather die! He'd be merciless. Life as she knew it would end. She'd spend too many grueling hours with Turner the Tormenter!

"Cat got your tongue?" he asked as he followed her to the door.

"You'll regret this," she warned.

"Oh, I don't think so," he drawled with a sparkle of devilment lighting his eyes. "Matter of fact, lady, to tell you the truth—I'm lookin' forward to it!"

## CHAPTER TWO

TURNER SLAPPED HIS HAT against his thigh and dust swirled to the heavens. Why in God's name had he told Zeke he'd like to show Heather how to handle a horse? She must've made him crazy last night, because this was the worst idea he'd come up with in years! It didn't help that he hadn't slept a wink the night before. Nope. All night long he'd thought of her, how her white skin had looked in the darkening water. He'd seen her nipples, hard little buds in the frigid depths, and he'd grown hard at the sight. She'd done her best to cover up, but he'd noticed the slim length of her legs as she'd tried to tread water and cover her breasts at the same time. The sight had been comical and seductive. Had she been a different kind of woman, he'd have spent the night with her.

But Heather Tremont had been like no woman he'd ever met before. She'd been indignant when she'd spied him and when he'd tried to tease her, she'd refused to laugh. But she'd challenged him. By taking his horse. And he'd never yet come up against a challenge he hadn't taken and won.

Now, as he watched her try to keep her balance upon a high-strung gelding, he almost grinned. Served her right for keeping him up all night wondering what it would feel like to kiss her lips, to drown in her sky-blue gaze, to touch her man to woman in the most intimate of places.

He shifted, resting his back against the fence and forcing his thoughts away from his sudden arousal.

"Pull back on the reins," he said. "Let him know who's boss."

"That's the trouble," she threw back at him. "He already knows! And it's not me!"

Turner swallowed a smile. She had guts—he'd give her that. She'd blanched at the sight of Sundown, a burly sorrel with a kick that could break a man's leg, but other than inquire about Nutmeg, her usual mount, she'd climbed into the saddle and gamely tried to command a horse who was as stubborn as he was strong.

"Uh-uh. No hands on the saddle horn," he reminded her as Sundown gave a little buck of rebellion and her fingers searched frantically for any sort of purchase. "That goes for the mane, as well."

"I know, I know!" she snapped.

She pressed her legs tighter around the gelding, and Turner's eyes were drawn to the tight stretch of denim across her rump. Her waist was tiny, but her hips were round and firm, in perfect proportion to her breasts. He saw the stain of sweat striping her back and the resolute set of her mouth.

He wondered what she would taste like. Yesterday, riding so close to her, the scent of her skin had driven him mad and he'd thought long and often about pressing his lips to hers. But, so far, he hadn't gotten close enough or been stupid enough to try to kiss her.

"How long is this going to take?" she asked, yanking hard on the reins and swearing under her breath when Sundown didn't respond.

"As soon as I think you're ready to take him out of the paddock."

"Humph." She set her tiny little jaw and a gleam of

determination flared in her eyes. She worked the reins again and the gelding reared, but she hung on, refusing to be dismounted.

Turner forced his mouth to remain grim, though he wanted to smile. Crossing his arms over his chest, he settled back against the fence to enjoy the show.

Heather decided the lesson was a disaster.

While he leaned his back against the rails of the fence and watched her put her mount through his paces, she tried to stay astride Sundown, who fought the bit and pranced this way and that.

"You know, I'd work a lot better with Nutmeg," she grumbled when Sundown tried to buck her off for the third time. She managed to stay in the saddle, but only because she finally grabbed hold of the saddle horn.

"You'll never make a rodeo queen," Turner said. He shifted a piece of straw from one side of his mouth to the other.

"Oh, gee, all my dreams, down the drain," she tossed back, but laughed a little. She was hot and dirty and tired. After spending most of the day in the kitchen, she'd changed into jeans and had been astride Sundown for two hours, and her legs ached.

"You know, Heather, you might like me if you let yourself."

She nearly fell off the horse. The last thing she expected was any conversation from him about their relationship—or lack of one. "Me? Not like you? Whatever gave you that impression? Just because you invaded my privacy, forced me to ride with you and then came up with this harebrained idea of having you teach me, on *my* free time, mind you, all I wanted to know about horses but was afraid to ask, now, why would you think I didn't like you?"

A bevy of quail suddenly took flight and Sundown leapt high. Heather scrabbled for the reins and the saddle horn, but the horse shifted quickly. She pitched forward. The ground rushed up at her and she hit the dirt with her shoulder, landing hard. Pain exploded through her arm, and she sucked in her breath.

Turner was there in a second. Concern darkened his eyes as he reached to help her to her feet. "Are you okay?"

"You're the teacher," she snapped. "You tell me." But her arm throbbed and she held it against her body.

"Seriously, Heather." With a gentle touch she thought he reserved only for horses, he poked and prodded her shoulder. Eyebrows knit, he watched her reaction. "Hold your arm up, if you can."

Wincing, she forced her elbow high into the air. Like fire, pain shot through her bones. She gritted her teeth. Again his fingers touched her shoulder. "Ooh!"

"That hurt?" he asked.

"It all hurts." Especially her pride. The last thing she wanted to do was fall off in front of him. She sent Sundown a scathing look. "Idiot."

"Well, I see your sweet temper is restored," he said, and relief relaxed the hard contours of his face. For a second she was lost in his silvery gaze and her silly heart skipped a beat. His hands were warm and tender, and beneath his rough cowboy exterior Heather spied a kinder, gentler man—a man with a sense of humor and a man who did seem to care.

"Good as new," she said sarcastically, for she didn't want to glimpse into Turner's soul. It was easier to hate him than to have a current of conflicting emotions wired to her heart.

He tried to help her up, but she ignored his hand and found her feet herself. The less he touched her, the better.

"I think that'll do it for tonight."

"Oh? You're not one who believes that you have to climb right back on a horse if you fall off?"

He eyed her speculatively, his gaze searching her face, and her breath was suddenly constricted in her throat. "You enjoy putting me down, don't you?" When she didn't answer, he stepped closer and the twilight seemed to wrap around them. "What is it you've got against me, Heather?" he asked, and his hand reached upward, barely touching her chin.

"I don't have anything against you," she lied.

"Oh, yes, you do, lady, and I intend to find out just what it is." His thumb stroked the edge of her jaw and she felt as if she might collapse, so weak went her knees. Instead, she knocked his hand away.

"Don't touch me," she said, her voice breathless.

"Afraid?"

"Of you? No way."

"You're a liar, Heather Tremont," he said slowly, but didn't touch her again. "And I don't know what you're more scared of. Me or yourself." He whistled to Sundown and caught the gelding's reins in the hand that had so recently touched her skin. "You'd better go into the house, Heather, and have Mazie look at your shoulder." His lopsided grin was almost infectious. "Unless you need the paramedics, I'll see you same time, same place tomorrow."

"How long will these lessons last?" she asked, rubbing the pain from her upper arm.

His gaze focused on hers again—hot, flinty and male. With a sardonic twist of his lips, he said, "We'll keep at it for as long as it takes."

Heather's heart dropped to her stomach and she knew she was in trouble. Deep, deep trouble.

LUCKILY, HER SHOULDER WASN'T sprained. Mazie clucked her tongue, Jill was absolutely jealous that Heather was spending so much time with Turner, Maggie didn't much care, but Sheryl, the girl who'd been with the Lazy K longer than any of the others in the kitchen aside from Mazie, seemed to grow more quiet. Heather caught Sheryl staring at her several times, as if she wanted to say something, but the older girl would always quickly avert her eyes and hold her tongue. Heather didn't pay much attention.

Even with her bruised upper arm, Heather was still able to do her kitchen duties, sketch without too much pain and meet with Turner every evening. Despite telling herself that being with him was a torture, a punishment she was forced to endure, she began looking forward to her time alone with him.

They rode through the forest on trails that had been ground to dust by the hooves of horses from the Lazy K. He showed her an eagle's nest, perched high over the ridge where she'd first spotted him astride his horse all those days ago.... It seemed a lifetime now. He pointed out the spring that fed the river and let her wade in the icy shallows. They raced their horses across the dried pastureland, laughing as grasshoppers flew frantically out of their way; and they watched the sun go down, night after night, a fiery red ball that descended behind the westerly mountains and brought the purple gloaming of dusk.

Often he touched her—to show her how to hold the reins, or tighten the cinch, or guide the horse, but the impression of his fingers was always fleeting and he never showed any inclination to let his hands linger.

One night, when they were alone in the woods, standing at a bend in the trail, she felt the tension that was always between them—like a living, breathing animal that they both ignored.

He was on one knee, pointing to a fawn hidden in the undergrowth. Heather leaned forward for a better view and her breast touched his outstretched arm. He flinched a little, and the tiny deer, which had stood frozen for so many seconds, finally bolted, leaping high as if its legs were springs, and making only the slightest sound as it tore through the scrub oak and pine.

The wind died and the hot summer air stood still. Heather felt droplets of sweat between her shoulder blades, and she moved a step back as Turner stood. "I—uh, guess we scared him off," she said, her throat as dusty as the trail.

"Looks that way." He was so close, she could smell the scents of leather and horse that clung to his skin.

She moistened suddenly dry lips and wondered why she didn't walk back to her gelding, why she didn't put some distance between herself and this man she barely knew. There was something reckless about him, an aura that hinted at danger and yet was seductive. He touched her shoulder, and she nearly jumped at the heat in the pads of his fingertips. From the corner of her eye, she noticed the raw hunger in his stare.

She expected him to yank her close, to cover her yielding lips with his hard mouth, to feel the thrill of passion she'd read about in so many books. The naked hunger in his expression tightened her diaphragm about her lungs.

"We'd better get back," he finally said, his hands dropping.

Disappointment ripped through her.

"It'll be dark soon." Still he didn't move.

Heather's throat constricted at the undercurrent of electricity in the air. She licked her lips and heard his breath whistle past his teeth.

"Come on!" Grabbing her arm roughly, he strode back to the horses. "We don't want to be late."

"No one's waiting up for us," she replied, surprised at her own boldness as she half ran to keep up with him.

"For the love of Pete," he muttered. Stopping short, he pulled on her arm, whirling her so that she had to face him. The darkness of the forest seemed to close in on them and the night breathed a life all its own as the moon began to rise and the stars peeked through a canopy of fragrant boughs. "You're playing with fire, here, darlin'," he said, his voice tinged with anger.

"I'm not playing at all."

He dropped her arm as if it were white-hot. "Then let's go home, Heather, before I start something neither one of us wants."

She wanted to argue, to protest, but he scooped up the reins of his horse, climbed into the saddle and kicked Sampson into a gallop.

Heather was left standing in the darkening woods, wondering why he seemed to want her desperately one second, only to reject her the next. She was certain she hadn't misread the signals. Turner wanted her; whether for just a night or a lifetime, she couldn't begin to guess. But he wanted her.

Yet he wouldn't break down and admit it.

She hoisted herself onto Sundown's broad back and followed Sampson's angry plume of dust. Turner was probably right, drat it all. Whatever there was between them was better left untouched.

THE NEXT MORNING, HEATHER and Sheryl were assigned to inventory the pantry. The room was close and hot and Heather counted while Sheryl wrote down the information.

"Sixteen quarts of beans...three tins of beets...five carrots—"

"You've been spending a lot of time with Turner," Sheryl said suddenly, causing Heather to lose track of her tally of the corn.

"I—well, I've been taking riding lessons from him."

Sheryl lifted an arched eyebrow. "And that's all?"

"Yes—"

"Good," she said, seeming relieved. "The man's trouble, you know."

Heather bristled a little. "His reputation doesn't interest me."

"Well, it should, because Turner Brooks is bad news. He doesn't care about anyone. I've seen the girls come here, year after year, and without fail, one of them falls for him. They get all caught up in the romance of loving a cowboy, and he ends up breaking their hearts. Not that he really intends to, I suppose. But they all start seeing diamond rings and hearing church bells and the minute they start talking weddings and babies, Turner takes off. He's out for a good time and that's it," Sheryl said, shaking her head. "And it's not really his fault. His dad's a drunk and his mother's dead. Some people say that the old man killed her—either from neglect or booze, I'm not really sure. But she's gone, and before she died, they had horrible fights. Turner never lets himself get too involved with any woman."

"Is that so?" Heather responded, wanting to close her ears. Why should she believe this girl?

Sheryl's eyes were suddenly clouded, as if with a

private pain. She touched Heather lightly on the shoulder. "Look, for your own good, stay away from Turner Brooks. He'll cause you nothing but heartache. You can't expect a commitment from a man who'd rather sleep on a bedroll in the snow and cook venison over an open fire than enjoy the comforts of a feather bed and hot shower. You like the good life—I can tell. You want to be an artist and live in a big city and show your work in some fancy gallery, don't you?"

Heather could barely breathe, but she managed to nod.

"And Turner? What do you think he'd do in the city? Take you to the theater? Do you see him standing around an art festival and listening to jazz music? Or do you see him dancing in a tuxedo in an expensive restaurant?"

"No, I don't think—"

"He belongs to the open range, Heather, and to the mountains. His idea of a wild time is having a couple of beers after a rodeo in a small town in the middle of nowhere. He'd never be happy in the city."

Heather's heart nearly stopped. She wanted to say something, to defend herself, but her tongue was all tied in knots.

"There was a time when I thought I could change him," Sheryl said softly. "I've been working here since my senior year in high school and I guess I had a crush on him." She fingered her pencil nervously and avoided Heather's eyes. "I thought...well, that given enough time...he'd grow up or away from ranch life. I was wrong. I've been here six summers. This spring I'll have my master's in architecture. I've already started looking for jobs in L.A. Two years ago, I gave up on Turner. I knew I couldn't change him." Tears filled her eyes. "God, he's got a girl in just about every town from here to Alberta! I was crazy. I...I just don't want you to make the same mistake I did."

"I'm not—" Heather protested, but knew she was lying.

"You belong in the city, Heather. Don't kid yourself." Clearing her throat, Sheryl motioned toward the cans of corn stacked on one of the deep shelves. "How many tins have we got?" she asked, and Heather, shaking inside, her dreams shattered, started counting again.

IN THE NEXT COUPLE OF DAYS, Heather thought about Sheryl's warning, but she couldn't help herself where Turner was concerned. She knew she was beginning to care about him too much, looking forward to their time alone together, and she refused to let Sheryl's confession change her. Besides, she couldn't. She'd waded too far into emotional waters and there seemed to be no turning back.

Every evening, when the heat of the day fused with the coming night, Heather felt that she and Turner were alone beneath a canopy of ever-growing stars. They weren't alone, of course. Laughter and the rattle of the coffeepot could be heard from the ranch house and every so often one of the hands would come outside to smoke or play harmonica or just gaze at the stars. But it truly *seemed* as if nothing else existed but the horse, Turner and herself. Silly, really. Nonetheless she did feel a change in the atmosphere whenever she was with him, and she began to notice him not so much as an adversary or a teacher, but as a man.

The lone rider on the ridge.

Yet he never so much as touched her again.

"He's such a hunk," Jill said after work one evening as Heather changed for her lesson. "God, Heather, you're so lucky! I'd give anything to spend a few hours alone with him."

Heather fought down a spasm of jealousy. "I'm sure he'd like that," she said, brushing her hair and noticing the little lines between her eyebrows. Those little grooves always seemed to appear when Jill was gushing about cowboys in general, and Turner in particular.

"Oh, no. He's half in love with you." From her bed, Jill sighed enviously.

Heather nearly dropped her brush. It clattered on the bureau. "You're crazy," she said, but felt a warm glow of contentment at Jill's observation.

"No way." Ripping a black headband from her hair, Jill offered Heather a conspiratorial smile before tossing the headband onto the bureau and rummaging under her bunk for a well-worn magazine. "I've seen it before."

Turner? In love with her? Absolutely ridiculous! Still, the idea had merit. "He doesn't like me any more than I like him."

"That's what I said. He's half in love with you," Jill replied, licking her fingers and flipping the page. In the mirror, Heather saw the wash of scarlet that was causing her cheeks to burn just as Sheryl walked into the room. Her lips were pressed into a hard line, and if she'd heard any of the conversation, she pretended she hadn't.

However, Jill thought Heather cared about Turner. Heather glanced at Sheryl, but the girl was fiddling with her Walkman and fitting the earphones over her head. Heather fingered her brush and tried to convince herself that Turner wasn't her type. Too cynical. Too hard. Too... threateningly male. His sensuality was always between them, always simmering just below the surface of their conversations, always charging the air. And yet she'd wanted him to kiss her when they were alone at the deer trail. She wouldn't have stopped him.

The next few lessons were more difficult than ever.

Though she tried not to notice, Heather found herself staring at the way his jeans rode low on his hips, the magnetism of the huge buckle that fit tight against his flat abdomen, the insolent, nearly indecent curve of his lips and his eyes…. Lord, his eyes were damned near mesmerizing with their cynical sparkle. Worse yet, whenever she had a few moments alone and she began to sketch, it was Turner's face she began to draw, Turner's profile that filled the pages of her book.

Was she falling in love with a man who was only interested in the next rodeo? A cowboy who had seen too much of life already? He was a little bit mystery, and a lot rawhide and leather.

It was dusk again—that time of day she seemed destined to spend with Turner. A few stars dappled the sky and the wind, blowing low over the Siskiyou Mountains, tugged wayward locks of her hair free of her ponytail. Clouds had gathered at the base of the mountains and the air felt charged, as if a storm were brewing.

Turner was waiting for her in the corral, arms crossed over his chest, back propped against the weathered fence. His eyes were dark and serious, his expression hard as granite.

"You're late."

She felt the need to apologize, but shrugged and said, "Large dinner crowd."

As she reached the corral, he opened the gate. Sundown stood in the far corner, no bridle over his head, no saddle slung across his broad back.

"Aren't we going to ride?"

"You can—soon as you catch your horse."

"Oh, no way..." She started to protest, knowing how stubborn the sorrel could be and how he hated to be saddled. Always before, Turner had seen that the gelding was ready to start the riding lesson. Tonight was obviously different. "What if he decides that—"

"Do it." Turner yanked the bridle from a fence post and threw it at her.

She caught the jangling piece of tack by the bit and, stung by his attitude, said crisply, "Anything you say, *boss*."

His lips flattened a little, but he didn't reply. Arms over his chest, a piece of straw in one corner of his mouth, eyes narrowed, he glared at her.

"Are you angry with me?"

"Has nothin' to do with you."

"What doesn't?"

His eyes flashed fire for a second, then he tamped down his anger and glanced pointedly at his watch. "I don't have all night. Go on—get him."

The task was an exercise in futility. Sundown had it in his thick skull that he wasn't going to let Heather touch him. In fact, he seemed to enjoy the game of having Heather chase him around the corral. Nostrils flared, tail aloft, he pranced around the corral as if the evening wind had rejuvenated his spirit.

"Come on, you," she said, clucking softly to the horse, but no matter how she approached him, he let her get just close enough to nearly touch his sleek hide, then he bolted, hoofs flying, as he sent a cloud of dust swirling in his wake. Heather was left standing in the middle of the corral, her hand outstretched, the bridle dangling from her fingers.

"Nice try," Turner remarked on her third attempt.

"Look, I'm doing the best I can."

"Not good enough."

Damned cowboy! Who did he think he was? How in the world had she fancied herself in love with him? Humiliation burned bright in her cheeks, and she decided right then and there that she'd show Turner Brooks what she was made of. Even if it killed her. Gritting her teeth, she started after Sundown again, slowly clucking her tongue, her gaze hard with determination. He breezed by, nearly knocking her over.

"I'm gonna win," she told him, and again the horse took off in the opposite direction.

By the time she finally cornered the horse and threw the reins over his neck, the big sorrel was soaked with lather and she, too, felt sweat clinging to her skin and beading on her forehead. "You useless piece of horse-flesh," she muttered, but gave him a fond pat. Despite his temperament, or maybe because of it, she felt a kinship with this hard-headed animal.

She adjusted the chin strap of the bridle and led a somewhat mollified Sundown back to the side of the corral where Turner was waiting.

"'Bout time," Turner had the gall to remark as Heather tossed the blanket and saddle over Sundown's glistening back. She tightened the cinch, making sure the horse let out his breath before buckling the strap. Thrilled at her small victory, she climbed into the saddle and picked up the reins. This was the part she loved, when she was astride the horse and she and Turner rode the night-darkened trails. "Now what?" she asked, her hopes soaring a bit.

"Now take his gear off and groom him."

"But—"

Turner looked pointedly at his watch and swore under his breath. "I can't hang around any longer." Without another word, he put two hands on the top rail of the fence and vaulted out of the corral. Once in the yard, he strode straight to a dusty blue pickup and hauled himself into the cab. There were a few silent seconds while Heather, still astride Sundown, sat stunned, disbelieving; then the pickup's old engine turned over a few times and finally caught with a sputter and a roar of blue smoke. Turner threw the rig into gear and, spraying gravel, he drove off.

"Terrific," Heather muttered, patting the sorrel's shoulder as the pickup rounded a bend in the lane and disappeared from sight. The rumble of the truck's engine faded through the trees. "Just terrific!"

Turner had been different tonight and Heather wondered if she'd pushed him too far in their last lesson, but she couldn't think of anything she'd said or done that would provoke this kind of treatment. True, they had nearly kissed—she was certain of it—but nothing had happened. She kicked Sundown gently in the sides and rode him the short distance to the stables. Why did she even care what was going on with Turner?

She spent the next half hour grooming the gelding and stewing over the cowboy who had touched her heart. Her emotions seemed to change with the wind that blew off the mountains. One minute she was angry with him, the next perplexed and the next she fantasized about loving such an unpredictable man.

Telling herself to forget him, she walked back to the ranch house and swatted at a bothersome mosquito that was buzzing near her face. Muttso, a scraggly shepherd with one blue eye and one brown, was curled up on a rug on the porch near the screen door. He yawned lazily as she passed. Inside the kitchen, Mazie was washing a huge kettle she'd used to cook jam. The fruits of Mazie's labor, twelve shining jars of raspberry preserves, were labeled and ready to be stored in the pantry.

"How'd the lesson go?" Mazie asked as she twisted off the taps. The old pipes creaked and the faucet continued to drip. "Damned thing." Mazie swiped her hands on her apron, then mopped her sweaty brow with a handkerchief. Her face was the color of her preserves and she was breathing hard.

"The lesson? It was fine," Heather hedged.

"Turner take off?" Mazie asked. Without waiting for a reply, she shoved aside the muslin curtains and looked out the window to the parking lot and the empty spot where Turner usually parked his truck. Absently, she reached into a drawer for her cigarettes. "That boy's got a lot to carry around," she said as she lit up and snapped her lighter closed. Letting out a stream of smoke, she said, "His pa's got himself in trouble again." Mazie untied her apron and hung it on a peg near the pantry door, then turned toward Heather.

"Booze. Old John can't leave it alone, and when he goes on a bender, look out!" Mazie pressed her lips together firmly and looked as if she was about to say something else, but whatever secret she was about to reveal, she kept to herself. "It's a wonder that boy turned out to a hill of beans. You can thank Zeke Kilkenny for that. Never had a son of his own—took his sister's boy in when he needed it."

"So Turner went to meet his father tonight?"

"Your guess is as good as mine. Long as I can remember, Turner's been bailing John out of jail. Looks like nothin's changed." Mazie, as if suddenly realizing she'd said too much, waved toward the preserves. "Now, you put those jars where they belong in the pantry. I don't have all night to sit around gossipin'."

Heather did as she was told, but she couldn't help wondering where Turner was and when he'd be back.

Later, she climbed into her bunk bed and picked up her sketch pad. Gazing through the window, she began to draw idly, her fingers moving of their own accord. Soon, Turner's face, scowling and dark, was staring back at her.

Sheryl, face scrubbed, walked into the room. She glanced up at Heather, her gaze slipping quickly to the sketch pad propped by Heather's knees. Sadness darkened her eyes. "I heard that Turner left," she said, flopping onto her bed. The old mattress creaked.

"That's right," Heather replied.

"Is he gone for good?"

Heather's heart froze. "For good?"

"For the season. His shoulder's healed up and I thought he'd entered a few more rodeos—that he'd be leaving soon."

"I—I don't know," Heather admitted, her insides suddenly cold.

"Well, even if he comes back, he'll be leaving soon. Believe me. He always does."

There was no riding lesson the next day, nor the following evening, either. Turner hadn't returned, and Heather silently called herself a fool for missing him. Was Sheryl right? Had he just taken off without saying goodbye? Her heart ached as if it had been bruised. She hadn't realized how much she'd looked forward to their time together.

"You must really be bored," she told herself on the third evening when Turner's pickup rolled into the yard. Her heart did a stupid little leap as she watched through the dining-hall window and saw him stretch his long frame out of the cab. He looked hot and tired and dusty, and the scowl beneath three days' growth of beard didn't add to his charm.

He spent the next hour with his uncle in the office and when he emerged, Heather, from the kitchen window, saw him head straight for the corral. Though she still was supposed to wipe down the tables, she tore off her apron and ran upstairs. Within minutes she'd changed into jeans and a blouse and was racing down the back staircase. She practically flew out the back door, nearly tripping over Muttso. The old dog growled and she muttered an apology as she flew by.

But the corral was empty and her heart dropped.

Turner's pickup was still parked in the yard, but she didn't think he'd gone to the bunkhouse. "Damn," she muttered under her breath. Why she felt so compelled to talk to him, she didn't understand, and yet compelled she was. She hurried to the stables, flipping on the lights and disturbing more than one anxious mare.

A sliver of light showed beneath the tack room door, and Heather hurried past the stalls and through the short hallway. Her boots rang on the concrete floor and she ripped the door open. Billy Adams, a boy of about nineteen, and one of the younger ranch hands who worked at the Lazy K, was seated on an old barrel and furiously polishing a bridle. He looked up and his freckled face split with a smile at the sight of her.

"Have you seen Turner?" she asked, and tried not to notice that Billy's boyish grin wavered a bit.

"He just took off."

"To where?"

"I don't know. He just saddled his horse and headed into the hills."

"North?" Heather asked, her mind racing.

Billy lifted one scrawny shoulder. "Guess so."

"Thanks!" She didn't pause to hear if he responded, just headed back to the stables. Sundown was a range horse and wasn't put in each night and Nutmeg was sadly missing, as well. But Heather wasn't to be thwarted. Bridle in one hand, she ran back to the kitchen, slunk into the pantry and stole several sugar packets. Feeling like a thief, she raced back to the paddocks and spied Sundown lazily plucking grass in the pasture.

"Come on, you old mule," she said with an affectionate smile. "Look what I've got for you."

Sundown nickered softly and his ears cocked forward. His eyes were still wary, but he couldn't resist the sweet temptation she offered, and soon Heather snapped the bridle over his head. "Your sweet tooth's going to be your downfall," she chided.

She didn't bother with a saddle, just led the big sorrel out of the pasture, and closed the gate. Swinging onto his broad back, she gave a soft command, and Sundown, bless him, took off. She didn't know where Turner had gone, but she crossed her fingers, hoping that he'd returned to the bend in the river where they'd first met.

Her heart was racing in tandem to the thud of Sundown's hoofbeats as he tore through the forest, along the trail, guided by the fading light of a dying sun. She didn't think about what she would say when she caught up with Turner, didn't dwell on the disappointment of not finding him at the swimming hole. She knew only that she had to see him.

The smell of the river was close, and the hint of honeysuckle and pine floated on the air. Heather pulled hard on the reins as the trail widened and the trees gave way to the rocky bank where Sampson was tethered.

Heather's gaze swept the river and she spotted Turner as he broke the surface near the rocky ledge that jutted over the water. His eyes met hers for a brief instant before he placed both hands on the shelf and hauled himself out of the water. Naked except for a pair of ragged cutoff jeans, he tossed the water from his hair and wiped a hand across his face.

Heather's throat went dry at the sight of his wet, slick muscles moving effortlessly as he shifted to a spot where he could sit comfortably. She noticed for the first time a purple scar that sliced a jagged path across his tanned abdomen.

"You lookin' for me?" he asked, his gaze piercing and wary, every lean muscle taut.

She would have liked to lie, but couldn't very well deny the obvious. "We, uh, we haven't had a lesson for a few days." Dismounting quickly, she tied the reins of Sundown's bridle to a spindly oak and wondered how she was going to reach Turner and why she bothered to try. He wasn't happy that she'd shown up; in fact, he seemed to be trying to tame a raging fury that started a muscle leaping in his jaw.

"Thought you hated the lessons," he observed.

"Thought you did, too."

The ghost of a smile touched his lips. "I've been busy."

"I heard."

He froze, and his eyes drilled into hers. "You heard what?" he said, his voice so low, she could barely hear it over the rush of the river.

She wanted to squirm away from his stare, and yet she stood, stuffing her hands into her pockets for lack of anything better to do, trying to keep her chin at a defiant angle. "I heard you had some trouble."

"That damned Mazie," he growled. "Doesn't know when to keep her mouth shut."

"Seems as if it's common knowledge."

"Or common gossip. Christ, I hate that." He picked up a smooth stone and flung it so hard that it flew across the river and landed with a thunk against a tree trunk on the opposite shore. Throwing his arms around his knees, he glowered mutinously across the rushing water. "What is it you want, lady?" he said without so much as tossing her a glance.

"I just thought you might want to talk."

"I don't."

"But—"

He swiveled around so fast to stare at her that she nearly gasped. "You made it perfectly clear what you thought of me the first time we met, and every day thereafter. Now you'd better climb on that damned horse of yours and ride out of here or I might just show you how much of a gentleman I ain't."

"You don't scare me," she said, though her insides were quivering.

"Well, I should."

"Why?" She walked up to the ledge where he was sitting and stared down at his wet crown. Drops of river water still clung to his hair, causing the gold streaks to disappear. He leaned back, his eyes focused on her so intently that her heart nearly stopped. With eyes that smoldered like hot steel, he studied her for a long, breathless moment.

"Because," he said, rising to his more than six feet and taking his turn to stare down at her. "Because I think about you. A lot. And my thoughts aren't always decent."

Oh, God. Her knees threatened to crumble.

"So, what're you really doing here, Heather?" Reaching forward, he touched the edge of her jaw, drawing along the soft underside with one damp finger. She trembled and swallowed hard as his gaze searched the contours of her face. "Because we both know that you and I, alone, can only mean trouble."

Her heart was pumping, its erratic beat pounding in her eardrums and her skin, where he touched it, felt on fire. Knowing she was stepping into dangerous, hot territory, she decided to plunge in further. "I came here because I care, Turner."

He snorted in disbelief.

"Mazie said that you were having a rough time of it, and I thought I...I hoped that I could help."

He barked out a hard laugh, and the finger that was traveling along her chin slid lower, down her neck, pausing at the slope of her shoulder before sliding down between her breasts. "And how did you think you'd do that, eh?" he asked, but his own breathing seemed suddenly as uneven as her own.

She grabbed his wrist and held his hand away from her. "Don't try to cheapen this, okay? I'm here as a friend."

"Maybe I don't need a *friend* right now. Maybe I need a lover."

Her stomach did a flip. Sheryl's warning flitted into her head then disappeared like morning fog. "Maybe you need both."

He eyed her silently, his gaze moving down her body slowly, then up again. "I think you'd better get on your horse and leave, little girl, while you still can."

"I said it before, Turner Brooks. I'm not afraid of you."

"Then you're a fool, Heather." Reluctance flared in his eyes for just a second as he grabbed her and yanked her body hard against his. Before she could utter a word of protest, he pressed his hot lips to hers, molded his wet body against her own and kissed her with such a fevered passion, she thought she might pass out. His arms were strong and possessive, his body as solid and hot as she'd imagined.

Closing her eyes, she swayed against him. The river seemed to roar in her ears and the thunder of her heart was only eclipsed by the sound of his, beating an irregular tattoo. His tongue pressed hungrily against her teeth, and she opened her mouth, feeling the sweet pressure of his hands against the small of her back. She felt weak and powerful all at once as emotion upon emotion ripped through her.

She thought of denial, of surrender, of love and of hate, but she was powerless to do anything but return his kisses with her own awakening passion which exploded like a powder keg at his touch. One of his hands lowered, cupping her buttocks, lifting her from her feet so she could feel his hardness, his desire. Still she wasn't frightened, and all her doubts seemed to float away into the twilight. She was a virgin, a girl who had never experienced the thrill of a man's passion and for the first time in her life, her virginity seemed no longer a virtue, but a prison.

With Turner, she could be freed of the bonds. She ran her fingers down his shoulders, feeling the corded texture of his skin, tasting the salt on his lips, smelling the powerful scents of maleness and river water.

Lifting his head, he stared down at her for a second. His eyes were no longer angry but glazed. A red flush had darkened the color of his skin. "Do you know what you're doing?"

"I don't care...."

"This is insane—"

She kissed him again, and with all the strength he could muster, he grabbed her forearms and held her at arm's length from him.

He was breathing hard now and his lips were pale with strain. "Listen to me, damn it! We're playing with fire, here, and one of us is gonna get burned."

Her senses were spinning wildly out of control, but slowed instantly as she realized that he was rejecting her. She, who was ready to offer him her body as a means to balm his wounds, was being told that he didn't want her. Tears, unwelcome drops of misery, suddenly filled her eyes. "Turner—"

"Don't you see, Heather? I'm just using you!" he said, though the pain in his eyes wouldn't go away.

"I don't believe—"

"I don't want *you,* I just want *someone.* Got it? Any woman would do."

Her heart crumbled into a million pieces; he couldn't have hurt her more if he'd thrust a white-hot knife into her chest. "You don't mean—"

"We're not the same, you and I. Men don't think like women. So if you want me just because you want to experiment with sex, or you don't really give a damn and just want to get laid, then we're okay. But if you think that what's happening here has anything to do with love or romance, then you'd better get on that damned horse and hightail it out of here."

A small cry escaped her lips.

"I mean it, Heather," he said, squeezing her arms so hard that they hurt. Pain swept through his eyes, but he didn't back down.

"I...I...I just wanted to help you," she whispered, tears drizzling down her face.

"Don't sacrifice yourself. I'm not worth it," he said bluntly as he dropped her arms. "No one is. Save yourself for your boyfriend back in Gold Creek."

"I don't—" she said, but bit off the rest. Somehow he'd heard about Dennis. "We broke up."

"Then don't *use* me to get even with him."

Without thinking, she raised her hand and slapped him so hard the smack echoed through the canyon. "I'm not using you."

"You're right about that, darlin'," he drawled, rubbing the side of his face.

Emotions all tangled, her vision blurred, she ran and stumbled blindly. The horse was where she'd left him, and she threw herself across his back, swung one leg over and kicked with all her might. Holding back sobs of humiliation, she headed back to the ranch house.

TURNER WATCHED HER GO, with a mixture of anger and relief. He'd almost lost himself in her. It wouldn't have taken much more to forget about his father, forget about his problems and make love to Heather Tremont.

It had taken all of his worthless upbringing to be able to say the cruel things—the lies—that had forced her away. He kicked at a stone and swore under his breath, not sure that he'd made the right decision. His face still stung where she'd hit him. He may have hurt her, but he kept telling himself he'd done the right thing. She was a small-town girl with dreams of the good life, a cute little thing who was bored to tears on the ranch. He'd become her distraction, and though she might have had the best intentions in the world, he didn't trust her. No more than she trusted him. And he wasn't going to treat her like a whore, not even if she wanted it. Because, deep down, when all was said and done, he did believe she was a lady.

## CHAPTER THREE

HEATHER, HER PRIDE WOUNDED beyond repair, managed to avoid Turner for the rest of the week. She heard the gossip surrounding him, knew his father had been hurt in a barroom brawl and tossed in the local jail. Turner had been absent several days, without explanation, but the gossip was that he was trying to help his old man dry out and avoid another jail sentence.

Only Sheryl didn't buy into it. Peeling apples at the sink, the water running slowly, Sheryl shook her head. Her lips compressed and she attacked the apples with a vengeance. The Rome Beauties were on the soft side— having wintered over in the fruit cellar. While Sheryl worked to remove the Romes of their skins, Heather was at the next sink, slicing the apples into thin slivers for the pie filling.

"If you ask me," Sheryl said, "Turner took off because of woman trouble."

Heather's stomach knotted, and Jill, mixing sugar and cinnamon, shot her a knowing glance.

Sheryl went on. "Oh, his father might have got into some trouble, Lord knows that's possible, but I'll bet there's a woman involved— Oh! Damn." She dropped the apple peeler and sucked in her breath. "Cut myself." Snatching a kitchen towel, she blinked back sudden tears, then dashed up the stairs toward the bathroom.

Mazie sighed. "If you ask me, she never got over him."

Clucking her tongue, she picked up the dropped peeler and started stripping the apples of their tough skins. "Turner and Sheryl were...well, I don't think you'd say they were in love. Leastwise he wasn't, but Sheryl, I'm afraid she fell for him." Mazie smiled sadly. "Just like half the other girls around here."

Jill, suddenly red-faced, handed Mazie the bowl of sugar and cinnamon, then set about wiping down the wood stove, which was only used when the power went out.

Heather bit her lip and kept working, afraid that if she said anything, she'd look as foolish as the other girls who'd thought themselves in love with Turner Brooks.

With her tongue still clucking, Mazie dried her hands quickly and left the rest of the apples to Heather. "Yep, that Turner...he's somethin'. I don't know how many girls fall for him." She grabbed her old wooden rolling pin and a bowl of pie dough from the refrigerator. Measuring by handfuls, she dropped several lumps of dough onto a flour-covered board, then started stretching and flattening the dough. "Well, speak of the devil," she said, glancing up as Turner's pickup wheeled into the yard.

Heather's stomach dropped to the floor as she watched the headlights of the pickup dim and Turner step down from the cab. Averting her eyes, she continued working on the remaining small mound of apples while Jill turned her attention to filling the salt-and-pepper shakers for the next day.

Mazie frowned as Turner started for the house. "He's got his share of troubles, that one."

"I heard his dad will spend a year in jail," Jill said, eager for gossip.

Mazie frowned. "I doubt it. Seems old John's always

slippery enough to get off." She worked the dough to her satisfaction and folded the flattened crust in half.

"So Turner's father is an outlaw," Jill whispered with a deep sigh.

"Nothing so romantic. John Brooks is a drunk and a crook who depends upon his son to get him out of one jam after another." Scowling, Mazie draped several pie plates with the unbaked crusts. "If he were my brother-in-law—"

"Mazie…" Zeke Kilkenny's voice was soft but filled with quiet reproof. Heather's head snapped around and Mazie's spine stiffened.

She started shaping the edges of the crust as if her very life depended on it. "Well, it's true, and if you won't admit it, Zeke, I will!" She finished with one pie, and started working on another, twirling the pan as she cut off the excess crust. "Margaret might have been your sister, but she was my cousin, damn it, and my best friend and that…that drunk of a husband of hers killed her!" Mazie's chin wobbled, and she turned toward the window, dropping the pie pan and spilling the crust onto the floor. "Oh, God, now look—"

"I'll get it," Heather said quickly, grabbing a broom and dust pail and scraping away the ruined crust.

Zeke shoved his hat off his head and ran a hand through his thick white hair. "You girls go on," he said, as Heather did her best to clean up the fine film of flour on the floor. "You're finished for the night. Mazie and I—we'll take care of this." The look he sent them brooked no argument. Heather didn't waste any time. She was up the stairs like a shot. She yanked the band from her ponytail and stripped out of her apron. Jill followed her into the room, but Sheryl was missing.

"Wow! Can you believe what we just heard?" Jill said.

She walked to the mirror and plucked a contact lens from her eye. "Melodrama at the Lazy K! Just like a soap opera!"

"You hear so much around here, you really can't believe it all."

But Jill wasn't listening. "No wonder Turner's so... distant. Such a rebel."

"You're making more of it than there is," Heather said, trying to think of a way to change the subject.

"I don't think so." Jill removed her second contact and found her glasses. "What do you think? Turner's dad killed his mother? But how? Did he take a gun and shoot her or beat her or—"

"Enough! I...I don't think we should talk about this. It's just gossip!"

"Where there's smoke, there's fire!" Jill said. "And Mazie said—"

"Mazie talks too much," Heather replied, inadvertently paraphrasing Turner as she hurried down the stairs. She avoided the kitchen and slipped through the dining room where some of the guests were watching television, or playing checkers or cards.

The French doors were open, and a breeze filtered into the ranch house, stirring the crisp muslin curtains as she dashed outside. Muttso growled from the bushes somewhere, but Heather didn't pause. She ran down a well-worn path leading to the stables and corrals. Outside she could breathe again. The claustrophobia of the ranch house with its gossip and conjecture slowly ebbed away. Heather slowed her footsteps and closed her eyes for a second. She needed to be calm, because beneath her determination to see Turner again, she felt a sense of dread. What if he rejected her again? Not that she was going to throw herself at him, of course. But he needed a friend. And she was willing to be that friend.

*And how much more?* her mind niggled, but Heather shoved that nasty little thought aside. She pressed her palms to her cheeks and waited for the heat to disappear from her skin. Her breathing was normal again, though her heart was pounding about a thousand beats a minute.

She found him in the stables, pitching hay into the mangers of the brood mares. He'd taken off his jacket, and the sleeves of his work shirt were rolled over his forearms, showing off strong muscles and tanned skin. He didn't look up when she entered, but his muscles flexed, his jaw grew tight and he hurled his pitchfork into a bale of straw. The seconds ticked slowly by. Heather hardly dared breathe.

"Didn't you get the message?" he finally asked as he turned and faced her. His eyes were the color of flint and just as explosive.

"I didn't think we were through with our lessons."

He let out a long, low breath and forced his eyes to the rafters where barn swallows swooped in and out of the open windows.

Again the silence stretched between them—as if they were awkward strangers. Heather fidgeted.

Turner hooked a thumb in his belt loop. "You know enough about horses to get by."

"Do I?"

He trained his eyes on her, and his expression was a mixture of anger and desire. "Look, Heather, I just don't think it's such a good idea—you and me."

"All I was asking about was riding lessons…" Her voice drifted off when she noticed the tic at the corner of his eye. The lie seemed to grow between them.

"Don't play dumb," he said, his jaw shifting to one

side. "'Cause I won't buy it. You and I both know what's going on here and I'm just tryin' to stop something that you'll regret for a long, long time."

Unconsciously, she bit her lip. "I didn't come here to try and seduce you, if that's what you're getting at."

A thin smile touched his lips. "Good."

"I just thought you could use a friend. Someone to talk to."

"And that's what you want to do. Talk...oh, and ride, of course."

She shrugged. "Why not?"

"I can think of a million reasons." But he didn't voice any of them, and despite all million, he muttered a curse under his breath, threw her a dark, brooding look and saddled their two mounts. "I should be hung for this," he said, as he led the horses from the barn and swung into the saddle.

"Not hung. Shot, maybe, but not hung," she said, offering a smile, and Turner laughed out loud. Some of the strain left his features as they headed through a series of paddocks to the open pastureland.

Soon, the horses were loping along the westerly trail, skirting the pastures and keeping to the edge of the forest.

"Where're we going?" she asked, hardly daring to break the companionable silence that had grown between them.

Turner's grin widened. "Wait and see."

"But—"

He spurred his horse forward, and Heather had no choice but to follow. The path thinned as it wound upward, through the hills and along the rocky banks of Cottonwood Creek.

Turner didn't say much and Heather didn't dare. The

night was too perfect to be broken with words. The moon, full and opalescent, hung low over the hills and thousands of stars studded the sky like tiny shards of crystal. Every so often, a shooting star would streak across the black heavens in a flash of brilliance that stole the breath from Heather's lungs.

The hum of traffic along a distant highway melded with the chorus of frogs hiding in the shallow pools formed by the creek.

All the while they rode, Heather couldn't take her eyes off Turner. Tall in the saddle, his shoulders wide, his waist narrow, his hips moving with the easy gait of his horse, he rode as if he belonged astride a horse. She imagined the feel of his hard thighs pressed against the ribs of the horse and her mouth turned to cotton.

"Here we go," he finally said, when the trees parted to reveal a clearing of tall grass and wildflowers. A lake shimmered, reflecting the black sky and tiny stars. Moonlight streamed across the surface in a ghostly ribbon of white, and fish jumped at unseen insects, causing splashes and ripples along the glassy surface.

Lithely, Turner hopped to the ground and tethered his horse on a nearby sapling. The animal snorted, then buried his nose in the lush grass.

"What is this place?" Heather asked, mirroring Turner's actions by tying Sundown to a scraggly pine.

"My mother's favorite spot in the world. She brought me up here a lot in the summer." He stared across the night-darkened landscape and a sad smile crossed his lips. "The Lazy K was where she and Zeke grew up. It was just a working ranch then—no boarders or tourists. But then my grandparents died and left the place to Zeke." He glanced over his shoulder. "They cut Mom out of the will because she married my old man."

"Oh," Heather said weakly.

"That's what this is all about, isn't it?" Turner shoved his hands into the back pockets of his jeans. "You heard some gossip about me and you want to know what's true."

"No, I—I just wanted…"

He turned and faced her, his hair ruffling in the slight breeze, his face taut and hard. "What, Heather? You wanted what?"

Time seemed to stand still. The air became suddenly quiet aside from her own frightened breathing. Swallowing hard, she decided that she had to be honest with him. "I just wanted to be alone with you," she whispered, feeling an odd mixture of shame and excitement.

"Don't you think that's dangerous?"

No time for lies. "Probably," she admitted.

"I don't get involved—"

"I know, Turner," she snapped. "Listen, I didn't want to like you and I hated the first few times we had lessons, but…day after day, I started to look forward to being with you."

"Because you're bored."

Licking her lips, she shook her head. "I don't think so, Turner. I think I…I think I'm falling for you." Her voice, though a whisper, sounded deafening.

He didn't move. Aside from the breeze tugging at the flap of his shirt, he stood stock-still, as if carved in stone.

She took a tentative step forward, walking close enough to touch him.

"What about the guy in Gold Creek?" he asked.

"I told you. It's over."

Biting her lip, she reached upward, touching the thin curve of his lips. With a groan, he grabbed her hand, holding it away from him. "You're playing with fire here, Heather."

"I know what I'm doing."

"I don't mess with women who are involved with other men."

"I'm not!" She turned beseeching eyes up to him. "Believe me, Turner. Just trust me."

He wanted to. She could see the passion stirring in his night-darkened eyes. And yet he held back, his fingers surrounding her wrist in a death grip, his emotions twisted on his face. "Don't play with me."

"I wouldn't," she said, and all at once his arms were around her, his lips molded over hers in a kiss that robbed the breath from her lungs. His lips were warm and supple and his tongue gained easy access to her mouth when she parted her lips.

Her thoughts swirled and blended with the night and a warm ache started somewhere deep in her abdomen. He explored and tasted and she moaned softly, unconsciously winding her arms around his neck, pressing her body closer still, feeling her nipples grow taut.

Groaning, he dragged them both to the ground, to the soft bed of bent grass and fragrant flowers, and still kissing her, he slowly removed her T-shirt, kissing the tops of her breasts, rimming the circle of bones at her throat with his tongue, creating a vortex of heat in her center that she didn't protest as his hand slid beneath the waistband of her jeans and toyed with the lacy edge of her panties.

"You're sure?" he asked, his breath ragged against her ear.

She kissed him hard on the lips and he let out a deep sigh, the flat of his hand pressed intimately to her lower abdomen.

"I mean it, Heather, because if we don't stop now, I won't be able to."

It was already too late for her. The fires within her had been stoked and now were white-hot and ready to explode. She pulled his head back to hers and kissed him with parted lips. "Don't ever stop," she whispered into his opened lips.

His hand slid deeper into her jeans, teasing the apex of her legs, creating a liquid need so intense that she was squirming and writhing beneath him. In the darkness, he smiled. "Take it easy, darlin'," he drawled, kissing the beads of sweat dampening her forehead. "We've got all night."

His lips found her again, and he began his magic. Hands, callused and rough, were gentle as they unclasped her bra and held her breasts, pushing the soft mounds together, kissing her skin and causing her nipples to turn to hard little nubs.

"That's a girl," he whispered before his mouth closed over one dark peak and he teased and played, his tongue and teeth nipping and laving until the pressure within her was so hot she bucked beneath him.

He stripped her of her jeans, his large hands sculpting her buttocks, his face buried in the soft flesh of her abdomen.

Heather's mind was spinning; she'd never been so reckless, never wanted more of the touch, feel and taste of any man. He guided her fingers to the buttons of his shirt, and she quickly undressed him, her hands running eagerly over the sinewy strength of his muscles.

His fingers tangled in her hair and she ran her palms down the springy hair that covered parts of his chest. His lips were on hers again and he kicked off his jeans. The back of her throat tightened at the sight of him—she'd never seen a man completely naked before. A warning pierced her mind, but she ignored it.

"I've wanted you since the first time I saw you skinny-dipping in the river," he admitted, kissing her eyes, her lips, her throat and moving lower still.

"And I wanted you," she whispered, her mind racing in romantic fantasies of a cowboy and his lady. She wound her arms around his neck as he settled over her, gently prodding her knees apart.

"You're sure about this?" he asked again, though his voice shook and his control seemed held by a rapidly fraying thread.

"Oh, yes, Turner. Yes."

He kissed her forehead and eyes before his mouth claimed hers with a possession that reached to her very soul. She felt him shift, the tensing of the muscles of his back as he entered her. She cried out, for the pain was blinding, but he didn't stop, and with each thrust there-after the pain lessened, balmed with pleasure, driving all thoughts from her mind as she gazed up at him. His hair fell over his forehead and his body was backdropped by the jewel-like stars. She met each of his strokes with her own increasing tempo, and without realizing it, she clung to him, her fingers digging into his shoulders.

With a shivering explosion, he climaxed. She, too, convulsed in a shattering, dizzy burst of color and light that erupted behind her eyes and sent shock waves through her limbs.

"Heather, sweet lady," he whispered between tattered breaths.

"Oh, Turner, I love you," she cried, holding him close, listening to the wild cadence of his heart, smelling the earth and water and wind on his skin.

"Shh." He kissed her so tenderly that she thought she would die.

Tears sprang to her eyes for the cowboy and all the pain he'd suffered. She would change things—change him. No longer would he have to wear a cynical shield... she would be there.

Slowly he rolled off her and cradled her in his arms. Together, without a sound, they watched the shooting stars streak through the heavens and listened to the soft sounds of their horses plucking grass, bridles jangling quietly, hoofs muffled by the thick turf of the meadow.

"You didn't tell me you were a virgin," he finally said.

"You never asked."

"I just assumed that..." His voice drifted off.

"You assumed that because I'd been engaged, I'd experimented with sex," she finished for him. "Well, it didn't happen."

"Why not?"

She levered up on one elbow and stared down at him. "Does it matter?"

"Just curious." His gaze touched hers, and her heart missed a beat.

"I wasn't interested."

He lifted a skeptical eyebrow.

"I only really dated Dennis and...well, our relationship wasn't all that physical."

"What's wrong with the guy?"

"Nothing! Everything! I mean—I just knew it wasn't right."

He snorted. "But with me?"

"I love you, Turner," she said again, hoping to hear the magic words returned. Instead she felt him stiffen and the arms that had held her so tenderly suddenly seemed like lead.

"You don't."

"Yes...I love you."

"You don't even know me."

Her heart turned stone cold. "But I...we...I thought..."

"You thought what?" he asked, his arms slowly withdrawing from her as he sat and stared at her. "That we had something special? That we were in love?" His voice was filled with a cold incredulity that drove a spike straight into her soul.

"Of course—"

"Hey, wait a minute. I like you and hell, yes, I wanted you, I mean wanted you in the worst way. Damn thing of it is, I still want you. But love... Heather, you're kidding yourself."

Her throat seemed strangled and she wanted to die.

"Look—" He reached forward as if to touch her, but she drew away, as if he'd burned her. "I care about you and we can be friends, but—"

"Friends?" she whispered, her throat catching in disbelief. "Friends? I don't make love with my friends!" Oh, God, what a mess! What had seemed so remarkable, so incredible only moments before, now seemed cheap. And to think of how she'd thrown herself at him. She thought of her sister, Rachelle, and all the pain and embarrassment she'd suffered at the hands of Jackson Moore, a boy she'd slept with only one night, a boy who had left her with her reputation in tatters.

"Don't get me wrong," he said. "I care for you. I do—"

"But you don't love me."

"I don't love anyone," he said flatly. "I don't believe in it."

She closed her eyes on the horrid words, felt hot tears in her eyes. "Then I feel sorry for you, Turner," she said flatly.

He tried to touch her again and she recoiled. How could she have been so stupid? After Sheryl had warned her, how could she have thought she would be the one who could change him?

"I don't know what you were expecting, Heather, but I'm not the kind of man to settle down with a wife and kids and picket fence and station wagon. I ride rodeo. In two weeks, I'll rejoin the circuit. I'll be in Oregon, Colorado, Wyoming and Alberta. And then—"

"I don't need to know what you'll do after that," she said.

He grabbed her then, and though she tried to squirm away, he held her tight. Aware of her nudity, of his strength, of the love she still felt deep in her heart, she closed her eyes.

"Look at me, damn it," he said, shaking her a little.

When she lifted her lids, she found his face only inches from hers, his expression filled with concern, remorse dark in his eyes. "What do you see?"

"I don't underst—"

"What do you see?"

"You," she said, her throat tight.

"And what am I?"

"A…"

"A cowboy, right? The kind of man you wouldn't really want to be caught dead with, not to mention spend the rest of your life following around. I have nothing, Heather. Nothing except a drunk for a father and part of a ranch with a mortgage against it that rivals the national debt. I own a broken-down pickup, a saddle, a damned good horse and the shirt on my back. That's it. Is that what you want?"

She didn't answer, couldn't speak past the dam of tears that filled her throat.

"Well, is it?"

"Yes," she cried, tears streaming down her cheeks.

"Oh, lady," he whispered, and suddenly she was deep in his arms again. They were warm and tender and loving, and the kisses he placed in her hair and on her cheeks eased the pain in her heart. She tasted the salt of her own tears when his lips found hers again and she didn't think about the future as she kissed him back and made love to him again. Tomorrow didn't matter. As long as she could have him this one night, she'd live with her memories forever locked in her heart.

# CHAPTER FOUR

TURNER GAVE HIMSELF A mental kick. Astride Sampson, he threw out his arm and sent the lasso whizzing through the dusty air. The rope loop landed with a thud on the ground, inches away from his target, a bawling Hereford calf. It was the second time he'd missed, and several of the guests as well as some ranch hands were watching.

"Hey, Brooks, he's gittin' away," Hank hooted from the other side of the fence.

"Yeah, maybe you should stick to tying something you can handle—like your shoes!"

Color washed up the back of Turner's neck. He gritted his teeth and hauled the rope back. With lightning-quick speed, he spun the rope again, urging Sampson forward with his knees as they chased the calf and, just at the right moment, he let loose. The lasso snaked through the air, landing squarely over the surprised calf's neck.

Sampson started stepping backward instinctively, tightening the loop as Turner vaulted from the saddle, ran through the dust, and over the cheers and jeers of the onlookers tied the Hereford neatly.

Damn, what a job! He stepped back from the struggling calf and yanked his hat from his head. His life seemed to be turned upside down. Ever since making love to Heather, he hadn't been himself. He'd been gruff and surly with some of the hands, his duties at the Lazy K had suffered and the skills in which he'd prided himself for years seemed to have escaped him. All because of some female!

But not just any female. No, Heather Tremont was different from all the women Turner had known. A small-town girl who had dreams of fame and fortune and the glitter of the city life. A woman who wanted to be an *artist* for God's sake. A female who believed in romance and love. Hell, what a mess! What he needed was a drink and maybe a good hard kick in the head to make him wake up.

"'Bout time you roped him," Bud yelled, cupping his hands around his mouth.

Turner ignored the gibe. He deserved it. A few days ago he could've lassoed that calf with his eyes blindfolded. But not now. Not since Heather had wormed her way into his heart.

He knocked his hat against his leg, sending dust up in a cloud, then jammed the Stetson back onto his head and walked back to untie the calf. He didn't know what he was going to do about Heather. Had no idea. He didn't believe in love or marriage, and even if he did, he realized she'd never be satisfied with him. So that left him with the obvious option of continuing the affair he'd so reluctantly started. But his reluctance was now long gone. Even now, just thinking of her, he ached. Never, *never* had he experienced such intense passion with a woman, never had he felt so sated. And yet, he couldn't stop thinking and plotting how he was going to get her alone again.

"Miserable bastard," he muttered at himself. Everyone who heard him probably thought he was talking to the calf. With a flip of his wrist the rope fell away and the Hereford was free. Bawling and scrambling to his feet, the whiteface ran to the far end of the corral.

"Y'all done?" Bud hollered. "We were hopin' for another demonstration. These here guests paid good money to see you miss that calf."

Turner grinned lazily. "Maybe I should practice a little more."

"Ah, hell. Ya got a lot on yer mind," Hank said as he opened the gate and Turner, leading his buckskin, walked through.

"That I do," Turner agreed, letting Hank and Bud and the others think that his problems all stemmed from his father. Not that John Brooks wasn't on his mind. The old man had given him nothing but grief over the years, but right now his problem was Heather.

He'd never planned on marrying or even settling down with one woman. But Heather turned his thoughts around. He suddenly was questioning everything he'd ever believed in.

After turning Sampson out to pasture, he brushed the dust from his jeans and started for the kitchen. But he stopped short when he saw the black Porsche roar into the yard. The car looked like liquid ebony under the sun's hot rays. It rolled to a stop, and the engine, along with a hard-rock song that had been thrumming from the sports car's speakers, died.

Turner stopped short and he felt the ghost of dread crawl up his spine as a tall man about his own age rolled out of the plush leather seats. Mirrored glasses, a smooth leather jacket, polo shirt, slacks and expensive shoes covered the man from head to foot. A gold watch strapped to the man's wrist glinted in the sun's rays.

Turner had never seen the guy before in his life, but he wasn't surprised to watch as Heather, wiping her hands on her skirt, ran out of the house to greet him.

Turner's gut twisted. Heather didn't run to the man's

open arms, but didn't protest too much when he grabbed her and spun her off the ground. He caught her lips in a kiss and she pushed away.

So this was the man she was supposed to marry. Dennis something or other—Italian sounding, if he remembered right. His back teeth ground together and he wanted to wring the man's neck. Turner started toward the couple, then thought better of it. What did he have to offer Heather? Nothing. But this guy—he could give her the world.

His mood as dark as the Porsche's gleaming finish, Turner swung toward the ranch house, washed his hands in the basin on the back porch and, feeling dirt-poor and ranch-bred, dared walk into Mazie's kitchen.

She was smoking at the table, going over some sort of list. "What's on your mind, Turner?" she asked, eyeing his boots critically as if to make sure he didn't drag any dirt or manure into her kitchen.

"Nothing." He checked the cooler and found a bottle of beer. "Just a little thirsty," he said, slamming the door shut and twisting off the top from his bottle.

"You don't want to talk about anything?"

"Nah." In the past, he'd confided in Mazie. She was kin and the only mother figure he could remember. Zeke's wife had left him years before and eventually died and Turner's mother had been killed when he was twelve. That left Mazie. His mother's cousin. And a woman who had trouble keeping her mouth shut.

"Thinkin' of movin' on?"

Turner took a long pull on his beer. "In a couple of weeks." Funny, the thought wasn't as appealing as it had been. When his old man had been thrown into the slammer, Turner had sworn to leave the Lazy K as soon as his shoulder was well, but since he'd become involved with

Heather... He glanced out the window and saw Heather and her boyfriend. They were standing several feet apart and she looked guiltily over her shoulder. The rich guy took a step toward her, but she held up her hand, said something and spun on her heel, running back to the house.

"You could stay on," Mazie said, as she always did, and Turner barely heard her his heart was slamming so loudly.

"What? Nah. I don't think so."

"Zeke needs good hands."

"Not me." His heart was beating like a drum as the man, his face dark red with fury, climbed into his fancy car and started the engine. With a spray of gravel, the sleek car and its driver were gone. The front door slammed shut and quick footsteps pounded up the stairs. Heather!

"And you'd be closer to your ma's place," Mazie pointed out.

Turner didn't look at her, could barely concentrate. She'd pushed the city boy out of her life! But why? For him? Pride mingled with self-disgust; he knew he would never be able to make her happy.

"Turner? You listening to me? I said 'you'd be closer to your ma's place!'"

Forcing his attention back to the conversation, Turner frowned and took a long swallow from his beer. While his mind was occupied with Heather, Mazie was talking about the run-down ranch where his father lived. Turner had grown up there and his father had rented the place from Thomas Fitzpatrick, a wealthy Gold Creek businessman who had gotten the ranch by some shady means. John Brooks had always wanted to own that miserable scrap of earth and when his wife had died, he'd managed to buy out Fitzpatrick with the life insurance proceeds coupled with a huge mortgage from the Bank of The Greater Bay.

Turner had done his best to pay off the mortgage. He scowled as he thought of it.

"Someday, son," his father had told him when he was barely thirteen, "this will all be yours." John Brooks had waved expansively to the acres of green grass and rolling hills. "And that's the way your ma, rest her soul, would've wanted it. Oh, I know she took out that policy for you, so you could go to college, earn yourself a degree, but she would've known that you weren't right for schoolin', that you needed some land, some roots." He'd slapped Turner on his shoulder. "That's right, boy. Your ma, now she was a smart woman. Had her own degree, y'know. In music. Could've been a teacher, but she married me instead—and me, I wasn't about to have my wife workin' and supportin' me. No way!" John had leaned over the fence rails, cradling a beer and smiling into the western hills. The tears in the corners of his eyes were probably from the intense light of the afternoon sun. Those telltale drops probably had nothing to do with remorse for being drunk behind the wheel of the pickup when it had rolled down an embankment, flipped over and killed his wife. "She would've wanted you to own something, kid, and there's nothing more valuable than land. Yesirree, Margaret would've approved."

Turner doubted it. He finished his beer in one long swallow and tossed the empty into the garbage can. In his peripheral vision, he caught Mazie studying him through a cloud of cigarette smoke.

"It won't work, y'know," she said kindly, and in that instant he realized that she could read his mind. "She wants the fine things in life, has her sights set upon being an artist."

"I don't know what you're talking about."

"Sure you do. I see the way you look at Heather when you think no one's watchin'. And she feels the same. But it won't last, son. Think of your poor ma—"

He rammed his hat back onto his head. "I'll be leavin' before the end of the month," he said suddenly. "Don't want to miss the final days of the rodeo season." Without waiting for a reply, he headed back outside and refused to think about Heather. Mazie was right. Heather complicated his life, and right now he had more than his share of complications.

HEATHER COULDN'T SLEEP. Dennis's surprise visit had caught her off guard. He'd come hoping to patch things up and she'd had to be firm. She didn't love him. Never had. Never would. She'd tried to be gentle, but he'd understood and he'd been angry when he'd left. Dennis Leonetti was used to getting what he wanted.

What had she ever seen in him? Compared to Turner... well, there was just no comparison. Sighing, she threw off her blankets and let the brisk night air that stole through the open window cool her body.

Her roommates didn't share her problem with insomnia. They were all tucked under their covers, snoring softly, dreaming whatever dreams filled their heads. But Heather was restless. She tossed and turned.

Ever since the night she and Turner had made love, he'd been avoiding her. She was hurt, and the ache in her heart wouldn't go away. Getting through the days had been difficult, and she'd just gone through the motions of her work. Mazie had been forced to scold her more than once and even Jill had noticed her bad mood. Sheryl hadn't said a word, but her blue eyes had been filled with silent accusations.

All because of Turner.

What a fool she'd been. She loved him. She was sure of it now. The fact that he was a cowboy was no longer repulsive—she even found his livelihood intriguing and romantic. "You're being as silly as Jill," she muttered to herself as she climbed from her bunk. She felt bottled up—claustrophobic—and she had to get outside for some fresh air. Throwing a robe over her nightgown, she stole down the back stairs.

The ranch house, filled with noise during the day, seemed strangely quiet. The hall clock ticked, the refrigerator hummed, the old timbers groaned and creaked, but still the house was different, the dark shadows in the corners seeming close.

Holding her robe together with stiff fingers, Heather dashed through the kitchen and outside. Muttso growled from somewhere in the bushes, but she ignored him and ran to the paddocks, her bare feet scraping on the stones and packed earth of the paths and walkways. The air was filled with the drone of insects and an owl hooted from an upper branch of a mammoth pine tree situated behind the pump house.

Heather breathed deeply of the pine-scented air. She ran her fingers through her hair, shaking the loose, tangled curls that fell down her back. The notes of an old country ballad drifted from a forgotten radio left on the windowsill of the tack room.

She wondered about Turner. Was he in his bed—sleepless as she? Was he packing to leave, for she'd heard he would soon rejoin the rodeo circuit? Or was he sleeping soundly, maybe with some other woman in his arms?

That thought caused a particularly painful jab in her heart.

"Don't you know it's dangerous slinking around here in the middle of the night?" Turner's voice was soft and close, and for a minute she thought she'd imagined it, had conjured the deep sounds as her thoughts had drifted to him.

Turning, she saw him, shirt open and flapping in the gentle breeze, Levi's riding low over his hips. She forced her gaze to his face, expecting hard censure. She wasn't disappointed, his gaze was stony, his jaw set.

"I couldn't sleep," she said, hoping her voice didn't betray her.

"Seems to be contagious." His voice was low and supple and seemed to whisper up her spine.

Heather gripped the top rail of the fence so hard she felt splinters against her fingers. "Did you think about the other night?"

"Can't think of much else."

Her heart took flight. "Me, neither."

He hesitated a second. "You had a visitor today."

Her stomach turned over and she bit her lip.

"Your boyfriend."

"Ex," she said automatically.

"He didn't seem to think so."

"Look, Turner, it's over. I know it and I think he does now, too."

He turned halfway, leaning an elbow on the fence rail and studying her face as if it held a vast secret he hoped to expose. "You're a hard woman to forget."

"Is that a compliment?" she asked, her voice tremulous.

"I'm just pointing out that your 'ex' didn't look like the kind who gives up easily."

"He's not."

"But you convinced him?" His voice was edged in skepticism.

"All I can tell you is that it's over between me and Dennis. It has been for a long time. And now…"

"Now what?"

Curling her fists, she sent up a silent prayer for strength, for honesty took more strength than she knew she possessed. "And now I only want you."

He let out a long low whistle. "You don't—"

She stepped forward, touching the rough stubble on his face with her hand. "I do, Turner. I want you."

She felt him smile in the darkness, a slow, sexy grin that brought an answering smile to her own lips.

"So what're we going to do about it?" he drawled.

She turned and looked across the rolling acres of night-darkened grassland. Her throat felt thick and tight. "You tell me," she finally whispered, swallowing hard and afraid that he would tell her that he didn't want her again, that it would be best if they stopped seeing each other. Her heart was knocking against her ribs, her hands sweating.

"I think the less we talk about it, the better." His arms suddenly surrounded her. He pulled her backward a bit, so that her buttocks pressed against his thighs, and he bent his head and kissed the crook of her neck. She went liquid inside, her knees giving way as his hands slipped beneath her robe, wrapping possessively around her abdomen. Through the thin fabric of her nightgown, she felt his fingertips, the hot pinpoints stretching from beneath her breasts to the top of her legs.

"I've missed you, Heather," he murmured, his lips hot and hungry.

"I…I've missed you, too."

His hands moved, stroking the skin over her belly, the thumb of one hand grazing the underside of her breasts, the fingers of his other swiping the apex of her legs.

Her blood began to pulse as he shifted, his hardness firm against her buttocks.

Closing her eyes, she knew she couldn't resist, that as long as Turner and she were together, she would surrender to him, even seduce him, time and time again. As they tumbled into the dry grass, she realized that loving him was her destiny as well as her curse.

For the first time in her life, Heather felt weak. She knew she should avoid Turner, for he would certainly leave and leave soon.

"YOU'RE MAKING A BIG MISTAKE," Sheryl told Heather as they basted chicken with tangy barbecue sauce. Over fifty fryer quarters sizzled over the huge barbecue pit in the backyard. Tonight was the last evening at the ranch for many of the guests. Balloons and torches lined the back porch and a huge barbecue and dance were planned.

"What kind of a mistake?" Heather asked innocently as the sweat ran between her shoulder blades. She picked up the tongs and began turning each quarter. The sun was blindingly hot. Grease spattered loudly and smoke billowed into the blue sky.

"You know what I mean. About Turner. You should avoid him. He'll only cause you heartache."

Jill, balancing a tub of sauce on her hip, heard the last of the discussion. "I don't know," she said, sending a wistful glance in the direction of the corral where some of the cowboys were branding calves. "I'd take his kind of heartache any day of the week."

"That's crazy," Sheryl muttered, as she brushed more sauce onto the chicken.

"Crazy like a fox," Jill replied, tossing her head and lowering her voice. "But I tell you, if I wanted to tie Turner down, I'd trick him."

"I don't want to tie anyone down," Heather snapped, hating the conversation. "I don't think we should be talking about—"

"Trick him?" Sheryl repeated. "How?"

"By telling him I was pregnant."

Heather dropped the tongs.

"Oh, God," Sheryl whispered. "That's insane."

"Not if you really want a man. You know what they say, 'all's fair in love and war.'"

"But he'd find out—" Sheryl said.

"By then it'd be too late, or I would be pregnant," Jill replied with a smile.

Sheryl and Heather stared at each other as Jill flounced up the stairs. "She'd do just about anything to leave home, I guess," Sheryl said, biting her lip. "Even trap a man."

Heather felt sick. She finished basting the chicken, then helped bake corn bread as Mazie stood over a massive tub of chili. Even with the windows thrown wide, the kitchen seemed well over a hundred degrees. Heather tried to keep her concentration on her job, but her eyes kept wandering to the window and beyond where calves bawled and sweaty men tended a small fire and pressed the hot brand of the Lazy K into living rawhide.

Turner was there. She could see him leaning over a frightened calf, talking softly, untying quick, flying hooves and stepping back swiftly as the calf scrambled to its feet.

"If you don't watch out, that bread'll rise three feet," Mazie admonished. "Just how much baking powder you figure on adding?"

Heather jumped, nearly dumping the contents of the baking powder can into her mixture of cornmeal, flour, milk, sugar and egg. "Sorry," she said, recovering.

"Just keep your mind on what you're doing."

That wasn't easy advice to follow. For the next few hours, her eyes worked as if they had a mind of their own, searching the corrals, always seeking out Turner. Just as some of the guests were leaving tonight, Heather had a horrible premonition that Turner, too, would try to say goodbye. He'd been hinting at it for the past two days. It was only a matter of time.

The girls were given time to change after the food had been served, and they, along with the hands and guests, danced on the plank deck while the flames of the torches gave off a flickering light. The music was a blend of country and old rock and roll, and Heather danced with several of the ranch hands and guests before she found herself in Turner's arms.

The lead singer, as if on cue, started singing a slow ballad by the Judds that nearly broke Heather's heart.

Turner's arms folded around her and she clung to him with a desperation born of fear. Tears burned behind her eyes. Soon he would leave. As surely as the sun would rise in the east, Turner would be gone.

And what was she supposed to do? Live her life as if she'd never met him? Pretend that their affair hadn't existed? Save enough money for art school and find an apartment in the city? She thought of her sister's lifestyle, once so envied, that now didn't have the same fascination for her. The bright lights of the city, the dazzle of theater openings, the glitter of dance clubs had dimmed as she'd come to know and love Turner.

She snuggled deeper in his arms, closing her eyes as his scent enveloped her. Leather and denim and smoke from the branding fire mixed with soap and horses to create a special male aroma. His body molded against hers, and beneath the sundress she wore, her skin turned warm. His lips pressed against her bare neck and she tingled all over....

The song ended, and Turner whispered, "Meet me in the barn at midnight," before they parted and found new partners. She fell into the arms of a hefty guest named Ron, who stepped on her toes, and Turner wound up dancing with Sheryl. Heather gritted her teeth and forced a smile and tried not to watch as Sheryl smiled up at Turner and whispered something in his ear. Turner laughed and Sheryl cast a superior glance in Heather's direction.

Heather turned her attention back to her partner and started counting down the minutes until midnight.

TURNER WAS WAITING FOR HER. His silhouette was visible against the window as she stepped into the darkened barn.

"I thought you might have changed your mind," he said.

"Never." Running to him, she threw herself into his open arms and met his hot lips with her own.

"Not here.... Come on," he whispered, taking her hand and leading her to the ladder that stretched to the hayloft. He followed her into the bower of fragrant hay and together they tumbled onto a mattress of loose straw. His lips found hers again and the hunger in his kiss told her that he would leave soon. There was a surrender in his movements that she'd never felt before, as if he hoped in one night to take his fill of her.

She met his fevered lovemaking with her own flaming desire. She closed her mind to the future, lost herself in the here and now and made love to him with all the passion and fear that tortured her heart.

"I love you," she whispered recklessly, as she straddled him and her hair fell around her face and shoulders in thick golden waves.

Turner gazed up at her, his eyes glazed, his face flushed with desire. "Don't say—"

"But I do, Turner," she gasped.

He placed a finger over her lips, and she caressed it with her mouth and tongue, convulsing over him as he bucked upward and released himself deep within her. "Heather," he cried. "Sweet, sweet, lady." His arms were around her and he pulled her sweat-soaked body down to rest on his.

She felt tears fill her eyes, but she wouldn't cry, not in front of him. Together they lay, entwined, their hearts beating rapidly, their breath mingling in the warm summer air. Turner's arms were wound possessively around her and his lips touched her hair. They lay on their backs, staring through the open window near the apex of the roof, and watched the stars wink in the dark sky.

"I can't stay here forever," Turner said as he kissed her temple and plucked a piece of straw from her hair.

Her throat was so tight, she could barely whisper, "Why not?"

"I've got a life out there."

Oh, God, not now! Please not now! Her world seemed to crack. "So you're just a ramblin' man," she said, fighting tears and the sarcasm that poisoned her words. She'd promised herself that when he wanted to leave, she wouldn't tie him down, but now she felt desperate to do anything, *anything* to stop him.

"I guess."

She squeezed her eyes shut and told herself she wouldn't break down, wouldn't shed one solitary tear for this man whose heart was hard enough that he could walk away.

"You'll leave soon anyway, too," he said calmly, though his voice was rougher than usual. "You've got school in the fall—"

"It doesn't matter now."

"Sure it does." He levered up on one elbow and studied the features of her face so intently she looked away. "Heather, you have a chance—to do what you want. Go for it. Don't let anyone take your dreams away from you."

"Like someone took yours from you?" she guessed, and he stiffened.

"I always wanted to be a cowboy."

"Little boys want to ride horses and shoot guns," she said, touching his arm, feeling the downy hair beneath her fingers. "Grown men like to sit in offices, order their secretaries around and play golf."

"Not this one." He flopped onto his back and stared at the dusty rafters where a barn owl had tried to roost. "That's the problem, Heather. I *like* my life the way it is. I'd die in a three-piece suit and a tiny office on the forty-third floor of some high rise. I'd rather hassle with my old pickup than drive a Mercedes. And I'd take a camp stove and a tent over a house in the suburbs any day. I wouldn't be any good at frying hamburgers on the backyard grill and I don't see myself coachin' Little League."

"You're telling me there's no room in your life for me."

"Nope. I'm telling you there's no room in *your* life for *me*."

"I love you, Turner."

"You don't—"

"Shh." She pressed a finger to his lips and fought back

the urge to cry. He didn't love her. Oh, he cared for her. That much was evident. But to him she was no more than his girl at one of the many places he called home. He probably had women waiting for him in every rodeo town in the West. Tears clogged her throat and burned her eyes. She leaned over and kissed him.

He responded, but his eyes were open and he saw the tears that she fought so bravely. With a sad smile, he wiped a tear from her cheek. "Don't cry for me, darlin'. Believe me, I'm not worth it," he said before his lips found hers again and he showed her a way to forget the pain.

HEATHER DIDN'T SEE TURNER the next day. He didn't come in for meals and his pickup wasn't in the yard. If Mazie knew anything, she was keeping her lips buttoned and Zeke wasn't around.

All day long Heather's stomach was queasy and her heart felt as if it had turned to stone. But he wouldn't have left without saying goodbye.

The day dragged endlessly, and when finally she was finished shaking the rugs, hanging the kettles and mopping the floor, she tossed her apron into a hamper and ran outside. Heart in her throat, she walked to the stables.

Sampson was missing.

And Turner's saddle wasn't slung over the sawhorse near the corner of Sampson's stall. She hurried down the cement walkways, her boots ringing hollowly beneath the glare of single bulbs.

In the broodmare barn she found Billy, pitchfork in hand, tossing fresh hay into a manger.

"Is—have you seen Turner?" she asked when Billy glanced her way.

"Not since daybreak. He's gone."

"Gone?" she replied, panic causing her heart to beat so fast she could barely breathe. Maybe Billy meant that Turner had driven into town for supplies with Zeke. Or maybe he meant that Turner had taken some of the guests on an overnight campout. Or maybe his father had gotten himself into trouble again and Turner had to bail the old man out. That was probably it. John had gotten drunk, thrown a few punches in a bar and—

"He took off just after dawn," Billy volunteered, jabbing another forkful of hay.

"When will he be back?"

Billy's jaw tightened. He stuffed the pitchfork into a bale of straw and yanked off his gloves. "I don't reckon he's comin' back. Leastwise not this summer."

Her heart dropped to the cold cement floor. "You're sure?"

"Hell, I don't know." Billy shrugged and tossed his hair out of his eyes. "But his shoulder isn't hurt anymore and he paid a lot of money for entry fees and everyone knows he likes to keep some distance between himself and his old man, so you figure it out."

He yanked on his gloves and began spreading straw in some of the empty stalls. Heather's throat squeezed shut and tears stung her eyes. So he'd gone. Without telling her. Well, maybe he'd tried last night, but she'd expected more than a "I'll be leaving soon."

She battled tears all the way back to the ranch house. She wanted to throw herself onto her bed and kick and scream and sob until all her tears were wrung from her body. But she couldn't go upstairs and run into Sheryl or Jill or any of the girls who worked at the ranch. No, she'd have to do her grieving by herself. Maybe he'd call. Or write. She could cling to those frail hopes.

Feeling more miserable than she'd felt in all of her

life, she saddled Sundown and rode to the bend in the river where she'd first spied Turner. "The beginning of the end," she whispered, patting the gelding's neck and hopping to the ground while tears streamed down her face.

She tried to be strong because she faced more than a single fear. Not only did she realize that he'd used her, that she'd been nothing more than one of the girls he'd met on the road, that he'd never loved her, she also suspected that she might be pregnant.

She touched her flat abdomen and tried not to cry for the baby who would never know his father. For the baby, she had to be strong; for the life beating within her, she had to find a way to survive. Without Turner.

## BOOK TWO

*Badlands Ranch, California*
*The Present*

# *CHAPTER FIVE*

THE BRONC LEAPT HIGH, twisted in midair and kicked toward the sun, but Turner held on, his fingers twined in the bridle and mane of his furious mount. "That's it, you bastard. Show me what you've got," he gritted out. His hat flew off, skimming through the dry air to land in the center of the paddock. The roan, a nasty beast named Gargoyle, landed with a bone-jarring thud before he became airborne again, bucking and rearing, fighting to dislodge his unwanted rider.

Turner gritted his teeth and ignored the grime and dust of a day's work. This ugly stallion was the best of the lot he was to train, a fiery-tempered quarter horse who didn't give up, the kind of do-or-die animal that Turner had always found a challenge.

Hooves found earth again and the roan took off, running the length of the paddock, kicking up dust and nearly smashing Turner's leg against the shaved poles of the fence.

Grinning wickedly, Turner clamped his thighs tighter, shifting his weight, letting the horse know who was boss.

Gargoyle careened to a stop, wheeled on back legs and took off again, running and bucking and tearing up the arid ground.

"I think that's enough." Turner reined in, and while the horse took a minute to shift gears, Turner hopped to the ground and wrapped the reins around the top pole of the fence. Man and beast were both sweating and breathing hard.

Turner retrieved his Stetson and slapped the dirty hat against his thigh. A cloud of dust swirled upward. "Tomorrow," Turner promised.

The horse glowered at him, flattening his ears and shifting his rear end to get a clean shot at Turner's shin.

Sidestepping quickly, Turner avoided the kick. "You lazy no-good son of a bitch," Turner muttered, though he was amused by the stallion's spirited antics. With a little work, this quarter horse would be one of the best he'd ever ridden—ugly or not. "You won't win, y'know." With an eye to the horse's back legs, Turner loosened the cinch and slid the saddle from the roan's back. "And I'm considering changing your name to Silk Purse. You know the story, don't ya?"

Gargoyle swung his broad head around and tried to take a nip from Turner's butt, but the reins restrained the stallion and he was left to stomp the hard earth in frustration.

"Serves you right." Turner hoisted the saddle to the fence rail, then quickly unsnapped the bridle. Gargoyle didn't need any more encouragement. He took off, bucking and kicking across the dusty paddock, snorting and galloping with as much speed as any stallion Turner had come across in a long while.

"Remember—tomorrow!" Turner called out as he vaulted the fence. The roan huffed, fire in his eyes, as if he were already anticipating the outcome of their next encounter. Turner laughed. "Yeah, well, I'm lookin' forward to it, too."

"Quite a show you put on."

The voice was soft and feminine, and Turner glanced up sharply to find Nadine standing in the shadow of the barn. He'd forgotten this was her day to come and clean his place. "Didn't know anyone was watchin'," he drawled as she crossed the gravel lot, her red hair catching fire in the sunlight. She was a pretty woman with big green eyes, an easy smile, and a smattering of freckles across the bridge of a straight little nose. Divorced, with two small children, Nadine made her way in the world alone.

"I thought you might need this." She handed him a cold bottle of beer, right from the refrigerator. "And I didn't want you tracking dirt on my floor."

"And here I thought that floor was mine," he replied, taking the bottle and twisting off the cap.

"Not until the wax is dry, it isn't." She reached into the pocket of her denim jacket and withdrew a stack of envelopes. "Mail call." Slapping them into his callused palm, she motioned toward the stallion. "Not too handsome, is he?"

"He'll do." Turner couldn't help baiting her a bit. "Don't you know that the uglier they are, the better they look flyin' out of the chutes?"

"He flies all right. I'll give him that." She squinted up at Turner, and for a minute he caught a glimpse of some emotion she usually hid. She'd been his housekeeper for four years, long before she was divorced from Sam Warne, but lately he'd gotten the feeling that she was interested in more than wiping the grime from his windows. "By the way, she called again," Nadine added, and Turner's gut turned to stone.

"Who?"

"As if you didn't know. Heather, that's who. Seems as if she's trying pretty hard to reach you."

Turner didn't respond. No reason to. As far as he was concerned, Heather didn't exist—hadn't for a lot of years.

"And the Realtor for Thomas Fitzpatrick hasn't let up. He phoned, too. Fitzpatrick wants this ranch back in a bad way."

Turner's glower increased. "I already told him—it isn't for sale."

"Thomas Fitzpatrick doesn't give up easily."

"He doesn't have a choice."

She lifted a shoulder. "Just thought you'd want to know."

"Only good news. That's all I want to hear about," Turner said, his eyes narrowing.

"Well, you may be waiting a long time."

Though she was only teasing, he knew she was right. He closed his eyes for a second. Damn, he didn't need either Heather Tremont Leonetti or Thomas Friggin' Fitzpatrick fouling up his life. He was capable of fouling it up himself without anyone else's help. When he opened his eyes again, he watched Nadine as she waved and moved toward her car, a beat-up old Chevy filled with mops, brooms, soap and wax.

Turner's gaze followed after her as she climbed behind the wheel, fired the engine and tore off down the lane, leaving a plume of dust behind her. She was a good-lookin' woman, a woman any man would be proud to claim as his wife, but Turner wasn't interested. Besides, she deserved better. He took a long swallow of the beer and wiped the sweat from his brow. Leaning both arms over the top rail of the fence, he eyed the stallion. "You are a mean beast, you know," he said.

A soft nicker whispered over the dry fields, and Gargoyle lifted his head, nostrils extended, ears pricked forward, in the direction of the sound. Turner followed the stallion's gaze to the small herd of mares, sleek hides gleaming in the afternoon sunlight as they grazed near the ridge. Backdropped by a copse of cedar and pine, they plucked at the dry grass, oblivious to the stallion's interest.

Gargoyle tossed back his head and let out a stallion's whistle to the mares. Beneath his dusty, reddish coat, his shoulder muscles quivered in anticipation.

"You poor bastard," Turner said with genuine regret because he liked the feisty roan. He watched as Gargoyle pranced along the fence line, whinnying and snorting, head held high, tail streaming like a banner as he showed off for the lackadaisical females. "So you like the ladies, do you? It's a mistake, you know. Can only get you into trouble."

The stallion nickered again and the mares, flicking their ears toward the noise, continued to graze and swat at flies with their tails.

Turner had seen enough. Wiping his hands on the thin denim covering his thighs, he started for the small ranch house he called home. It wasn't much, but it was bought and paid for and all Turner needed now that his old man was gone. The mortgage had nearly sucked the life blood from him, but he'd used every penny he'd earned to pay back the bank—Leonetti's bank. Dennis's grandfather and father had owned and run the bank and when old John had taken out the mortgage, Turner hadn't yet met Heather or known of Dennis Leonetti. But once he'd figured it all out, he couldn't pay off his debt fast enough. The thought that he owed any Leonetti money galled the life out of him.

What comes around goes around, he thought. Now Thomas Fitzpatrick was interested in the ranch again— wanted to run some geological tests on the land beneath the ridge, scouting around for oil—but Turner held firm. This was his place, bought with his mother's tears and his own blood and sweat. He wasn't going to allow the likes of Thomas Fitzpatrick to get his hands on it again.

As he headed along the weed-choked path, his body, jarred from two hours in the saddle, ached. Old pains, "war wounds," as he referred to them, reappeared. His hip hurt so badly he nearly limped again, but he gritted his teeth against the pain. He was barely thirty, for God's sake—he wasn't going to start walking like a run-down old man.

Kicking off his boots on the back porch, he swatted at a bothersome yellow jacket, then shoved open the screen door to the kitchen. The house reeked of lemon, pine and cleaning solvent—in Turner's opinion, a stench worse than horse dung and sweat.

He didn't breathe too deeply, but as he crossed the gleaming floor, he noticed the white rose propped in a cracked vase, giving the kitchen "a woman's touch." As usual. And as usual, the rose would wither and die until Nadine came back and put another flower of some sort in its place. As if he cared.

Settling into one of the chairs at the table, he took a long swallow from his bottle. The beer was cold and slid easily down his parched throat. A little too easily. He wiped his mouth with the back of his hand.

He was careful with liquor, because of his old man. He knew how the beast in the bottle could drive a man— how it could break him. But, though he hated to admit it, he had a fondness for beer. One of his weaknesses. His first was—or had been—a woman. He'd given up on one, so he felt no compulsion to forsake the other. But he'd be careful. No way was he going to end up like John Brooks—in and out of the drunk tank all of his life, dying before he was fifty because his overworked liver just gave up and quit.

He took another pull, drained half the bottle and felt his muscles relax. Shuffling through the mail, his hands leaving smudges on the white envelopes, he eyed the sorry stack of bills, advertisements, a magazine and one lone letter—written crisply in a woman's hand. Heather's hand.

The return address was San Francisco—where she'd moved to escape the small-town poverty and boredom of Gold Creek. For that, he didn't blame her. Nothing but trouble ever came out of Gold Creek, California. Including himself.

Memories of Heather skittered like unwanted ghosts through his mind. He finished his beer and reached into the refrigerator before curiosity overcame good sense.

His mouth went dry for just a second.

Heather Tremont. No, Heather Tremont Leonetti. She was married now. Had been for years. Her husband was Dennis Leonetti. Big name; big money. A slick-talking banker who had inherited his money, could give his beautiful young wife anything her heart desired—as long as it had a price tag attached. Even an art gallery. And a son. The same SOB she was supposed to have broken up with when he'd come careening into the yard of the Lazy K in his rich boy's machine. Well, Heather had shown her true colors, hadn't she? All that talk about not caring about money. About trust. About love. All BS!

Not that it mattered. Not that he cared. He let the door of the refrigerator swing shut.

Peeling the label from his empty bottle, he noticed the message written on a notepad by the phone—Heather's name and phone number written in Nadine's no-nonsense scrawl. In his mind's eye, he compared Heather to Nadine. Nadine was so simple, so earthy, so straightforward. Heather had always been complicated, beautiful and manipulative. An *artist* for God's sake—with the temperament to match. So why was it always Heather's gorgeous face that disturbed his dreams? Why couldn't he take a chance on a simple, good-hearted woman like Nadine Warne?

He reached again for the refrigerator. This time he didn't stop when he opened the door. He pulled out a tall, dewy bottle and twisted off the top as he glanced again at the letter.

Heather.

He wondered if she'd found happiness with all her money. Not that he gave a damn. Crumpling the letter in a grimy fist, he lobbed the wadded, unread note into a corner where it bounced off the wall and landed on the gleaming floor, six inches from the basket. Well, he'd never been good at basketball. In fact, he hadn't been much good at anything besides staying astride a stubborn rodeo bronc. Now, even that was gone.

He glanced through the window to the rolling hills of his ranch; he'd kept it running with the stubborn grit that told him he had to make something of himself, something to break the legacy that he'd inherited from John Brooks. He had all he wanted right here.

He didn't need Heather Leonetti or her money to remind him of that.

Frowning darkly, Turner took another long tug from his beer. He'd finish this one, take a shower and maybe drive into town—do anything to stop thinking about Heather.

HEATHER HAD NEVER BEEN to Turner's ranch. Never had the guts. She'd put their past in a neat little package of memories that she'd locked in a closet in her mind and had never dared examine. Until recently.

She'd been married and tried to make the marriage work. It, of course, had been doomed from the beginning. Without love, the walls of her marriage had cracked early on only to crumble later. Now, as she squinted through her sunglasses, her hands were sweating on the wheel of her Mercedes. She'd let the top down and felt the wind tug at her hair and whip across her face.

The landscape was dry; the grass already bleached gold, the dust a thin layer on the asphalt as the wheels of her Mercedes flew over the country road leading north from Gold Creek to Badlands Ranch. Once called Rolling Hills, Turner had renamed it for who knew what reason. Heather didn't understand why and didn't care.

She only had to face Turner again because of Adam. At the thought of her son, she caught her lip between her teeth. His disease wasn't, at the moment, life threatening. But at any time his remission could be reversed and then…oh, God, and then… She shuddered though the interior of the car was warm.

Her own bone marrow didn't match that of her son. And, of course, Dennis's wouldn't, either. That left Turner. For, if Adam should need a donor and was unable to donate enough good tissue to himself, Turner was the next logical choice.

He deserved to know.

She pushed a little harder on the throttle, and her car leapt forward, exceeding the limit. She couldn't seem to get to Turner fast enough. She'd been in Gold Creek long enough to know that he wasn't married, that no woman openly lived with him, but she wasn't sure that he wasn't in love with someone and that whoever the woman was, she wouldn't want Heather showing up on Turner's doorstep with the news that not only was he a father, but that the boy needed him.

She tasted blood and forced herself to relax, removing her teeth from her lip and easing up on the throttle. The ranch was just ahead. She spotted the turnoff to a long dirt-and-gravel lane that wound through a thicket of trees. The ranch house was probably beyond. She turned into the lane. The tire of the Mercedes hit a pothole and shuddered, and Heather sent up a prayer that when she faced Turner again, she wouldn't break down.

THE TEMPERATURE IN THE barn hovered around a hundred degrees. Dust filled the air that was acrid with the smells of manure and oil from the broken-down tractor. Yellow jackets buzzed near the filthy windows and swallows flew in and out the open door. The light from the lowering sun seeped through the cracks in the old siding and faded in the recesses of the interior. A headache thundered behind Turner's eyes. He needed a shower and a drink and then maybe a woman. Not necessarily in that order. He'd be lucky if he got the shower.

Sweat ran down the back of his neck and over his bare back as every one of his muscles strained while he pitted his will and strength against that of the stallion.

Gargoyle wasn't going to win this round, Turner decided as he held the roan's bent foreleg tightly between his thighs and carefully, so as to avoid being nipped in the rear, tapped the nails of the horseshoe back into Gargoyle's hoof. The roan snorted, shifting his weight against the man and looking for a way to take a piece out of Turner's hide.

"Relax," Turner muttered around a mouthful of nails. His muscles ached, but he didn't give in. For his efforts, he was flicked in the face with the coarse hairs of the horse's tail. "Cut it out!"

*Tap, tap, tap.* He drove the nails into the hoof. The

horse was nervous. Lather greased his coat and his ears were flat with hatred for the man intent on taming his wild spirit. "You'll live. Believe me," Turner told the roan as he drove the last nail into place.

"Turner?"

The feminine voice, so familiar in his distant memory, caught his attention. He looked up and saw her silhouetted in the open door, her figure dark in contrast to the fading sunlight, her skirt moving slightly in a tiny ghost of a breeze. The hairs on the back of Turner's neck lifted one by one. It couldn't be...

"Turner Brooks?" she repeated, stepping into the shadows of the barn, closer now so that he could see her face, the same damned face that he'd tried so hard to forget.

Gargoyle shifted, his head swinging around. And Turner, thighs still clamped over the horse's foreleg, sidestepped the nip. He spat the nails into his hand, all the while never letting his gaze wander from the doorway. "Well, well, well," he heard himself saying. "If it isn't Mrs. Leonetti?" She winced a little at that, and he wondered where was the satisfaction he should have felt in wounding her. Letting the roan's leg drop, he vaulted easily over the railing of the stall. She was still a few feet away, but he noticed her eyes widen a bit, and the quick intake of her breath, as if she were frightened. "You know, I never thought I'd see you again."

"I...um...I know." She licked her lips—from nerves or in an effort to play coy, he couldn't guess. His gut tightened, warning him that she was trouble. Always had been. Always would be. Her blond hair, the color of winter wheat, stirred in the breeze, and in the half light of the barn her eyes were as dark as the stone cold hue of an arctic sky. Fitting. "You haven't returned my calls," she accused, though her words weren't harsh.

"Nothin' to say."

"And my letter?"

One edge of his lip lifted sardonically. God, she was beautiful—frigidly so. The layer of sophistication she'd so carefully wrapped around her made her seem ice-cold and untouchable—like a marble statue. She'd changed over the years, and not for the better. "You sent me something? Must've got lost," he drawled, and they both knew it was a lie.

"You should've read it."

"Why?" He folded his arms over his chest, waiting with measured patience.

Her mouth moved, but she didn't speak.

"Look, lady," Turner said irritably as he remembered using that very word as an endearment in the past. She froze for a second and he mentally kicked himself. "Is there something you want? If so, just spit it out and then leave me the hell alone."

"I just...I... Oh, drat!" She rolled her eyes to the ceiling, and for the first time he noticed the lines of strain near her mouth. Maybe being married to Mr. Big Bucks wasn't all it was cracked up to be. "I had to see you again."

His body turned rigid. Every sweat-soaked muscle grew taut with suspicion. She was playing with him. A bored housewife looking for a quick thrill. "So now you've seen me," he said, with as much malice as he could muster. May as well have a little fun with her. She deserved it. "Now what?"

"I, um, thought we could talk."

He sauntered closer to her, aware that he smelled of sweat and horse and dirt. He hadn't shaved in three days, and his faded jeans, threatening to bust through in the knees and butt, were streaked with grime. A pretty sight he made, he thought as he stopped only inches from her and stared down into her cobalt-blue eyes. In his peripheral vision, he caught a glimpse of a sleek, silver Mercedes—a rich woman's car.

"Talk?" He lifted a dubious eyebrow and smiled inwardly when her pulse, visible in her throat, leapt. So she was either scared or nervous. Good. "I'm not in the mood to talk. There's only one thing I've ever wanted to do with you," he said cruelly, keeping his voice low while sliding one long finger along the V of her neckline. "And you know what that is. So, let's either get down to it or you can get the hell out of my life."

Shuddering, as if from revulsion, she drew in a long breath and focused her eyes directly on his. "Don't try to scare me, Turner. It won't work."

So she did still have some gumption. She tossed her thick blond hair away from her face and didn't flinch, not even when his finger slipped beneath the clear button and the blouse opened a slit. He told himself she could never arouse him again, but the pad of his fingertip pressing against the taut skin over her sternum caused a reaction elsewhere in his body, and when he noticed that her expensive white blouse was dirty where he'd touched the lapel, his groin tightened. He always had liked a challenge and she seemed intent on giving him one.

So what the hell? Even if she were here for a quick roll in the hay—why not? So she was married. He'd always drawn the line at married women before, but with Heather, when she was practically begging for it...

He grabbed the front of her blouse in his fist and drew her close, intent on kissing her.

"Don't even think about it," she warned as he lowered his head.

"No?"

Her own fingers wound around his wrists. "I didn't come here to seduce you, Turner and, in fact—" she managed to rake her gaze down his filthy body "—if I were in the mood, you'd be the last man I'd want."

"I doubt that," he replied, his eyes slitting as he stared down at this rich little bitch who had the nerve to stride onto his ranch, uninvited, and insult him.

"I'd heard that you were a broken-down cowboy, a man who was on the verge of pouring his life into a bottle, but I didn't believe it. But now—" she skated that haughty gaze over the rough planes of his face "—I see that I was wrong."

He wasn't going to argue with her. So he'd inherited his old man's reputation. Big deal. He knew that he'd never, *never* follow the same path as John Brooks. What other people thought—including Heather Leonetti— didn't matter.

"Then why the hell are you here, *lady?*" he asked, spitting out the final word.

"Because I need your help!"

His fist uncoiled and he stepped away from her, noticing the fire in her eyes. "From a 'broken-down cowboy'? From a man who's on his way to 'pouring his life into a bottle'? I don't think so." He glared at her as if she were dirt. His lip curled in disgust. He was tired of the game and furious that just the sight of her could arouse him. "Go home, Heather. Go back to your fat-cat husband. I don't really give a damn what you want. I wouldn't help you if you crawled back to me on your hands and knees."

"Well, think about it, Turner, because that's exactly what I'm doing," she said, holding her wobbling chin a little higher. Tears filled her blue eyes and he felt his pride start to shatter. "I'm begging you because I need your help."

"I don't think so—"

"We have a son, Turner," she said quickly, and all sound inside the barn seemed to cease. He stared at her as if she had gone stark, raving mad. "He's five. His name is Adam. And regardless of what you think of me, he needs you very much."

# CHAPTER SIX

BENEATH HIS TAN, TURNER'S face drained of color. "A son," he repeated, when he finally found his tongue. Disbelief clouded his eyes and his voice was deadly. "I have a son?"

"Yes and—"

"And you haven't told me about him for six years and now, all of a sudden, out of the clear damned blue, I have a son." He looked at her long and hard, his face harsh and flushed with fury. "Come on, Heather, you can do better than that. Just try."

"I'm telling the truth!" She didn't panic. Not yet. She'd known he wouldn't believe her, not at first.

"Sure. Well, for your information we have three daughters, too. I just never got around to tellin' you 'bout 'em." He offered a cold smile, and it was all Heather could do not to grab him by his filthy collar and shake some sense into him.

"It isn't impossible, you know."

His cruel grin faded, and she knew he, too, was remembering all the times they'd made love that summer.

"Why would I lie?"

"You tell me." Yanking a handkerchief from his pocket, he wiped the sweat and grime from his face. His hands shook a little and she knew she was finally reaching him.

"I wouldn't be here if I didn't have to be, Turner. You know that."

Time seemed to spin backward six long, lonely years. The air was thick with old, tangled emotions that seemed to creep into the barn and bring sweat to Heather's brow. Turner's expression turned from wary to a thundering rage that knotted his features as the truth finally hit home. "Are you trying to tell me that I've had a kid for five years and you've kept it a secret?"

Heather's heart ripped.

"That you married a rich banker so that my kid wouldn't have to be raised by a poor cowboy? Is that it?"

She choked, her throat swollen, her heart shredding.

"Are you trying to convince me that you're so callous—so friggin' manipulative that you would pass off another man's son as his?"

She couldn't help herself. With a smack that resounded to the dusty rafters, she slapped him hard across his dirty face. He caught her wrist, and the ugly horse in the stall snorted and stamped impatiently. "It wouldn't be wise to get physical with me, lady," he warned, the tension in the barn snapping as with the current of an electric storm.

But Heather barely heard his warning. She yanked back her hand and glared at him. "You weren't interested in commitments, Turner, remember? You didn't want a family. No strings to tie you down. You were too busy chasing cows and riding bucking horses and being a loner to think about…about…"

"About the fact that I had a kid? How the hell would I know?"

"You didn't stick around long enough to find out, did you?" she accused. Her fury suddenly grew to a living, breathing beast that roared within her. All her pent-up rage exploded. "You don't think I wanted to tell you? I tried, Turner. But you were gone."

"Seems to me you found yourself a patsy."

"A patsy? All I wanted was a father for my child! A man who would care for him, a man who *wanted* him—"

"All you wanted was a rich man, Heather. That's all you've ever wanted. I knew it then and I know it now. But I'm warning you, if you're lyin' to me—"

"I'm not. Adam's your son," she said flatly. "And believe me, if I could change that, I would."

For the first time, he actually seemed to see past his anger. A vein ticked in his forehead and sweat drizzled down his neck. "And why, after six years, do you want to see me now?"

Her stomach knotted with the pain of the truth. "Adam's sick, Turner," she said, her voice barely a whisper.

His spine went rigid and his eyes turned black as night. "Sick?"

"He has leukemia," she said, deciding that it was now or never. She saw the fear flare in his eyes. "The disease…it's in remission. He's been through hell fighting it, but the drugs have seemed to work. Now the doctor is talking about a possible bone-marrow transplant. But Adam has no siblings and…well, I don't match. Even though it's a slim chance, I was hoping…I thought that you might…" She threw her hands up toward the rafters and tears filled her eyes. "Oh, Turner," she whispered, her voice cracking as she thought about losing Adam. "I wouldn't have come, but you're Adam's best hope."

"*If* I'm his father," he said coldly.

"You are, damn it! Do you honestly think I would've wasted my time driving up here, dredging up everything again?" Blinking rapidly, she fingered the clasp of her purse. "I've got a picture—"

"I'll need more proof than that."

"Anything," she whispered, glad that at least they were making headway.

Turner's gaze shifted around the barn quickly, as if he were sizing up his own operation. Nervously, he rubbed the top rail of the stall. "They have tests now—genetic tests that would prove without a doubt—"

"I *know* that, Turner. That's why you should trust me. If I'm lying, I'll be found out. But I'm not. Believe me, I wouldn't have bothered."

That stopped him. His fidgeting hands quit moving. "Does your husband know?"

"Of course my *ex*-husband knows. He knew I was pregnant when we got married. I told him about you." She thought fleetingly of Dennis, of his reaction when she'd first told him she was pregnant with another man's child. He'd been angry, even wounded, and he'd left her mother's house with a screech of tires. But he had come back. Swearing that he loved her. Vowing to look after her and the baby. Promising to give the infant everything it could ever want. And she'd stupidly believed Dennis Leonetti, a man obsessed with her. It all seemed like such a long time ago. And now, staring at Turner, she wondered how she'd ever let the world think that Adam had been Dennis's son.

Turner's jaw tightened, and before he could say anything hateful, she said, "I didn't really know that I was pregnant until you were gone. Then I tried to contact you…but it was impossible. I called the Lazy K. Zeke wouldn't say where you were and for once Mazie kept her mouth shut. Even the other ranch hands played dumb."

"So you married Leonetti," he said, his voice cold as stone.

Why bother explaining? He'd set himself up as judge and jury, tried her and found her guilty. But she couldn't expect much more, she supposed. She dug into her purse, found the picture of Adam and held it out to him. "This... this is our son," she said.

Turner swept the snapshot out of her fingers, and in the half-light within the barn, he squinted at it. His eyebrows knotted in concentration.

*Can't you see it, Turner? Doesn't the resemblance leap out at you? He has the same straight, light brown hair, the same gray eyes, the same little cleft in his chin? Oh, God, Turner, he's yours!*

A dozen emotions flickered in Turner's eyes. Emotions that were dark and dangerous. His voice, when he spoke, was thick. "How do you know?" he asked, and though she'd been prepared for the question, it startled her.

"I was a virgin, remember? You were the first. The only."

His mouth tightened. He remembered all right. Everything about her. Loving any other woman had never felt so right. Even now, in her expensive clothes and soft leather shoes, she was as attractive to him as she had been as a girl in cutoff jeans and halter tops. "There could have been others."

Her steady blue eyes held his. "There weren't."

"How do I know—"

"You don't. You have to trust me on this one, Turner. I never made love to anyone but you until I married Dennis—two weeks after the doctor confirmed my pregnancy. You can think what you want of me, but that's the God's honest truth. Adam's yours."

His heart was pounding so hard he could hear the blood pumping at his temples. She leaned closer to him, and he could see the golden crown of her head, could smell the provocative fragrance of her perfume. Just as before, he found her impossible to resist.

"I wouldn't have come here unless you were my only hope, Turner. It's just that I'm out of options and I would risk anything, even facing you again, to help my boy. I was hoping you'd feel the same way."

Turner's guts twisted. Leukemia! Wasn't that fatal? His mouth turned to sand as he thought about a boy he'd never had the chance to know, a son that he could lose before he'd ever really found him. Damn Heather and her lies! She should have told him. She'd owed him that much. His fingers curled possessively over the slick snapshot. "What if he hadn't gotten sick? Would you have ever told him about me—or let me know I had a kid?" he asked, rage beginning to swell inside him.

"Yes."

"When?"

She hesitated just a second. "When he was eighteen."

"Eighteen!" She had it all planned out. And she'd intended to rob him of ever seeing his boy as a kid. So that they'd never play catch, never ride trails and camp out on the river, never even meet. "Eight-friggin'-teen?" he said in a voice so low he saw the fear register in her eyes.

"He'd need to know someday."

"And me? Did I need to know?"

She shook her head, and there was a trace of sadness in her cold blue eyes. "You gave up that right when you walked away from me and acted as if what we'd shared never existed," she said as icily as if she meant every word.

He started to argue with her. To ask why she'd never

returned his calls, why she'd never answered her mail, but he already knew the reasons. By the time he'd returned and started looking for her, she'd already married the son of one of the richest men in the bay area.

Pregnant or not, she'd realized even then what she'd wanted and it had come with a price tag. A price tag he could never afford. He handed her back the picture of Adam and watched as the disappointment registered on her face. "I want to see him," he said, trying to keep his voice level. "Face-to-face. I want to meet my son."

"You will."

"You'll bring him here?"

She was startled. Again, fear registered across her beautiful features. Nervously, she licked her lips, and Turner's diaphragm slammed up to his ribs. "I thought in the city, in the hospital…"

"Does that have to happen immediately?"

"No, right now he's better, but—"

"Then I want to meet him, but not in some sterile hospital room with a bunch of doctors and nurses stickin' tubes and needles in him."

To keep his hands busy, he grabbed a pitchfork and tossed hay into Gargoyle's empty manger. He felt trapped, felt as if he had to move on, and yet he wouldn't have it any other way. If the kid was his, and he was starting to believe Heather, then Turner planned to include the boy in his life.

He shoved the pitchfork in a split bale and leaned upon it. Heather was waiting, her elegant features tense. "Look, no matter what happened between us, I'll do what you want," he said, his heart twisting as the tension left her pretty face. "I'll go to the city, have the tests done. No reason to hold this thing up. If the kid needs a donor and I'm a match, I'll do whatever I have to. No problem."

Relief brought a tremulous smile to her lips, and he anticipated the words of gratitude that were forming on her tongue. She misunderstood and he had to set her straight.

"But that's not the end of it, Heather. As soon as he's well enough and the tests have proven that he's mine, then I want you to bring him back here…and not for an afternoon."

The color in her face turned pasty and her fingers curled into tight little fists. "That might take a while. I don't know when he'll be well enough. The doctors might decide to do the transplant—if it's possible—and he'll need a long recovery."

"Then I'll meet him at your place, but not the hospital. Afterward, when it's all done, and he's well enough to come to the ranch, I want to spend some time with him. Two, maybe three weeks—enough time to get to know the boy."

"That's impossible—"

He picked up the pitchfork and hung it on a nail on the wall. "The way I figure it, you've had him for five years. Now it's my turn."

Panic registered in her eyes. "But he's sick—"

"I wouldn't do anything to jeopardize his health, Heather, but I have a right to know my own boy."

She swallowed hard and sweat collected on her forehead. His reasoning was sound, but a deep fear started to grow deep within her, a fear that if she didn't lose her son to this horrid disease, she might very well lose him to his father. But it was a chance she had to take. She was all out of options. "I…I…suppose if the doctor will approve."

"He will."

She licked her lips and glanced anxiously around the run-down old barn. "But he can't stay here alone."

"I'll be here."

"I know, but he'd be frightened. He doesn't even know you!"

"Whose fault is that?"

"We're not talking about laying blame, Turner. We're talking about my son's well-being!"

"You're not going to bring up some damned nanny to this ranch," he warned, and watched as she squared her shoulders.

"No, Turner, I'm not. But if Adam stays here, so do I."

He started to argue. Hell, the last thing he wanted here was Heather Tremont Leonetti. She'd be in the way. She'd be a distraction. She'd interfere with him getting to know the boy, always overplaying the part of the mother. But he could see by the set of her small jaw that it was all or nothing, and he wasn't enough of a bastard to barter with the boy's health. No way could he say that he'd only agree to the tests if the kid would be allowed to come here alone. A son! He had a son. The very thought knocked the breath out of his lungs. He noticed her watching him and rubbed a hand over his chin.

"All right, lady, you've got yourself a bargain," he said, letting a slow, lazy grin drift across his face. Deliberately, he let his gaze rest for a long moment on the hollow of her throat. "But it's not going to be easy."

"With you, nothing is," she said, not backing down an inch. He approached her and she didn't move; in fact her eyes widened and she parted her lips ever so slightly. If he didn't know better, if he didn't still feel the sting of her hand against his cheek, he'd swear she was coming on to him. But that was crazy, or was it?

The look she sent him fairly sizzled. "I'll call and set up an appointment with the doctor and the hospital," she said, and impulsively he touched her arm.

"I think we should talk some more."

She paused just a second, as if deliberating. "I don't see what good that would do."

"Give me a break, Heather. It's been six years. I think we have a lot to discuss."

"I—I don't know—"

"We'll call a truce. Temporarily at least. There's a lot I want to know." The fingers curling over her forearm tightened and she stared deep into his eyes. "You *owe* me this much."

Quickly, she yanked her arm away. "Let's get something straight, Turner. I don't *owe* you anything. But I know that you have a lot of questions. I—I'll be back later. Right now, I've got to go into town and talk to my mom. Good enough?"

"I guess it'll have to be."

"What time?"

"I'll be through with my chores around seven."

"I'll be back at seven-thirty." With that, she was gone. In a cloud of tantalizing perfume, she stormed away, never even looking down at her blouse where the dirt from his fingertips still stained the silken fabric.

She'd gotten tougher over the years as well as more sophisticated. To Turner's mind, she was more deadly than before, because now, unless she was lying through her beautiful teeth, she had his son!

HEATHER SQUINTED THROUGH the dust that collected on the windshield. Badlands Ranch was located to the northwest of Gold Creek, and the main road leading back to the town was a narrow ribbon of asphalt that wound around the western shore of Whitefire Lake. Through the trees, Heather caught glimpses of the water, now blue and pristine, unlike the white misty lake from which she'd taken a long sip this morning. It had been a foolish ritual, and now, if she hadn't felt so desperate, she would have laughed at herself. But she could barely concentrate on anything except Turner and the fact that he wanted to make love to her again. She'd seen it in his eyes—the passion rising to the surface. And he'd even tried in a crude way to suggest that they could make it happen again. He'd been bluffing at that point, trying to force her out of his life by proving he wasn't the kind of man she wanted.

But he hadn't known how desperate she was. And he hadn't known that this would have been the perfect time to make love to him. And he hadn't known that should she make love to him and become pregnant with his child, she would be giving their only child another chance for survival. But she hadn't been able to do it. She couldn't deceive him so coldly, nor could she plan to conceive one child just to save the life of another.

Or could she?

She'd always wanted another baby. The fact that Dennis had been unable to father children had been a big disappointment for them both. And the thought of giving birth to another son or daughter with Turner as the father touched her in a romantic way that bordered on lunacy. Just because Adam had turned out so well was no reason to think that another child would fit into the life she'd carved out with her son.

But a sibling could save his life. Every doctor she'd talked to had stressed that donors for bone marrow are usually a brother or sister of the recipient. The more siblings a recipient had, the better the chance for a match.

Already she knew that she couldn't help her son; there was a strong chance Turner couldn't, either. But a sibling...

The thought turned her stomach. She wouldn't, *couldn't,* even think about another pregnancy, another child.

*But if it means Adam's life? And why not have another baby to love? Adam needs a sister or brother and you need another child.*

"Another child without a husband. No way," she told herself as she approached Gold Creek. She followed the road past the dip beneath the old railroad trestle and through the sprawling suburbs that were growing eastward into the foothills of the mountains. Several homes were for sale, white-and-red signs for Fitzpatrick Realty posted on the front lawns. She drove past the park where children played in the playground and concrete paths crossed the green, converging in the center where a white gazebo had become a shrine to Roy Fitzpatrick, eldest legitimate son of Thomas Fitzpatrick and the boy Jackson Moore had once been accused of killing.

But that was a long time ago, and now Heather's sister, Rachelle, was planning to marry Jackson. His name had been cleared and some of the scandal of the past had been erased.

She slowed for a stoplight, then turned onto Main Street, past the Rexall Drugstore where, sometimes after school, she and Rachelle and Rachelle's friend, Carlie, had bought sodas at the fountain in the back. Rachelle hadn't much liked Heather tagging along, but Carlie, whose mother had worked at the fountain for years, hadn't seemed to mind that Rachelle's younger sister was always hanging around.

A few blocks farther and she passed the Buckeye Restaurant and Lounge. Her stomach tightened as she heard the country music filtering through the open doors. More than once she'd had to wait at the back door while a busboy or kitchen helper had searched out her father, who, smelling of cigarette smoke and liquor, had stumbled into the parking lot and walked the few blocks back to their house with her.

She pulled up in front of the little cottage where she'd grown up. One story, two bedrooms, cozy but in need of repair, the bungalow had been home, but Heather had only wanted out. Away from a mother and father who bickered continually, and later, away from the scandal that had tainted her family.

Her mother didn't live here now. In fact, Heather owned half the cottage, so all that running hadn't done anything. This still could be her home. She shuddered at the thought. Could she bring Adam here, to grow up riding his bike along the same cracked pavement where she'd cruised along on her old hand-me-down ten-speed?

She didn't stop to think about it for too long. There was a lot to do. Her insides were still in knots because of her having seen Turner again and presenting him with the truth; now she had to do the same with her mother.

"God help me," she whispered as she turned around in the driveway and drove the two miles to her mother's small house on the other side of town. Recently separated from her second husband, Ellen Tremont Little would be in no mood to hear about her youngest daughter's problems.

"I DON'T BELIEVE YOU!" Heather's mother reached into the drawer where she kept a carton of cigarettes. "This... this story you've concocted is some crazy fantasy." She clicked her lighter over the end of her cigarette and took a long drag.

"It's the truth, Mom."

Ellen wrapped one arm around her thickening middle and squinted through the smoke. "But Dennis—"

"Dennis isn't Adam's father."

"He *knew* about this?"

"Yes. From the beginning. Remember the night he left here so angry with me. It was right after I got home from working at the Lazy K. I told him about Turner—"

"Turner?" Ellen's head snapped up. "Not—"

"Turner Brooks."

"Oh, God." She sank into a chair at the table and cradled her head, her cigarette burning neglected in her fingers. "John Brooks's son."

"Yes."

Her mother let out a long, weary sigh, then drew on her cigarette. Smoke drifted from her nostrils. "How will I ever hold my head up in church?" she asked, staring out the window to the bird feeder swinging from the branch of a locust tree. Several yellow-breasted birds were perched on the feeder. "Cora Nelson will have a field day with this. And Raydene McDonald... Dear Lord, it will probably be printed in the *Clarion!*"

"I don't think so," Heather said, and saw her mother attempt a trembling smile.

"Why would you ever want a boy like Turner Brooks when you had Dennis?"

"Don't start with me, Mom," Heather said with a smile, though she meant every word.

"He's never done anything but ride horses and get himself busted up."

"He took care of his father."

Ellen stubbed out her cigarette. "I suppose he did."

"He's not a bad man, Mom."

"So where was he when you were pregnant? He didn't marry you, did he? No...Dennis did." Shoving herself upright, she turned to the dishwasher and started taking out the clean dishes. "We Tremont women have a great track record with men, don't we?" she said, her words laced with sarcasm. "Well, without us, what would the gossips in town do?"

"I'm not ashamed that Turner is Adam's father."

"No, I suppose you're not. But what were you thinking, Heather? Why fall for a rodeo rider when you could have had any boy in town including..." Her voice drifted off. "I guess I'm beginning to sound like a broken record, aren't I? Well...we'll just have to change that. After all, nothing matters but Adam's health, and if Turner's willing to do what he can to save my grandson, then I'll just have to quit bad-mouthing him."

Heather chuckled. "Do you think that's possible?"

"I don't know. But I've accepted Jackson. I *never* thought that would happen."

"Neither did I."

"And he and Rachelle are getting married." She stacked two glasses in the cupboard and wiped her hands. "You know, I was wrong about Jackson—the whole town was wrong about him. Maybe I'll be wrong about Turner, too."

"You are, Mom," Heather said with more conviction than she felt.

"I hope so. For everyone's sake. I hope so." She hung her dish towel on a rack. "Now tell me, what happens if Turner's tissue doesn't match Adam's?"

"Don't even think that way."

"But it's a possibility."

*A good one,* Heather thought to herself. *What Adam needs is a sister or brother... Oh, God, not this again!*

"He's not in any immediate danger," Heather heard herself say as she repeated the pediatrician's prognosis. "His remission could last for years. If so, he won't need a transplant."

"But if he does?" Ellen persisted.

"Then we'll cross that bridge when we come to it," Heather replied, while she tried to tamp down thoughts of a sibling for her son.

Ellen's brow was drawn into a worried frown. "We'll have to talk to your father and anyone else in the family—any blood relation—who might be able to help the boy."

"Turner will be the most likely donor," Heather said, and tried to still the beating of her heart. She thought of facing him again and her insides went cold. There was still the attraction; she'd felt it in the barn. Now she had to decide how she would deal with him. Would she keep him at arm's length or try to seduce him?

## CHAPTER SEVEN

TURNER WAS WAITING FOR her. Seated in a worn-out old rocking chair on the front porch, a bottle of beer caught between his hands, he watched as she parked her Mercedes near the barn. "It's now or never," she told herself as she climbed out of the car and slung her purse over her shoulder. She'd changed into a pair of white slacks and a wine-colored T-shirt, pulled her hair back into a ponytail and left her jewelry in her makeup bag back at the cottage.

The evening air was heavy, weighted with the coming night. Insects droned and lavender clouds shifted across the darkening sky. Twilight. A summer evening and she was alone with Turner. Just as she had been six long years before. But now they had a son—a son with an illness that could be fatal. Oh, God, why?

"I thought maybe you'd chicken out," he said, the old chair creaking as he stood.

"Not me." She forced a smile she didn't feel and realized just how isolated they were. No bunkhouse full of ranch hands, no attic rooms with kitchen help, no guests dancing or laughing or playing cards in the dining hall, no Zeke, no Mazie. Just Turner and the windswept hills that were Badlands Ranch.

Her heart drummed loudly and she only hoped that he couldn't hear its erratic beat over the sigh of the wind.

"You didn't have to show up," he said, finishing his

beer and setting the empty bottle on the rail of the porch. As he walked down the stairs, she noticed his limp, barely visible, but evidence of the pain his body had endured for a life he loved. "I would have gone through with the tests, anyway."

"I figured I owed you this much," she said, trying not to observe his freshly shaven jaw, or his slate-colored eyes, or the loose-jointed way he sauntered across the hard earth. Or his limp. The reminder of the life he led. In jeans and a faded shirt, with a backdrop of a run-down ranch house and acres of grassland, he was, without exception, the sexiest man she'd ever seen. That was the problem. What they'd shared had been sex—in its young, passionate, raw form. Naively she'd thought she'd loved him, that he'd loved her, but all that had been between them was a hunger as driven as the winds that blow hot through the California valleys in August. Even now, as she tried to seem relaxed, she felt that tension between them, the tug of something wild and wanton in her heart, the hot breath of desire tickling the back of her neck.

"Tell me about Adam," he said. "Where is he now?"

"He's with the babysitter, Mrs. Rassmussen. She lives two houses down from mine."

"How sick is he?"

Her heart twisted. "He's in remission. It could last indefinitely, but then again..." She shook her head and bit on her lower lip. "Adam's pediatrician's name is Richard Thurmon—he's the best in San Francisco. I've told him about you and all you have to do is call him. He can tell you anything you want to know."

"I will."

They stood in awkward silence and Turner stared at her, sizing her up, as if he still didn't believe her. "I tried to call Zeke today."

"To check my story."

His lips twitched. "He's in Montana. Won't be back for a couple of weeks."

"What about Mazie?"

"She doesn't remember much about that summer, but she does think you called, that you wanted to talk to me."

"She doesn't remember me practically begging her for your address—for a phone number where I could reach you?" Heather said in disbelief. Though she hadn't confided in Mazie, she'd been near tears, her voice choked with emotion. But Mazie had probably taken more than her share of teary phone calls from women Turner had left behind.

"She didn't say."

"Well, it's the truth, damn it!" Heather cried, then threw her hands up in despair. Turner still acted as if she were a criminal, and she was no better about trusting him. One minute she was fantasizing about him, the next she wanted to wring his neck. "Why don't we go for a ride," she suggested.

"A what?"

"A trail ride. Like we used to."

"Why?" The look he sent her silently called her a lunatic.

"Because I can't just stand here and have you start accusing me of God only knows what! It used to work, you know. Whenever we were angry with each other, we'd ride—get rid of our aggressions. You do have horses around here, don't you? What about Sampson?" She didn't wait for a response, just stormed off toward the barn where she'd seen the ugly reddish horse earlier in the day.

He caught up with her in three long strides. "You're crazy, lady," he accused, as she flung open the barn door and stepped into the dark interior. She reached for a switch, found none and fumbled in the dark. "We have a son, a kid I didn't know about, a boy who needs a transplant, for God's sake, and you want to ride?"

"I just don't want to argue anymore!" She swung around and faced him. High in the rafters of the barn a bat's wings fluttered. "I'm scared, Turner. Scared out of my mind. And I don't want you or anyone else to start in on me about what I did or didn't do wrong. I only want to deal with the here and now!"

"You want me to forget about six years?" he asked, his voice low and angry.

"Yes. Because it doesn't matter. Nothing matters except Adam's health!" She found the latch to a stall and opened it, but the stall was empty.

"For God's sake, Heather, I have questions. A million of them."

"What you have is accusations!"

He grabbed her so quickly that her breath came out in a rush. Suddenly she was slammed against his chest, her back pressed into the rough boards of the barn walls. "I've spent the last six hours wondering how the hell this happened and why you didn't tell me about Adam."

"I explained that I—"

"I heard your story, Heather, but it doesn't wash. You didn't have to jump into marriage right off the bat. You could've waited."

"For how long, Turner?" she asked, tears clogging her throat. "Until you got back to the Lazy K? Until you were through with the circuit? Until you couldn't ride anymore because you'd suffered too many injuries? I had a baby to think about. I didn't have any time to waste."

His lips curled in disgust and his fingers dug into the soft flesh of her arms. "You weren't thinking about the kid. You were worried about your reputation. You'd told me often enough about your sister and what she'd suffered in Gold Creek—and then you turn up pregnant, with no husband. You couldn't face the thought of being a single mother. People would talk. Everyone in Gold Creek would know. You probably couldn't face your parents!"

"Oh, Lord," she whispered, shaking her head. How far apart they were and yet how close. She swallowed the hard lump in her throat and lifted her chin a fraction. "I thought I loved you, Turner. I had myself convinced that you were the man I wanted to spend the rest of my life with. And you walked out. It's that simple."

"Not quite. You were pregnant. I'd say things got a lot more complicated."

She felt the heat of his body, smelled the scent of soap on his skin and stared at the small cleft in his chin. Her breasts were flattened against his chest, her thighs imprisoned by his legs. She ignored the tingle that swept through her blood and told herself that he no longer attracted her. He was a broken-down cowboy, cynical and cold.

"Just what kind of a woman are you?" he asked, but his hard grip loosened a bit.

"I just want to start over," she said. "For Adam's sake."

"Like nothing between us ever happened." His hands moved down her arms to manacle her wrists, and a thrill shot through her—a thrill she refused to acknowledge.

"I...I can't forget what happened, Turner, and I don't expect you to. But if we could just start out without being enemies, it would be best for Adam."

His hands, warm as the breath of summer, tightened a little, and pulled her even closer. She noticed the thin line of his lips, and her stomach seemed to be pressing hard against her lungs, her blood heating despite her determination to ignore his sensuality.

"So what're you going to do, Turner?" she asked with surprising calm. "Are you planning to keep punishing me for the rest of my life—are you going to try and find ways to make me atone for my mistake?"

"Is that what I'm doing? Punishing you?"

His voice was so low, so sexy against her ear that she could hardly respond. But she forced the words past her lips. "I think you plan on making me pay for my mistake for the rest of my life."

He stiffened, and she knew that she'd finally gotten through to him. But he didn't move away, and his body molded over hers as closely as if they were making love. Hard contours pressed intimately to hers and she could hardly catch her breath. The smell of him, the heat of his body, his dark looks as he stared at her assailed her senses, and her mind wandered dangerously backward in time to when she and he had so innocently, so desperately made love. She licked her lips and wondered if he was thinking of kissing her again. Somewhere in the barn a horse snorted.

"My mistake wasn't sleeping with you, Turner. My mistake was loving you and thinking I could make you love me." Her voice was low and she forced her gaze to his. "I was wrong. All you wanted from me was what I gave you—a summer fling. A distraction from hard work at the ranch."

His back teeth ground together and she saw the protests forming on his tongue. "I cared about you—"

"Don't lie, Turner. It belittles us both and only makes things wor—"

His mouth slanted over hers and his arms tightened around her body. His hands pulled her tighter still and her breath was lost between her throat and her lungs. Raw passion surged between them, racing hot as wildfire through her blood, pounding in her brain, shutting down all her defenses. The taste and feel of him brought back memories she'd tried for years to forget. Her body responded of its own accord, knowing instinctively that this was the man, the only man, who could arouse a desire so torrid, she lost all reason and abandoned herself to him.

*This can't be happening,* she thought wildly, and yet she was unable to stop the seductive assault of his tongue pressing hard against her teeth, gaining entrance to her mouth and exploring her with exquisite little flicks that caused her to tremble inside.

His hands caught in the silver-blond strands of her hair, forcing her head back farther so that he could kiss her throat and neck, as if he had every right to kiss her, to touch her, to make love to her.

*Stop him! Stop him now! This can only lead to trouble!* one side of her mind cried desperately, but another part of her melted against him, thrilled by the sensations he aroused in her, toying with the idea that making love would be a good way to bury the pain of the past, to start a new relationship, to...to conceive a child.

She yanked herself away. "No!" she cried, and he jerked back, lifting his head. What was she thinking? Conceiving a child. Oh, God, no! She couldn't deceive him. He already thought she'd used him. She wouldn't do this.... She was shaking so badly, she had to touch the side of the barn for support.

"What the hell?" Turner took a step back and shoved his hands through his hair. He kicked at the stall in frustration. A frightened horse whinnied nervously. Outside a dog barked and in the barn bats took flight yet again.

"I'm sorry, Turner," she said, then hated the weak sound of her apology.

"Hell, Heather, I wasn't going to force you to—"

"Oh, I know that," she said, flustered. Her hands trembled as she finger-combed her loosened hair back to her ponytail and felt like an awkward teenager. "I—I—just don't know if this is such a good idea."

His lips twisted into a cold smile. "I understand," he said, and there was something in his words that forewarned her of dangers to come. "You still don't want a cowboy."

"That's not true—"

"Oh, so you do want a cowboy?"

"Of course not."

A trace of sadness touched his eyes. "There's the problem, Heather. Always has been. You have trouble admitting exactly what it is you do want. You claimed you loved me—yeah, I remember. And you probably believed it yourself. But all along I knew that you thought I wasn't good enough."

"Oh, Turner, that's not true—"

"Of course it is! I wasn't blind, damn it!"

"I loved you!"

"You convinced yourself you loved me so that you wouldn't feel so guilty about what we were doing. You confused love with lust—"

"I never—"

"Oh, yes, Heather," he hissed. "You did. We both did. What we shared, hell, it was the best sex I've ever had—the kind of passion that cut right to the bone and turned me inside out. And you felt it, too." He touched her neck, rubbed the tiny pulse at the base. "You still do. We both do."

She couldn't argue with his logic. Even now, when

she burned with fury, his hand touched the hollow of her throat and she wanted to melt. Instead, breathing hard, she swiped his arm away and stepped back from him.

He held up both hands, as if in surrender. "I've never wanted a woman the way I wanted you, Heather. The way I still want you, but I knew, even then, that it wouldn't work between us. All we had was sex—great sex, but that's not enough."

His words stung as surely as if a dart had pierced her heart, draining it slowly of lifeblood. She ached, because he was telling the truth, at least as far as he knew it. Tears welled behind her eyes and she stumbled forward, her hands brushing against the rail of the stall. She had to get out, get away; coming here had been a vast mistake.

His voice jarred her. "The problem was, I didn't have this all figured out then, at least not clearly. I had a gut feeling that you weren't the right kind of woman for me, but I had trouble convincing myself." He leaned his back against the stall and closed his eyes, as if willing his passion to rest. "At least I didn't know until it was too late."

"And then?" she asked, her voice quavering.

"And then I decided I'd take a chance. Hell, why not? It wasn't as if I had this terrific life or anything. I came back home and you were gone. Married already."

"So I was just an alternative to a lonely existence."

"I wasn't sure what you were, Heather, but I couldn't stop myself from coming back." He threw a dark look to the ceiling as if condemning himself. "I draw the line with married women—always have. But with you, it was hard. I even thought about kidnapping you away from Leonetti, just to talk to you, but..." His jaw slid to the side at the irony of the situation. "I heard you were pregnant."

"Oh, God, you thought—"

"I didn't know what to think."

"Turner." She reached for him then, took his callused hand in her smaller fingers and squeezed. Torment wound through her soul. He'd thought she was pregnant with Dennis's child. And why wouldn't he? "I...I'm so sorry."

"So am I, Heather."

"If I'd known you'd come back..."

In the half-light, he stared at her with disbelieving eyes. "What would you have done, Heather? Waited for me?"

"I—I don't know," she admitted, realizing that she couldn't lie ever again. Tears glistened in her eyes and impulsively she threw her arms around the neck of her child's father. She held him close, refusing to sob for the years they hadn't shared together, forbidding the tears to drizzle from her eyes. Her lips moved of their own accord, gently kissing his cheek, and his arms wrapped around her—strong and warm and secure.

Without thought, she closed her eyes and tilted her face upward, molding her mouth to his. A tremor ripped through his body, and his kiss became harder, more insistent.

His arms held her possessively and her knees turned weak. Heat rushed through her veins and his mouth explored the hollows of her cheek and her ears. Desire spread through her veins like liquid fire. She trembled as his hands found the hem of her T-shirt and touched her skin. Sucking in her breath, she felt the tips of his fingers scale her ribs and move upward to cup her breast.

"Heather," he whispered into the shell of her ear, and her legs gave way. Together they tumbled onto the hay-strewn floor of the stall, legs and arms entwined. Dust motes swirled upward and the horse in the stall next door shifted, snorting loudly.

A thousand reasons for stopping him crowded in her mind, but as he lay over her, his rock-hard body fitting against hers, the reasons disappeared and desire, long banked, burst into flame.

As he lifted her shirt over her head, he stared down at her and a small groan escaped him. He pressed his face into the cleft between her breasts and he sighed against her skin. Her nipples grew taut as he removed the rest of her clothes and kissed her flesh, sending shock wave after shock wave of delicious hunger through her.

Her own fingers stripped him of his shirt and trailed in wonder over the hard, sinewy strength of his arms and chest.

Turner's mouth covered hers as he tore off her slacks and underwear and he kicked off his boots and jeans to lie beside her. She circled his chest with her arms and kissed the sworling mat of hair that hid his nipples. He groaned again and trembled.

"I've dreamed of this," he muttered into her hair as he poised himself above her. "I don't think I can...I can't stop."

"Don't stop," she whispered. "Please, don't ever stop."

His mouth slanted over hers and he parted her legs with his knees, hesitating just a second before entering her in one hard thrust.

"Turner, oh, Turner," she cried. The sounds of the night faded, and Heather, driven by a desire so hot she was certain she was melting inside, moved to meet the rhythm of his strokes. She clung to him, her fingers digging into his shoulders, his muscles contracting and flexing as she soared higher and higher, like a bird taking flight, rising to some unseen star until the night seemed to explode around them. And Turner, his body drenched in sweat, fell against her, crushing her breasts and breathing as if he'd run a marathon.

"Oh, God, Heather, what're we doing?" he whispered, kissing her naked chest. Hay and straw stubble poked at her skin and she almost laughed.

"Making up for lost time." She held him close, kissing his crown, smiling sadly as she noticed the stubborn swirl of light hair at his crown—so like Adam's. Her throat grew thick and tears once again threatened her eyes as she realized that she was now, and forever would be, a part of his life. His lover. The mother of his child. The woman he alternately hated and made love to. But she would never be his wife, would never be the woman to whom he would turn when he needed compassion or empathy or comfort.

He rolled off her and cradled her head against his shoulder. Together they stared through the darkness up to the rafters. Turner's voice was still raspy when he said, "This was probably a mistake."

"Probably." Her heart felt bruised.

"But not our first."

"No."

"And certainly not our last." He sighed heavily. "You've always been a problem for me, Heather," he admitted. "I've never known exactly what to do with you."

*Just love me,* she silently cried, but knew her sentiment was foolish, the product of an emotion-wrenching day mixed with the slumberous feel of afterglow. "All I want from you is what you've already agreed to do," she said softly. "You don't have to worry about anything else."

"But I will want my time with him. You've had him a long time. Now it's my turn."

"I can't—"

"Shh." He said, kissing her again and stoking the long-dead fires to life once more. Heather couldn't stop herself, and saw no reason to. She'd leave a little later, resume her life in San Francisco and deal with the aftermath of making love to Turner then. But for now...she pressed her lips to his.

# CHAPTER EIGHT

TURNER THREW A CHANGE OF clothes into a battered old duffel bag and caught a glimpse of himself in the mirror. He didn't look any different than he had a week ago, and yet now he was a father...or at least it was beginning to look that way. And he was involved with Heather Tremont—make that Heather Leonetti—again. Even now, at the thought of her lying in his arms, his loins began to ache.

He forced his thoughts away from her lovemaking and concentrated on her tale about him fathering Adam. He couldn't see any reason Heather would lie, no angle she could play for her own purposes. He still didn't trust her, but he did believe that she was telling the truth about the boy—and that, yes, he was a father. He also didn't doubt that she loved the boy very much. He'd recognized the fire in her eyes when she'd talked of saving Adam's life, seen the fear tighten the corners of her mouth when she'd thought Turner might try to take the boy away.

He'd considered it, of course. For hours on end. His initial shock at having learned he was a father had given way to a quiet rage that swept through his bloodstream and controlled his mind. She'd had no right, *no friggin' right,* to keep Adam's existence from him.

And then to marry Leonetti and pass the kid off as his. He'd thought a lot of things about her in the past, but he hadn't really blamed her for their breakup. He'd been the one who had taken off, and though he'd been furious to find out that she'd gotten herself married before he returned to Northern California, he'd felt as if he'd asked for it.

He had felt a little like a fool, for he'd half believed her when she'd vowed she loved him six years ago. She'd seemed so sincere, and she'd given herself to him without any regrets, so he'd been confident that he'd been first in her heart.

Then she'd refused to answer his letters or return his calls and within weeks married the boy she'd sworn she didn't care a lick about. It had seemed, at the time, that she'd only been experimenting with sex, sowing some wild oats with a cowboy before she turned back to the man and the lifestyle she'd always wanted.

But he'd been wrong. Because she'd been pregnant with his kid. Her pregnancy didn't change the fact that she hadn't wanted anything more to do with him—hell, she admitted it herself that she would have kept Adam's parentage a secret for a long time if it hadn't been for this illness. This damned illness. He'd read up on leukemia and it scared him to his very soul.

It seemed too cruel to believe that he would be given only a short time with the boy and then have him snatched away.

Turner didn't believe in God. But he didn't disbelieve, either. He'd been raised a half-baked Protestant by his mother, but had developed his own reverence for the land and nature after her death, blaming God as well as John Brooks for taking his mother from him. In the past few years he hadn't thought about religion much one way or the other, but now, when his son's life was nailed on the hope of a team of doctors in San Francisco, Turner wanted very much to believe in God.

Frowning at the turn of his dark thoughts, he grabbed his duffel from the bed and tossed it over his shoulder. He shot a glance to the sturdy oak frame of the double bed he'd slept in for as long as he could remember and tried to picture Heather lying with him on the sagging mattress, beneath the faded old patchwork quilt his grandmother had pieced. Heather with her calfskin shoes, diamond earrings and expensive suits. No, that mirage wouldn't come to life before his eyes. He was just being foolish.

He walked down a short hallway to the kitchen where Nadine was scrubbing an old kerosene lamp he used when the power went out. She'd tied her hair back into a ponytail and her cheeks were flushed from working on the floor and counters. Seeing his reflection in the brass works of the lamp, she smiled. "Thomas Fitzpatrick called while you were in the barn."

Turner's jaw tightened. "Some people just don't know when to give up."

She looked at him quickly, then her eyes fell on his duffel bag and her lips turned down a little at the corners. "Sometimes, when people want something desperately, they can't quit."

"Fitzpatrick never gives up."

"So they say. So…you're all packed?"

"I guess."

Turning, she attempted to hide a sliver of sadness in her eyes. "You're going to the city?"

"Hard to believe, isn't it?"

"There must be a reason."

Turner offered her his lazy grin. "Maybe it's time I got more sophisticated."

She swallowed a smile. "Well, be sure to tell me all about the opera and the ballet when you get back."

"I will."

She set the lamp on the windowsill and snipped off the extra leaves of three roses she'd left in the sink. "Why do I have the feeling that your trip has something to do with all those calls from Heather Leonetti?"

"I don't know. You tell me," he teased, then regretted the words when she pricked her finger on a thorn and avoided his eyes as she muttered something under her breath. She placed the roses in a vase and set them on the table—her last chore before she left each week.

"You don't really have to bother with those," he said, motioning to the heavy-blossomed flowers. "I'll be gone—"

"I like to," she cut in. "You could use more of a woman's touch around here."

"You think so?"

"I know it."

"Then why am I happy with the way things are?"

"'Cause you're a bullheaded fool, Turner Brooks, and if you think you're happy, I strongly suggest you take a good long look in the mirror." She grabbed her bucket and supplies and swung out the door.

Turner watched her leave. He should've told her the truth, explained about Heather and the boy. But how could he, when he barely understood it himself? It was his problem, keeping things bottled up, never sharing with anyone, but he didn't figure now was the time to tell Nadine his life story.

Right now, all he could worry about was the son he'd never met. And there was other, unfinished business he had to deal with. As he watched Nadine's dusty Chevy pull out of the yard, he picked up the phone and dialed the number of the Lazy K.

Mazie answered on the third ring. After a short discussion on the fact that she hadn't seen Turner for too long a period, she told him that Zeke was still in Montana, scouting up livestock, where he'd been for the past week and a half. If Turner would like, Mazie would give him a message.

"I'll call back," Turner replied, as he had the other two times he'd called. He didn't want Mazie or anyone else from the Lazy K involved. If Zeke had lied way back when, if he hadn't bothered to tell Turner that Heather had been looking for him six years ago, Turner wanted to hear it from the older man himself.

Heather wasn't lying about Adam. Turner had determined that she loved the boy and would never have sought Turner out unless she was desperate, which she was. No—he was certain now that the boy was his, but he still didn't trust her—not completely.

But if she only wanted Turner for his bloody bone marrow, then why make love to him—nearly seduce him? It didn't fit. He wanted to believe that she still cared for him, but he'd been fooled once before. No. Heather wanted something from him, something more.

He glanced at the acres of ranch land he owned free and clear. Thomas Fitzpatrick was more than interested in the land—the old man had called him just yesterday with another ridiculous offer, but Turner had held firm. A strange, uncomfortable thought crossed his mind and drew his brows into a knot of concentration. Jackson Moore, the man Heather's sister was planning to marry, was Thomas's son, his firstborn, the only decent male descendent left since Roy had been killed and Brian had bilked his father out of part of his fortune. Was it possible that Heather was trying to get close to Turner to get him to sell his land to Fitzpatrick? Maybe the old man had offered her a cut of the profits. Turner wouldn't be surprised. Fitzpatrick would stoop as low as a snake's belly to get what he wanted, and Heather—well, her track record proved how she felt about money and what it could buy. If Fitzpatrick had gotten to her... But that was too farfetched. Or was it?

Bile rose in the back of Turner's throat as he climbed into his pickup. First things first. He'd do what he had to do for his boy, and then he'd deal with Heather, find out just exactly what made her tick.

"HE WON'T SELL." BRIAN FITZPATRICK pulled at the knot of his tie as he flopped into one of the plush chairs near his father's desk on the third floor of the old hotel that now housed Fitzpatrick, Incorporated. "For some reason, Turner Brooks has decided to keep hold of that miserable scrap of land for the rest of his damned life."

Thomas studied his son carefully. Brian had never been his favorite; in fact he'd once, years ago, referred to the boy as a "backup" for his firstborn, golden boy, Roy. Although Roy hadn't really been his eldest. Thomas's firstborn had been a bastard, born out of wedlock to a woman Thomas had never been able to forget. Oh, he'd stopped his affair with Sandra Moore thirty years before, but he couldn't kid himself. Never once in all his years of marriage to June did he feel that same exquisite passion he'd had with Sandra.

And June had never let him forget it.

Oh, well, it was all water under the bridge, but it seemed ironic that of his only two living sons, one hated his guts, and the other was a weakling, a boy who'd never grown up, a man who had skimmed money from the logging company. Thomas was torn. By greed and the need to pull his family—all of his family—together. As much as he wanted the Brooks ranch, he wished he could make things right with Jackson. But what he'd put the boy through was unthinkable. He didn't blame Jackson for despising him.

It seemed as if his life had turned upside down ever since that Tremont girl—the reporter—had come back to town, wagging her cute little tail and luring Jackson back here.

*Jackson.* His insides shredded. Now there was a son of whom a man could be proud. But he couldn't think of pride right now. His mind was boggled with more important matters. Though few people knew it, Fitzpatrick, Incorporated was teetering on the brink of bankruptcy. Thomas had spent a lot of money greasing some palms in a senatorial bid that hadn't gotten off the ground. Now, with the truth about Roy's death, any political chances he'd had were gone. Besides which, logging was off and Brian had skimmed enough off the top to break a weaker company and the rest of his businesses were recession-weary. June was talking about an expensive divorce, and the cost of defending his son and daughter-in-law for their part in Roy's death was crippling.

And he'd made a decision about the house at the lake. He and his wife had never gone there, not since Roy was killed over twelve years before. It belonged to Jackson— if he'd take it—for all the pain he'd suffered at his father's hand. It wasn't much and Jackson would probably laugh in his face, but in Thomas's mind the land and house were the boy's.

But that didn't stop his need for dollars. Though the house and grounds at the lake cost him money in taxes and upkeep every year, they were valuable and June would hit the roof when she found out. Too bad. She was to blame as much as he.

And there were ways to make money. If Thomas knew

nothing else, he knew how to turn a buck. He knew there
was oil on Badlands Ranch. The geological tests he'd
done on the surrounding acreage that he already owned
had proved him out. If only he could find a way to make
Turner Brooks budge. Money didn't seem to matter to
Brooks—the damned cowboy was as stubborn as some
of those sorry animals he tried to tame.

"So what have we got on Turner Brooks?" Thomas
asked as Brian, restless, had shoved himself to his feet
and walked to the bar. Brian poured them each a shot of
Scotch.

"Not much. His old man was a drunk—killed his
mother in that pickup wreck years ago."

"I remember," Thomas clipped out, irked that he'd
sold the ranch for the pitiful amount of insurance money
John had inherited at his wife's death. Brooks had mort-
gaged the rest of the debt and Thomas had been sure that
John would drink himself into oblivion and default on
the note. At which point Thomas had planned to step in
and buy the place back for a song. That way, the Fitzpatricks would have collected the insurance money as
well as ended up with the ranch. But Turner—damn that
cowpoke—had always scraped together enough cash to
keep the place afloat. How he'd done it, Thomas couldn't
figure out.

"Well, when Turner sets his mind to do something, it
would take an act of God to change it," Brian observed,
handing his father the drink. "Brooks spent a lot of time
taking care of his old man, getting him out of jams. Then
John's liver gave up the ghost a few years back. I don't
think there's more to his life than that."

"Everybody's got a past," Thomas said. He sipped
the Scotch and enjoyed the burn that followed the liquor
down his throat. "My guess is that there's something

more important to Brooks than the ranch. All we have to do is figure out what it is."

Brian shrugged. "I'll look into it."

Not good enough. Brian was a bumbler. He'd cut corners. "Hire a detective."

"Do you really think—"

Thomas slammed his empty glass onto the desk. "Get the best P.I. that money can buy! Once we find out what skeletons Brooks has tucked away in his closet, then we can deal with him!"

Brian didn't need to be told twice. He finished his drink and was out the double doors of Thomas's office. But the old man wasn't satisfied. He walked to the window, where he could spy down on the parking lot. His white Mercedes hadn't moved and Brian's sleek green Jaguar was parked in the next spot. Within seconds Brian emerged from the back of the building. But he wasn't alone. Melanie Patton, Thomas's secretary, was with him. They shared a stolen kiss and Thomas's stomach turned to ice. No wonder the boy couldn't keep his mind on anything important.

Brian climbed into his Jaguar and roared off, but Thomas knew that he'd have to handle Turner Brooks himself.

HEATHER DROVE HOME FROM her gallery by rote, stopping automatically at the stop signs, slowing for corners, accelerating up the steep streets of San Francisco without even thinking. Pictures of Adam flashed through her mind. She remembered bringing him home from the hospital, giving him his first bath, watching anxiously as he tried to skateboard at four.... Oh, God, her life had been empty until he'd arrived. A lump settled in her throat. By the time she'd parked in the garage, on the lowest level of

her home in Pacific Heights, the reality that Adam's life
was in jeopardy nearly incapacitated her. What if she lost
Adam? What if the boy died? Her own life would be over.

Her heart froze and she could barely breathe. A cold,
damp sweat clung to her skin as she sat behind the wheel,
unable to move. "You can't let it happen," she muttered,
not knowing if she was talking to herself or to God.

She was in her mid-twenties and she suddenly felt ancient. Her legs barely carried her up the first flight, from
the garage to the kitchen level, above which two more
stories loomed in this prestigious part of the city.

"Mommy!" She heard Adam's squeal as she opened
the door. Fifty-three pounds of energetic five-year-old
came barrelling toward her, nearly throwing her off balance as Adam flung himself into her waiting arms.

*Oh, precious, precious baby,* she thought, squeezing
her eyes against tears. Her throat worked over a huge
lump. "How're ya, sport?" she said, managing a smile.

"Good!" he replied, though his skin was pale, and
dark smudges beneath his eyes belied his insistence that
he felt fine.

"And you were good for Aunt Rachelle?"

"Of course," he said, his impish eyes gleaming. He
wrinkled a freckled nose. "She's crazy about me."

"Is she?" Heather couldn't help laughing, despite her
fears about Adam's future. Adam was precocious and she
overindulged him terribly, but she couldn't help herself.

"You bring me a treat?" Adam demanded.

"Did I ever," she replied, opening her purse and finding a minuscule little car, part of a set. She had the entire
collection hidden in a closet upstairs, and when she left
Adam, she always slipped a tiny car into her purse to
surprise him when she returned. Today's gift, a candy-

apple-red racing car, was unlike the taxi, ambulance and garbage truck he'd already placed in his toy box.

"Oh, wow!" Adam's eyes, gray and round, lit up. He scrambled out of her arms and began moving the tiny vehicle over the floor, the tables, the plants and everything else in his path as he made rumbling race-car noises deep in his throat.

The stairs squeaked. Heather glanced up as Rachelle descended from the upper living room level. Sunlight refracting from the leaded windows over the landing turned her hair a reddish mahogany color for an instant. Tall and willowy, with intense hazel eyes, the "level-headed one" of the two Tremont sisters, Rachelle was four years older than Heather and soon to be married to Jackson Moore, a New York lawyer who had once been the bad boy of Gold Creek.."I thought I heard you," Rachelle said, questions in her eyes. Though Heather had confided to her older sister about Adam's paternity, Rachelle was still a little hurt that her younger sister hadn't told her the truth long ago.

"Turner will be here a little later." Heather's nerves were strung tight. "He's already at the hospital, being typed." She thought about her conversations with Turner—short and to the point. All business. As if they'd never kissed, never touched, never made love in the hay...

"What happens then?"

Heather snapped herself back to the present and caught Rachelle observing her. Damn her sister's reporter instincts. Heather sometimes felt she couldn't do anything without Rachelle guessing her motives. "If the marrow's a match, we go through the procedure—when the doctor says it's the right time. Once Adam's given a clean bill of health, so to speak, we all go back to his ranch."

"And if the tissue doesn't match?"

"Don't even think that way," Heather said softly. "This has got to work." Her fists closed in silent determination. "It's got to!" There were no other alternatives.

Rachelle skated a glance down Heather's sleek dress and coordinated jewelry. "And then you're off to the ranch? Why is it I can't see you branding calves or hauling hay or whatever else it is they do at a place named Badlands?"

"You'd be surprised," Heather replied.

"I'd be flabbergasted."

Adam ran his racing car around a potted fern, and Rachelle hugged her sister. "We'll get through this. All of us," she insisted. She was always so positive and level-headed, though now her hazel eyes were shadowed with worry.

"I will—"

"Hey, lookie, Auntie Rachelle!" Adam held up his new prize, the little red Porsche. He was beaming ear to ear.

"Boy, isn't that something?" Rachelle bent on one knee to examine the tiny car. "I bet you could win the Daytona 500 with that rig."

"I could even win the 'Tona five million!" Adam assured her confidently and snatched his small prize from her hand.

Rachelle glanced over her shoulder to Heather, still standing near the stairs. "You spoil him, you know."

"I know." Heather felt that infinite fear again, that she was tumbling through dark space to a cold, black hole where she would never see her son again. "But it won't hurt him."

"Don't worry, Heath. We'll work this out," Rachelle

said firmly, as if she could read Heather's mind. "Come on, I'll buy you a cup of coffee."

"With a shot of brandy?"

"Whatever you want," Rachelle agreed, walking quickly into the kitchen. Heather followed behind, her own steps seeming to drag on the shiny mahogany floors. This house, once her pride and joy, seemed lifeless, as if it, too, had lost its vitality. The antiques and objets d'art were meaningless; even her own work, paintings created with love and patience, seemed frivolous. All that mattered was Adam.

Rachelle was already pouring black coffee into heavy mugs as Adam careened into the room. "Hot chocolate for me," he ordered. "With marshmallows."

"You got it, kid." Rachelle winked at her nephew.

Heather slid into a chair and Adam crawled into her lap. He suddenly wrapped his arms around her neck. "Mommy, you sad?" he asked, wide eyes searching hers.

"No," she lied, her heart wrenching.

"Good. I don't like it when you're sad."

Rachelle turned to the cupboard, ostensibly to find the marshmallows, but not before Heather noticed the tears shining in her older sister's eyes. Even Rachelle, stalwart and sane in any crisis, was shaken this time.

Heather hugged her boy closer. *Just let him live,* she silently prayed, *and I'll be the best mother in the world.*

# CHAPTER NINE

THE DOORBELL CHIMED FOR the second time as Heather raced down the stairs. She checked the window and felt her heart take flight as she saw Turner, his arms crossed over his chest, his face shadowed by the brim of his Stetson. He was dressed in a clean pair of jeans and a blue cambric shirt, open at the throat. His eyes were dark and guarded but he didn't seem as threatening as he had when they'd first met in his barn. Neither were they glazed with passion as they'd been when she'd last seen him.

He'd had time to pull himself together, she realized, and they'd talked several times on the phone—short, one-sided conversations where she'd explained what he would have to do once he came to the city. He'd accepted her instructions with only quick questions and no arguments.

She opened the door. "Turner," she said, and hated the breathless quality in her voice. "Come in. Are you finished at the hospital?"

"For now. There was some sort of delay, then it took longer than they thought. The doctor will call us both when the results are in." He glanced at the exterior of the house. "Had a little trouble finding this place."

"Well, you made it." His gaze touched hers and her lungs seemed tight. She held the door open for him and he crossed the threshold slowly, his gaze moving up the polished walnut banister, over the gleaming wainscoting and wallpaper, resting for a second on one piece of art or another, before traveling to the Oriental carpets that covered the hardwood floors.

She'd never been self-conscious of her house before, but under his silent, seemingly condemning stare, the baskets filled with cut flowers and live plants seemed frivolous, the matching overstuffed furniture appeared impractical, the shining brass fixtures ostentatious.

"Adam's in his room."

"Asleep?"

"Not yet. I just put him down. I knew you were coming, but it was so late..." Her words trailed off and she licked her lips nervously. Lord, this was awkward. "Come on up." She led him up another flight of stairs and pushed open the door to Adam's room. The bedside lamp was still lit. Adam lay under a down comforter, his light brown hair sticking at odd angles. He was breathing loudly, nearly snoring, and Heather guessed he was pretending to be asleep. His red bedspread matched the curtains surrounding his bay window and contrasted to the border of wallpaper that rimmed the top of his walls. A built-in desk and bookcase housed toys, books, blocks and an ant farm. "Adam? Honey, are you awake?" He snored loudly as she crossed the room and touched his shoulder.

Two bright eyes flew open and he giggled. "I tricked you!"

"You sure did." As Heather sat on the edge of the bed, she caught a glimpse of Turner from the corner of her eye. Her heart felt as if it would break. Here they were, a family, at least in biological terms, together for the first time. "There's someone I want you to meet."

Adam shoved himself up from his covers and cocked

his head up to see the big man standing behind his mother. "Who're you?" he asked, rubbing his eyes and yawning.

For once Turner didn't have a quick comment. He glanced at Heather, who shook her head ever so slightly, and he extended his hand to Adam's. "Turner Brooks. I...I knew your mother a long time ago." Slowly he released his son's hand.

Heather's throat swelled shut. She had to blink back unnecessary tears. "There's a chance Mr. Brooks—"

"Turner, for now," he cut in.

Heather stiffened. "There's a chance Turner might be able to help us when you go to the hospital."

"I *hate* the hospital!" Adam said firmly.

"You and me both." For the first time, Turner grinned. "They stuck a needle in me this long," he said, spreading his hands wide.

"Turner!"

"They did?" Adam was suitably impressed.

"Mr. Brooks tends to exaggerate," she said, though Adam's eyes gleamed.

"Only a little bit," Turner said. He sat on the edge of the bed and the mattress creaked a little. "When you get the okay from the doctor, your mama promised that you can come visit me at my ranch. Would you like that?"

"A ranch? You got a ranch? With horses and tractors and cows and Indians and—"

"No Indians," Turner said. "The rest comes with the place."

Adam's eyebrows drew together and he looked at his mother. "We goin' on a vacation?"

"Something like that."

"Is Daddy coming?"

Heather's heart nearly stopped. She noticed Turner

stiffen and a muscle suddenly came to life, working reflexively in his jaw. "No, honey. This time it'll just be
you and me."

Adam glanced warily at Turner, as if for the first time
suspecting a threat to his mother's affection. "When?"

Heather stole a quick look at Turner. "As soon as Dr.
Thurmon says it's okay."

"I *hate* the doctor."

Turner ruffled the boy's fine hair. "The doctor's a
good guy. He's gonna help us all."

Adam yawned.

"You'd better go to sleep," Heather suggested. She
didn't know just how much of this tender scene she could
take. Turner wasn't her husband, he'd never met Adam
before in his life, and she was beginning to feel maudlin,
as if this were some great reunion.

"I'm not tired," Adam argued, though he tried vainly
to swallow another yawn and his eyelids drooped. "Read
me a story."

"Honey, it's late and—"

"Oh, pleeease!"

"I'll tell you a story," Turner offered, and Heather's
throat turned to cotton. Turner's campaign to win his son
was starting already.

"It's late. I don't think—"

"It'll be all right," Turner said with a quiet authority
that caused fear to settle in her heart. He sat on the edge
of the bed looking too tall, too ranch-tough, too damned
cynical to be thinking of bedtime stories.

"Tell me about the Indians!"

"I already told you there aren't any Indians at the
ranch, and besides, I think the term is Native American.
So unless you want to get scalped—"

"Turner!" Heather cut in again.

"Just joking."

"He's only five, for crying out loud!"

Turner clucked his tongue and smiled at Adam. "What's wrong with your mom? No sense of humor?"

"I have—"

"Tell me! Tell me!" Adam demanded, bouncing on the bed.

This was going from bad to worse and quickly. Heather tried to intervene, but Turner grabbed hold of her hand and stared up into her eyes. "It's all right," he said calmly, though his voice sounded deeper than she remembered. Her pulse jumped where his fingertips brushed her wrist. "The boy and I need to talk."

Her heart tore a little. "But—"

"But nothing." The fingers around her hand tightened ever so slightly and she was reminded of the power he had over her. Turner's gaze slid back to his son. "How about if I told you about the wild horses I've ridden?"

Adam's eyes rounded. "Wild ones? Really?"

"Broncos, mustangs, you name it!" Heather heard the ring of pride in his voice.

"No way," Adam said, but his face was filled with silent adoration.

"Yes way." Turner smiled at his boy and Heather's insides shredded. When Turner glanced back at her, she received the unspoken message. "I remember one particularly wild bronco named Daredevil. Coal black. Eyes that were nearly red, he was so mean."

"Turner, please!" she cut in, shaking her head. "Horses aren't mean."

"You've never tried to tame Gargoyle," he replied with a lopsided grin, then shrugged. "Well, your mom's right. Most horses aren't mean, but old Daredevil, he had the worst reputation on the rodeo circuit. No one wanted to ride him. But I didn't have a choice, when they drew my number in Pendleton that year, I ended up on Daredevil."

"Tell me! Tell me!" Adam said, wiggling up to a sitting position, all thoughts of sleep driven from his mind.

Heather started to protest. "This wasn't the idea—"

"Sure it was," Turner replied, his face etched in stone. "This was all part of the bargain. Remember? I go through with the tests and you—"

"Scaring Adam wasn't part of the deal."

"I'm not scared!" Adam protested, his brow furrowing in disgust.

"Leave us alone, Heather. The boy wants a bedtime story."

The small of her back turned to ice at the warning hovering in the air. With a few simple words he could destroy her entire life. All he had to do was tell Adam he was his father. Everything she'd worked so hard for would crumble and she would be the bad guy—the creator of the big lie.

"Just remember, he's only five!" Her heart heavy, she walked out of the room with leaden footsteps. A thousand emotions knifed through her. This was only fair, one part of her screamed. Turner deserved to know his boy and Adam had the right to know his father. There was also Turner's sacrifice to consider. He'd agreed to leave his ranch, come to San Francisco and help her—perhaps save the life of a boy he'd never known existed.

And yet she was petrified. Afraid that Turner, with his ranch and horses and tales of wild West stories would seduce her son from her. Though Adam had been raised with anything money could buy, he wasn't always happy and Heather knew she spoiled him rotten. Ever since Adam had been born and Dennis's reaction to his "son" hadn't been as enthusiastic as he'd promised, Heather had overcompensated, indulging the boy. And then the first signs of his illness and the horrid diagnosis. She'd been alone then. Dennis had lost his fascination with her.

"I'm sorry, Heather," Dennis had apologized, looking weak, his dark eyes frightened. "I just didn't figure on this.... I don't know what to do."

"He needs you now," Heather had told him, and Dennis had nodded, but never once picked up the boy he'd claimed to be his son. Almost as if he were afraid he'd catch the disease, Dennis had become more and more absent. They were separated soon after the diagnosis, divorced not long after. Dennis hadn't even fought her for custody. In fact, he'd given her the house, her car and the gallery just to end it quickly.

As anxious as he'd been to marry six years before, he'd been even more anxious to divorce. He'd found someone else, someone less complicated, someone without a sick child.

She heard the scrape of Turner's boot as he entered the room, and when she turned to face him, she found a new determination in his gaze. "This can't go on, you know."

"What can't?" she asked, hoping to sound naive, when she knew with a certain dread what was coming. Her hands trembled a little and she motioned him into the living room. Deciding that playing coy with Turner had never been a good idea, she admitted, "You don't have to explain—I know." She felt as cold as ice as she stared out the window to the winking lights of the city and the dark, reflective waters of the bay. Wrapping her arms around her middle, she told herself that it would be all right. That as long as Adam was healthy, nothing else mattered. That it was important for the boy to have a father—a man he could look up to, a man who would love him. But still she was frightened. "What do you want, Turner?" she asked again, in a voice that seemed detached from her body. A few cars passed on the street below the window, their headlights causing an uneven illumination in the room.

"After this is over, I want to be part of his life."

"How big a part?" She reached for a lamp switch, but Turner's hand stayed hers.

"I want to be his father."

"You are—"

"I mean day-to-day, Heather. Every day."

"But that's impossible," she said, her throat catching.

"Not if you move to Gold Creek."

She felt as if she'd stopped breathing. Move to Gold Creek? Oh, Lord. She couldn't speak for a minute, but finally found her tongue. "Are you out of your mind?" She whirled on him and saw that his eyes were dark and serious. "Are you really suggesting that…" Her voice failed her. He wasn't kidding. The look on his face was deadly serious, and Heather was suddenly very frightened. She'd known he'd demand partial custody, but she'd thought he'd only want a few weeks in the summer—maybe Christmas vacation and those would be hard enough to give up—but *this,* this insane plan for her to move back to the small town where she'd been raised… It was impossible. "I'd die in Gold Creek."

"Adam would be closer to me."

"Until a few days ago, you didn't even know you had a son and now—"

"Yes, and now I want him. And I'll do anything, got it? I mean *anything* to have him close."

"You can't be serious," she whispered.

"Oh, but I am, Heather," he said with a deadly calm that drove a stake of desperation into her heart.

The room was dark, and now the shadows seemed to

envelop them. "You can't walk into this house and turn my life upside down just because—"

"—because I found out I have a son. Because for six years we've both been living a lie? Because I've discovered that my kid, *my* sick kid, is the most important thing in my life?" His hands were suddenly on her forearms, gripped in the fury that consumed him. "You walked into my barn and turned my life inside out, lady."

"You left me!"

"I never said I'd stay."

"Then don't start interfering now."

His eyes slitted and the hands upon her forearms clenched harder. "This isn't about sex. This isn't about love. This is about our child. And if you have some lame-brain notion that I'll do my part as a biological parent, donate whatever it is Adam needs and then just leave you alone until you have another crisis, guess again. I'm here for the duration, Heather, and you'd better get used to that idea."

"I—I know," she said, her throat catching. "But don't think you can start bossing me around, Turner. You're not my husband!"

As soon as she'd said the words, she wished she could call them back.

Turner's eyes flashed fire.

A knot formed in her throat, but she wasn't going to break down. She had shed her tears for Turner a long time ago and she was through. Wrenching free of his grasp, she turned on the switch to the gas starter in the fireplace and struck a match. Immediately the room was lighter, the gas flames flickering blue and yellow against an oak log. She felt him watching her. Nervous, she asked if he wanted a drink and when he declined, she reached into a liquor cabinet, found an old bottle of bourbon and

poured them each a splash in the bottom of two glasses.
"You may not need a drink, but I think I do," she said,
handing him one of the glasses.

"No one *needs* a drink."

"Okay, so I want one." She sipped the hard liquor, and
it burned the back of her throat, scorching all the way
to her stomach. With a hiss and crackle, the moss on the
oak log caught fire and sent out an orange glow throughout the room.

Turner sipped his drink, but his face muscles didn't
relax and he looked out of place, a range-hard cowboy
caught in a frivolous living room filled with women's art
and furniture. "I think you'd better explain a few things,"
he said quietly.

"Like what?"

"How about starting at the beginning. Tell me why
you married Leonetti. Why you didn't contact me."

She wanted to scream at him, to tell him to leave them
both alone, that she didn't need this emotional torture,
but she knew in her heart she was wrong. Adam needed
him, and a deep, traitorous part of her needed him, too.

Unsteady at that realization, Heather sat on the wide
windowseat, her knees tucked up beneath her chin, her
drink forgotten. She began to tell him everything she
could remember. Turner lowered himself to the floor,
propped his back against the couch and stretched his legs
toward the fire.

And for the next hour and a half, Heather explained
about her realization that she was pregnant, of her calls
to Mazie and Zeke at the Lazy K, of Dennis's anger, then
acceptance. "Believe it or not, he wasn't a monster. He
was obsessed with me back then, though I really don't
know why, I guess because I was the only girl who'd ever
said no to him and because I wasn't acceptable to his

parents. They'd heard the gossip about my family, knew my sister's reputation was destroyed. Then there was the scandal with my dad when he married a woman younger than either of his daughters. We Tremonts weren't exactly blue bloods. So Dennis's folks were distraught to say the least. They were hoping he'd find some nice girl in college whose family was from 'old money.'" She laughed a little when she remembered the horror that the elder Leonettis had expressed at their son's choice of wife. "I wasn't even from 'new money.' Dennis's father offered to buy me out, but Dennis got wind of it and by the end of the week we'd eloped."

"How do they feel about Adam?" Turner asked, a possessive flame leaping in his eyes as he swirled his drink and watched the fire play in the amber liquor.

"Ambivalent, I guess. I would've thought they would have been all over the Leonetti heir, but, though they were never unkind to him, Adam just wasn't all that interesting to either of them. I expected some kind of custodial fight when we were getting divorced, but by then Dennis didn't want any part of Adam and his folks never once called him. My guess is that Dennis told them the truth—that Adam doesn't have a drop of Leonetti blood in him."

"So Dennis has given up all his parental rights?"

"He knew that sooner or later, with Adam's condition, the truth would bear out."

"So just because he didn't sire the kid, suddenly Adam's not good enough! Son of a bitch, what a great guy!" Turner's rage twisted his handsome features, making him seem fierce and dangerous. "You really know how to pick 'em, don't ya?"

"That I do," she replied, and the room grew quiet except for the soft hiss of the fire.

She twirled her drink in her hands, watched the reflections of the flames against the amber liquor. "We aren't here to discuss Dennis." She took another sip of bourbon and felt the first tingle of warmth run through her blood. "I'll tell you anything you want to know about Adam, but as far as my marriage is concerned, all you need to know is that it's over and Dennis doesn't have much interest in my son."

"Our son," he corrected quickly, and her throat tightened.

"Our son."

"Which brings us back to square one. What're we going to do about *our* son?"

"I guess that depends upon how he responds," she said, the darkness in her soul growing at the thought of Adam's illness. Turner's bone marrow had to match, it just had to. If not...oh, Lord, she couldn't think of the possibilities. Aching inside, she finished her drink in one swallow. "Until we know that he's well, I can't make any plans."

"I won't just walk out, Heather." Turner left his empty glass on the hearth and strode to the window. Outside, the summer wind stirred the leaves in the trees and a few pedestrians walked briskly up the hilly streets. Cars moved slowly. Streetlamps pooled warm light on the sidewalk and cars parked along the curbs.

"And I can't move to Gold Creek."

"You'll have to let him visit me."

"He will—"

"Every other week."

"No way." Her head snapped up. "He can't be uprooted half the time just so you can play father! He'll be in school and—"

"I don't *play*, Heather."

"But he'll need the security of a home and—"

"He's my kid, damn it."

"A kid you didn't want!" The words tumbled out of their own accord, and she saw him wince, as if he'd been stung by the bite of a whip.

His face flexed and he sucked in his breath. With fingers of steel he grabbed her arms and lifted her off the seat with such force she gasped.

"A kid I didn't know about."

"Let go of me, Turner. It's easy for you. Just turn your back and walk away. You've done it before!"

"I've been trying to let go of you for years, Heather." His voice was as rough as scarred leather, his eyes as hot as a branding iron, and when his lips found hers, there was a force behind them as primeval as the range he rode.

She didn't want to kiss him, didn't expect to find his arms wrapped around her with a passion that sang from his body to hers. She told herself that she wouldn't kiss him, would fight him tooth and nail, but as she pushed against his shoulders, her body yielded, as if it had a mind of its own. Memories, like a warm western wind, blew through her mind, and the taste of Turner, as fresh as yesterday, triggered hotter thoughts of that long-ago summer.

She tried to protest, but couldn't, and the smell and feel of him drove out all thoughts of denial. For she knew they would make love. Again. As if destiny were charting its own preordained course, she felt her knees give way, her mouth yield, her sigh of contentment as his tongue teased her lips open.

*This can't be happening,* she thought wildly, yet her arms, rather than shove him away, wound enticingly around his neck, and her face lifted for more of his sweet caress. Her skin quivered where he touched her, and as he lowered both their bodies to the floor, she clung to him.

She wanted to blame the alcohol, or the desperate emotions that had ravaged her since she'd learned of Adam's illness and had known that Turner would try to take the boy from her. She wanted to accuse fate for tricking her into wanting Turner again, and yet, deep inside, she knew that the seeds of love she'd buried so long ago had never died, were planted shallowly enough to sprout again.

She closed her mind to the doubts that crowded in her brain and let herself go, kissing this man who smelled of rawhide and soap and tasted of bourbon. As he stripped her of her blouse, her fingers unfastened the buttons of his shirt and pushed the fabric over muscles as hard and lean as a Nevada winter.

His lips trailed across her skin, leaving a path prairie-fire hot and twice as deadly. She touched his abdomen and chest as he kissed her bare flesh. His fingers were callused and rough against her breasts as they traced the edge of her bra and quickly unfastened the clasp.

Unbound, nipples erect, her breasts spilled free and he kissed each mound with hungry lips that gave as much pleasure as they took. His arms surrounded her, his hands splayed upon the small of her back as he drew first one pink-tipped nipple into his mouth, then the other. She squirmed against him, her own hands tracing the line of corded muscles and a chest that was covered with downy brown hair that had turned dark and thick over the past six years.

One of his hands dipped beneath the band of her slacks and cupped her rump, pulling her hard against him. She felt his own desire against her abdomen and the bandage on his hip binding the wound where he'd given a part of himself for his child. As he gazed into her eyes, searching as if for the portal of her soul, she knew there was no turning back. He kissed her again, hard and long, and flung off their remaining clothes and there, on the thick handwoven carpet, with the crackle of flames and the hum of slow San Francisco traffic, Turner Brooks once again claimed the lady he'd never been able to forget.

# CHAPTER TEN

HEATHER FELT LIKE A CAGED CAT. All morning she glanced at the clock and paced from the living room to the kitchen and back again. Turner, too, was tense. His jaw was tight, his lips thinned. Today they would find out about the tests.

"It's gonna be all right," he told her, but she saw the doubts in his eyes.

"What if you don't match? What then?" she whispered, her voice cracking.

Turner's eyes darkened. He folded her into his arms and his breath whispered across her hair. "Let's not borrow trouble. Not just yet."

They were still embracing, still holding each other, when the front door unlatched and Rachelle, hauling her briefcase, dashed up the stairs. "Hey, I'm here. Sorry I'm late—the crosstown traffic was murder—" She looked up at the last step, and her eyes landed on Turner, who by this time had released Heather, but looked guilty as sin.

Heather sent up a silent prayer as she felt heat climb steadily up the back of her neck. Rachelle wasn't known for her tact or her ability to hold her tongue. Outspoken since she'd been a kid, she wasn't one to mince words, and the look she gave Turner in his faded jeans, worn suede jacket, cream-colored rough-spun shirt and Stetson was harsh enough to send a rattlesnake scurrying back under a rock.

Heather started introductions. "This is—"

"Turner Brooks," Rachelle guessed, her eyes flashing. "Adam's father. The cowboy."

Turner's jaw tightened just a fraction.

"Turner, my sister, Rachelle. She's going to watch Adam while we're at the hospital."

Immediately Rachelle's expression changed to concern and she crossed her fingers. "I'm praying that this will work."

"So am I."

"Mom's been lighting candles all week."

"She's not even Catholic—" Never had Heather heard of candlelighting in the Methodist church they'd attended in Gold Creek.

"I know, but some of her friends are and she figured it wouldn't hurt." Rachelle glanced around. "Where's Adam?"

"Napping—"

"Auntie Rachelle!" Adam squealed from the upper landing. Legs pounding, he flew down the stairs, arms outstretched so that Rachelle could scoop him up and fling him high in the air before catching him again and holding him close.

"Howdy, kiddo," she said, kissing his mussed hair. "How about a date with your favorite aunt? We could go to McDonald's and the video arcade and then get ice cream—"

"All the culture of the city," Turner drawled.

Rachelle cast him a superior glance. "Who needs culture? We're just gonna have fun, aren't we, sport?"

"Can we go to the toy store?"

"You bet. I'm gonna spoil you rotten today."

Turner's look darkened, but Heather touched his arm. "Don't blame the city. You could do everything Rachelle's talking about right in good old Gold Creek."

At the mention of their hometown, Rachelle's expression turned sober. "Gold Creek? What's this?"

Heather couldn't help herself. "Turner thinks Adam and I should move back."

"Heather, no!" Protectively, Rachelle clutched her nephew closer to her breast. "Not after…well, now that you know, with Dennis not being Adam's…and…" Her gaze flew to Turner. "Oh, Lord! The gossips in Gold Creek would have a field day!"

"So what?" Turner glanced at his watch, then tipped the brim of his hat slightly. "Nice meeting you," he said with more than a trace of sarcasm.

"My pleasure." Rachelle mimicked him without flinching. Then, as if deciding she'd been a little too harsh, she blew a strand of auburn hair from her eyes and balanced Adam on her hip. "Look, Turner, whatever's happened between you two—" she motioned toward Heather "—it's really none of my business. I'm just glad you're here and I want to thank you for helping Heather and Adam."

"No need for thanks."

"Yes, there is." Her intelligent hazel eyes held his for a second. Biting her lip, she shot out a hand and glanced at her sister. "Please, I didn't mean to come on so strong and I know…well, that this mess isn't all your fault."

Heather watched as Turner's big fingers surrounded her sister's tiny hand. "Thanks."

"And would you…I'm getting married in a few weeks. Jackson and I would love it if you came."

Heather held her breath. This might be too much of a commitment for Turner. Just because he was going to help Adam didn't mean he wanted to be entangled with Heather any further—at least not publicly. Their love-making was another matter—it had nothing to do with their future.

"The wedding will be held in Gold Creek, up at Whitefire Lake," Rachelle said. "And we're inviting some old friends..." She glanced back at her sister. "Even Carlie's coming. From Alaska. She wrote me that she's moving back to Gold Creek. Can you believe that?"

Carlie had been Rachelle's best friend in high school, the one person in Gold Creek who had believed in Rachelle during the horrid period in Rachelle's life when Jackson had been accused of murder. After high school, Carlie, with her striking black hair and blue-green eyes, had sought her fame and fortune modeling in New York. But something had happened, something no one in Carlie's family would discuss, and the last Heather had heard was that Carlie was in Alaska, working on the other side of the lens as a photographer.

"I'll be glad to see her again," Heather said, still waiting for Turner's response.

"So will I." Rachelle looked directly at Turner. "Please...we'd love to have you."

Turner rubbed the back of his neck. "All depends, I guess, on what we find out today." He looked at Heather and cocked his head to the stairs leading to the garage. "We'd better git."

Heather's stomach twisted. Her eyes locked with Rachelle's for just an instant and the fear they both felt congealed in their intermingled gaze. Turner placed an arm over Heather's shoulders. "Don't worry," he advised, though his own expression was anxious.

Heather swallowed a lump in her throat, kissed Adam's cheek and with Turner's arm still securely around her, started for the stairs leading down to the garage. She closed her eyes and sent up a silent prayer—for the thousandth time that day.

THOMAS FITZPATRICK WAS A fastidious man who took care of himself. His body was honed by exercise—tennis, golf and regular workouts at a health club. He prided himself on his patrician good looks, his thick head of hair and his practiced smile. Therefore, he wasn't impressed with the private investigator Brian had hired.

Mr. Robert "Bobby" Sands was seated in one of the living room chairs, his dusty boots propped on one of June's white ottomans, his thick fingers webbed over a belly that was paunchy for a man not yet forty. His hair was greasy black and pulled into a ponytail and an earring winked from his right ear.

"...That's right," he was saying, as if he felt right at home. Thomas poured them each a drink. "Turner's clean. A few barroom brawls when he was younger, but mainly those were caused by his old man. No major scrapes with the law. Kept his nose clean on the rodeo circuit—no booze or drugs or doped-up livestock."

Thomas, disgusted, glanced in the mirrored bar. At least June wasn't here to see their visitor. She'd decided to take Toni, their daughter, and spend some time in San Francisco with Thomas's sister, Sylvia Monroe. Hopefully Sylvia could talk some sense into her. When she came back, they'd discuss their marriage or their divorce.

He'd never really loved June, but, damn it, this house seemed cold without her. A few years ago, the house was teeming with life and now, without the kids and his wife... Quickly he snapped to attention and pulled himself together. He would not, *would not* show any signs of weakness to this scum bag of an investigator!

In the reflection he noticed Sands pick up a lighter from the glass-topped table, eye the gold piece, flick the flint and watch the flame snap up. Quickly he set the lighter back. For a second Thomas was sure the man was going to pocket it.

"You're telling me Turner Brooks has no secrets." He crossed the room and handed Sands a drink. His skin crawled as he noticed the man's chipped and dirty fingernails.

"Nope. I'm saying he looks clean. But he's had his problems and they all started surfacing just recently. He's started spending a lot of time with a woman...." Sands's reptilian eyes slitted a fraction, as if he was enjoying stretching out this moment.

"What woman?"

"Heather Leonetti." Sands took a swallow from his bourbon and smiled as the liquor hit the back of his throat. "You know who I mean—Heather Tremont Leonetti, the girl who married that rich banker six years ago."

*Tremont.* The name sent a jolt through him. Jackson's fiancée was a Tremont. She had a younger sister... a pretty girl who had married well, above her station....

"It seems as if Turner and Mrs. Leonetti knew each other a few years ago. Before she was married. Met up on a ranch owned by Turner's uncle, Zeke Kilkenny. Now, Kilkenny won't say much, won't even return my calls, and his housekeeper, Mazie, usually a gossip, wouldn't breathe a word about what went on between Brooks and Heather Tremont, who, by the way, was in an on-again, off-again engagement with Leonetti, but I did some digging. Came up with a few names. One of the ranch hands who used to work for Kilkenny, Billy Adams—he said Heather and this cowboy were damned thick, and another girl who worked up there during the summers—" He set down his drink, reached into the front pocket of his jacket—a shiny pinstripe—and pulled out a small notepad. Licking his fingers, he flipped through the pages. "Here it is. Yost. Sheryl Yost. Seems she had a thing for our boy Turner, as well. Anyway, she was more than happy to tell me anything I wanted to know. According to her, Brooks and the Tremont girl had an affair, kind of a summer fling. Eventually he rode off into the sunset and left her—this seems to have been his M.O. at the time—and she ended up marrying Leonetti."

Thomas, who had been interested, wasn't impressed. "Lots of people have one last fling before they get married."

The fat man's lip curled outward and he moved his head from side to side. "Maybe. The thing of it is Mrs. Leonetti had a baby. Not eight months later. And the kid don't look all that Italian, if you get my drift."

Thomas held his glass halfway to his lips. "Brooks's?"

"Again, your guess is as good as mine," Sands replied in his oily voice. "But I found out that Dennis Leonetti had some tests done a few years back and he can't father children. His sperm count is near zero." Sands picked up his drink and finished it in one long swallow, then snapped open his ratty leather briefcase and fumbled through some papers. "Now, all of a sudden, Heather Leonetti, who's managed to ditch Leonetti and strip him of some of his money—she's shown up on Brooks's doorstep, at the very ranch you want to buy, and he practically does back flips. He's in San Francisco now—has a friend of his, Fred McDonald, run the ranch while he's gone." Finding his report, he slid it across the glass expanse of the tabletop.

Thomas picked up the typewritten pages. "In San

Francisco…to meet the child?" he asked, reaching into his pocket for his reading glasses.

Sands leaned closer. He grinned in pleasure. "He's there for tests. Been to a hospital. The staff is pretty mum, but my guess is it has something to do with the kid as the boy's got leukemia. Heather's kept it a secret, but she and Leonetti split up after the kid was diagnosed. My guess is Leonetti found out he wasn't the boy's dad and gave Heather the old heave-ho."

Thomas set his unfinished drink on the table. He didn't like this. Not when children, sick children, were involved. "The boy?"

"Is in remission, from what I get out of it. I don't know why she told Turner about the kid now, but she did…or at least it looks that way. Maybe she wants to take up with him again now that Leonetti's out of the picture. Again, your guess is as good as mine."

Thomas's voice was scratchy. Much as he wanted the Badlands Ranch, and the oil he suspected was pooled beneath the dried-out fields, a child complicated things. He'd always been a sucker for his own children, even Jackson, though he'd made too many mistakes where his firstborn, his bastard, had been concerned. He'd tried to atone, but Jackson hadn't heard of it. He sipped his drink, didn't taste the expensive blend. Hell, a kid. Brooks had a kid. A sick kid. This complicated things.

"You want me to keep digging?"

Thomas's head snapped up and he felt beads of sweat on his brow. "Yes. Please. Let's see if there's anything else." He folded the report neatly and stuffed it into the inner pocket of his jacket.

Sands grinned and plopped an ice cube into his broad mouth. "You're the boss."

CLOSED-IN PLACES MADE HIM restless, and this doctor's office, complete with diplomas on the wall and soft leather chairs, didn't ease the knot of tension between Turner's shoulder blades. He felt trapped and hot, barely able to breathe. His legs were too long to stretch between his chair and the desk, so he sat, ramrod straight, while the doctor shifted the papers in a file marked LE-ONETTI, ADAM.

That would have to change. Turner would rot in hell rather than have his son labeled with another man's name—a man who really didn't care one way or the other for the boy. As soon as possible, Adam's name would be Brooks. Heather would have to change it. There were no two ways about it; Turner intended to lay claim to his son.

Dr. Thurmon was a portly man with thin silver hair and a face right out of a Norman Rockwell poster. Behind wire-rimmed glasses, Thurmon had gentle eyes and Turner trusted him immediately. He'd always had a gut instinct about people, and usually his first impressions were right on target.

Thurmon took off his glasses. "Good news," he said, casting a smile at Heather, and Turner saw her shoulders slump in relief. "The marrow's a match and I didn't have a lot of hope that it would be. Siblings are the best source for transplants. But—" he lifted his hands and grinned "—we lucked out."

"Thank God," Heather whispered, tears filling her eyes. Without thinking, Turner wrapped a strong arm around her and they hugged. His own throat clogged, and he fought the urge to break down. His son was going to be well.

"While this is still very serious, Adam is in good shape," the doctor went on as he polished the lenses of his glasses with a clean white handkerchief. "We have his own marrow, taken while he's been in remission, and now Mr. Brooks will be a donor. And as well as Adam's doing, there's no reason to anticipate that a transplant is necessary, at least not in the near future, But Adam will have to stay on his medication for a while."

Heather's voice was shaky. "And if he relapses?"

Dr. Thurmon's lips pressed together. "Then a transplant will be likely. We'll reevaluate at that time." He closed the file. "But let's not worry about it just yet. Right now, Mrs. Leonetti, your son is as healthy as can be expected."

"Thank you!" Heather cast a triumphant glance at Turner and smiled through the tears shimmering in her eyes.

"Does this mean that Adam can do anything he wants?" Turner asked.

The doctor nodded. "Within reason. I wouldn't want to have him become overly tired. And I'd keep him away from anyone you know who has a contagious disease."

Heather froze as Turner said, "Then there's no reason—no medical reason—why Adam couldn't visit me at my ranch."

"Absolutely not," the doctor replied, and Heather's smile fell from her face as Turner and Dr. Thurmon shook hands.

She walked on wooden legs along the soft carpet of the clinic, past open doors with children sitting in their underwear on tables and mothers fussing over their kids as they waited. She turned by rote at the corner to the exit and found herself in the elevator before she let out her breath.

"That wasn't necessary," she said as the elevator descended.

"What?"

"I told you I'd let Adam visit."

"Just making sure you didn't find a reason to weasel out of it."

"I wouldn't—" She gasped and nearly stumbled as Turner slapped the elevator button and the car jerked to a stop.

"You kept him from me for five years. You admitted that you probably wouldn't have told me about him until he was eighteen if he hadn't gotten sick! You probably would have kept him from me if your bone marrow had matched. When I think about that—" He slammed a fist into the wall and Heather jumped. Turner's face suffused with color. "Well, things have changed. He does know me and soon you're going to tell him that I'm his father and—"

"I can't just blurt it out! He's only five!"

"Then he'll have fewer questions."

"But—"

"Don't fight me on this, Heather," he warned, leaning over her, his face set in granite. "I've lived up to my part of the bargain. Now I expect you to come through."

"Why wouldn't I?"

Turner stared deep into her eyes and some of his hard edges faded a bit. "Oh, hell," he muttered, trying to control himself. He flexed his hands, then shoved them impatiently through his hair. "Look, the last few days, we've both been worried—on edge and we...well, we fell into a pattern of trusting each other and playing house."

Stung, his words cutting deep, she couldn't respond, just swallowed at the swelling in her throat.

"But now we know that Adam's safe. You don't need me anymore. Or at least not right away. It would be easy to step back into our old lives—you go your way, I go mine."

*Oh, Turner, you're so wrong. So very wrong,* she thought desperately. Perhaps he could forget her easily, but she'd never forget him. Never! She'd already spent six years with his memory; she was destined to love him, if just a little, for the rest of her life.

"But that's not going to happen. Now that I know about Adam, my way—my path—is wound with his. That can't change."

Fear took a stranglehold of her heart. "What're you saying, Turner, that you want custody?" Her knees threatened to crumple, and she leaned hard against the rail in her back.

He slapped the button again and, with a groan of old gears, the elevator continued on its descent. "Not yet. I'm not stupid enough to try to take him from you, but from this point onward, I'm going to have some influence over him." He sent her a look that cut clear to her bones.

"How much 'influence'?"

"That's up to you, Heather."

"Meaning?"

"As long as I see him often, and I'm not talking one weekend a month, I won't challenge you in court. But…" His eyes glittered ominously, with the same gleam she'd seen whenever he was trying to break a particularly stubborn colt. "…If you come up against me, or try any funny stuff, you'll be in for the fight of your life."

The elevator landed and the doors whispered open to a crowd of onlookers. One man was frantically pushing the call button; other people whispered about the wisdom of getting onto a temperamental car.

Turner cupped her elbow and guided her through the crowd.

"You really are a bastard," she whispered under her breath.

"Why thank you, darlin'. I'll take that as a compliment." With a smile as cold as a copperhead's skin, he shoved open the doors.

Outside, fog had settled over the city, bringing with its opaque presence the feel of nightfall. Heather, shivering, slid behind the wheel of her Mercedes. Turner hauled his long body into the passenger seat, propped his back against the door and stared at her.

"If you moved to Gold Creek, I wouldn't feel any need to demand partial custody," he said.

She shot him a look of pure venom and switched on the ignition. "Me move back to Gold Creek? I'd rather die first."

"Are you willing to take a chance on a custody hearing?"

Her hands tightened over the wheel. *Please, Turner, just leave it alone!* "This wasn't part of the deal. You asked me to bring Adam to your ranch for a week or two and I intend to, but I'm not moving. Just because you're Adam's father, doesn't give you the right to bully me." Muttering under her breath, she eased the car into the flow of traffic traveling through the city.

"Is that what I'm doing?"

"From the first time I stepped into your barn."

He turned his attention to the roadway. In the fog, brake lights glowed eerily and crowds of pedestrians crossed the streets at the stoplights.

"You've got a week," he said as the light changed. "I'll expect to see Adam then."

"But I have work—"

"So do I." He rubbed a big hand over the faded spot of denim covering his knee. "I've been gone long enough already. Fred can't watch my place forever. Work out whatever you have to, but bring Adam to the ranch."

She wanted to argue, to find a way out of the deal because she knew that if she took Adam to Badlands Ranch, it wouldn't be long before she lost her son as well as her heart to Turner Brooks.

## CHAPTER ELEVEN

"I THINK YOU'RE MAKING a big mistake." Rachelle eyed her sister in the mirror of her bedroom, grimaced, then adjusted one of the shoulder pads in Heather's gown. Layers of raspberry-colored chiffon and silk, the dress was to be worn at Rachelle's wedding. "You can't let him have the upper hand."

"What choice do I have?" Heather asked, holding her hair up and frowning at the sight she made. Modeling the elegant dress only reminded her of weddings and just how far apart she and Turner had grown. The city girl and the cowboy. An unlikely combination. An unlikely *explosive* combination. "He's holding all the cards."

Rachelle shook her head furiously. "I saw him with Adam. He wouldn't do anything to jeopardize his son's well-being. Hold still, will you? I think this should be taken in a little in the waist...what do you think?"

"That you're being overly concerned. You're the bride. No one will be looking at me."

Rachelle's brow puckered as she slid the zipper down her sister's back. "If it were up to me, Jackson and I would've taken off on his Harley, driven straight to Lake Tahoe and gotten married without all this fuss."

"So why didn't you?" Heather asked, stepping out of the dress.

"Because *His Majesty* wants to make a statement."

"I heard that," Jackson called from the living room of Rachelle's tiny apartment.

"Well, it's true." Rachelle's eyes lighted as she zipped a plastic cover over the gown. "You're tarnishing your rebel image, you know, by doing the traditional wedding and all."

"Good! Keeps the people in Gold Creek on their toes."

As Rachelle hung up the dress, Heather slipped on her jeans and cotton blouse, then slid her arms through a suede vest.

Rachelle arched an eyebrow at Heather's getup. "Well, aren't you the little cowgirl?"

"I figured I better look the part." Together they edged along the hall, past the stacked boxes and packing crates. Jackson was on the floor near the bay window, black hair tumbling over his forehead, his sleeves rolled up as he wrestled with a red-faced Adam.

"I got you, I got you!" Adam chortled triumphantly as he straddled Jackson's broad chest. "One, two, three, you lose!"

"You're just too tough for me," Jackson said with a laugh. His dark eyes gleamed as Rachelle approached. "I think we should have a dozen of these."

"A dozen?" she said, grinning. "I don't know. Sounds like a lot."

"Well, maybe just a half dozen. When do we start?"

"When I've got a legal contract, Counselor. One that spells out how many times you change the diapers and get up in the middle of the night and—"

"Okay, okay, I've heard this all before." With a quick movement, he lifted Adam off his chest and rolled quickly to his feet. Adam squealed with delight as he was tossed into the air and caught in Jackson's strong arms.

"Legally binding, mind you," Rachelle said. "And I plan to have a *real* attorney check all the fine print."

A devilish grin slid across Jackson's jaw and he motioned to his fiancée as he stage-whispered to Heather, "She just doesn't trust me. That's the reporter in her."

"Give it up, Counselor," she said, but he grabbed her, twirled her off her feet and left her suddenly breathless when she finally touched down again.

"Never," he mouthed, his lips only inches from hers.

Heather felt her heart twist when she saw them exchange a sensual glance, the same kind of glance she shared with Turner. Yet, while Rachelle and Jackson were head over heels in love, she and Turner were worlds apart and had no chance of planning a future together. He'd never once said he loved her, and as far as she knew, he still didn't believe that particular emotion existed. He'd told her as much six years before and Heather doubted he'd changed his mind. She cleared her throat, and the two lovers finally remembered there was someone else in the room. "Well, I guess we'd better get going. Adam can't wait to see Turner's ranch, can you?"

Adam let out a whoop. "I'm gonna learn how to break a..." He glanced to Heather for help.

"Break a bronco," she replied. "But I wouldn't hold my breath if I were you."

Adam's eyes were shining. "You can come visit," he told his aunt. "Turner will probably let you break one, too."

"I'll remember that," Rachelle said with a chuckle. "And while I'm at it, I'll rope me a steer, brand half a dozen calves and spit tobacco juice!"

"You're lyin'!" Adam accused, but curious doubts crowded his eyes, and Heather imagined he was trying to picture his trim aunt wrestling with livestock and shooting a stream of brown juice from the corner of her mouth.

"You might be surprised, sport," Rachelle teased, her eyes glinting mischievously. "Oh, Heather, would you mind dropping these in the mailbox?" She rifled through the papers on the desk and came up with a stack of wedding invitations, already addressed and stamped.

"No problem." Heather took the stack of cream-colored envelopes and headed down the stairs. A post office was on her way out of town and she was glad to do a favor for her sister. Rachelle and she had always been close, though Heather had kept more than her share of secrets from her sister. Not only had she hidden the fact that Turner was Adam's father, but she'd also kept quiet about Adam's illness for a long time, until the doctors had started talking about bone-marrow transplants.

Though Rachelle had known that Adam wasn't well, Heather had kept the extent of the illness to herself, always telling herself that she couldn't burden her sister or mother with her problems. They had both experienced enough of their own. Rachelle had been horrified, when six weeks ago Heather had told her the truth.

After strapping Adam into the passenger seat, she wove the Mercedes through the traffic until she reached the nearest post office and pulled into the lane near a series of mailboxes. As she stuffed the thick envelopes through the slot, she saw the names of people she'd known all her life, people who had lived in Gold Creek. Monroe and McDonald, Surrett, Nelson, Patton and...the last envelope surprised her. Addressed in Rachelle's bold hand, the invitation was addressed to Thomas Fitzpatrick, Jackson's father. The man who had never claimed him. The man who had almost let Jackson twist in the wind for the murder of his legitimate son, the man who all too late tried to make amends, the man Jackson still professed to despise.

Had he changed his mind? Heather doubted it. No, this had all the earmarks of Rachelle deciding it was time her husband-to-be put old skeletons to rest. And it spelled fireworks for the wedding.

"Oh, God, Rachelle, I hope you know what you're doing."

Heather turned the invitation over in her hand and a sharp beep from the car in line behind her startled her. This wasn't any of her business. Heather jammed the envelope into the slot and edged the car back into the flow of traffic. Certainly Rachelle wouldn't have been so silly as to send the invitation behind Jackson's back. Or would she?

Rachelle had a reputation for being stubborn and bullheaded. She'd stood on principle once before—for Jackson—and it had cost her the respect of her friends and family and soiled her reputation. But surely she'd learned her lesson....

This was Rachelle's wedding—if she wanted to make it her funeral, as well, it was her choice. Besides— Heather stole a glance at her son, his face eager, a small toy car clutched in his fingers—she had her own share of concerns.

"I ALREADY SAID I WASN'T interested," Turner said, irritated beyond words. He'd made the mistake of picking up the phone as he'd walked through the house and ended up in a conversation with God himself: Thomas Fitzpatrick. Now the guy wasn't even working through his real-estate agent.

"I'm willing to pay you top dollar," Fitzpatrick argued smoothly. "Why don't you think it over?"

"No reason to think." He could almost hear the gears grinding in Fitzpatrick's shrewd mind.

"Everyone has a price."

"Not everyone, Fitzpatrick," Turner drawled.

There was an impatient snort on the other end of the line. "Just consider my offer. Counter if you like."

"Look, Tom," Turner replied, his voice edged in sarcasm. "With all due respect, I'm busy. I've got a ranch to run. If you wanted this place so badly, you should never have sold it in the first place."

"I realize that now. At the time, I wasn't interested in diversifying. I had timber. Now I've changed my mind. There might be oil on the land and I'm willing to gamble. I'm offering you twice what the land is worth, Mr. Brooks. You couldn't get a better deal."

"Good. 'Cause I don't want one."

"But—"

"Listen, Fitzpatrick, you and I both know you never cut anyone a deal in your life."

"But—"

"The answer is 'no.' Well, maybe that doesn't quite say it all. Let's make it 'No way in hell!'" With that, Turner slammed the receiver into the cradle, turned off the answering machine and strode to the bathroom. He didn't want to think of Fitzpatrick with his starched white shirts, silk ties and thousand-dollar suits. The man couldn't be trusted and Turner wasn't interested in doing any kind of business with him.

Still bothered, he cleaned the dirt, grime and horse-hair from his face and hands, then noticed the smell of oil that lingered on his skin from this morning, when he'd had to work on the fuel line of the tractor. Damned thing was always breaking down.

Scowling, he glanced at his watch. Three-thirty. She'd

be here any minute. Calling himself every kind of fool, he stripped quickly, leaving his clothes in a pile on the floor, twisted on the shower and stepped under the cool spray. Within a minute or two the water warmed and he scrubbed his body from head to foot. Wrapping a towel around his waist, he headed down the hallway and nearly tripped over Nadine, who was walking through the front door.

"Oh—God—I… Oh, Turner…I knocked but no one answered." She flushed at the sight of his naked torso and legs. "I didn't mean to—"

He grinned. "Sure you did, Nadine," he teased, and saw her face turn several shades of red.

"Believe me, Turner, I'm not that hard up," she threw back, her chin angling defiantly, though her eyes caught his mischief. "I haven't reduced myself to bein' a Peeping Tom, and even if I had, *you* certainly wouldn't be on the top of my list." Her eyes shifted away from his, though, and he felt that same uncertainty he had in the past. He guessed that she was half in love with him. The poor woman. Beautiful and bright, she could do better than Sam Warne or himself.

Through the window, he saw Heather's Mercedes roll to a stop. "Look, Nadine, I've got to change." Without another word, he half ran into the bedroom, slammed the door, let the towel drop and changed into clean jeans and a work shirt. He ran his fingers through his hair and was opening the bedroom door as the rap of a small fist banged against the screen door.

"Turner?" Adam's voice rang through the ranch house as he pushed the door open. Quick little steps hesitated in the entry hall.

Turner felt a strange tightness in his chest as he turned the corner and saw his son standing in the hallway of his house, looking confused and worried. This wasn't how it was supposed to be. Any child of his should feel at home on the ranch, know every rock and crevice in the land, spend hours in the barn or astride a horse or exploring the wooded hillsides. Any child of his should live here, no matter what the sacrifice. Turner could barely find his voice, and when he finally spoke, his words sounded hushed, choked by emotions he'd never experienced before. "I wondered when you were gonna git here, cowboy," he said.

Adam's freckled nose crinkled and he giggled. "I'm not a cowboy!"

"You are now." Turner reached onto the scarred wooden coatrack, where on the highest spindle a small brown-and-white Stetson had been placed. "All you need is this hat—" he plopped it on Adam's head "—and a pair of boots."

"I got high-tops!" Adam proclaimed, proudly displaying white basketball shoes with a famous insignia.

"We'll fix that." With a grin that seemed to light his very soul, Turner picked the boy up and hugged him close. It felt right holding his boy—like nothing he'd ever experienced—and Turner knew that with each passing minute he'd want more until he had it all. There was no turning back, no way he could pretend Adam didn't exist.

But he wouldn't rip a son from his mother. He'd lost his own mom when he wasn't all that old and he'd missed her every day of his life since. No, somehow Turner would have to work out a compromise with Heather, find a way that they each could spend as much time with Adam as possible.

For a second, he thought of marrying her. There were certainly worse twists his life could take, but he didn't believe for a minute that she would agree. She'd be bored to death here on the farm, and he'd curl up and die in the city. And she would want love—not companionship, not sex, not even friendship. She wanted to be loved. And she deserved that much. Hell, what a mess! For a second he was furious with her again. If only she'd been honest with him way back when, bridging this abyss wouldn't be necessary.

He spied Heather walking across the porch, and again his heart leapt to his throat. God, she was beautiful—too beautiful. A graceful, intriguing creature who should have been modeling for some highbrow agency in New York. Without makeup, with the layers of sophistication peeled away, she was still the most sensual woman he'd ever met. Her blond hair was pulled into a ponytail and held by a leather thong. She was wearing an outfit befitting a country singer. Stylized cowgirl. Earthy with a touch of glitz.

The kind of woman that stayed with you long after she'd said goodbye. The kind of woman a man could get used to. The kind of woman he would marry. The idea sent a jolt through his brain. He'd never considered marriage—not seriously, though once before, when he'd found out that Heather had left the Lazy K, he'd contemplated tracking her down and proposing. The urge had passed when he'd realized that she'd married Leonetti.

But now…marriage didn't seem so unlikely, though he doubted she would give up her fast-paced lifestyle in the city to become a rancher's wife. He kicked the idea of marriage around and found it wasn't as distasteful as he'd originally thought.

"Momma's a cowboy, too!" Adam chirped as Turner held the door open for Heather.

"I'll get the rest of your things," he said.

Heather's blue gaze touched his for a second, before

shifting to a point beyond him. Her smile faded, and the color seeped from her face. "Heather?" he asked, before glancing over his shoulder and spying Nadine, dust rag in one hand, mop in the other as she stood in the archway to the kitchen.

"Company?" Nadine asked, her smile frozen, her eyes dark with quiet emotions.

Turner couldn't stand the deception a second longer. He hated lies and wasn't about to let Heather's web of deceit tie him into knots—especially not where Nadine was concerned. He should have used his hard head and told her earlier. "Nadine, I'd like you to meet Heather Leonetti." Nadine's arched brows inched up a bit. "And this is Adam. My son."

Heather gasped.

Nadine's mouth dropped open and she quickly snapped it shut. "Excuse me?"

"Turner!" Heather cried, glancing in horror at her boy. Adam's little face was puckered a bit, but he didn't seem all that concerned about the fact that every grown-up in the room was nearly apoplectic.

"And this is Nadine Warne, my housekeeper."

Heather's throat closed in on itself. She wanted to strangle Turner right then and there. What right did he have to break the news to Adam this way? And Nadine, who from the knowing glance she cast Turner, cared more for him than she did for mopping his floors...what did she think?

After a second's hesitation, Nadine left her mop in the kitchen and stuffed her dust rag into a pocket. She managed what appeared to be a genuine smile as she walked toward Adam with her hand extended. "Well, how are you?"

"He's confused, that's what he is," Heather cut in,

though she wasn't angry with Nadine. Obviously the woman was shocked and making the best out of a bad situation. But Turner...he was another matter. She'd love to pummel him with her fists, and the look she shot him told him just that.

"Maybe I'd better come back another time," Nadine said, her sad gaze landing on Adam.

"It's all right," Turner replied. His strong tanned arms surrounded his son with such possession that Heather didn't know whether to laugh or cry. Adam needed a father, a man to care for him, but Heather couldn't find it in her heart to let go of her boy even a little. "I'll bring in Heather's things and we'll be out of your hair. Adam wants a tour of the ranch, don't you, kid?"

"I want to break a bronco!"

Turner smiled and winked. "Slow down, son. We have to save something for tomorrow."

"I won't let him—"

"Enough," Turner said sharply, then at Heather's gasp, added in a gentler tone to his son, "Come on, let's bring the rest of the bags inside." Hand in hand, father and son walked through the door, leaving Heather standing in the entry hall, trying to think of some kind of conversation she could drum up with Nadine.

"I would've known anyway," Nadine admitted to Heather. Through the window, she watched Turner as he stepped out of the shadow of the house, into the dry dust of the yard. He set Adam on his feet and the boy took off, pell-mell to the fence nearest the barn. "Adam's the spitting image of his pa."

"I think so, too."

Nadine nodded. "I grew up with Turner, you know. Seeing Adam...well, it takes me back about twenty-five years." She wiped her hands on the rag in her pocket. "I'm surprised he didn't tell me."

"He didn't know," Heather said, deciding it was time for the truth to be told. There was no reason to lie any longer. Even if Nadine didn't turn out to be the biggest gossip in Gold Creek, the news was bound to get out. Turner would see to it. "It...it's complicated," she added.

"With Turner, it always is," Nadine replied. Then, as if shaking herself out of a great melancholy, she cocked her head toward the kitchen. "Come on inside. Look around. I don't know if he's got anything in the refrigerator but beer and milk two weeks beyond the pull date, but there might be a soda."

Heather followed Nadine into the kitchen, where a bucket, mop and basket of cleaning supplies had been set. She envied Nadine's familiarity with the house, with the routine, with Turner, and yet she knew that she had no one to blame for the distance between herself and the father of her child but herself. She could have told him the truth anytime in the past few years, but she hadn't. *Coward! Now, look at the mess you're in!*

"I met your sister when she was back in Gold Creek," Nadine said, opening the refrigerator and searching at the meager contents. "How about that? He knew you were coming. Pepsi all right?"

"Fine. You know Rachelle?"

"Mmm." Nadine popped the tabs on two cans of soda and handed one to Heather. "I have a lot of respect for her. Stood up for what she believed in and came back to prove it. I was there, you know, the night Roy was killed. God, it was awful." She shook her head and sighed. "And now things are really jumbled up. Who would've believed that Jackson was Thomas Fitzpatrick's son? Believe me, that little bit of news set the town on its ear. Those Gold

Creek gossips couldn't talk of much else for three or four weeks." She managed an amused smile. "Not that Gold Creek didn't need to be set on its ear, mind you. But for years the Fitzpatricks and the Monroes have owned and run everything in this town. Aside from your husband's family—"

"My ex-husband," Heather clarified.

"Well, aside from the Leonettis, the Fitzpatricks and Monroes own Gold Creek lock, stock, and barrel. I just find it hard to believe that old Thomas Fitzpatrick let Jackson, his own son, take the rap for Roy's death."

"I think Thomas believed it because of June," Heather said, a little uncomfortable with the subject. Mention of the Fitzpatricks always made her skin crawl.

Nadine shrugged and took a long swallow of her drink. "Well, I'd better get to work so I'm not late for my own boys." She reached for her mop and smiled wistfully. "I've always thought that Turner could be the best father in the county. He just didn't know it. Now, maybe, he'll really settle down."

"Hey, Mom! Come on!" Adam yelled from the back porch. He was waving furiously. "We're gonna go see the life stock."

"Livestock," Turner corrected, holding the door open for Heather. Adam was already leading the way, running through the dappled sunlight, dust kicking up behind his new shoes. Turner and Heather fell into step together.

"She's in love with you, you know," Heather finally said, worried that Nadine had a place in Turner's heart and sensing that down-to-earth Nadine, the woman who spent a lot of her time here, would be a perfect mate for him.

"Who? Nadine?" He swatted at a wasp that flew near his head.

"Don't pretend you haven't noticed."

Brackets tightened around the corners of his mouth. "She deserves better."

"Maybe she doesn't think so."

Turner stopped and stared down at Heather. "Don't be playing matchmaker," he said, his voice steely with determination. "And don't try to get me interested in another woman or her kids. It's Adam I want."

She felt her face drain of color. What did he think? "I was only saying—"

"I know what you were doing, damn it, and it won't work. Now that I know about Adam, I'm not going to fill in with some substitute."

"I didn't..." But her words faded when he opened the barn door and the scents of dust and hay, horses and leather assailed her. She walked past the very stall where they'd made love and her throat caught at the vivid memory. Adam dashed deeper into the interior, sending dust motes into the air and mice scurrying. "I didn't suggest that you should be a father to just any child," she said indignantly. Several horses snorted, and Heather caught Turner staring at her, his eyes dark and serious.

"Good," he drawled in a low, emotion-packed voice, "because Nadine Warne isn't the woman for me."

The walls of the barn seemed to close in on them. Heather's breath was lost in her lungs at the words he hadn't spoken, the insinuation that hung, like a thin diaphanous cloud, between them.

Heather fought the thrill of hope in her heart that she might just be that woman. Angry with that thought, she shoved it out of her mind. Would she be happy here, in a run-down ranch house, living less than five miles from Gold Creek, with a lifestyle made up of horses, leather, bacon grease and P.T.A. meetings? Where would she paint? She'd have to have a studio.... She glanced back, through the still-open barn door to the weathered sheds and barns and rambling ranch house. Where would the best natural light filter in? She'd need water and light and privacy and... She caught herself up short.

What was she thinking? That Turner would ask her to marry him? Gritting her teeth, she changed the course of her thoughts and watched Adam scamper along the stalls, petting one velvet-soft nose of a horse before hurrying on to the next. His cheeks were rosy, his eyes alight with anticipation. He looked happier and healthier than he had in weeks, and Heather's heart twisted.

As she walked to the first stall, she noticed the horse within, a stocky sorrel mare, was saddled. The mare shook her head and the bridle jangled. "What's going on?"

"Seems to me the last time you came here, you wanted to ride."

She flushed at the memory.

"Least I could do is accommodate you."

"Adam doesn't know how to stay astride a horse," she protested.

"He'll be with me." Turner didn't wait for another argument. He opened the stall gate, grabbed the reins of the mare's bridle and stuffed them into a surprised Heather's fingers. "This is Blitzen." His lips twitched a bit. "I didn't name her. She came that way."

"But—"

He walked to the next stall, and a tall buckskin nickered softly. Heather smiled as she recognized Sampson. Turner patted the big horse fondly on the shoulder.

"I didn't think you still had him," she said.

Turner's eyes flashed. "He's the best horse I ever owned. I'd never sell him." One corner of his mouth lifted. "Don't you know by now that I'm true-blue, Heather?"

A basket of butterflies seemed to erupt in her stomach, but he didn't miss a beat and swung Adam up into the saddle.

"Hold on, honey," Heather said automatically, her eyes riveted to her son's precarious position.

"Oh, Mom!" Adam actually rolled his eyes.

"He'll do fine." Turner tugged gently on the reins and the horse's hooves rang on the concrete as they headed back to the door. Outside, the daylight seemed bright, and Turner spent a few minutes explaining to Adam about the horse and how he could be controlled by simple tugs on the reins.

"Just don't whistle," Heather added, and was rewarded with a sharp look from her son's father. They were both reminded of the first time they met and Heather's misguided attempt to steal Turner's horse from him.

With Adam propped in the saddle, Turner tied Sampson to a rail of the fence. "I'll be right back. Don't go anywhere."

"Where would we go?" she called after him as he dashed along a well-worn path to the back porch and disappeared around the corner.

"What's he doin'?" Adam asked, frowning slightly as the screen door creaked and banged shut. His little fingers held on tight to the saddle horn and a perplexed look crossed his freckled features. "And why'd he say he was Daddy?"

*Oh, Adam, what have I done to you?* she wondered silently. "I don't know," she said, unable to tell her son the truth of his parentage while they sat astride two separate horses. When it came time for telling the truth, she wanted to be able to hold him and kiss him and tell Adam that he was the most loved child on this earth.

Damn Turner. Why did he think he had the right to blurt out that—

*Because he's Adam's father.*

Still that didn't give him the right to go spouting off—not until the time was right.

*And when would that be? When would the time ever be right?*

Before she could answer her own question, Turner strode back with sacks he'd stuffed into the saddlebags that were strapped to his horse. He swung into the saddle behind Adam, and led the way, through the sprawling acres of the ranch.

Despite her worries, Heather felt herself relax. The day was warm, sunlight heated the crown of her head. Bees floated over the few wildflowers caught in the dry stubble of the fields, and a bothersome horsefly buzzed near Blitzen's head, causing the little mare's ears to flick in irritation.

The ranch, in its rustic way, was beautiful. The buildings were time-worn and sun-bleached, but sturdy and practical. Rimming the dry fields, thin stands of oak and pine offered shade while the sun sent rippling images across the dry acres. Turner stopped often, pointing out a corral where he trained rodeo horses, a field that was occupied by brood mares and their spindly legged colts, and a pasture that held a few head of cattle. Adam's eyes fairly glowed as he watched the foals frolic and play or the calves hide behind their mothers' red flanks. His small hands twisted in Sampson's black mane and he chattered, nearly nonstop, asking questions of Turner or laughing in delight when a flock of pheasants rose before the horse, their wings flapping wildly as they flew upward.

"Like in the park!" he exclaimed, obviously delighted.

"Yeah, but those are doves. These are pheasants. Ring-necked Chinese," Turner told him.

When Turner released the reins and kneed Sampson into a slow lope, Heather panicked, sure that Adam would fall. She started to cry out, but held her tongue when she saw the strong grip of Turner's arm around his son's chest. If she was sure of nothing else in this world, she was certain Turner wouldn't let Adam fall. The thought was comforting and unsettling alike. Things were going to change. Her life with Adam would never be the same.

She urged her mare into an easy lope and the wind tugged at her hair and brought tears to her eyes. She felt eighteen again and couldn't keep the smile from her lips. "Come on, girl, you can keep up with them," she told her little mount, and the game little mare didn't lose much ground.

Turner pulled up at the crest of a small hill. A crop of trees shaded the grass, and a creek, dry now, wound jaggedly along the rise. From the hilltop, they could see most of the ranch. As he tethered the horses, Turner glanced at her over his shoulder. His eyes were thoughtful and guarded as he looked at Heather. "My mom and dad rented this place for years," he said, frowning slightly as he revealed more of himself than he ever had. "From Thomas Fitzpatrick. Dad bought it from him with the proceeds of the life insurance he had on Mom. Now Fitzpatrick wants it back."

"Why?"

"Don't you know?"

Heather lifted a shoulder. "How would I?"

"The man who's going to be your brother-in-law is Fitzpatrick's son."

"A trick of fate," Heather replied, surprised at the train of Turner's thoughts. He seemed to be asking deeper questions, questions she didn't understand. "Jackson and Thomas Fitzpatrick are related by blood only. There's no love lost between those two."

Turner opened the saddlebags and pulled out brown sacks filled with sandwiches, fruit and sodas. Adam wandered through the tall, dry grass, trying to catch grasshoppers before they flew away from his eager fingers.

Stretching out in the shade of an oak tree, Turner patted the ground beside him, and Heather, feeling the need for a truce between them, sat next to him, her back propped by the rough bark of the tree.

"Fitzpatrick says he's interested in the mining rights to the place, thinks there might be oil. My guess is he already knows as much, though how he goofed and sold the place back to my old man beats me. Either John Brooks was sharper than we all thought, or Fitzpatrick made a mistake that's been eating at him for years. Old Tom never likes to lose, especially when money's involved. He made a bad decision years ago—concentrating on timber. Now he realizes with all the environmental concerns and restrictions, he'd better find new means to keep that Fitzpatrick wealth." He plucked a piece of grass from the ground and twirled the bleached blade between his thumb and forefinger. "What do you think?"

"I wouldn't even hazard a guess." She drew her knees up and stared after Adam, though she was all too aware of Turner and that he was watching her reaction, as if he expected her to start telling him everything she knew about Thomas Fitzpatrick. Which she had. What she knew of the man was common knowledge to the citizens of Gold Creek. "Ever think about selling?"

"Nope." He leaned back against the tree, his arm brushing hers as he squinted into the lowering sun. Smiling slightly, watching Adam squeal and run, he seemed more content and relaxed than she'd ever known him.

"What about joining the circuit again? Ever consider it?"

He shook his head. "Busted my knee too many times already. And my shoulder's not in the best of shape."

"So you're going to live out the rest of your days here?" It all seemed too pastoral, too quiet for the Turner she knew.

"That's the plan."

It didn't seem so horrible, she thought, staring at the rolling hills and fields. The sounds of birds in the trees and the relaxing view of horses and cattle grazing brought a sense of peace she hadn't felt in years. Deep down, she knew she could lose a little bit of the frenetic pace of the city and enjoy the leisure that she'd somehow lost.

But to live in Gold Creek? Seeing Turner day in and day out and knowing that their relationship would go nowhere?

"This place is special to you."

"It's all I've got," he said simply, then frowned. "Or it was. Now there's Adam."

Heather's heart twisted. "Yes, now there's Adam."

He glanced at her from the corner of his eye. "I've thought a lot about this, Heather. Ever since you showed up here. I told myself it would be best to leave it all alone. To see the boy occasionally. To pretend to be like a... well, a favorite uncle or something. But that won't work. And I told myself to stay away. Let you and Adam live your lives without me interfering." He glanced to the distant hills, and the breeze teased at the golden-brown strands of his hair, lifting them from his forehead. "But it won't work. It can't. I can't let it. It's not the way I'm made. Even if I'd convinced myself that staying away from him would be best, I couldn't do it once I'd laid eyes on him. It's...well, it's like nothing else in the world. I never planned on having kids—hell, I didn't think I'd be much of a father—but now that he's here and he's mine, I'm going to be the best damn dad this side of Texas."

Heather's throat closed in on itself. "That's what I've said about being a mother."

Turner's eyes narrowed on the horizon, as if he were wrestling with an inner decision. "I grew up without a mom, leastwise for the last half of my growing-up years. I wouldn't do that to a kid. And my old man..." He shook his head, his eyes troubled. "That son of a bitch was a piece of work. But he was my dad, and like it or not that's the way it was." He leaned back again, resting on an elbow and staring up at her, his gray eyes frank and serious. "You may as well know it right now. Nadine was just a start. From this point on, I'm claiming my boy to everyone I meet. And you can rant and rave and raise holy Cain, but I'm not backing down on this one." He stared at her for a long minute. "In fact, I think we'd better straighten out this whole mess with the person it means the most to."

"Turner, don't—"

But he didn't listen. "Hey, Adam, come on over and have some supper. We've got a lot to talk about."

"Turner, I'm warning you," she said, her motherly defenses springing into position.

"Warn to your heart's content, darlin'. This little man is gonna find out he's got a real pa!" Waving, he flagged his boy over, and Adam raced back to him, face red, legs flying wildly. The look of pure joy on the boy's face almost broke Heather's heart. She wanted to think that this visit to the ranch was just a lark, a diversion no more interesting than their trips to Candlestick Park or Fisherman's Wharf, but she had the deep, unsettling fear that what Adam was feeling was more—a deeper bond to the land that ran through his veins as naturally as his father's blood.

And in her heart, she knew that some of Turner's arguments were valid. She did spoil Adam. She did overprotect him. Because of Dennis's ambivalence toward the boy and then the horrid fear brought on by his disease, she had overreacted and coddled her sick son, praying that a mother's love could conquer all.

But maybe her love had overshadowed the fact that what he needed was freedom to explore, a chance to see the world away from the high rises of the city. Maybe what he needed was his father.

Adam, dust smearing his face and the brown "tobacco juice" of grasshoppers staining his fingers, landed under the tree with a loud thump. Automatically, Heather wiped his hands, but the brown dye didn't come off easily.

"Won't hurt him," Turner said. He'd unwrapped a sandwich and handed half to Adam, who promptly turned his nose up at it. "Don't like lettuce," he said.

"Adam…" Heather tried to step in, but Turner waved off her arguments, stripped the lettuce from the sandwich and tossed the green leaf over his shoulder.

"That's littering."

"Not out here," he said, stretching out in the shade of the tree. "Some rabbit or cow or crow or field mouse will find it." He handed Adam a can of soda and the boy grinned widely. "Now look, there's something your mom and I want to tell you."

While her guts wrenched, Heather shot Turner a look that spoke volumes.

Adam sat cross-legged and held his sandwich in two hands. "What?"

"From now on you can call me Dad."

"Why?"

"'Cause I'm your father."

Adam's brow beetled, and he sent Heather a glance that said he thought Turner had lost his marbles. "Already got a dad."

"And you don't want another one."

"Can only have one," he said, in simple five-year-old terms. Having set the older man straight, he took a big bite from his sandwich.

"Well, that's not necessarily true. Lots of people get married and divorced these days."

"My mom and dad are divorced."

"Right. But they may remarry, and when they do, you'll have a stepfather and a stepmother."

Adam chewed his ham sandwich thoughtfully. "So you're gonna marry Mom. Right?"

Turner's jaw slid to the side and Heather hardly dared breathe. "I don't think she'd have me," he said, and cast Heather a look that melted her insides.

"So how can you be my dad?"

"Your mom and I knew each other a long time ago," Turner said carefully, his voice oddly distant. "And... well, we fell in love, I guess, and she ended up pregnant with you, but I was far away. So she married the man you call your father."

"He *is* my father," Adam insisted, and Turner's muscles tightened a bit.

We fell in love? Heather wished she could believe the fairy tale he was spinning. Talk about lies! Turner was staring at his son, and Adam, arms crossed importantly over his chest, wasn't listening to any more of this craziness. He knew who his father was.

"I'm your pa, too," Turner told his boy.

Adam snorted. "Can't have more than one."

*Don't argue with him,* Heather silently pleaded, and for once Turner used his head.

"Sometimes things aren't so cut-and-dried. I know it'll take a little getting used to and you might still want to call me Turner, and that's okay." Turner's voice had thickened, and he looked down at the boy with an expression of concern and tenderness. "But I want you to know that I really am your pa."

Adam just shook his head and swallowed a drink of grape soda. When he set down the can, his lips were a pale shade of purple. He eyed Turner and Heather with unhidden suspicion. Obviously, he thought the grown-ups around him had lost any lick of common sense they'd been born with.

Heather ruffled her son's hair, letting the silky strands tickle her fingers. She forced words past her lips she hadn't planned on uttering for years. "He's telling you the truth, Adam. Turner is your dad." Looking at Turner, Heather smiled. Somehow this felt right.

"And what about Daddy?" Adam asked belligerently. His entire world had been turned upside down.

"He's your daddy, too. Your stepdaddy."

"I don't get it," he complained.

Heather offered him a tender smile. "Don't worry about it. Turner just wanted you to understand when he tells people you're his son why he's saying it."

"Sounds crazy to me," Adam said, but didn't seem

much concerned one way or the other. There was just too much to do here, too much to explore to worry about grown-up things. He left his sandwich half-eaten and ignored three quarters of his soda.

Turner, radiating pride, stared at the boy who was his son, and Heather felt the urge to kiss him, not with passion, but just to let him know that she appreciated the fact that he cared, actually cared, for his son. After so many years of Dennis's apathy, Turner's concern, though irritating sometimes, was a breath of fresh air. At least now, if anything happened to her, Adam would be with a parent who loved him. What more could she ask?

They ate in companionable silence, eating and watching their boy play in the tall grass while the sun lowered and a breeze laden with clover and honeysuckle danced through the dry leaves of the oak tree. Sunlight dappled the ground, shifting as the leaves rustled in the wind. The silence grew between them, and Turner rubbed his chin thoughtfully, as if wrestling with an inner dilemma.

Well, God knew, they had their share.

"Adam brought up an interesting point," Turner said quietly.

"Which is?" she hardly dared ask.

"That, in a perfect world, you and I would be married."

Her heart missed a beat and she looked up sharply to find flinty eyes regarding her without a trace of humor. He wasn't teasing her, but she had the feeling he was testing her. "It's not a perfect world," she said, meeting his gaze boldly.

"Growing up with only one parent isn't easy."

"Lots of kids do it."

His nostrils flared. "Not mine."

"If you're still trying to talk me into moving back to Gold Creek—"

"I think it's gone further than that, Heather. We both know it. Neither of us will be satisfied playing part-time parents, now, will we?"

Her throat was as dry as the last leaves of autumn. "What're you getting at?" she asked, her heart hammering wildly, her fingers nervously working the hem of her vest.

He eyed her long and hard, assessing her as he would a wild mustang he was about to break. "Well, Heather," he said, his gaze traveling up from the cleft at her breasts to settle on her eyes, "I guess I'm asking you to marry me."

# CHAPTER TWELVE

HEATHER ALMOST LAUGHED. Except for the dead-serious glint in his eyes, she would've thought he was joking. But marriage? She bit her lip. How long had she waited for a proposal from this lonesome cowboy? She would've done anything to hear him beg her to marry him six years ago. Now, however, she understood his reasons, the motives for making a commitment he would otherwise have avoided. "You don't have to do this," she said quietly, as she picked a flower from the dried grass and twirled it between her fingers. "I won't keep Adam from you."

His expression tensed. "You mean he can stay with me?" Unleashed anger sparked in his eyes.

"Part of the time, yes. When he's not in school." She swallowed back the impulsive urge to throw caution to the wind and tell him she'd gladly become his wife. However, she wouldn't allow his nobility, if that's what it was, or his love for his child, to interfere with his happiness.

"All summer long?"

"I—I can't promise—"

"Every weekend?"

"Well, no, but—"

Turner's expression turned as thunderous as a summer storm. "But nothing! The only way I'm going to see him as much as I want is for you to live with me."

"Here?"

"Is it so bad, Heather?" His voice was deeper than usual, and she saw the pride in his eyes when he looked over the acres that he'd sweated and bled for.

Hot tears filled her eyes. "No, Turner, it's good here. It's good for you. Maybe even good for Adam. I can feel it. But I don't know if I can fit in. I'd die if I had to spend my days making jam, or tending garden, or…or cleaning out stalls." She stared up at the sky, watching as a hawk circled near the mountains. "It's not a matter of not liking to make jam," she added. "Or even tending the garden. I…I'd enjoy it, some of the time. Even mucking out the stables. But…I need more. I'd go crazy if I couldn't paint, if I couldn't ever sculpt again, if I didn't have time to sit down with a sketch pad and draw." If only he could understand. "It's the same feeling you'd have if you knew you'd never climb on the back of a horse again."

He tipped back his hat and studied the horizon, his eyes narrowed against the sun. "Can't you do those things here?"

"I…yes."

"But you don't want to."

Close to tears, she offered him a tender smile. She'd never loved him more in her life, but she didn't want him to throw away his own lifestyle. His own needs. "This is no time to sacrifice yourself, Turner. You never wanted to marry. You as much as told me so."

"Maybe I changed my mind."

"Then maybe you'll change it again," she said, her throat closing upon itself as she stared into the intensity of his gaze. "And I'd hate to be the woman you were married to when you realized you wanted out."

"I won't."

"Oh, Turner—"

"Think about it," he suggested, bristling. He dusted his hands on his jeans as he stood.

She doubted she'd think of little else.

THAT EVENING, TURNER DROVE them into town. Heather's fingers tightened over the edge of the pickup seat as they passed familiar landmarks, the park with the gazebo built in memory of Roy Fitzpatrick's death, the yellow-brick building that had once been the Gold Creek Hotel and now housed Fitzpatrick, Incorporated, the post office on Main Street and the old Rexall Drugstore still standing on the corner of Main and Pine.

"I thought Adam would like one of the best burgers this side of the Rocky Mountains!" Turner said as he eased his pickup close to the curb.

They walked into the drugstore and a bell tinkled. The ceilings were high, with lights and fans, never renovated in the seventy years that the building had stood in the center of town. Shelves were neatly stacked; row upon row of cosmetics, medications, jewelry, paper items and toys stood just as they had most of the decade. The items had changed, turned over for new and improved stock, following the trends of small-town tastes, but the shelves were the same metal inlays that Heather remembered from high school.

The soda fountain in the back hadn't changed much, either, and Thelma Surrett, Carlie's mother, her hair grayer, her waist a bit thicker, was still making milk shakes. She glanced over her shoulder and offered Heather a surprised grin. "Well, well, well...look who's back in town," she said, turning on the milk shake mixer and snapping up her notepad as the blender whirred as loudly as a dentist's drill. "First Rachelle and now you. Don't tell me this town has changed its name to Mecca."

Heather grinned. "Rachelle said Carlie will be back for the wedding."

Thelma's eyes shifted a little, and her mouth tightened slightly but she nodded. "In a couple of weeks. Guess she got tired of those long nights up in Alaska. Uh-oh. Who's this?" she asked as Adam climbed up on a stool.

"This is my son, Adam," Heather said, unable to keep the pride from her voice.

"Well, howdy, partner," Thelma replied. She tapped the brim of Adam's hat. "Should I rustle you up some grub?"

"Three burgers, onion, fries, the works," Turner ordered, as Thelma turned off the blender and poured a thick strawberry milk shake into a tall glass.

"I want one of those!" Adam demanded, and Thelma, handing the drink to another customer, winked at the boy.

"You got it."

"Take off your hat while you eat, Adam."

"No!"

"Your ma's right," Turner added. "It's just plain good manners." He lifted the hat from his son's head.

Adam clapped his hands over hair that raised with static electricity. "I *hate* manners."

"Me, too," Turner said with a chuckle.

Heather felt as if she'd been transported back to high school and the days she'd walked to the pharmacy after school, tagging along with Rachelle and Carlie. Eventually Laura Chandler had joined the group and Laura had flagrantly ignored Rachelle's younger sister. "She's such a drag," she'd told Rachelle. "Can't we ditch her?"

Rachelle, none-too-thrilled to be stuck with Heather, had, nonetheless stood up for her. "It's okay," she'd argued, and Laura had pouted, though Carlie had never minded. Well, things had changed—turned around in the past twelve years. Laura had ended up married to Brian Fitzpatrick. Years later she'd been accused of killing Roy, the boy who, had he lived, would have become her brother-in-law.

Thelma started burgers sizzling on the grill, and soon they were eating again, laughing and talking, listening to Thelma go on and on about Rachelle's upcoming wedding and how she hoped Carlie would find a nice boy to settle down with and marry.

After finishing their meal, they wandered through the drugstore for a while, and as they were leaving, nearly ran into Scott McDonald. Turner's face stretched into a grin, but Heather had trouble finding a smile. Scott had been one of Roy Fitzpatrick's friends who had been with Rachelle the night Roy had been killed. After Roy's death, Scott had been vocal in pointing out Jackson's guilt, and had given Rachelle a rough time thereafter.

"I want you to meet someone, Scott," Turner said, and Heather thought she might drop through the yellowed linoleum of the drugstore's floor.

Turner introduced Scott to his son, and Heather managed a thin smile. Scott's eyes flickered with interest, but he congratulated Turner on such a "fine-looking boy." He and his wife, Karen, were expecting their first in February.

"I don't know if that was such a good idea," Heather said, as they wandered along the streets, window shopping at the bakery, jeweler's and travel agency.

"He would've found out anyway. He's Fred's brother

and Fred works for me." Turner slid a comforting arm around her shoulders. "Sooner or later it's all gonna come out."

"I vote for later."

"But it's easier now. Less to explain."

Her chest felt tight and worry crowded her brow as they strolled down the sidewalks. Adam found a pair of cowboy boots in the window of the shoe store, and Turner eyed a stove on display at the local Sears catalog store.

The town had a lazy summer feel. A few birds twittered and traffic rolled by at a snail's pace. The city lamps began to glow as dusk crept over the land and they walked unhurried to the park and past the gazebo erected in Roy's memory.

While Adam scrambled all over the playground equipment, Turner chased him, and Heather sat alone on a park bench. In the evening, with the wind soughing through the trees, Gold Creek didn't seem so horrible. She had fond memories of the town where as a child she'd drawn hopscotch on the cracked sidewalks, jumped rope and ridden her bike along the flat tree-lined streets. Her family hadn't had much money, but they'd made up for it in love.

And then her father had started drinking and his wandering eye had ripped apart that cozy blanket of security. Their mother had been devastated, the girls stunned. Tears and anger, pity and anguish had been followed by deep embarrassment. Gossiping tongues had wagged. Her father had filed for divorce and married a younger woman. The rumors had exploded. Later, Roy Fitzpatrick had been killed and Rachelle, alone, had stood up for Jackson Moore, the bad boy, telling the world that she'd spent the night with him, ruining her reputation.

Scandal had swept like a tornado through Gold Creek and the Tremonts were at its vortex. The friends and neighbors Heather had known all her life seemed to look at her differently, some with compassion, some with worry, others with out-and-out disgust. Life had never been the same. Heather had learned what it felt like to be an object of speculation while her sister became an object of ridicule. And Heather had begun to hate the small town she'd once felt was the center of the universe.

But now...if she faced the past, stood proudly with Turner by her side, maybe she could learn to feel comfortable in Gold Creek again. Not all the citizens were gossips. Not all were cruel. Not all had long memories. Not all cared. The people, and the town, had grown up, and Rachelle had been vindicated.

However, when the truth about Adam's parentage came out, she feared her innocent little boy would become grist for a long-dry gossip mill. But now she was stronger. She and Turner would protect their son.

For Heather, what people thought was no longer as important as it once had been. She'd survive, with her head held high. As for changing her lifestyle, there were drawbacks to living in the city where oftentimes she'd felt isolated. In San Francisco there were so many people, but so few good friends. Knowing people from the time they were children created a bond that was like no other in life.

Rachelle, though she hadn't seen Carlie in years, would never find a friend she understood better.

Wrapping her arms around herself, Heather watched as Turner pushed Adam on a swing. Adam shrieked in delight and Turner laughed, a deep, rumbling sound of pure happiness. In her heart, Heather knew she could never separate father and son. Now that they'd come to know each other, she wouldn't stand between them.

Stars winked in the heavens and other children played a game of tag on the baseball diamond near the equipment. Mothers and fathers pushed strollers down the cement walkways. Teenagers cruised by in cars, searching for their friends.

There was a charm to this town, and whether she liked it or not, it was, and always would be, home. Tears touched the back of her eyes. She could return. Her mother was here. Her father was in a town nearby. Jackson had told Rachelle he thought they should buy some property here eventually, though that might have been a joke. But if he was serious, there was a chance he and Rachelle would visit occasionally.

And Turner, bless and curse him, Turner belonged here.

The course of the rest of her life depended upon Turner. As it had since the first time she'd made love to him six years before.

It was after nine by the time they returned to the ranch. Nadine had made the spare room up for Adam, and after a quick bath, he was asleep as soon as his head hit the pillow.

Turner and Heather were alone. They sat on the porch swing, hearing the chorus of crickets and watching thousands of diamondlike stars glitter in the dark heavens. The old swing rocked slowly back and forth, creaking on rusty hinges. Roses, gone to seed, scented the air. Turner placed his arm over the back of the swing, gently holding Heather closer. "I wasn't kidding this afternoon," he said, his voice surprisingly rough. "I want you to consider marrying me."

She was touched, and her heart screamed "yes." "You wouldn't be happy," she said, her head resting against his shoulder.

"*You* wouldn't be happy."

Right now she was more content than she'd ever been. She couldn't imagine spending another day alone, without Turner. "I could be happy, Turner," she heard herself say, "with you. With Adam."

"But...?"

"But I'm not sure if I could live in the town."

"We're miles from the town, and there's a fairly substantial lake between the ranch and Gold Creek. It wouldn't be like before, when you were smack-dab in the middle of the city limits. And if you want to paint and draw, we'll find you a place. You could still keep the gallery in the city and go there anytime you got the urge."

Was it worth it? She gazed into Turner's steel-gray eyes and her heart swelled with love. She knew there was only one answer. "Of course I'll marry you, Turner," she said, as his strong arms surrounded her. His lips touched hers, gently at first, softly exploring, until he brazenly covered her mouth with his own.

FOUR DAYS LATER, HEATHER had settled herself into the ranch routine. Though she did cook breakfast and dinner for Adam and Turner, she drew the line at lunch for the hands. She figured they'd gotten along without her all these years and they could get along without her now. Besides, she planned to spend a lot of her time sketching or painting.

She and Adam had scouted through all the old buildings and finally, though it needed a lot of work, she'd settled on an attic over the stables for her studio. Every evening, Turner had helped her haul out the junk—books, magazines, old bikes, broken saddles, trunks of clothes and everything else under the sun. She was ready to start work refurbishing the room and she eyed it critically.

The attic was unique with its windows, pitched ceiling and inoperable ceiling fan. Though the room was smaller than her studio in the city, and it would require a lot of elbow grease to clean it up, the attic definitely had potential. With a couple of skylights, new paint and refinished floors, the room just might convert into an attractive workplace.

"I think you're right," agreed her mother, who had come out to the ranch for a visit. "But you might check for mice," she added, her practiced gaze sweeping the baseboards.

"I'll get a cat," Heather replied with a grin.

Ellen swiped at a cobweb dangling from the ceiling. "You know, I don't approve of you living here," she said, chewing nervously on her lip.

"Mom—"

"In my book you live with a man *after* you marry him, not before—and I don't care how much you're involved with him. It just doesn't look right!"

It was on the tip of Heather's tongue to tell her mother that she planned to marry Turner, but she didn't. She didn't want to steal any of her sister's thunder. Rachelle had waited too many years for the moment when she would become Jackson Moore's bride, so Heather and Turner had agreed to wait until after Rachelle's wedding to make an announcement about their own wedding plans. There wasn't any hurry. Despite what her mother thought.

"Living in sin is against everything I ever taught you."

"It's not sin, Mom."

Together they walked down the outside staircase and crossed the yard. Nearby, Turner was breaking a mule-headed colt and Adam was watching in rapt awe.

"Well, I will admit, Dennis didn't seem like much of a father," Ellen said as they walked onto the back porch. She glanced at her grandson. "I always wondered about that, you know. And I do believe that Adam deserves better."

Heather smiled.

"Maybe Turner isn't so bad, after all."

"He's not," Heather assured her mother as they entered the kitchen. "Here. Sit down. I've got ice tea. You drink and I'll start dinner." She poured them each a glass of tea, and while her mother lit a cigarette, Heather began slicing scallions and mushrooms. She nearly cut off her finger when Ellen announced that she was starting work as a clerk at Fitzpatrick Logging.

Heather dropped her knife and stared at her mother in disbelief. "But—"

"Look, I need any job I can get," Ellen said emphatically as she sat at the table in Turner's kitchen and ignored the glass of ice tea that Heather had set before her. The ice cubes were melting and her lower lip quivered. "That stepfather of yours is trying to make sure I'll have to work until I'm seventy," she said, trying to fight back tears of self-pity.

"I know, but I just find it strange. You applied at the logging company—what—six or eight weeks ago and you were told there were no positions, right? Fitzpatrick Logging was going to be laying off men, not hiring clerks."

"Well, things must've changed," Ellen said, a little miffed. "Anyway, I can't afford to be picky, and when Thomas called—"

"Wait. Time out. Hold the phone." Heather pointed the fingers of one hand into the palm of her other in an effort to cut her mother off, and her stomach began to knot. "Thomas Fitzpatrick called you himself?" Her suspicions rose to the surface. "Isn't that a little odd?"

"It is, but I thought, well, now that we're practically family..." Ellen let her voice drift off, and Heather decided not to argue with her mother, who had taken more than her share of heartaches in life.

"When do you start?"

"Tomorrow. Can you believe it? I was so worried that I'd have to get a job in Jefferson City or even farther away. This will be so close and handy." She stared up at her daughter. "It really is a godsend."

"Then I'm glad for you," Heather replied, though she felt uneasy. Thomas Fitzpatrick wasn't a man to be trusted, and her mother had always been susceptible to the rich—believing their stories, hoping some of their wealth and fame might rub off on her. Dennis Leonetti was a case in point. And the Fitzpatrick wealth was rumored to be much more than the Leonettis'.

Heather glanced out the open window to the corral where Adam was hanging on the fence and watching his father as Turner trained a feisty gray colt. Shirt off, muscles gleaming with sweat in the afternoon sun, Turner held the lead rope, coaxing the nervous animal to trot around him in a circle. In another pen, one of the men who worked for Turner, Fred McDonald, was separating cows from their calves. The fragrance of roses mingled with the ever-present smell of dust and filtered into the warm room. The cattle bawled, Adam yelled at his dad and Turner spoke in soft tones to the headstrong colt.

"He almost ran for state senator," Ellen said, still defending Thomas Fitzpatrick. Heather managed to change the subject as she heated a pot of water for the pasta and stirred the sauce. They talked about the wedding, less than a week away, and Ellen's face brightened at the thought that one of her daughters might find matrimonial happiness, an intangible thing that had eluded her in two trips to the altar. Ellen's opinion of Jackson Moore had turned around and she was beginning to trust Turner. A good sign. Now, if she'd just reform her opinion of Thomas Fitzpatrick…

"So how's my grandson been?" Ellen said, finally sipping her tea while Heather worked at the stove, trying, with Turner's limited cookware, to fix dinner. She'd invited her mother over for shrimp fettuccine, but cooking on the old range had been a trial. There were definitely some things about San Francisco that she would miss. In lieu of a whisk, she used a beat-up wooden spoon to stir the sauce.

"Adam?" she asked as the creamy sauce simmered. "He's been fine."

"And the surgery?"

"So far it's been postponed. As long as Adam's in remission, there's no reason…" She glanced out the window and smiled. Adam's new boots already were covered with a thin layer of dust, and his cowboy hat was, these days, a permanent fixture on his head.

Fred finished with the cows and waved to Turner as

he climbed into his old Dodge pickup. Turner let Adam help him cool down the horse.

"Boots off," Heather ordered as the two men in her life approached the back door. "And hands washed."

"Mine are clean," Adam replied holding up grimy palms for inspection as he tried to nudge one boot off with the toe of another.

"Not good enough," she said. "March, kiddo..." She pointed toward the bathroom with her wooden spoon.

"Drillmaster," Turner grumbled.

"You, too—oh!" He grabbed her by surprise and silenced her with a kiss that stole her breath.

"*I* don't take orders from no woman," he said, in a gritty voice. With a wink, he let her go, leaving her breathless as he headed for the bathroom.

"My goodness," her mother whispered. "I wondered what you saw in that man, but now, I guess I know."

PREPARATIONS FOR THE WEDDING started to pick up. Rachelle and Jackson had moved into Heather's cottage in town—the small house where she and Rachelle had grown up—and the old, forgotten summer camp on the edge of Whitefire Lake was being overhauled. Rachelle, usually calm under any condition, was a mess, and their mother, too, was a nervous wreck.

Heather imagined she might be a little more nervous, but she had her own problems to contend with. Doing a quick calculation with the calendar, she realized that she had missed the last menstrual period of her cycle.

She couldn't believe the cold hard facts of the calendar, so she counted off the weeks. No doubt about it. There was no disputing the fact that she was nearly two weeks late. And her periods had always come like clockwork. Except when she'd been pregnant with Adam.

Mentally kicking herself for not being more careful, she checked the calendar one more time. She'd just been too busy with her worries for Adam and her relationship with Turner to consider the fact that she might be pregnant. It had been stupid—as often as she and Turner made love. This was bound to happen…and deep down, she knew, she'd hoped it would occur. But not just yet. Not until things were settled.

A part of her thrilled at the prospect of pregnancy, but the saner side of her nature was scared to death. She wasn't married, for crying out loud. What would Turner do? What would he think? Just when everything was going so well…

She thought about confiding in him, but decided to wait until she was more certain. He had enough on his mind and shouldn't have to worry about another baby until Heather was positive of her condition, until she'd checked with a gynecologist or done a home pregnancy test.

While Turner was working with the cattle, she and Adam drove into town, and after a frantic meeting with Rachelle, who was dead certain the florist and band were going to foul up everything, Heather stopped by the pharmacy. She bought Adam a butterscotch soda, and while he was slurping up the gooey concoction, she purchased a few supplies—tissues, candles, wrapping paper and a pregnancy test. A young girl she didn't recognize helped her, and all her items were packed carefully in a brown sack before she returned to the soda fountain.

Glancing nervously over her shoulder to the pharmaceutical counter where Scott McDonald worked, she saw him at his elevated station, busy filling prescriptions. Though he had a bird's-eye view of the counters, fountain and shelves, she doubted he had paid much attention to her purchase.

As Adam finished his soda, she sipped a diet soda and chatted with Thelma about Carlie's arrival, which was scheduled for the very next day. Thelma and her husband, Weldon, could hardly wait to see their daughter again.

Hours later, when she returned home, Heather kept the pregnancy test in her large shoulder bag. She had to wait until morning to administer the test, so she planned to pick a morning when Turner got up early to feed the stock. A deceptive whisper touched her heart, but she told herself she was doing the right thing. No need to worry him without cause.

So why did she feel like a criminal?

POSITIVE.

The test results were boldly positive.

Heather, hand trembling, touched her abdomen where, deep within, Turner's child was growing. She leaned against the wall for support and didn't know whether to laugh or cry. A new baby! Ever since Adam had turned one year old, she'd hoped to conceive another child. But Turner's child? A full-blooded sister or brother to Adam—who would've ever thought? Certainly not Heather Tremont Leonetti.

Tears of happiness formed in her eyes. This unborn baby, this miracle baby, was a dream come true.

"Oh, God, thank you," she whispered. She'd bought the test three days before but had to wait until this morning. Turner hadn't woken her when he'd gotten up, and though she'd been awake, she'd feigned sleep until she'd heard the kitchen door close shut behind him.

He hadn't come back in yet, and Heather had enough time to perform the simple test and wait for the results. Without a doubt, the test told her she was pregnant, and with that knowledge came a contentment. Having her children growing up here on the ranch, where the air was fresh, the water clear, the work hard but satisfying, wasn't such a bad idea. They weren't that far from the city and could take weekend excursions to San Francisco or anywhere else they wanted to.

She could paint and sculpt and more importantly be a mother to her children and a wife to Turner Brooks.

Yes, life was going to change, but only for the better. Humming to herself, she threw on her robe and walked to the kitchen. Through the back window, past the heavily blossomed clematis that sprawled over the back porch and across a yard parched from the dry summer, she spied Turner deep in conversation with Fred McDonald. Fred had his own spread to run, but he spent his extra time here, with Turner, helping out and making a few extra bucks. Turner's ranch wasn't as large or as busy as the Lazy K, but it was paid for and, along with her own income, could provide well enough for a small family.

Smiling to herself with the knowledge of her secret, she plugged in the coffeemaker and added coffee and water. After checking on Adam, who was still sleeping soundly, she quickly showered and slipped into a sundress and planned what she would say to Turner and when. Maybe tonight. After Adam was asleep. She'd make a dinner, light candles, and in the warm candle glow, reach across the table for Turner's hand and tell him of the child…

*Pregnant!* The word whirled through her mind. She thought of her maternity clothes, sophisticated expensive outfits tucked away in her house in San Francisco. The silks, wool blends and velours would hardly do on the ranch. She didn't even own a pair of maternity jeans. That would have to change.

She combed her wet hair and decided to let it dry in the sun. With only a quick touch of lipstick and blush, she padded back to the kitchen, set out three empty cups and arranged the sugar and creamer and three spoons beside a vase she'd filled with roses the day before.

Feeling unusually domestic, she decided to bake biscuits. She was busy with her work, her mind already moving ahead to planning a nursery here on the ranch, as she rolled out the dough on an old breadboard.

She heard the grind of a pickup's engine. Looking out the window, she spied Fred's old truck lumbering out of the drive, which was strange, considering he'd just arrived. But maybe he was running into town for parts or supplies.... Turner's tractor was acting up again and he'd ordered a part from the farm machine store in Gold Creek. She'd convinced herself that she'd figured out the reasons for Fred's abrupt departure when she spied Turner walking toward the back porch. Smiling, she lifted her hand to wave to him when she noticed his expression—hard and grim, his skin stretched tight across his nose and the blades of his cheekbones. His mouth was a thin white line and his nostrils were flared in rage, not unlike those of an angry stallion.

Heather's heart plummeted. She barely noticed the dog romping at his heels, a half-grown puppy, part German shepherd from the looks of him, bounding playfully in the dust that Turner's furious strides stirred. Every once in a while the pup would stop, snap at the air to capture a fly, then romp forward again.

"What's going on?" she asked, as Turner shoved open the door and the dog followed him into the kitchen.

"You tell me."

"Fred left...and this dog...?"

"For Adam." He glared at her then, and her throat closed in upon itself, for the hatred that glittered in his gunmetal eyes was unmistakable. "Every kid needs a dog."

"Something's wrong..." The temperature in the cozy kitchen had seemed to plummet and Heather's stomach turned sour. She dropped her rolling pin and wiped her flour-dusted hands on a towel. "What is it, Turner?" she asked, her mind racing before landing upon the answer. There could only be one reason for the anger seething from him.

He knew. Somehow he knew about the baby. And rather than the happiness she'd expected he would feel, his emotions had turned the other direction until he was in a black rage.

"What, Heather?" he said, striding over to her and glaring down at her with condemning eyes. "What's wrong?"

"I...I..."

"Spit it out, woman. You're pregnant."

She felt like a Judas. All the happiness she'd felt just moments before melted away. "Yes, but I just found out—"

"Like hell! How come half the town already knows?"

"It couldn't...I mean I just took the test this morning..." she said, as her words faded, for she understood what had happened. This town. This bloody small town!

When she'd bought the pregnancy detection kit, some-one at the drugstore had put two and two together, and though most clerks weren't supposed to discuss their cus-tomer's purchases, someone had. The clerk at the drug-store, or Scott McDonald, or even Thelma Surrett, must have seen her and started speculating.

Heather's insides churned. Her hands shook.

"The whole damned town knows I'm gonna be a father before I do," he spat out, kicking the wall. The puppy, nervous already, slithered to a hiding spot beneath the table and cowered against the wall, whining pitifully. "Hell, Heather, didn't you think I might want to know?"

"I was going to tell you—"

He grabbed her then, his grip on her arms punishing, the fierce fire in his eyes reminding her of the very devil himself. "When?"

"As soon as I—"

"When we were married? Or before? You know, I've heard of a lot of low-down, despicable things to do, but to get pregnant, plan it all out, just to make sure you had a donor—"

"What are you talking about?"

His voice was as cold as a bottomless well. "Don't pretend, Heather. It belittles us both."

"What the devil are you talking about?" she de-manded, but back in the darkest corner of her mind, she knew, and, God help her, some of those very thoughts had been with her. Hadn't she once considered making love to him just to create a child so like Adam that the baby might be able to eventually become a bone-marrow donor? But that would never have been the sole reason. No. She'd wanted another child for years. Her thoughts must've reflected in her eyes, because he let go of her then and his lips curled in disgust. "I don't like being used, Heather. Not for any reason."

"I didn't use you," she protested.

"Like hell! I was a stud. Nothing more."

She felt as if he'd hit her hard in the stomach. "Oh, Turner, you can't believe—"

"Do you deny that you thought about this? That you hoped we could start a new child? A sibling for Adam? A damned *donor*?"

"Oh, God," she whispered, as the color drained from her body and she had to hold on to the counter for support.

"I just find it hard to believe that I fell for it."

"You didn't fall for anything—"

"Don't lie to me, woman!"

Something inside her snapped, and her temper exploded. "I'm not lying, Turner, and I shouldn't have to remind you that this baby wasn't created by me alone! You were there and, I might add, enjoyed doing your part!"

His breath came out in a hiss. "I don't object to a child! What's the difference between one or two? But it's the reasons for creating this child I hate. Cold and calculating. You didn't even consult me—"

"Why would I do it?" she nearly screamed. "Your bone marrow is a match!"

"Maybe you didn't want to be saddled with me. Maybe you didn't trust me."

"No, Turner, it's you who never trusted me," she said, wretchedness whirling deep in her soul. "You never loved me. And that was my mistake, because I loved you, Turner. For six years I didn't do right by Dennis, because it was you I loved, you I'd always loved. But you never have believed me." She was visibly shaking by this time, and she blinked hard against tears that burned her eyes. "With Adam or without, with this baby or without, I loved you. Stupidly, blindly, with no reason behind it, I loved you."

She noticed the muscle ticking near his eye, saw the contempt in his expression and knew all her plans for happiness had been shattered. She glanced away from him, unable to stare him down, and noticed the biscuit dough beginning to rise, smelled the warm scent of coffee she'd never drink, noticed the pathetic grouping of cups and spoons near a vase of freshly cut flowers that she would no longer enjoy. She felt more miserable than she had in her entire life.

"Mommy?" Adam's sleepy voice stopped her short, and she quickly cleared the lump of self-pity from her throat. She couldn't break down in front of her child. He needed to know that everything was all right, that he was secure. He'd already lost Dennis as a father; it wasn't going to happen again! Her fingers curled into fists of determination and she blinked back any remnants of her tears.

Turning, she managed a thin smile and thought her heart would break. He was getting well. Heather noticed the color in his cheeks and the dark circles beneath his eyes had disappeared. Living here, with Turner, had helped Adam. "Good morning, pumpkin," she whispered over a clogged throat.

"You sad?" He looked from Turner to Heather with worry etched in his small features, and Heather swept him into her arms.

"I'm fine, sweetheart. Look what Turner got for you—"

Adam's eyes rounded as he spied the puppy, still cowering under the table. Slowly the gawky pup inched forward one big paw at a time. Adam pushed his way back to the floor. "He's mine?" Adam whispered, his adoring gaze flying to Turner's hard face. For just a second, Turner's harsh visage cracked and he offered his son a smile as warm as a Western sunset. Heather's heart shredded.

"All yours."

"What's his name?"

"You get to name him."

"Can I really?" Adam looked to his mother as if he expected her to refuse.

"Of course you can."

Adam's freckled face squinched into a thoughtful frown. "Then I'll call him Daytona—that's where they have car races!" He reached out to pet the dog's broad head and was rewarded with a long tongue that swiped his skin. Adam shrieked in happiness and within minutes he and the dog were outside, running along the fence line, kicking up dust and trampling dry grass and wildflowers.

"I won't let him go, you know," Turner said in a low voice edged in steel.

She bit her lip to keep from crying. "I know."

Turner stormed out of the house and she didn't think twice, just turned on her heel, marched to the bedroom she'd shared with him and stripped her clothes from the closet and bureau drawers. He didn't love her, never had, never would—and she'd be damned if she'd spend the rest of her life with a man who couldn't return her feelings.

Call her a hopeless romantic, call her a fool, but call her a woman who knew her own mind. She packed her things quickly and did the same with Adam's. In short order she was ready to leave. She'd take Adam, she'd take her unborn child, she'd even take the dog, but she knew she'd be leaving behind a part of her heart.

## CHAPTER THIRTEEN

"YOU COULD DO WORSE." Thomas Fitzpatrick tented his hands beneath his chin and waited as Turner read through the offer. "That's two and a half times what the place is worth—four times what your dad paid for it when he bought it from me. Quite a profit."

Turner clicked his pen a few times. The papers looked straightforward enough, and he wanted to sell. Hell, ever since the fight with Heather three days ago, he'd thought of nothing but running.

But he hadn't. Because things weren't settled. Not only was there Heather and Adam, but now a new baby to consider. He and Heather hadn't talked; she'd packed up the boy and said something about visiting her mother until the wedding, and Turner, because of his stubborn streak, hadn't bothered to call. But he hadn't slept a wink, either.

Then, out of the blue, Thomas Fitzpatrick showed up on his front porch offering money, bigger money than before. His ticket out. Almost like destiny. Trouble was, Turner didn't believe in destiny.

"I thought I told you I wasn't interested," Turner said, slapping the contracts and deeds and all the rest of the legal mumbo jumbo onto the table.

"But that was before."

"Before? Before what?"

Thomas pulled at his silk tie. His silver hair, as always, was cut just above his collar. He smoothed one side of his trim white moustache, then spread his hands in a supplicating gesture. "Gold Creek is a small town. There are no secrets in small towns."

"Meaning what?" Turner didn't like the feel of a noose around his neck, and he definitely was feeling that he was about to be strung up—by one of the best.

"I've heard about you and the Tremont girl."

"What have you heard?" Turner demanded, the noose tightening and his rage turning black.

"Just that she left you. With your boy. Well, I know the cost of lawyers and I figure if you're planning a lawsuit—for custody, you could use some quick cash. And if you do end up with the kid, you'll have medical bills— more bills than you can imagine—"

Turner was on his feet in an instant. He kicked back his chair and grabbed Fitzpatrick by his fancy silk tie. It was his turn to pull the rope and he'd strangle the old man if he had to. "Where'd you hear all this—"

"Doesn't matter."

"Like hell it doesn't! Now, if you don't want to tangle with me any further, you'd better spill it, Fitzpatrick."

Beads of sweat dotted Thomas's brow and trickled down his temples. "You can't—"

"Tell me!"

"You have no right—"

Turner's cold smile moved from one side of his face to the other. "You're on my property, now, Fitzpatrick. Leastwise it's still mine until I sign your damned papers. So, while you're here, you're going to play by my rules. Who told you?" To add emphasis to his question, he jerked on the tie. Thomas came forward, falling onto the scarred table, sending documents scattering to the floor.

"Ellen Little," he finally said. "Ellen Tremont Little."

Deceit seemed to run in the family. Turner dropped the tie and Fitzpatrick fell back into his chair. "Heather's mother," he snarled. So Heather had run to Mama and told her everything and Ellen had seen fit to give Thomas the information he wanted. Turner's guts twisted into hard little knots and he could barely see beyond his fury.

Recovering somewhat, Thomas offered Turner a grin as icy as his own. "Ellen works for me now. Seems to think she owes me something for giving her a pathetic little job."

"You bastard!" Turner lunged for the man, but Fitzpatrick was out of his chair in an instant. He moved as quick as a sidewinder to the back door.

"Think about the offer. Believe me, it's the best one you're gonna get." He was gone as quickly as he'd come, and Turner looked at the scattered papers on the floor. Unfortunately some of what Fitzpatrick had said made sense. Heather had plenty of money from her divorce from Leonetti and she would use every dime she had to keep her child—his child—their child. His lungs felt tight and he could barely breathe. There was the chance that Adam would need more extremely expensive medical care—Turner's insurance company wouldn't touch a child already diagnosed with leukemia.

All he had was this ranch, and Fitzpatrick was offering him a fortune for it.

Bile rising in his throat, he grabbed up all the papers and without thinking too hard, started signing the documents wherever they were marked. With Fitzpatrick's dirty money, he could fight for custody of his boy and his unborn child; then he'd figure out how he'd spend the rest of his life.

"YOU'RE A FOOL!" NADINE scrubbed the stove as if her very life depended on it. "You let that woman go? Couldn't you see that she loved you, that she wanted to have your children, that she would've done anything... Oh, for crying out loud, why am I talking to you?" Still polishing the damned stainless steel, she hazarded a quick glare in his direction. "Men!"

Turner wasn't going to let Nadine rattle him. He wouldn't have confided in her at all except she already knew half the story and when she'd come here and found Heather gone, she'd guessed the rest. He grabbed a bottle of beer from the refrigerator, plopped himself down at the table and twisted open the cap.

"What about your son?" Nadine asked. "What're you going to do about him?"

"Probably sue for custody."

"Oh, great! Just wonderful!" Nadine didn't even attempt to hide her scorn. "Really confuse the kid." She threw her dirty rag into a pail and put her rubber-glove-encased hands on her slim hips. "First the man he thought was his father rejected him, and now the guy claiming to be his real dad is getting into a bloody legal battle with his mom. And he's the prize. 'Course he'll be pushed and pulled and put through a damned emotional wringer before it's all settled! Think, Turner! Use that brain of yours if you can find it! What's going to happen to Adam and, as far as that goes, not that it really matters, mind you, think what's going to happen to you!"

"I'm—"

"Miserable." Nadine yanked off her gloves, and her anger was suddenly replaced with a deeper emotion. She took in a long breath and said in a voice that was surprisingly even given the state of her emotions, "Look, Turner, believe me, I, of all people, wouldn't steer you into a relationship you didn't want. But for the past week or two, you've been different—a changed man. Whether you know it or not, Heather Leonetti got under your skin so deep, you'll never be able to shed yourself of her. So you'd better stop being a coward and face up to the fact." She made a quick motion to the bottle of beer he cradled, untouched, between his hands. "And that's not going to help. Your father was proof enough of that."

To gall her as much as anything, he took a long swallow. The beer tasted sour, and he hated to admit it but she was right, damn it. He missed Heather. He missed waking up with her; he missed hearing her sing; he missed the scent of her perfume on his pillow and the lilt of her laughter. He missed making love to her at night.

And that didn't even begin to compare to how empty he felt without Adam. Since the boy had been gone, Turner felt as if a hole had been torn from his heart.

"Don't let your pride be your downfall," Nadine said as she reached for the pile of papers he was about to throw out. "You know where you can find her." With a flip of her wrist, she sailed the wedding invitation for Rachelle Tremont and Jackson Moore onto the table. "That's all I've got to say."

Thank God she didn't know he planned to sell the ranch to Fitzpatrick.

He watched as she strode out the door in a cloud of self-righteous fury. She was right, damn it, Turner thought, picking up the invitation. Heather would be there. At the wedding.

Oh, to hell with it! He crushed the engraved sheet of paper in his fist and finished his beer. Then he picked up the phone and placed a long-distance call to the Lazy K Ranch. If Zeke wasn't there, he'd track him down all across the damned country, and Mazie was going to help him. He needed answers. Answers he should have had six years before!

"SOMETHING'S WRONG. I FEEL IT," Rachelle said as she eyed her reflection in a free-standing full-length mirror in the back room of the tiny chapel by the lake.

"You worry too much. Everything's perfect." Heather adjusted her sister's veil and sighed. Rachelle looked beautiful. Her long auburn hair, trained into loose curls that fell to the middle of her back, shimmered beneath the beaded veil and her dress, off-white with a nipped waist, lace and pearl bodice and billowing skirt, fit her exquisitely.

"Heather's right. You're always borrowing trouble," Carlie agreed. With sleek black hair and blue-green eyes, she smiled at her friend. What a fiasco Carlie's arrival had caused just a few days before the wedding. Rachelle had insisted Carlie become part of the wedding party. Somehow the seamstress had made the gown, another usher, a cousin of Jackson's, was fitted with a tuxedo and here she was, an encouraging smile in place.

"I don't know." Rachelle's forehead was lined as she looked from her best friend to her sister. "I did something I shouldn't have."

"You invited Thomas Fitzpatrick," Heather said.

"You knew?" Rachelle asked.

"It doesn't take an investigative reporter, Rachelle. You gave me the invitations to mail."

"Didn't you tell Jackson?" Carlie asked.

"Not until last night."

"And?"

"Let's just say he didn't jump for joy," Rachelle said, though she laughed.

"That takes a lot of nerve." Carlie tugged at her zipper, then smoothed her skirts.

"Or no brains," Rachelle joked.

"Or both." Heather tried to join in the fun. She wasn't going to ruin Rachelle's big day. She wasn't! And yet she had trouble thinking of anything other than Turner.

"Okay, so I've bared my soul," her sister said, eyes narrowing on Heather. "Now out with it. Something's bothering you."

"Nothing—really."

"Adam's okay?"

Heather managed a smile. "Adam's great! Now he thinks he's a cowboy."

"Because of Turner." Rachelle fiddled with the fasteners at her back. "Something's not right. Can you get that—?" She held her hair and veil out of the way.

"Here. No problem." Quickly Carlie took charge, hooking the fastener at Rachelle's nape into place. "These are always a pain," she said.

"You know about wedding dresses? Come on, Carlie. Were you married?"

For a second Carlie blanched but she recovered. "While I was modeling, I did a lot of bridal stuff."

"I'll just be glad when this is over." Rachelle let her hair fall down her back again. She sent her sister a side-long glance. "So tell me about Turner."

"I don't know if he'll show up," Heather hedged.

"Don't tell me you broke up." The dismay on Rachelle's face cut Heather to the bone. Carlie, who'd caught up with the Tremont girls' lives in the past three days knew most of the story.

"Don't worry about Turner. We just had a little argument," Heather lied, and hated the fact that, once again, because of Turner Brooks, she was stretching the truth. Her mother, bless her soul, had been right: one lie did beget another. She shrugged. "Really, that's all."

"It had better be," Rachelle said, her lips tightening a bit.

With a sharp rap, the door flew open and Ellen stormed inside. "I can't believe it! What was he thinking! That father of yours brought—"

"I know, Mom, I invited her," Rachelle admitted, wincing a little at the hurt in her mother's eyes. "She's his wife, whether you like it or not."

For a second, Heather thought their mother might break down and cry, but Ellen, made of stronger stuff, squared her shoulders. Her hair was freshly done and she was wearing a gold suit. "You look great, Mom," Heather told her, and kissed her cheek.

"Thanks, honey." Ellen's eyes glistened with pride as she looked at her two daughters.

"Places, everyone," the minister's wife called through the partially opened door.

Impulsively Rachelle hugged her younger sister. "You and Turner will work things out, I just know it." The sound of music drifted into the little room, and Rachelle took a deep breath. "I guess this is it."

"Good luck!" Heather said. She squeezed Rachelle's hand.

They emerged from the small room near the back of the crowded little chapel. Near the altar, backdropped by long white candles, Jackson Moore fidgeted in his black tuxedo as he waited for his bride. His hair was shiny and black, his eyes anxious, and if he saw Thomas Fitzpatrick sitting in the fifth row, he didn't show any sign of emotion other than love for the woman who planned to spend the rest of her life with him.

Heather's throat was in knots. Taking the arm of Boothe Reece, Jackson's partner in his New York law firm, she began her hesitation step to the music. Soon Rachelle would be starting her new life with Jackson, and Heather would have to begin again, as well—a life without Turner, a life with a new baby, a life of sharing her children with an absent father. Heather forced a smile, and the tears that shimmered in her eyes were tears of happiness for her sister. Nothing more. Or so she tried to convince herself.

STRAINS OF ROMANTIC MUSIC drifted on the air, and the breeze, smelling of the fresh water of the lake, was cool against Heather's face. The sun had dropped beneath the ridge of westerly mountains and the sky was ribboned with brilliant splashes of magenta and pink.

Twilight was coming. That time of night—dusk really—when her thoughts would always stray to Turner. Stars were beginning to wink, and the ghost of a crescent moon was rising. She wrapped her arms around herself and began walking along the sparsely graveled path toward the lake, the very same lake she'd sipped from only a few weeks earlier. Drat that darned legend! She'd been a fool to think there was any hint of truth in the Indian lore.

With a rustle, the wind picked up and the chilly breath of autumn touched her bare neck. Still wearing her raspberry-hued gown, she picked her way along the ferns and stones.

She'd stayed at the wedding and reception as long as she could, watched Jackson and Rachelle exchange vows, witnessed them place rings upon each other's fingers, smiled as they toasted their new life together and laughed when they'd cut the cake and force-fed each other. All the old traditions. New again.

She'd even watched as Rachelle had tossed her bouquet into the crowd and a surprised Carlie Surrett had caught the nosegay of white ribbons, carnations and baby pink roses only to drop the bouquet as if it was as hot and searing as a branding iron. Rachelle, good-naturedly, had laughed and tossed the bouquet over her shoulder again and to everyone's joy their mother, Ellen, had ended up with the flowers.

"Can you believe this?" she'd said. "Well, maybe the third time's the charm!"

The big moment, when Thomas Fitzpatrick had shaken his bastard son's hand and wished him well, had come afterward. Thomas had seemed sincere, and Jackson, his face stony, hadn't made a scene. He'd even accepted the envelope Thomas had given him and had said a curt "thanks." It hadn't been a joyous father-son reunion, but it hadn't turned into the worst disaster since the *Titanic,* either.

Now, as she glanced back over her shoulder, Heather noticed that a crowd had joined Rachelle and Jackson on the portable dance floor they'd had constructed for the ceremony. Tucked in the tall pine trees, with torches and colorful lanterns adding illumination, the old camp was a cozy site for a wedding. A great way to start their lives together.

Heather had her own set of plans. Tomorrow she'd return to San Francisco, the city she loved, and start her life over. Without Turner. Her heart wrenched and her throat thickened. Tears burned behind her eyes. Why couldn't she find any comfort in the thought that she was going home? Why couldn't she find any consolation that she wouldn't have to move back to Gold Creek? Why wasn't she happy? The answer was simple: Turner Brooks.

Gathering her skirts, she followed the path until the trees gave way to a stretch of rocky beach. The wedding was far behind her now, the music fading, the laughter no louder than the sound of crickets singing in the dusk.

Twilight had descended, and the stars reflected in the purple depths of the lake. "Oh, Turner," she whispered, kicking a stone toward the water and watching as it rolled lazily into the ebb and flow of the lake.

Again she felt a tickle of a breeze lifting the hairs at her nape. She looked to the west and her breath caught in her throat, for there, just as he'd been six years earlier, was the lone rider, a tall cowboy on horseback, his rangy stallion sauntering slowly in her direction.

Her heart turned over and she wanted to hate him, to tell him to stay out of her life, but she couldn't. Staring up at his rugged features, her heart tumbled and she knew she was destined to love him for the rest of her life.

She waited, unmoving, the wind billowing her skirts until he was close enough that she could see the features of his face. Strong and proud, he'd never change. Her throat closed in on itself, and it was all she could do not to let out a strangled sob.

She thought for a moment that he was coming for her, but she knew differently. He'd known where she would be and was probably here to tell her that he'd talked with a lawyer and was going to sue her for custody of their children. Oh, Lord, how had it come to this? Her fingers twisted in the fabric of her skirt and she wished she could hate him, could fight him tooth and nail for her children, but a stubborn part of her wouldn't give up on the silly, irrational fact that she loved him. As much as she had six years ago.

His jaw was set and hard, but his eyes were dark with an inner torment. Heather braced herself, refused to break down. He slid from the saddle and, without a word, wrapped strong arms around her. Pressing his face into the crook of her neck, he held her, and the smells of leather and horse, sweat and musk, brought back each glorious memory she'd ever shared with him.

She clung to him because she had no choice, and tears filled her eyes to run down her cheeks and streak the rough suede of his jacket. Her heart ached, and she wondered if she would ever get over him.

As the night whispered over the lake, Turner's voice was low and thick with emotion. "I love you," he said simply.

Heather's heart shredded. "Y-you don't have to—"

"Shh, darlin'. Don't you know I've always loved you? I was just too much a fool to admit it."

"Please, Turner, don't—" she cried, unable to stand the pain.

He pulled back and placed a finger to her lips. Staring straight into her eyes, with the ghosts of Whitefire Lake as his witnesses, Turner repeated, "I love you. Believe me."

"But—"

"Don't fight it."

Tears slid down her cheeks. Could it be true? She hardly dared believe him, and yet the gaze touching hers—caressing hers—claimed that she was and always had been his whole life. "Oh, God," she whispered, and threw her arms around him. "I love you, too, Turner. I always have."

"Then marry me," he said simply. "Let's not wait. It's time we gave our son a family and time we built a life for our new little one."

"But—"

"Now, marry me."

Things were going so fast. Heather's mind was spinning. "Now?" she repeated as he kissed away her tears.

"Isn't there a preacher over there?" He cocked his head toward the old summer camp and the lights flickering through the trees.

"I don't know.... Yes, I suppose, but do you think—?" Without another word, he lifted her onto his horse, then swung into the saddle behind her. Wrapping one solid arm around her middle, he urged the horse forward toward the bobbing colored lights and the music. "Where's Adam?"

"With my mother—"

He grimaced at that. "Well, as soon as we find him and a preacher we're getting married."

"But Rachelle...Jackson..."

Turner laughed low in his throat. "Somehow, I don't think they'll mind. They seem to like to cause a stir."

"But why—why now?" she asked.

"You're as bad as Mazie with all your questions," he said, but chuckled. "I finally got hold of Zeke, and the next time I see that old coot, I intend to fill his backside with buckshot."

"Why?"

"He admitted you called, that you were frantic to reach me, but by the time I returned, you'd already married. As for the letters I sent you, I mailed them to the Lazy K with instructions to forward them 'cause I didn't have your address. Zeke, thinking he was doing us a big favor, burned every last one."

"Oh, no—"

"As I said, 'buckshot.'" But he smiled and kissed her temple.

Then, as if he'd truly lost his mind, he reached into the inner pocket of his suede jacket, withdrew a crisp white envelope, and while Sampson broke into a lope, started shredding the neatly-typed pages.

"What—?"

"Confetti, for the bride and groom. Compliments of Thomas Fitzpatrick."

"I don't understand—"

He let the torn pages disperse on the wind, the ragged

pieces drifting to the lake. "All you have to understand, lady, is that I love you." With a kiss to her rounded lips, he spurred the horse forward. The wind tore at her hair, and the waters of Whitefire Lake lapped at the tree-studded shore. Turner's arm tightened around her, his lips buried against her neck, and they galloped toward their future as husband and wife.

Together forever, she thought, as the lake flashed by in a blur, and she thought she heard laughter in the trees. Hers? Turner's? Or the ghosts of the past who knew the powers of Whitefire Lake?

* * * * *

*A Short History of*
*Gold Creek, California*

THE NATIVE AMERICAN LEGEND of Whitefire Lake was whispered to the white men who came from the east in search of gold in the mountains. Even in the missions, there was talk of the legend, though men of the Christian God professed to disbelieve any pagan myths.

None was less believing than Kelvin Fitzpatrick, a brawny Irishman who was rumored to have killed a man before he first thrust his pickax into the hills surrounding the lake. No body was ever found, and the claim jumper vanished, so a murder couldn't be proved. But rumors around Fitzpatrick didn't disappear.

He found the first gold in the hills on a morning when the lake was still shrouded in the white mist that was as beautiful as it was deceptive. Fitzpatrick staked his claim and drank lustily from the water. He'd found his home and his fortune in these hills.

He named the creek near his claim Gold Creek and decided to become the first founding father of a town by the same name. He took his pebbles southwest to the city of San Francisco, where he transformed gold to money and a scrubby forty-niner into what appeared to be a wealthy gentleman. With his money and looks, Kelvin wooed and married a socialite from the city, Marian Dubois.

News of Fitzpatrick's gold strike traveled fast, and soon Gold Creek had grown into a small shantytown. With the prospectors came the merchants, the gamblers, the saloon keepers, the clergy and the whores. The Silver Horseshoe Saloon stood on the west end of town and the Presbyterian church was built on the east, and Gold Creek soon earned a reputation for fistfights, barroom brawls and hangings.

Kelvin's wealth increased and he fathered four children—all girls. Two were from Marian, the third from a town whore and the fourth by a Native American woman. All children were disappointments as Kelvin Fitzpatrick needed an heir for his empire.

The community was growing from a boisterous mining camp to a full-fledged town, with Kelvin Fitzpatrick as Gold Creek's first mayor and most prominent citizen. The persecuted Native Americans with their legends and pagan ways were soon forced into servitude or thrown from their land. They made their way into the hills, away from the white man's troubles.

In 1860, when Kelvin was forty-three, his wife finally bore him a son, Rodwell Kelvin Fitzpatrick. Roddy, handsome and precocious, became the apple of his father's eye. Though considered a "bad seed" and a hellion by most of the churchgoing citizens of Gold Creek, Roddy Fitzpatrick was the crown prince to the Fitzpatrick fortune, and when his father could no longer mine gold from the earth's crust, he discovered a new mode of wealth and, perhaps, more sacred: the forest.

Roddy Fitzpatrick started the first logging operation and opened the first sawmill. All competitors were quickly bought or forced out of business. But other men, bankers and smiths, carpenters and doctors, settled down to stay and hopefully smooth out the rough edges of the town. Men with names of Kendrick, Monroe and Powell made Gold Creek their home and brought their wives in homespun and woolens, women who baked pies, planned fairs and corralled their wayward Saturday night drinking men into church each Sunday morning.

Roddy Fitzpatrick, who grew into a handsome but cruel man, ran the family business when the older Fitzpatrick retired. In a few short years, Roddy had gambled or squandered most of the family fortune. Competitors had finally gotten a toehold in the lumber-rich mountains surrounding Gold Creek and new businesses were sprouting along the muddy streets of the town.

The railroad arrived, bringing with its coal-spewing engines much wealth and commerce. The railway station was situated on the west end of town, not too far from the Silver Horseshoe Saloon and a skeletal trestle bridged the gorge of the creek. Ranchers and farmers brought their produce into town for the market and more people stayed on, settling in the growing community, though Gold Creek was still known for the bullet holes above the bar in the saloon.

And still there was the rumor of some Indian curse that occasionally was whispered by the older people of the town.

Roddy, always a hothead and frustrated at his shrinking empire, was involved in more than his share of brawls. Knives flashed, guns smoked and threats and curses were spit around a wad of tobacco and a shot of whiskey.

When a man tried to cheat him at cards, Roddy plunged a knife into the blackguard's heart and killed him before a packed house of gamblers, drinkers, barkeeps and whores. After a night in jail, Roddy was set free with no charges leveled against him by the sheriff, who was a fast friend of the elder Fitzpatrick.

But Roddy's life was not to be the same. One night he didn't return home to his wife. She located Kelvin and they formed a search party. Two days later, Roddy's body washed up on the shores of Whitefire Lake. There was a bullet hole in his chest, and his wallet was empty.

Some people thought he was killed by a thief; still others decided Roddy had been shot by a jealous husband, but some, those who still believed in the legend, knew that the God of the Sun had taken Roddy's life to punish Kelvin Fitzpatrick by not only taking away his wealth but the only thing Kelvin had loved: his son.

The older Fitzpatrick, hovering on the brink of bankruptcy, took his own life after learning that his son was dead. Kelvin's daughters, those legitimate, and those who were born out of wedlock, each began their own lives.

The town survived the dwindling empire of the Fitzpatricks and new people arrived at the turn of the century. New names were aded to the town records. Industry and commerce brought the flagging community into the twentieth century, though the great earthquake of 1906 did much damage. Many buildings toppled, but the Silver Horseshoe Saloon and the Presbyterian church and the railroad trestle survived.

Monroe Sawmill, a new company owned and operated by Hayden Garreth Monroe, bought some of the dwindling Fitzpatrick forests and mills, and during the twenties, thirties and forties, Gold Creek became a company town. The people were spared destitution during the depression as the company kept the workers employed, even when they were forced to pay in company cash that could only be spent on goods at the company store. But no family employed by Monroe Sawmill went hungry;

therefore, the community, which had hated Fitzpatrick's empire, paid homage to Hayden Garreth Monroe, even when the forests dwindled, logging prices dropped and the mills were shut down.

In the early 1960s, the largest sawmill burned to the ground. The police suspected arson. As the night sky turned orange by the flames licking toward the black heavens, and the volunteer firemen fought the blaze, the townspeople stood and watched. Some thought the fire was a random act of violence, others believed that Hayden Garreth Monroe III, grandson of the well-loved man, had lost favor and developed more than his share of enemies when the company cash became worthless and the townspeople, other than those who were already wealthy, began to go bankrupt. They thought the fire was personal revenge. Names of those he'd harmed were murmured. Fitzpatrick came to mind, though by now, the families had been bonded by marriage and the timber empire of the Fitzpatricks had experienced another boom.

Some of the townspeople, the very old with long memories, thought of the legend that had nearly been forgotten. Hayden Garreth Monroe III had drunk like a glutton from the Whitefire Lake and he, too, would lose all that he held dear—first his wealth and eventually his wife.

As time passed, other firms found toeholds in Gold Creek and in the seventies and eighties, technology crept over the hills. From the ashes of Kelvin Fitzpatrick's gold and timber empire rose the new wealth of other families.

The Fitzpatricks still rule the town, and Thomas Fitzpatrick, patriarch of the family, intends one day to turn to state politics. However, scandal has tarnished his name and as his political aspiration turns to ashes and his once-envied life has crumbled, he will have to give way to new rulers—young men who are willing to fight for what they want. Men like Jackson Moore and Turner Brooks and Hayden Garreth Monroe IV.

Old names mingle and marry with new, but the town and its legend continue to exist. To this day, the people of Gold Creek cannot shake the gold dust of those California hills from their feet. Though they walk many paths away from the shores of the lake, the men and women of Gold Creek—the boys and girls—can never forget their hometown. Nor can they forget the legend and curse of Whitefire Lake.

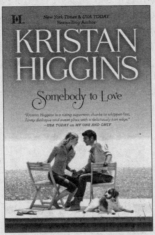

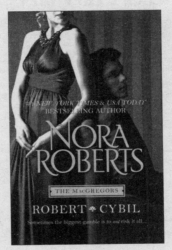

# REQUEST YOUR FREE BOOKS!

## 2 FREE NOVELS
## FROM THE ROMANCE COLLECTION
## PLUS 2 FREE GIFTS!

**YES!** Please send me 2 FREE novels from the Romance Collection and my 2 FREE gifts (gifts are worth about $10). After receiving them, if I don't wish to receive any more books, I can return the shipping statement marked "cancel." If I don't cancel, I will receive 4 brand-new novels every month and be billed just $5.99 per book in the U.S. or $6.49 per book in Canada. That's a saving of at least 25% off the cover price. It's quite a bargain! Shipping and handling is just 50¢ per book in the U.S. and 75¢ per book in Canada.* I understand that accepting the 2 free books and gifts places me under no obligation to buy anything. I can always return a shipment and cancel at any time. Even if I never buy another book, the two free books and gifts are mine to keep forever.

194/394 MDN FELQ

| Name | (PLEASE PRINT) | |
|------|------|------|
| Address | | Apt. # |
| City | State/Prov. | Zip/Postal Code |

Signature (if under 18, a parent or guardian must sign)

### Mail to the **Reader Service:**
**IN U.S.A.:** P.O. Box 1867, Buffalo, NY 14240-1867
**IN CANADA:** P.O. Box 609, Fort Erie, Ontario L2A 5X3

Not valid for current subscribers to the Romance Collection
or the Romance/Suspense Collection.

**Want to try two free books from another line?**
**Call 1-800-873-8635 or visit www.ReaderService.com.**

* Terms and prices subject to change without notice. Prices do not include applicable taxes. Sales tax applicable in N.Y. Canadian residents will be charged applicable taxes. Offer not valid in Quebec. This offer is limited to one order per household. All orders subject to credit approval. Credit or debit balances in a customer's account(s) may be offset by any other outstanding balance owed by or to the customer. Please allow 4 to 6 weeks for delivery. Offer available while quantities last.

**Your Privacy**—The Reader Service is committed to protecting your privacy. Our Privacy Policy is available online at www.ReaderService.com or upon request from the Reader Service.

We make a portion of our mailing list available to reputable third parties that offer products we believe may interest you. If you prefer that we not exchange your name with third parties, or if you wish to clarify or modify your communication preferences, please visit us at www.ReaderService.com/consumerschoice or write to us at Reader Service Preference Service, P.O. Box 9062, Buffalo, NY 14269. Include your complete name and address.

ROM11

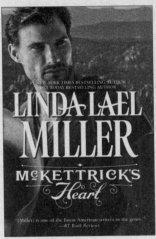

# LISA JACKSON

| | | |
|---|---|---|
| 77650 ABANDONED | ___ $7.99 U.S. | ___ $9.99 CAN. |
| 77578 STRANGERS | ___ $7.99 U.S. | ___ $9.99 CAN. |
| 77489 STORMY NIGHTS | ___ $7.99 U.S. | ___ $9.99 CAN. |

*(limited quantities available)*

| | | |
|---|---|---|
| TOTAL AMOUNT | | $ _____ |
| POSTAGE & HANDLING | | $ _____ |
| ($1.00 FOR 1 BOOK, 50¢ for each additional) | | |
| APPLICABLE TAXES* | | $ _____ |
| TOTAL PAYABLE | | $ _____ |

*(check or money order—please do not send cash)*

To order, complete this form and send it, along with a check or money order for the total above, payable to HQN Books, to: **In the U.S.:** 3010 Walden Avenue, P.O. Box 9077, Buffalo, NY 14269-9077; **In Canada:** P.O. Box 636, Fort Erie, Ontario, L2A 5X3.

Name: _____
Address: _____ City: _____
State/Prov.: _____ Zip/Postal Code: _____
Account Number (if applicable): _____

075 CSAS

*New York residents remit applicable sales taxes.
*Canadian residents remit applicable GST and provincial taxes.

PHLJ0512BL